GHOSTS OF SAINT-PIERRE

A NOVEL

DUANE PONCY

PATRICIA J MCLEAN

Rainy Nights Press

ISBN: 979-8-9861523-3-2 (print); 979-8-9861523-2-5 (ebook)

Disclaimer:

This is a work of fiction, although much of it is based upon the life events of a real person, my grandfather, Paul Poncy, who grew up in Martinique, and whose first family perished there on May 8, 1902 in the eruption of Mont Pelée. As far as we know the factual details of his life, and those of other known members of my family, we have attempted to stay true to them. Nearly all of the mentioned individuals in Paul's, Stephanie's, and Clara's family were real people.

Other characters in the novel, like Ludger Sylbaris and Vachal Lindsey, were also real people, but are used here in a largely symbolic way. I have no knowledge of my grandfather actually knowing any of them.

A number are totally fictional, such as Amanda Laviolette and her coterie in Buffalo and Paul's school friends in Martinique.

We have tried to not minimize the issues of race, class, and colonialism, which are integral to this story and to the history of Martinique and the Americas.

—Duane Poncy, May 2021

In loving memory of nephew
Joseph Paul Poncy
1975 — 2022

PART 1
LA MAISON DES REVENANTS

L'HABITATION SABLON

There once was a villa on the Rivière Montauban, in Martinique, near Ajoupa-Bouillon, where Paul spent a few languorous summers as a child. L'habitation Sablon, Maman's childhood home, was once the manor house of a small plantation that had been in her papa's family since the early days of French settlement. Granmé Jeanine continued to live there for a few years after the death of her husband in 1881, before returning to Morne Rouge to be near her birth family, the Petits. Paul's other grand-mère, on Papa's side, it might be noted, was also a Petit, and the auntie of Granmé Jeanine.

L'habitation Sablon was a shambling old country mansion full of guest rooms and ghost rooms and mysterious hallways in which a young boy could lose himself for hours in play and exploration under the watchful eye of Emmaline. Emmaline was the family's household manager, a sort of head maid with no subordinates, because the Fauvé-Sablons could no longer afford a staff of cooks and maids. But to Paul and his brother, Mannie, she was simply Emmaline, the woman who cared for them during those long summers—Granmé's version of their own Sandrine, back home in Saint-Pierre.

Emmaline's own children, Daniel and Euphrasie, were among their playmates, and when they were allowed out into the fields, Emmaline watched over them with a keen eye, never allowing them too far from her sight. Snakes sometimes slithered through the old overgrown cane fields, including deadly fer-de-lance, although every year there were fewer of them, as the humans encroached on their tropical forest habitat. But the reptiles appeared occasionally in the fields, and the children, being too young to be trusted on their own, were seldom allowed far from Emmaline's sight.

There were times, however, when the children would slip away, as Paul and Mannie, along with their visiting cousines, Léonie and Alix, did one August day. Mannie and Alix were the oldest, and Mannie, because he was a boy, was leader of the pack. He should have known better.

"I bet you're too scared to go into the forest," he taunted Paul.

"I'm not."

"By yourself?"

"I'm not scared of some trees." Young Paul marched with false bravado toward the treeline.

"But there are snakes," warned Léonie, the youngest but most sensible among them, giving name to one of his biggest fears.

"You'll be in so much trouble, Paul," Alix said. "Don't be stupid."

Paul faltered.

"They're just girls," Mannie scoffed, a fact which, of course Paul knew. But he also knew his brother had challenged him to not be a sissy. And what seven-year-old boy wants to be a sissy? So Paul charged ahead into the forest, until his foot slid over the edge of a muddy pit, the kind that was called a bouillon. He would have gone right in, been swallowed by the mud, if he hadn't grasped a liana on his way down and clung to it with all his seven-year-old strength. But as hard as he tried, he didn't have the stamina to hoist himself up to safety. Each time he gained a centimeter his hand would slip on the vine's slick green skin and the fibers cut into his skin.

"Mannie!" he yelled, on the verge of tears, "I need your help."

"I told you," Alix scolded, and he heard her feet running toward the house as she called out for Emmaline. Paul was certain they had abandoned him until he looked up to see Mannie standing above. "Hang on, Paulie."

"Are there snakes in there?" Paul cried out.

"Probably," Mannie said. Then, thinking better of it, "I doubt it. I don't see any. Hang on. The girls are getting help."

Within minutes, Daniel arrived with Emmaline close behind. Paul could only think about snakes, but he should have been worrying about Emmaline, because she was furious with them when she reached down with her strong black arms and pulled him roughly from the pit.

After all these years, he still recalled Mannie's cries that evening from the switching given to him by their eldest brother, Eustase.

THE SABLON HOUSE was long gone, swept away by time and the ravages of tropical weather, gone even before he had abandoned his homeland for America, and before the volcano tried, without success, to lay all that history to rest. But Paul still visited the old house sometimes in his quiet hours, unable or unwilling to let it go. In this house in his mind he'd lodged not only the good times but also the painful things, ones he could not face in his daily life, things only called up in the darkness of the night when nothing stirred but the beating of his heart.

The spirit of Eustase lived in that house, and when he opened the door to Eustase's room, he entered his long-dead brother's domain. Though Eustase's world could be a happy, nostalgic place, Paul did not open that door often, because he could as easily stumble into that bloodstained field in Sainte Philomene as into Eustase's arms.

Papa and Tata Elmire, bless their souls, had rooms there as well. And after the volcano, he'd made a place for Stéphanie and Maman; for Mannie and Joseph and Alice Germaine and Adrien; and for André Paul and Yvonne. Little Yvonne, whom he can only imagine now, but will never know, because she was less than a month old when he abandoned her for America.

And then there were all those others, all the family, friends, and acquaintances lost forever from this world. All lost in the fury of Montagne Pelée. *But perhaps many of them were somehow saved,* he tried to tell himself in those first years, *gone to relatives in Fort-de-France or Lamentin or Sainte-Anne. Perhaps this cold dread is only a misplaced feeling.* But this was his fairytale. Of course, they were all gone. All of them. Swept away by the nuée ardent – that blast of searing ash and poisonous gas. There were so many spirits shaking the doorknobs and rattling the windows. But even his ancestral house of revenants could not hold the entire city of Saint-Pierre. Martinique was only a brittle memory now—an island that he had no place for in his daily life, no room for in his cluttered mind. So he locked the door to that house. Visited it only in rare dreams or when he came home exhausted and his family left him in solitude, allowing his mind to wander.

But now, as Paul was about to lay yet one more child to rest, his ghosts rose in their unpredictable way, not in the darkness of night, or in those rare quiet hours, but during the day, interrupting his morose thoughts. *When can I meet my new brother, Papa?* said Alice Germaine, appearing from nowhere as he sat in the living room with his family in mourning, only hours after the funeral service for Francis Paul.

"This is a living room, child," he chastised. "Not a dead room."

His wife, Clara, shot him a concerned look, and eleven-year-old Theresa said, "Are you alright, Papa?"

"I'm fine, mes chères." He was mortified that he had spoken out loud.

His family did not know about Alice Germaine, or her Maman, Stéphanie, or his other children. They knew almost nothing of Martinique. He could not bring himself to talk about it. Of all his ghosts, though, it was little Yvonne who troubled him the most. Try as he would, he could not conjure a mental picture of his baby or imagine what she might have become had the volcano not taken her away. He'd tried over the years to put these memories to rest. But here they were, slipping like smoke through the shuttered windows, beneath the bolted door, rising on this new wave of grief.

FRANCIS PAUL

"ARE YOU ALRIGHT, PAPA?" Theresa asked for the second time. No acknowledgement came, no nodding of the head, nor any sign that Papa had heard her. It was as if he inhabited another world entirely. *But we all are in another world, aren't we? Another world where everything is cold and lonely and unreal.* She thought these things but didn't feel them — not really. It was like a dream, this other world. It had always seemed to her, since she was a tiny girl, that Papa was lost in a dream, and now she had joined him there. Trapped, no longer able to touch the actual world, which lay just outside her grasp.

Throughout her big brother's funeral service, she had not felt sad or angry. She felt nothing until the very end when she stood before his closed coffin and looked at that beautiful photograph Papa had taken just a few months before any of them had gotten sick. In it, Frank was smiling, happy, the way he was before that grotesque infection ate away his ear. She broke down crying. Even then, she didn't know if she felt anything. It seemed this thing had built up inside her and she'd released it, and now she was empty again. She wondered if there was something wrong with her.

After the mass for Frank, they had all gone to the hospital to see her brother, Clair, who was still deathly sick with pneumonia. The Spanish flu had devastated the family for three months now and it seemed as if it would never end.

Everyone was exhausted from the horribly long afternoon. Mom was on her bed resting with the baby nearby asleep in his crib and the boys were off in their rooms, napping. Theresa was alone with Papa. He sat in his chair staring, his mind a million miles away. She thought she should talk to him and comfort him, but she wondered if she could even reach him out there in his other world.

"Papa…" she said, tentatively.

Papa didn't respond, so she said it again, a little more forcefully this time. "Papa."

"Yes, mon ange?" Papa said after a moment, which seemed like forever. He spoke with no emotion, as though he were reciting a rosary or answering the telephone. It was exactly the same way that she felt.

"Never mind," she said. "Ce n'est rien."

She couldn't even get angry. It was Papa, after all—he had always been like this. Remote. There, but not there. When she was little, he had held her on his lap and told her stories, but even when she remembered those peaceful years of her childhood, his sadness was always there, hovering.

Now she thought perhaps she understood better because they had this thing in common. She wondered what happened to him in the past, what kind of loss had taken all the joy from him?

Of course, she knew about his brother Eustase, who had died in a hunting accident when Papa was about her age. And to see that must have been as terrible and traumatic as watching your big brother waste away in a hospital bed. But did that mean that this would never end for her, too? This cold, empty nothing that had become her heart? Would there never be healing?

She watched Papa slumped in his chair, too sad to even light his pipe. She wanted to sit on his lap and hug him, just like she did when she was six, but she was too old for that now.

"Papa," she said, "do you think Frank is in heaven?"

"Papa doesn't even know if there is a heaven, ma chère."

"I think there must be," she said. "I don't want to think he is just gone."

"He will be in our memories, sweetheart. He will always be there."

Papa was trying to make her feel better, but she was afraid for her memories; afraid of forgetting all those little things that endear one person to another.

"But being in my memories is not the same as being *some*where," she said.

"I'm not so sure of that," Papa said. Finally, he picked up his pipe and bag of tobacco and loaded the bowl, tamped it down. She didn't know what Papa meant, but she was glad to see him preparing his pipe. It was a tiny sign that things might be normal again one day.

It had no effect on the emptiness she felt inside.

NOW THAT THEY were old enough to take some responsibility, the children were required to help with household chores. And because of Mom's childhood polio, which had left her crippled, Theresa had extra duties, as well. The thing Theresa resented the most about being a girl was that she had to take on so much burden for the family.

But when her thoughts turned to Frank, some of her resentment fell away. Her older brother had always been there for her.

She recalled the brief time they'd lived in Winslow, Arizona —it was in the fall just before Clair was born, because Mom was big and pregnant. Tata Berthe had ridden the train all the way from Canada to help Mom in the last months of her pregnancy. It was that morning the circus came to town and they were all waiting for Papa to arrive so they could watch the parade together. Mom and Auntie became distracted by a dress or a hat or something in a shop window. Theresa had been monkeying around and tumbled off the boardwalk, landing inches from the hooves of a horse tied to the rail. She'd cried out and the horse became skittish, and Frank, barely four years old himself, had jumped down and pulled her from under the horse's hooves, perhaps saving her from being trampled. All of this occurred before Mom and Auntie even knew what had happened.

Frank had always been kind to her and their little brothers. He loved his family, even though he refused to speak French any longer. "I am an American," he said when Mom asked him why. Her folks were a little sad, because they didn't see why you couldn't be an American and speak French, as well. But Theresa figured it was just Frank's way of becoming the person everyone thought he would one day grow into.

But now he would never grow into that person, and she would never see him again.

Afraid her thoughts had become maudlin, Theresa turned her attention back to Papa, who was puffing his pipe, his eyes still in some undefinable distance. She recalled Papa as he was when she was still that little girl, the curl of smoke rising from his cherry-wood pipe, the smell of the sweet tobacco, the wooden rocking chair where he held her on his lap, rocking slowly, seldom talking, except on those occasions when he would tell her tales about another little girl named Yvonne and her many adventures. Something he would often do if she were to ask.

At other times, Papa would shake his head and say, "Not now, mon ange. Papa needs to think." And then he would slip off into a silent reverie, pipe smoke billowing around his head. She couldn't imagine what he had to think about, back then. But he was an adult, so she didn't dare ask him. She would just put her head back and listen to his breathing, sometimes imagining little Yvonne and the adventure she might be missing.

If restless, she might go find Mom in the kitchen where she was preparing lunch, hoping for a treat. But Papa's stories were even more of a treat than some sugary pastry from the oven.

~

LONG AGO, the story began, *there was a little girl named Yvonne who lived on an island in the blue Caribbean sea with her maman and her older brother, André.*

Her papa had gone far away to another land in the north where he had taken a job, so that he could make money to send home to Maman. Yvonne had not seen Papa since she was just a tiny waddling. Maman, who was an artiste, often drew pictures of Papa and told stories about him and the wonderful land of Bordeaux, where Papa was born.

Ladies in Bordeaux, Maman said, wear the finest hats and go to the ballet in the evening, and speak only the most sophisticated French. They smoke cigarettes in cigarette holders as long as a little girl's arm, which they hold just so.

Papa would pause and demonstrate before continuing.

"One day we shall move to Bordeaux," said Maman, her eyes fixed on her distant dream, "and we shall live in the house where Papa was born, and then, someday soon after that, Papa shall join us there."

· · ·

PAPA WOULD OFTEN PAUSE in the story. Perhaps he was lost in memory, his mind wandering wherever it wandered.

"Weren't you born in Bordeaux, Papa?" Theresa recalled asking him.

"Yes, mon ange."

"Bordeaux is in France, isn't it?"

"Yes, Té. Have you learned about France in school?"

"No," she said. "I'm only in second grade, Papa. I learned about it from Mom."

"Your mother has been talking about me, again, has she?" he said, his voice mock indignant.

She giggled. "I didn't get her in trouble, did I?"

Papa laughed. "Of course not, mon ange. Shall I continue the story?"

She nodded her head and laid it back against his soft cotton shirt, which smelled of sweet Prince Albert tobacco, and he would go on in his graveled voice, telling the story of how the little girl Yvonne meets the pirate captain, Marie Le Méchant, who imprisons her mother in the ship's galley, and sails away with them across the sea to Bordeaux. His chair rocking back and forth like a creaky ancient schooner on the gentle Caribbean Sea.

"POPS," Theresa said. "Do you remember when you used to tell me stories about that little girl, Yvonne?"

Papa sighed. "Oui, ma chère," he said, "I remember."

"Would you tell me one now?"

"Not now, Alice. Perhaps later when your Papa's not feeling quite so sad."

Why had Papa called her Alice? She wanted to say something about that, but she was too miserable and tired to pursue it.

"Okay." She was too old for those children's stories, anyway. But a tiny resentment had crept into her thoughts. *Would they grieve like this for me, if I were the one? Boys are always more important. Frank left us all behind, left me behind, and no one cares about me, about how I'm feeling, they only care about their own unhappiness.*

How quickly her resentment had blossomed into anger. Anger at Papa, anger at her dead brother. It seemed to her there wasn't an ounce of fairness in the world. She couldn't bear to stay in this room with him any longer.

"My name isn't Alice," she hissed from the doorway.

GHOSTS

Paul listened to his daughter's footsteps retreating down the hall, her retort stung him and he thought he ought to call out to her. He hadn't meant to ignore her. He knew she was hurting. *I will make it up to her soon,* he told himself and turned his thoughts back toward the children he had abandoned in Martinique. Alice Germaine, Adrien, André Paul, Yvonne — left to the fate of the mountain. He had vowed to protect these children, to never leave them. And now, Francis had been sacrificed to this Spanish contagion, and perhaps Clair, as well. He could not keep them safe.

Was this God's revenge for his broken promise? A child's promise abandoned, not all at once, but slowly and without struggle, much in the same way as his faith had been replaced by his love for Stéphanie. A priest, had he confessed, would have pointed out that he was risking his immortal soul to turn his back on God for a woman, especially one who had two children already without the benefit of marriage. He may have been a heartbroken foolish child when he vowed to become a priest, but nothing he'd ever learned about God suggested that was grounds for forgiveness. He laughed at these unbidden thoughts. *What a conceit! That God would murder* 30,000 *people to teach me a lesson. Who do you think you are, Paul Poncy?*

Ah, it was so much easier to believe that God didn't exist at all, wasn't it?

God may not exist, but Paul's ghosts certainly did. As real in his mind as flesh and blood. And as much as he tried to banish them, they insisted on taunting him. Alice Germaine, in particular, who wanted to know when she could meet her new brother. She disturbed him to where, several times now, he had become confused between the dead Alice and the living Theresa. Had he actually called Theresa, "Alice?" That would never do.

Alice, he said after his living daughter had left, *you must go away when I am with my family.*

But why, Papa? Aren't I your family, too?

Of course, my love. But you are a spirit. I don't think they would understand.

Alice Germaine pouted dramatically, but her glower soon transformed into a sly smile.

Tell me, Paul prompted, *what do you find so amusing?*

I can visit you even when they can't.

The thought unsettled him, if he could be more unsettled than he already was. *No, Alice,* he said, *you must not do that.*

She looked accusingly. *But Papa, why don't you want them to know about me? Is it because of my skin?*

Somewhere, far off in his distant past, he heard the hurt voice of his first love, Sophie. "Go marry your white cousine! I don't care."

No, no, please don't take me to that place, Alice. Let me love you for the little girl I remember. Those are adult things.

He cried quietly.

Francis had never known about his Martiniquais siblings. Too late to tell him stories about his father's childhood in Saint-

Pierre. Therese should know the truth, at least. He shouldn't let that happen to her, to let her live her life without knowing them. But how could he? How could he after all this time? After all the lies?

He no longer knew why he had left his family behind to come to America. His motives were all hidden in layers of guilt and regret and rationalizing. And all of this guilt bubbled up whenever he thought about it. Times had not been easy in those years in Martinique, but not so hard he couldn't have stayed. It hadn't been a lack of love. Had it?

He had living children now. There was no time for these regrets. For these revenants. But what do you do with the dead? The body of his son lying in the mortuary had reminded him how quickly one becomes the other. And now he must make room for Francis, there among his other spirits. If that meant dredging up the past, well, that was what he would have to do. How else would he ever make peace with it?

But he couldn't help thinking that Francis did not belong with those others in l'habitation Sablon.

THAT NIGHT he returned to the Sablon house for the first time in a long while and he dared to go walking the halls looking for stories about Saint-Pierre. He checked in on Maman in her sitting room where she chatted with Tata Elmire. He peeked into Mannie's room, but realized he had nothing to say to his brother, so he left, quietly, without disturbing him. He walked by Joseph's door and Eustase's, afraid of what he might find there, not wanting to stir it up, whatever it might be.

On his way to Stéphanie's room, he passed the cellar door with its padlock. Far in the depths of the house, chains rattled, voices cried out, and he shivered. This is where he kept the darkest of secrets, those things not to be acknowledged except in times of deepest reflection. If at all. He had never met his grandfather, Jean Joseph Poncy, in life. But those shameful stories about him, about his gold and his crimes, tales too painful to think about, resided there in that caliginous lodging. Along with the slaves tortured and murdered on the plantations the old man had managed. And the ghosts of the hanged of Place Bertin, executed in part because of his grandfather's testimony in the court of Orleans.

There lived all those nasty things that might have reminded him of his family's guilt. He didn't deny that these were terrible crimes, but he was Grand-pére, after all. And family is family. And things done in the name of family are done for the survival of the family. Isn't that what they tell you? They still tell you. And no matter how hard he'd once tried to un-tell those stories of his family, the truth of them always snagged him.

No, it didn't have to be done that way. *Perhaps.* But it was the way it was, and now it could never be undone. The powerful currents of history are unforgiving, and what is the use of agonizing over it?

There were other, more pleasant, rooms in that house, such as the attic filled with ephemera. On makeshift plank shelves sat dusty boxes of lost photographs, childhood toys, books he'd once read: Jules Verne and Emile Zola and Victor Hugo. *Bouvard et Pécuchet,* leaning there against *Le Triomphe d'Eglantine,* a novel by René Bonneville he'd never finished. A tin flute, bent where he'd stepped on it in frustration at the age of five, a hand-woven bracelet given to him by Sophie. She was somewhere in this house too, but he never stopped to talk to her. She'd become merely a shadow of a ghost, a revenant of youthful longing.

And then there was Stéphanie's room, and whenever he walked into her room, he entered a world of wonder. Outside of her balcony bustled the fashionable Rue Sainte-Catherine, in the old city of Bordeaux, and he knew he could follow Stéphanie through her secret passages out onto the street below. They might take Alice Germaine or the boys, or they might go alone, arm-in-arm, like young lovers, weaving through the crowds of shoppers and the horse-drawn carriages making their way along the narrow, cobbled streets.

But he'd always felt guilty when he conjured these things. It was as though he were cheating on Clara. On his living children. And he couldn't abide that in himself. But it was something else, too. It was the way he had left them all to the mercy of the volcano.

Mon cher, said Stéphanie, as though it had been yesterday. *I am glad you dropped in. Would you like to take a stroll with me and Alice?*

Alice Germaine again appeared from out of nowhere, as his visitants invariably seemed to do.

Did you bring Francis with you?

Not yet, Alice, he said, sensing the slight irritation in his voice. *I must find Yvonne first.*

Stéphanie and Alice gave him a puzzled look, as they always did when he mentioned his missing daughter.

Alright Papa, said a disappointed Alice, giving him a long face.

He was sorry. He wanted to tell all his children, living and dead, just how sorry he was, but he didn't know how to do that.

Stéphanie kissed his cheek. *Au revoir, mon cher,* she said. Her look now expressed concern. Then mother and daughter walked out the door, hand in hand, leaving him to stew in his forgetfulness. He would tell them soon how much he loved them.

But first, he must find Yvonne.

THE TROUBLE WITH PAPA

By morning, Theresa had forgotten about the world's unfairness and gone back to worrying about Papa, who sat rocking in his chair, with his pipe in his mouth, as though he had never left it to go to bed last night. She knew he had, because she'd heard him walking up the squeaky stairs in the late hours as she lay awake feeling sorry for herself, which she was now ashamed of in the light of morning. It was her dear brother who had died, and she had no right to wallow in pity for herself.

Maman, she thought in French, because some mornings she woke up thinking in French, *is so strong, despite her difficulties. She doesn't mope around like everyone else. She takes her lumps and soldiers on.* Which she was doing this morning by making poached eggs and toast with maple syrup for everyone. And bacon, which sizzled in the skillet.

"Theresa," Mom called out as she came down the stairs, "put plates on the table, s'il-te-s'il-te-plaîtplaît."

"Oui, Maman," she said, and began to set the table.

Theresa felt as though she, herself, was a thoroughly modern American. But she had never rejected her Quebec side like Frank had. She thought of Papa in French, because he was so old-fashioned Français, it seemed to her. Most of the time Maman was simply Mom, but Papa was almost always Papa, unless she was teasing him by calling him Pops, a recent habit she'd picked up from Frank. No matter, Papa always called her mon ange or ma chère, not ruffled in the least, so she didn't know if her teasing really had an effect or not.

She had almost laid all the place settings out when she realized she had too many. Clair was still in the hospital. Frank would never be eating with them again. The thought was distant and emotionless and she didn't understand. She loved her brothers. So what was wrong with her?

She let it pass without further examination. She decided to put the settings all out, anyway. A kind of memorial to her missing brothers.

"Pops," she called out when the table was set, "breakfast."

Just then, Raymond began crying and Theresa went off to fetch him, as Art, followed closely by Henry, darted in front of her on their way to the table. "Slow down, petits démons."

Mom tut-tutted from the kitchen, but Theresa ignored it, making her way upstairs to the baby's room. *What a madhouse I'm living in,* she thought.

BACK IN THE DINING ROOM, Theresa passed baby Raymond to her mother, who spoon fed him some egg, as she continued talking about a letter from Uncle Edgard. "He will be moving to Los Angeles later this year or next. As soon as this pandemic has passed." Mama had a soft spot for her eccentric uncle, whom Theresa had met a few years ago. "He will be moving with his new bride, Irene, and setting up an art studio."

"Will we visit him in Los Angeles?"

"Of course, my dear. Maybe he will paint your picture."

Theresa liked this idea, imagining a beautiful portrait of herself in her best Sunday dress hanging in the hall.

Mama finished setting the food out, balancing baby Raymond on her free arm. "Papa," Theresa called out as she sat down to eat, but Papa was in his world again.

"Your Papa can eat later," scolded Mom. "Don't worry about him. He has a lot on his mind."

"Okay," said Theresa, but it didn't seem right to her, somehow, Papa sitting there like that, comatose. *He should be here with us.*

She broke her egg with her fork and watched the lazy yellow yolk drip down over the edge of the toast. Then she put the bacon on top and poured syrup over it all. This was the way to eat breakfast. She noticed Papa's newspaper folded in his empty chair and she called out again, "Pops, your newspaper's getting yellow edges."

"Theresa Marguerite," said Mom. "Please leave your Papa alone. He doesn't need you nagging him."

"But he should be having breakfast with us," she insisted.

Her mother emitted a small, sad sigh of exasperation. Theresa backed off. Mom was hurting, too. They were all just living in this bad dream, weren't they? Trying to get through another day.

It had been like this for months. Even before the contagion struck down her brother, they'd been isolated in this small house, Mom and Pops and six children, afraid to go out without masks, unable to attend school, because school was closed, unable to play with their friends, many whose families were in mourning for lost brothers and sisters and mothers and fathers and aunties. Only Papa must work, because of the trains, so what good had it all done? This flu had ruined Christmas, as her brothers wasted away in the hospital. Would the world always be this sad? Would there ever be better times?

She thought there might not be. *C'est la vie*, says Papa. *C'est la vie*, says Mom.

SHE CURLED up on the couch, as close as she could to Papa's rocking chair. "Papa," she said, "who is Alice?"

Papa closed his eyes, and for a moment Theresa thought he was going to ignore her. Was that a tear in his eye?

Then he said, "Alice Germaine was a little girl I once knew. She was about your age when I saw her last."

"Was this in Bordeaux, Papa?"

Papa sighed. "Oui," he said. Then after another moment, he added, "No, mon ange. It was Saint-Pierre."

"Oh," she said, not understanding why Papa said one thing, then another. "Is that the place where Eustase died?"

"Oui," he said with another deep sigh. She sensed his reluctance to talk about this, but it only made her want to know all the more. "Is that an island?" she asked, remembering the story from long ago.

"Martinique is an island, yes."

She thought she remembered something about Martinique from school, but she couldn't remember what it was. It was in the Caribbean, wasn't it? She recalled Papa's stories.

"Is Yvonne a *real* little girl?"

Papa was silent for a very long time before he said, "Yvonne was Alice Germaine's baby sister. She was only a month old when I left Martinique."

"So André was real, too," she said, recalling the older brother in Papa's stories.

"Oui," said Papa, clearly fighting back his emotions. "And Adrien, Alice's younger brother."

Theresa thought maybe she should leave Papa alone, but

he'd never talked about his earlier life before. She was amazed that he even had one. And she wanted to know everything there was to know.

"So why isn't Alice Germaine in the story about Yvonne, Papa?" It would be nice to have a story about someone her own age.

Papa looked troubled. "Maybe," he said, "your Papa isn't clever enough to juggle so many children in his head at one time."

The answer did not completely satisfy her, but she decided to let it go. The tears in Papa's eyes told her she'd pushed it as far as she dared.

LIFE GOES ON

Once again, Paul observed Theresa Marguerite walk away, disappointment marring her pretty face. He must be more present for her, and for his boys, or he would lose them. He must push away these revenants for the last time, push away that house and all of those memories that wouldn't let go of him. Because life goes on, and as much as he dreaded the thought, he must return to work soon. The trains must run, and as lead machinist at the Santa Fe shops, that responsibility belonged to him, and he couldn't help but take it seriously. It was part of the legacy passed down to him by generations before him: responsibility, commitment, and family. They were everything.

Clara returned from the hospital in the afternoon with the good news that their son, Clair, had improved. The pneumonia which wracked his lungs had cleared. A few more days are needed, the doctor said, to be certain. But it looked as if Paul wouldn't be losing a second son.

Now he must only come to peace with the loss of one. How would he do that when the old sorrow, that suit he wore just beneath his skin, still ate at him all these years later? Would it be easier to let Francis Paul rest than it was to bury Alice

Germaine and Adrien who were not even his blood children? And what of André Paul and the elusive Yvonne, only a month old when he last saw her? He recalled the day he left his family there on that dock in Saint-Pierre as clearly as if it had been a week ago. They'd all been there, Stéphanie and their sons and daughters, Maman, Emmanuel, Raphaël, and Samuel. Léonie had been there, as well. Even Joseph had wished him the best of luck in America, because his big brother, despite his resentments and prejudices, had been instilled with that same trilogy of responsibility, commitment, family. And all said goodbye to him with the belief in their hearts that he would return to Martinique in a few years, return to his family. Return to the land of his birth. That there would be a future together once he'd fulfilled his obligation to learn his trade. An obligation he'd taken on for his family and his island.

He accepted the fact that had he indeed returned before the eruption, he would also be dead in the ashes of Saint-Pierre. Yet he could not rid himself of this guilt. This belief that somehow he let them all down. That he'd been unfaithful to them.

He'd put that all away once, after Francis and Theresa were born. But it hadn't stayed buried. He wasn't certain when the obsession returned, perhaps when Theresa was five or six, always wanting her papa to tell her stories, and then one day out of the blue she asked about his life before he came to America.

"Papa," he remembered her asking, "can you tell me a story about before you came to America?"

He hadn't been ready for such a question. It shook him, to tell the truth. And it had been so long now since Martinique even entered his thoughts.

"I will try to remember one, mon ange," he'd said.

That night he'd found himself in l'habitation Sablon for the first time since he last locked those doors so many years before. And he'd rediscovered his sadness because he still couldn't see the face of his little girl, his Yvonne. Perhaps he might draw a face for her, not with his clumsy hand, with his mind. She'd have Stephanie's forehead, his own hazel eyes. She'd be smart and brave.

HE ATE dinner with his family that night, though he had no appetite, really, and he mostly nibbled at the edges of his meal. He put minimal effort into being social, and after a while, Clara and the children steered their conversations around him. His mind became a fog once more. Or more accurately, had never emerged from the fog where it had been lost for weeks. He felt feverish and confused, and he hoped it wasn't another relapse of the flu, like the one he'd suffered in early December.

Paul excused himself from dinner. "I am not feeling well," he said and returned to his chair in the living room, fumbling with his pipe and tobacco.

Something had gone terribly wrong in his mind. Something important, but he had no clue how to fix it. He'd never been whole since the volcano. And it was almost as though this family, this life, this world, all these things were not real. They were just some passing dream because when he looked back on his life, he saw only this tiny baby girl in her mother's arms as she stood on the dock in Saint-Pierre waving goodbye.

YVONNE MEETS CAPTAIN MARIE
THE ADVENTURES OF YVONNE

Long ago, there was a little girl named Yvonne who lived on an island in the blue Caribbean sea with her maman and her older brother, André.

Papa had gone far away to another land in the north where he had taken a job, so that he could make money to send home to Maman. Yvonne had not seen Papa since she was a tiny waddling. Maman, who was an artiste, often drew pictures of Papa and told stories about him and the wonderful land of Bordeaux, where Papa was born.

Ladies in Bordeaux, Maman said, wear the finest hats and go to the ballet in the evening, and speak only the most sophisticated French. They smoke cigarettes in cigarette holders as long as a little girl's arm, which they hold just so.

"One day we shall move to Bordeaux," Maman said, her eyes fixed on her distant dream, "and we shall live in Papa's house, and then, someday soon after that, Papa shall join us there."

Yvonne wasn't sure about cigarette holders and never speaking Matinik, but she wanted like nothing else to see her Papa, whom she hardly remembered.

And an adventure on the high seas might be fun, too. Boring steam liners were of no interest to Yvonne. Those were the ships that took Papa away. She wanted to sail with pirates on a schooner, like those which often filled the harbor of Saint-Pierre.

One summer day, Maman went out and left Yvonne and André with Tata Rosa, Maman's sister. Yvonne liked Auntie Rosa, who read stories to them, and never allowed André to tease her when he insisted on being troublesome.

But today, something bothered Yvonne. She didn't know what it was, exactly, but she thought it might be the woman who had come to the door to escort Maman to lunch. There was something a bit off about that woman. She looked mean, not the sort of person with whom Maman normally had lunch.

Maman returned in the afternoon, all ajite and bossy. *Do this, do that, go brush the ashes out of your hair, girl.*

Yvonne wondered what had happened between Maman and the woman, but she didn't find out anything until dinner time.

"We are going on a journey tomorrow," Maman said, taking a bite from her buttered brioche. "I have secured us passage on a sailing ship. We must all pack tonight, without delay."

"Where are we going, Maman?" Yvonne said.

"We are going to Bordeaux, mon ange," said Maman, smiling at last.

Yvonne was so excited, she couldn't believe her ears. She knew it was Mama's dream to go to France. She never imagined that they would actually do so. Dreams are only stories, after all. Yvonne never thought they could be true.

~

THE NEXT MORNING, the roosters were still crowing, and Tata Rosa came by with a small cart like the one which Uncle Auguste used to carry his carpenter tools to work. Uncle Auguste was Maman's brother.

They carried their bags out and loaded them onto the cart. Yvonne noticed that Auntie Rosa did not have any bags. Not only that, she was crying.

"Aren't you going with us, Auntie Rosa?" Yvonne asked. It hadn't occurred to Yvonne that Auntie might stay in Saint-Pierre.

"I cannot, my darling," Auntie said, wiping away a tear with the skirt of her dress. "I will miss you children so very much. But I shall come visit someday as soon as I can."

Yvonne was sorry that Auntie Rosa wouldn't be going with them to Bordeaux.

"Don't be sad, Auntie," she said. "This is only an adventure. I'm certain we will come home again."

Auntie Rosa kissed Yvonne on the cheek, and together they pulled the cart to the mouillage, where the ship awaited them.

Then it was Maman's turn to cry, and Auntie Rosa hugged them all and bid bon voyage.

~

A JOLLY BOAT took them to the ship, piloted by two big gabariers. The ship was enormous, with many large sails and some smaller ones. The crew were huge and scary looking men with tattoos and earrings. Something about them made Yvonne want to turn around and flee back home.

Maybe they really were pirates, she thought, shivering. But, wasn't that just what she had wanted, to sail with pirates across the Atlantic Ocean to Bordeaux? Maybe she should be careful what she wished.

The woman who had met Maman for lunch was waiting for them at the passenger ramp, which the crew lowered to the jolly boat.

"Yvonne, André," Maman said, "this is Captain Marie le Méchant."

Yvonne did not know there could be a woman captain. And with a name like Marie le Méchant, which means Marie-the-Mean-One, she *must* be a pirate, Yvonne thought.

"Pleased to meet you, Monsieur André," the captain said. "Pleased to meet you, Mademoiselle Yvonne. You may call me Captain Marie. I shall strive to make your journey as pleasant as possible."

Captain Marie gave Yvonne a sly wink, and once again, Yvonne felt a strange squirmy feeling deep down inside of her belly.

Two big brawny men with earrings came down from the ship and grabbed the family's heavy bags, lifting them as though they were as light as chicken feathers.

Yvonne wanted to tug at Maman's arm and tell her that something was very wrong and they should go back home at once, but she knew Maman would be cross with her if she did this in front of the captain.

So Yvonne put on a brave face and marched up the gang-way. André had already raced ahead to the top.

Maman was chatting companionably with Captain Marie. It must be alright, thought Yvonne. Maman wouldn't take us into danger, would she?

Captain Marie showed them to their cabin, which seemed small for three people.

"I shall come for you at 11 hours, précis," Captain Marie said to Maman. "The crew will show you the galley."

What did the captain mean about showing Maman the galley? Yvonne knew from Auntie Rosa's pirate book the galley was the kitchen. Perhaps she just wanted Maman to know where she could prepare some tartines for le déjeuner.

After Captain Marie said goodbye and left them, Maman had them choose their bed. Yvonne, being the youngest, of course, had to choose last, but she was happy to have a small window from which she could see the ocean.

After the children unpacked their bags and put their clothes in wooden drawers, Maman told them to sit down, that she had something to tell them.

"Captain Marie has hired me to cook meals for this ship," Maman said. "It's very hard and long work cooking for three dozen big men. So, I will be away from you children for much of the day."

"What shall we do all day?" André said, looking glum.

"You shall have to entertain yourselves when you are not working."

"Working?" Yvonne said, alarmed.

"Yes," said Maman. "We must pay our way to Bordeaux with our sweat."

André became excited as he pictured himself hoisting the mainsail.

But Yvonne did not like this at all. Not that she hated hard work, but what could a little girl like her do on this large ship full of big grown up sailors?

Maman saw the concern on Yvonne's face and put her arm around Yvonne.

"Don't worry, mon ange," Maman said. "Captain Marie promised me you could be the navigator's assistant and help keep the maps and logs in perfect order."

Yvonne's face changed from a frown to a huge grin. She now pictured herself sitting on the bridge, learning about navigating by the stars, and all the other things a navigator needed to know.

Perhaps this voyage wouldn't be so terrible, after all.

PART 2
JOURS D'ÉCOLE

TATA'S FUNERAL

SAINT-PIERRE, 1892

So many things are easy in Martinique. So many are hard. There is no trouble staying warm, there's no trouble getting drunk. The nights are noisy; the mosquitos are terrifying, but who notices these things? That's just life, isn't it? The way things are. It always rains on Montagne Pelée too, and the Rivière Roxelane turns brown with mud washing off the slopes. She rolls, ripples, and tumbles past le Pont Roche to the sea.

Paul paused on the bridge sometimes, on his way from running one errand or another. Perhaps to the boulangerie in the morning. In such case, he would have a baguette or two under his arm. A bag of croissants in his hand. If he had been to the mouillage market, he might carry manioc flour in a sack slung over his shoulder for Sandrine to make island bread, or precious wheat from America, if a shipment had arrived in the harbor.

He was hardly more than a boy, but at his age his older brothers, Eustase and Joseph, were preparing for work in the Plissoneau shipping firm, and for the Dupouys.

Eustase had been gone for three years. Paul lingered on the

pont and watched the Roxelane until he grew dizzy. He would not be going to work, even though at thirteen he would soon finish with école primaire. Times were different, and there were now two secondary schools in Saint-Pierre. His brother, Emmanuel, a year older, attended the Lycée Saint-Pierre. But Paul would go to Saint-Louis-de-Gonzague in the fall with the béké boys and France blancs and the sons of rich mulâtre merchants. It was good. He was glad to attend séminaire. The other young men would study so they could enlarge their families' fortunes. Some would even go to the Métropole to l'université and learn about the science of agriculture or perhaps medicine. Maybe one of his friends might someday find a cure for yellow fever or malaria. Who knows who could be the next Louis Pasteur? But Paul wanted to be a priest, to unlock the secrets of death, to know about the life of the soul. About Eustase, so that the image of him in Emmanuel's blood-soaked arms, the image of him laid out on the platform their father constructed, of Maman and Aunt Elmire washing him as if he were a baby could be erased — so that he could see Eustase in all his heavenly raiment, then Paul could ease his mother's heart.

Long before Emmanuel's last days at primary school, his father was planning for him to join the extensive network of family businesses. If not Plissoneau, then Dupouy, if not Dupouy, then the Petits, if not Petits, then Caminade or Assier du Pompignan. There were distilleries, plantations, shippers, importers — was there, in fact, any business on the entire island where his father's family, the Poncys, or his mother's, the Fauvé-Sablons, did not have a connection? Or so it seemed to Paul. In some ways, he was entangled in this web of family ties stretching back to the first years of the French in Martinique. Family lore even spoke of a Caraïbe ancestor, if one was to believe such rumors.

It's not at all that he was not ready to take on the responsibilities of a man. Though some of his cousins accused him of it, half joking. "What do you want to be a priest for?" said cousin Raphaël. "There's no future in it, is there? Not like the old days."

They'd taken to calling him Father Paul. It was all good-natured. Paul was the youngest of the first cousins, the one who had always been indulged — especially after the hunting accident. Everyone knew how much Eustase meant to him.

Behind him, the roofers and carpenters and other workers laughed and called to one another in Matinik Kréyol as they arrived at the cathedral to begin their day's work repairing the damage from last August's terrible storm. The wind had torn off the roof of the church as it had many of the roofs in Saint-Pierre, including his own family home. So many, in fact, that there were not enough skilled roofers on the island to repair them.

Paul turned away from the river. The distinctive dome of Eglise Saint-Pierre, the oldest surviving church on the island, built in 1680, loomed between him and the ocean, its grounds littered with storm debris. He had time to light a candle for Eustase. Maman would not scold him. The bread would be almost as fresh. Maybe even still warm.

THE DEAD RABBIT *is on the far side of the fence. You do what you always do, you lean the shotgun against the wire, next to your brothers' guns. You are eager to retrieve your prey, so you don't set your safety lock. You never do. No one ever does. You have all done this dozens of times. You just need to cross the fence with your brothers. Your eleventh birthday is two weeks away and you are still a little awkward and the fence snags on your trousers. Your brothers, Eustase, and Emmanuel, and cousin Raphaël are already on the other side of the fence, waiting for you.*

"Hurry up, Paulie," jibes twelve-year-old Emmanuel. "Why are you being so slow?"

"I'm caught up in the fence," you say, a little miffed at his taunting.

"Don't hurry him, Mannie," scolds Eustase. Eustase reaches over the fence to retrieve his shotgun, just as the barbed wire that is holding you back rips free of your trousers, throwing you forward. The shotgun's discharge roars in your ear as you lurch into the grass. Mannie screams. Why is he screaming? Why did Eustase fire the shotgun? Your first thought is a snake. You imagine the body of the fer-de-lance in the pasture, torn to pieces by the shotgun pellets.

Then you lift yourself, still a little stunned by your clumsy fall and confused by the surrounding commotion.

You rise and you see him lying there, his arm torn away, his face freckled with the wounds of stray pellets, his eyes open in surprise and glassy with death. Eustase. Emmanuel stands over his body, mouth open, frozen in shock.

Raphaël shakes Mannie from his stupor. "Go get help. Hurry."

Raphaël tries to stop the bleeding, but you can see it's futile. Eustase twitches on the ground, still in the throes of death. You know there is no saving him. He's gone.

THIS SCENE PLAYED out repeatedly in Paul's mind, ending always with that glassy, morbid stare. He thought, *was it my fault?* He told himself, *It might have been my shotgun.* He wondered, *why Eustase?* Why this big brother he idolized? The big brother who had always given him, the youngest, respect.

Then finally, he asked, *what kind of God is it who treats his children like this?*

So his candle's light cast small flickering shadows of uncertainty. His prayers were less like prayers and more like questions.

But still he lit the candle. Said the prayer. *I will become a priest,* he thought, *and perhaps someday I will understand these mysteries.*

~

IT WAS JANUARY, and a hundred varieties of liana bloomed in shocks of brilliant color on the hillsides. Purples, reds, blues, golds. In the city, roses and lilies and orchids were everywhere aflame. Bananes still flowering as they offered their yellowing fruit. Sweet mangues in their trees awaiting winter harvest.

The city was emerging from the shadow of the mornes, and Paul took in the colors and the smells and the sounds of morning in Saint-Pierre. From the old market of the Fort, the fishermen called out their morning catch. The market had been closed for over two years, but the fishermen didn't care. They must sell the fish. And the gendarmes and soldiers, by some agreement, refused to bother them. They liked their fish, too.

Paul turned up his street, carrying Maman's baguettes and a few sweet brioche buns to share with his brothers, Mannie and Joseph, who were both home this morning. Many of the houses still had no roofs, and piles of storm rubble adorned the neighborhood streets and gardens. His family home was less badly damaged than some, and Papa had hired roofers to replace the slate tiles blown off in the hurricane.

Paul climbed the stone steps up to the door of their two-story townhouse at number 15 Rue Castelnau. In the planters by the door, Maman had raised beautiful Martinican roses, which somehow survived the wind. Some were now taller than a full-grown man, all blooming in crimsons and vermilions. He pulled open the big mahogany door and called out for Maman, but there was no answer. He took the bread into the kitchen and called out again. But it was Joseph, not his mother, who came to the kitchen door.

"Maman is at the Dupouy's," his oldest brother reported, displaying an uncharacteristic sadness.

Paul thought of his auntie who had been bedridden for several weeks now. "Tata?" he asked. Hoping it wasn't so. Knowing otherwise. They all loved Tata Elmire, who was Papa's dearest and only remaining sibling, except for an older brother, Raphaël, who left for Paris and London years ago and who never wrote, so no one knew if he was alive or dead.

"Yes," Joseph said, running his fingers through his dark hair. "She passed this morning. Samuel came by to let us know. Maman is helping Adèle prepare her."

Prepare her for the priest's rites. Prepare her body for the cimetiére. *So many deaths in my family,* thought Paul. *So many taken by the storms, and by the disease they bring in their wake.*

But this is life, yes?

MAMAN CLÉMENCE, Cousine Edith, and Cousine Té would work all day helping Adèle with the house, Joseph told him. There would be a wake for Tata in the evening, with relatives and well-wishers arriving today and the next day, bringing food and kind words for the grieving family. Marceline, the Dupouy children's caretaker, and Edith's thirteen-year-old daughter, Léonie, had taken the little ones to the Mouillage market for the morning, primarily to get them out of the women's hair. It was quite a task—between the Dupouys and the Caminades, there were a half-dozen young children from the ages of one to six years old.

Paul wanted to help, but he knew the women would object to him hanging around underfoot. For a moment, he considered leaving to find the children. He enjoyed his cousine Léonie, who was his own age, but she would be busy herding the little ones, so he decided to stay at home and read, maybe kick around a little later with Mannie, when he returned from wherever he was off to.

Laying on his bed, Paul picked up his latest Jules Verne novel, *L'Étoile du Sud,* about a French engineer in South Africa who sets out to make an artificial diamond. It promised to be an even more exciting adventure than *La maison à vapeur,* his last Verne, which featured a house that traveled across India, pulled by a mechanical, steam-powered elephant.

To be part of the new scientific machine age, that was a dream. If only Martinique wasn't so backward. If only there were railroads here, like in civilized countries. Or moving pictures like those le Frères Lumière were making in Paris.

Paul lost himself in his book, only pulling himself away for a few moments to spread some cheese on a baguette. Cyprien Méré, the hero of the novel, has just met Alice Watkins, the beautiful daughter of a wealthy landowner in the diamond fields of Griqualand. He imagines Alice with pretty blonde hair and blue eyes full of longing, peering into his own brown Martiniquais eyes, her lovely lips whispering, "Mon cher," into his ear.

His heart fluttered. He closed the book and his eyes, lost in a daydream.

Later, when he emerged from his room, it was afternoon. He called out to Emmanuel, but his brother was nowhere about. So he put on his sandals and walked out to the small back garden. Even Louis, the gardener, had left, and Paul felt like the world came to a stop to honor Tata.

He returned inside and dressed for the evening without waiting for Mannie. The family would begin arriving at the wake in a few hours. The men, Papa, Samuel, and Gustav might already be there.

When he finished dressing, he would take a leisurely walk up toward the séminaire before going on to the Dupouy house on Rue des Bons Enfants.

PAUL CLIMBED the slope of Rue Castelnau, stopping now and again to wipe the sweat from his forehead. His suit was warm, and he regretted not wearing something cooler. Madame Pelée loomed in the north, her secret face hidden behind a veil of fog, so you couldn't tell if she was laughing at you or crying. *Surely you are crying for Tata today.*

He rounded the corner on Allée Pecoul and crossed over by the Grainau house on Rue Montnoël. Three-year-old Alice Germaine was playing by the side of the street. "Bon aprés-midi, Mademoiselle," said Paul, crouching to make himself child height.

The little girl grinned at him with her chubby brown face and turned shyly away.

"Bon après-midi, Monsieur Paul," the little girl's mother, Stéphanie, called from the front stoop. "I am so sorry to hear about your dear Tata."

"Bon après-midi, Madame," he replied. "Merci."

"Please extend my sincere condolences to your family."

"I will, Madame. That's very kind of you."

He waved goodbye before crossing over Rue Montnoël to the séminaire. Stéphanie waved back, and little Alice Germaine called out in Matinik, "Orevwa, Misye Poncy."

The Grainau family had lived here in this house since he could remember. Stéphanie had always been sweet to him, and today she seemed beautiful as well. He was a little surprised and self-conscious, because he had never thought of her in this way before.

He dawdled along the perimeter of le Séminaire-Collège Saint-Louis-de-Gonzague, thinking about his future. Perhaps he would be an engineer like Cyprien Méré. If being a priest didn't work out, that is. And didn't the church need engineers, as well? Even in Martinique, there must be engineers for the roads and bridges and dams. And for the electrification, which will come someday soon. And for the many not-yet-invented machines that the future will bring into their lives. Perhaps Papa would send him to America to study once he learned English at Collège. Or maybe the Church would send him to America, to some frontier outpost where there were Indians and mountain men and no one remembered God.

Paul turned away from these thoughts and looked up at the windows of the school. *Next year,* he thought, *I will be here, in this school, making new friends, learning new things.* That idea made him happy.

LA MAISON DUPOUY was buzzing with activity when Paul arrived. Mannie and Joseph sat on the balcony with Fernand Billioti. Pretty Lucie Plissonneau Duquène stood in the doorway, talking to Mannie. She held a bowl of fruit in one hand, on its way to the bouffé table at the far end of the large balcony, which wrapped around the house like a veranda.

"Bonjour, Paul," Lucie greeted as he mounted the stone steps. "Hi Lucie," he said. Mannie peered over the wrought-iron railing at him, "Hey, Paulie, come join us."

"I'll be up in a moment." Paul waved and walked past them into the house. Papa sat in the parlor with Gustav Caminade, Samuel Dupouy, Samuel's younger brother, Raphaël, and

Georges Plissonneau Duquène. It surprised him to see Uncle Edgard, Maman's brother, as well. The men, all very somber, talked about politics and business, as always. In the kitchen, Maman, Adèle, Edith, Té. Alix Biliotti cuddled Adèle's new baby, Robert, and the mothers were all cooing at him. Some of the older girls were standing around talking as well. Woman stuff.

Léonie Billioti wasn't in the kitchen, so she must still be with Marceline and the younger children. He could hear them out back in the garden, shouting and playing. He loved being around the little ones, and he would rather be there than on the balcony with the boys. But as the youngest Poncy boy, they already teased him enough. Mannie was the worst of them. *Priest. Daydreamer.* He didn't need to be taunted by his brother for some imagined childishness, as well. Or worse, *girlishness.*

He stood at the kitchen door just long enough for Maman to note that he'd arrived. He gave her a brief wave before he returned and leaned in the doorway to the parlor to listen to the men. To them he was still a child, and he didn't expect to be invited into adult conversation. But he could stand quietly and listen.

They were talking about the poor harvest, devastated by the August hurricane, and the perennial problem of getting the cane from Trinité and Basse-Pointe to the distilleries of Saint-Pierre. Once rebuilt, that is. It was a slow process, given the lack of money and shortage of skilled labor. Still, many would be back by summer with some grudging help from the Métropole. The Atlantic coast had no natural harbors, and its brutal tides could wreck a ship of any size. But the mountain roads, while well kept, were steep and impossible, as well. "The harvest will return, but we desperately need that railroad into Saint-Pierre, Georges," Uncle Edgard said. "The damn nègres are letting this country fall apart."

The dark-skinned Gustav raised an eyebrow, but said nothing.

"We shall have one," cousin Georges said. "By the fin de siècle, I wager. It is being discussed, tentatively, in the General Council at this moment. The progressives are ready to align with us on this. And there's money in Paris, if we take the lead."

"In a few years," Samuel said, "we will have the groundwork laid and the backers we need to convince the Métropole to support us. A decade at the most."

"A real railroad!" Paul burst into the conversation, unable to control his enthusiasm. "I would like to help build that!"

Papa gave him a stern look for speaking out of place. But Uncle Edgard said, "I thought you were going to be a priest, Paul."

"Oui," said Paul, now given tacit permission by his uncle to speak. "But I can build a railroad at the same time. Yes?"

"You certainly have ambition," Gustav said. "Maybe we can find a place for you, somewhere."

Papa smiled for just an instant before giving him another cross look, warning him to not interrupt again.

Time to join the boys out front.

The thought of his potential future delighted him. In his mind, he pictured the big American steam locomotives in one of Monsieur Verne's romances. Ah, to build one of those.

JOURS D'ÉCOLE

MOST OF THE boys at Saint-Louis-de-Gonzague were boarders. They came from Fort-de-France and Sainte-Marie and Lamentin. From every quarter of Martinique, in fact, and even a few from Guadeloupe or Sainte-Lucie or other neighboring isles. They were mostly the sons of wealthy white planters and rich créole entrepreneurs of all colors. Some were from good Catholic families and had come for religious instruction. But like all elite educational institutions, Saint-Louis-de-Gonzague existed to build lifelong school ties, and for introducing new friends to sisters and cousines to construct potential family ties as well. In a nutshell, the school's primary function was to maintain the considerable political influence of the conservative békés, the rural white créole elite, and so protect the endangered Faith. Or so reasoned the old men of the Church.

Paul didn't yet understand the powerful forces that ruled his world. But what he knew now, on the eve of his fourteenth birthday, was that he was going to learn English and science and mathematics and things spiritual. That he would soon make new friends. That it was an exciting time to be alive, to be taking these first steps into the future and adulthood.

He eagerly donned his school uniform, lingering in front of the mirror, making sure everything was just right before saying goodbye to Maman and Sandrine and setting out on this fine Martinique morning for his first day of classes. The city was still in the shadow of the hills, but the drone of the night insects had given way to morning songbirds as the first light crept in from the sea. Bread-sellers called out as they made their way through the rues of the Quartier du Fort. The washerwomen carried their baskets of laundry to the rivière Roxelane.

Stéphanie Grainau sat on her balcony as he passed by, Alice Germaine beside her. He waved, and mother and daughter returned his greeting in kind. "Bonjou, Misye Poncy," the little girl called out.

"Bonjou Mamzel — et Madame."

"I wish you the best at school, Monsieur Poncy," Stéphanie said.

"Merci, Madame. I am looking forward to it."

She smiled at him with her warm smile, and he sauntered off across Rue Montnoël and, taking two steps at a time, ascended the stairway up the hill to campus.

ON PAUL'S FIRST DAY, morning prayers were followed by the presentation of the annual curriculum. "For your first year," Père François said, "you will be studying the liturgy and the important figures and events of the Old Testament. And, of course, Latin. Religious instruction will occupy your mornings. After midday meal and afternoon prayers, you will study literature, mathematics, and science."

It sounded boring to Paul, and he was distressed at the proportion of religious instruction to his other studies, particularly science and mechanics, though he felt guilty about it. He knew he must forge ahead with what was given him if he wished to learn. And he wanted to learn.

Paul tried to keep focused on the morning lessons, and some of it was quite interesting. Many of the Old Testament stories were new to him. The père-professeurs insisted the students pay close attention so they might add to a lively discussion with the class afterward. But the instructor, Père Tomàs, was very strict in his interpretation of the Bible, and some students were sternly reprimanded for trying to argue a point. Paul hoped that all of his religious instructors were not so narrow minded.

At Tata's funeral, his cousin, Raphaël Dupouy, an adamant republican, had tried to convince him he should attend the secular lycée if he wanted to study science and engineering. "You know, Paul, those priests would like to stop the whole of modernity if they could. They only teach science and technology because the Republic requires it of them."

"But Maman would not allow it," Paul said. "She insists I go to a Catholic school. Besides, how can I be a priest if I go to a public school?"

Raphaël sighed. "Young cousin, the country needs progress, not priests. You'll see."

Paul harumphed and left to join the boys on the balcony. He did not believe that the priests could be so bad.

Still, a seed had been planted in his mind by cousin Raphaël. A seed not yet ready to grow. But already, in the first week of school, the Fathers were watering it.

AFTER A FEW DAYS OF CLASSES, Paul fell into a routine:

Each morning he rises in the early hours before the sun has emerged. The roosters are crowing, and the songbirds singing from the garden where he breakfasts. Sandrine, their servant, has set out bread and coffee, some mango juice, which he consumes in a leisurely fashion. Then, when the morning bells ring out across the town of Saint-Pierre, he returns to his room and gathers his bag of school books. He kisses Maman, who is usually in the parlor. "Au revoir, Sandrine," he calls out before he goes through the door, so she will know he has left the house, and he climbs the slope of Rue Castelnau to the Allée Pécoul. "Good morning, Étienne," he may call out to the bread seller if he passes him on the street. If Madame Marlet is out purchasing a loaf of levain, Paul tips his hat to her, "Good Morning, Madame." Or Alexandrine, the fruit seller may greet him as she passes. "Bonjou, Mesye Poncy." And if they are on the balcony in the early hours, which they often are, he stops for a moment at the corner of Rue Montnoël to greet Stéphanie and Alice Germaine before climbing the stairs to Saint-Louis-de-Gonzague.

Paul was one of a few day students, spending nights with his family, making his way home for dinner with Papa and Maman and his brothers on Rue Castelnau. Cousin Samuel had offered to pay his tuition if he had wished to board, but he declined. "You won't have the full advantage of discipline and camaraderie with the other students, Paul," Samuel insisted. But, in Paul's mind, it was just a matter of which bed you slept in at night. Priests telling you to dampen the light, when you would rather be reading an adventure novel. Besides, he could still attend lectures and social occasions in the evening. "Perhaps next year," he told his cousin.

What Samuel didn't tell him, in so many words, was that he would be an outsider in the eyes of the other boys. The day student who was different, who didn't quite fit in.

Paul crossed the campus and entered the grand chapel for morning prayers. Its arches of black basalt gave the impression of a dark grotto, lit by torches and candles and stained glass windows set into its thick volcanic walls. Its vestibule was adorned with crucifixes and crimson and purple tapestries, and the chapel itself bore long mahogany pews, adding to the darkness. It was not as beautiful and grandiose as the nave at the eglise. It was smaller and gloomier and, Paul thought, medieval.

The priests intoned their Latin prayers, which dragged on for far too long, until the students were at last dismissed. *"Veni, vidi, fessus sum,"* a fellow student quipped as they filed from the vestibule. Paul knew just enough Latin to laugh at the joke.

"Must we do this every morning?"

"It will keep the knees limber," Paul said with a chuckle. He tried to remember the mulâtre boy's name, but couldn't quite bring it to mind.

"Climbing these stairs every day should be enough exercise for that," said the student, who Paul recalled was from the south somewhere. Lamentin, or some other flat land. His name was Arnaud or Armand or something, and his father was a négociant in Fort-de-France.

Paul extended his hand. "Paul Poncy. I'm afraid I've forgotten your name."

"Armand Toussaint." The young man shook Paul's hand.

"Good to meet you, Armand."

"Likewise, Paul. Say, aren't you a day student?"

"Oui, my home is a few streets away."

"Tremendous," Armand said. "Perhaps you can show me around Saint-Pierre sometime, if we're ever allowed a day off, that is."

"I'd love to show you the town," Paul said, excited that he'd met his first new friend.

"Great." Armand suddenly veered off the path. Turning to face Paul, he deftly danced backward without a misstep. "Liturgy class this morning. Père Tomàs. Ugh."

He waved and Paul waved back, laughing.

ONE WEDNESDAY, a few weeks later, when no important school activities were planned, Paul took Armand on a tour of Saint-Pierre, leading him along the beach toward the mouillage. When they reached Place Bertin they veered off through the knots of soldiers and gendarmes one always found at the fountain, back up to Rue Bouille, where they could wind their way around the pier where the giant rhum barrels were stacked and waiting to be loaded onto the boats in the harbor. They continued up the hill to pass by the lycée, where students were milling around. Some were engaged in organized activity of some sort—the same sort of games and study groups he would be involved in at the séminaire on a Wednesday. He cast around for Mannie, but didn't see him, so the boys returned to the waterfront, where they purchased accras at a food stall on the beach and ate them while watching rhum barrels being ferried out to a ship bound for Bordeaux.

As they considered leaving the beach for other destinations, Paul spied Samuel outside the Bourse house and hailed him. Samuel smiled and strolled over to where the boys were sitting in the black sand.

"I haven't seen you in a while, cousin," Samuel said. "How is school?"

The boys stood and brushed off the sand, and Paul shook his cousin's hand. "Très bien," he said. "Especially math. I think I have a knack for it."

"It's good to hear you're doing well, Paul. Look, boys, I would love to stay and talk, but I'll be late for my meeting if I do."

"Before you leave, cousin, I'd like to introduce you to my friend, Armand. Samuel, this is Armand Toussaint. He is a student at the séminaire. Armand, my cousin, Samuel Dupouy. Armand's father is a proprietor in Fort-de-France."

"Very glad to meet you, Monsieur," Armand said, shaking hands with Samuel.

"A pleasure to meet you, too, Armand. Now, I must apologize again, cousin. I'm running late." Samuel nodded toward the distillery and rushed off.

Paul watched his cousin disappear up Rue Bouille before turning back to his friend. "Monsieur Dupouy is a financier," he confided, "as well as part owner of the distillery, which is a family enterprise. He is a good person to know if you wish to go into business."

"Thank you for the introduction. Perhaps it will be useful one day." Armand looked as though he wasn't convinced of his own words.

"You never know. Perhaps you will need a lender someday."

Armand sighed. "Please don't take this the wrong way, Paul, but my family has never been treated well by the béké bankers."

"Samuel is not a béké," Paul protested. "Besides, he is not that way. He's fair. He is republican. And his sister is married to Monsieur Caminade, who is also mulâtre, you know."

Armand looked as though he was about to say something more, but refrained "Well, thank you, anyway. I suppose it is good to know people with money."

Paul let Armand's statement hang in the air between them, another reminder of the difference between the white boy and his mulatto friend.

The boys ended their tour at the Jardín Botanique and were heading home when Paul extended Armand an invitation to dinner. The sun hung low over the bay of Saint-Pierre, lighting the sea on fire, as they made their way along the Rue des Trois Ponts. "Why don't you come over for supper, Armand?" Paul said. Seeing his friend's hesitation, he added, "There is always plenty of food."

Armand gave a little snorting laugh. "I mistook you for a poor boy, Monsieur."

Paul laughed, although a little self-consciously. "What is your hesitation, mon ami?"

"There may be other reasons I will not be welcome than lack of food."

"Oh," Paul said, "my parents are not like that." He hoped it was true. Armand must have seen his doubt, because the boy said, "Perhaps another time. It has been a very nice day, but I am too tired to be good company."

Paul felt a moment of disappointment. But maybe Armand was right. Why risk spoiling a beautiful day?

IT WAS difficult finding time to get to know his new friend. School days were broken only by a few brief moments of respite and nourishment. While Wednesdays were more relaxed, and often filled with organized recreation, Armand was usually in the company of a small group of mulâtre boys from the south, and Paul was hesitant to insert himself into their world. *There is the natural tendency of people to stick to their own kind,* Paul reasoned. A few of the priests frowned upon the mixing of the races outside of class, contrary to official school policy. And these conservative curés were vocal in their opinions. Some of the more troglodyte students would be more than happy to enforce the judgement of these priests on everyone, if it would not get them expelled from school.

Paul found extending a second dinner invitation to Armand troubling and awkward. Armand wasn't his only friend, of course, but he had especially taken to the boy, and he wanted a deeper friendship between them.

Paul believed his family was not like the planters and békés clinging to the old notions of race. They were good people. Naturally, he'd picked up nuances of household opinion, which he often discounted because they were the opinions of the old generation. His father was born in the time of the Bourbons and came of age under the reign of Orléans. Anatole Poncy wasn't exactly a monarchist, but neither had he wholeheartedly embraced the republican cause. He was more a Bonapartiste, Paul thought. Even so, there was always a copy of *Les Colonies* lying about the house, alongside the more conservative newspaper, *Les Antilles*. And Papa did not object when Paul read its republican opinions. Or when he buried himself in the sultry Jenny Manet serials carried in its pages.

Maman was Catholic, on the other hand. A Catholic of the conservative, créole kind, who thought that Republicanism and progress were suspicious ideas, possibly promulgated by the Enemies of the Faith. A belief not unfamiliar in the halls of séminaire.

Maman grew up among the planters of the Capisterre, during the time of slavery. She spent much of her childhood in Ajoupa Bouillon, in the care of Euphrasie, the Fauvé-Sablon children's beloved Da.

Although old-fashioned, Papa and Maman were not particularly strict. They treated their boys with a certain liberality and offered them an affectionate household in which to find shelter. Paul and his brothers were encouraged to speak their minds, within certain limits as to time, place, and manner, of course. They were encouraged to bring home friends.

But he had occasionally overheard Maman and his older brother Joseph make comments about the gens de couleur knowing their place, about their negative influence on the white youth of Saint-Pierre. But cousin Gustave is mulâtre, Paul thought, as are many of the businessmen Papa deals with. And, surely, these comments wouldn't apply to a nice Catholic boy like Armand, son of a successful business owner.

It may be hard for the old to change, Paul thought, but his was the new generation. The one that would build the future—the modern Martinique. The more forward looking of his generation struggled against the attitudes of the ancien régime, which stubbornly hung on two decades after the declaration of the Third Republic. Not only in his parents, but in the priests and in the béké boys and even among the mulâtre shopkeepers' sons.

Yet there was this tiny hesitation each time he thought about Armand and dinner. He really just wanted his family to know he had made a new friend. That everything was going well at school. And yet...

LE CERCLE

Paul put off inviting his new friend home until the matter was nearly forgotten, although he still felt occasional guilt. He wondered how the races would ever come together with all of this weight between them. So, he was pleasantly surprised one Wednesday afternoon in early May, when Armand introduced him to a small group of his mulâtre friends.

"Paul, I would like you to meet Alexis Cardin from Fort-de-France. His father works for the Ministry of the Colonies. Paul Poncy is the local boy I told you about." Paul shook hands with a tall, light-skinned mulatto with glasses whom he'd seen in English class. Alexis gave the impression of squinting, as though the light was too much for him. "Pleased to meet you, Alexis."

"Pleased to meet you as well, Paul," the boy said. "Everyone calls me Alex, by the way."

"And this is Eugène Legeay," Armand said, turning to the second boy. "His father owns a market in Fort-de-France."

Paul shook hands with Eugène. "A pleasure to meet you." Eugène merely nodded in response.

"We are forming a small Republican study circle," Armand said. "We want to discuss the future of Martinique."

"And support the workers," Alex whispered, his voice all hushed excitement.

Paul hadn't been shy about his liberal opinions in class, but he was still taken by surprise, and somewhat dumbstruck by the offer to include him in this study circle.

"Consider it, my friend," said Armand. "We meet on Sunday evening."

Paul was excited. He really wanted to be part of an organized social group like the other boys. But would Maman allow it? Sunday evening was traditionally spent at home with family. He was too embarrassed to express his concerns to these new friends, so he just nodded his head without committing.

"We are meeting at the lycée," Alex said. "There are students from there and a few young people from town as well who are interested."

"Girls." Armand winked.

AT HOME THAT EVENING, Paul was astonished when Maman didn't forbid him to go, although she was rather cool to the whole idea.

"I suppose you are a young man, now, and your opinions are your own," she said. "France is a republic," she continued, her mouth and nose clenched, as though fortified against a bad smell, "so I imagine a republican study group will help you understand how this infernal system works. Just be careful to not become involved with radicals."

"I will be careful, Maman," said Paul, who understood that by radicals, Maman meant blacks, whom she feared would use the guillotine on the heads of all white people if they ever came to power. He hadn't told her that his new friends were bourgeois mulâtre. And mulâtres were not the same as nègres, in any case. Not even in Maman's mind.

Maman still held fond memories of her childhood Da, Euphrasie, a mulâtress, rumored to have been sired by her own grandfather, François Xavier, which would make Euphrasie an aunt, but Clémence did not acknowledge such things. Paul wasn't sure how he knew this. Perhaps Mannie told him or Eustase — it wasn't the sort of thing Joseph would mention. Her memories of childhood often seemed so innocent and carefree, yet Paul sensed his maman avoided examining them too closely. He knew her childhood memories brought up a deep longing in her. But only those pleasures which reside on the surface. Long afternoons in the country playing with her cousins in the yard of l'habitation Sablon, riding bareback through the pastures. Teasing and later, flirting with the local boys. Yes, even the mulâtre boys.

The end of all that, she would say, was signaled when the Second Republic came to power, forcing the white créoles to give new rights to the blacks and free mulâtres. She was eight years old when the republicans deposed the Orléans monarch, ending the time of slavery. Her carefree childhood lasted a few more years, but it was never the same again, even after Bonaparte III returned some order to France and her colonies. "Maman and Papa would never let me go anywhere alone, even in the cane fields. We never knew when our very lives would be threatened, our homes burned." Sometimes Clémence paused her reminiscence, at other times she would continue on, "Whenever the republicans return to power, the blacks rise up and burn everything down, clamoring for their so-called freedom. And what's that earned them? Inept leaders who don't know how to run a country. Youth who leave the Church, who fornicate without marriage, who disrespect their elders."

Clémence worried that her sons, too, would lose the Faith.

Not so much Joseph, who was less influenced by the changed world. Paul and Emmanuel were the vulnerable ones. So open to these new ideas. And Anatole let Paul read that trash he left laying about the house. But what could she do? He was old enough now that she would only drive him away from home if she did not give him his opinions.

But she was not required to be happy about it.

SUNDAY EVENING. Paul slipped from the house, avoiding an uncomfortable conversation with Maman, who had given him disapproving looks all afternoon, or so it seemed to him. Maybe it was only his imagination, but he was not in a mood to listen to her anxious fretting.

It was a quiet night in late May, after sunset, and the streets were already dark as he wound his way through the quartier, and across the Roxelane, where business owners and laborers and gendarmes stood in small groups gossiping about the day's news, and the comings and goings in Saint-Pierre. He saw Raphaël Dupouy and waved to his cousin, but he didn't stop to chat or pause on the far side of the bridge to hear the black boy telling a zombi story to a group of youth, although, on another evening, he wouldn't have hesitated to join them. He didn't want to be late for the study circle at the lycée. There was to be a guest tonight, according to Armand, a Pierrotin local who had been organizing with the socialists against the colonial expansion in Africa.

Paul made his way down the slope to Rue Dauphin, where he hastened toward the mouillage and the lycée. A few people were out and about in le Figuier, mostly warehouse workers, wrapping up their day, or men leaving the bars and brothels around Rue Bouille, where it merged into Rue Dauphin. He tried to avoid them, half afraid, more than anything, that he might run into his brother Joseph, or one of the fourth-year students from school, out for an evening of debauchery. And what would he say to them?

If she knew, Maman would scold him for walking through the warehouse district at night, but it was dimanche and the rough men who worked there were mostly pious and would be going home to their families. Well, maybe he needed to keep his eyes open, just a little. But Rue Victor Hugo was boring and the world down here between the warehouses and the docks seemed so much more alive. And there were gendarmes about if he needed to call out. The real business of the world unfolds in places like this, he thought. And the harbor is beautiful at night. The refracted light and lapping of waves, the silhouettes of steamers and clipper ships and the shouts of stevedores working through the long hours until the cargo is loaded and bound for North America or Bordeaux or wherever in the world it might be going. He couldn't help, just a little, longing for those places.

When he passed the Bourse, Paul turned up Rue Précipice toward the lycée. He thought he saw Armand ahead of him on the street and picked up his pace to overtake him. But it wasn't Armand, and he remembered his friend was to come early with Alex and Eugène to meet with tonight's special guest. Armand had invited him to join them, but Paul declined, a little put off by Eugène's coolness toward him. "I can't leave early," he'd said. "I have some things I need to do at home."

Paul was now beginning to understand what Samuel was talking about, feeling like an outsider.

THE PLASTER WALLS and black stone foundations of the lycée were not dissimilar to the séminaire, Paul thought. And a classroom is a classroom. Only missing were the crucifixes and the omnipresence of priests. More people had shown up at the study circle than he expected. More than a dozen. As Armand promised, a handful of them were girls, whom his friend was busy chatting up in the back of the room. Henry Rose Marlet, Stéphanie's cousin, sat near the door, which surprised Paul. Henry was older, about Joseph's age, and long out of school. There was a lighter-skinned woman with him, who might be Camille Bouché, another of Stéphanie's cousins. He didn't know them well, even though they were his neighbors.

The chairs had been arranged in a circle, and most of those seated were his own age or slightly older. School kids. Scanning the room, he spotted Armand sitting with two girls. His friend beckoned him. "This is Sophie," he said, "and Désirée. They are students at the girl's school. This is my friend, Paul. He thinks he wants to be a priest, but we are trying to talk him out of this misguided plan."

The girls laughed. Sophie was a pretty mulâtre girl, with a bit of shyness about her. She was wearing a yellow dress, modern, like the schoolgirls wear, and a blue beret. Désirée was lighter skinned with sharp, chiseled features, and dressed similarly. "So," Désirée said, teasingly, "what is a béké choir boy doing hanging around with dangerous revolutionaries?"

Paul blushed and studied the floor. He hated being called a béké, partly because he recognized the grain of truth that lived within it. He knew she was teasing, but didn't know how to answer. "I'm a republican," he managed at last. "I believe this is the future of Martinique. *Egalité, Fraternité, Liberté.*" He made a sweeping, dramatic bow and smiled a little self-consciously.

The girls laughed again. "I like your friend," Sophie said to Armand. She smiled shyly at Paul.

Just then Eugène walked in, followed by Philippe Guillaume, Stéphanie's amour and father of Alice Germaine.

Behind him came Stéphanie. *So, this is the reason her cousins are here.* Was Philippe the mysterious guest of honor? Paul knew Philippe had been away for a long time in Bordeaux, but he had no clue that the man was a radical socialist.

Paul waved at Stéphanie, and she smiled and approached the small group of young people gathered around him. "Monsieur Poncy," she said, "how very nice to see you here. Are these your friends?"

"I just met Sophie and Désirée. This is my friend, Armand, from school. This is Stéphanie Grainau. She's my neighbor."

"Pleased to meet you," Armand said.

"Likewise," said the girls.

Suddenly, Philippe was standing beside Stéphanie. "Hello, Paul," he said. "I wasn't expecting to see you here tonight. Are you part of this group?"

Paul choked up, unsure of his place here. He looked at Eugène across the room, who glared back at him. Clearly, he wasn't welcomed by all.

"Paul is our chaplain," Armand deadpanned, rescuing him. "He keeps us on the narrow path."

The girls giggled.

"Do they always tease you so shamelessly?" Stéphanie said with amusement.

"Oui, they're merciless."

Across the room, Eugène coldly watched the scene of the béké boy chatting with the guest of honor. He folded his arms tightly across his chest.

The members of the study circle finally seated themselves and made introductions around. Eugène introduced Philippe, who spoke about the politics in Bordeaux, where the socialists and the radical republicans were agitating for a new united party of the left. But the students wanted to hear about the anti-colonial organizing among the troops in Senegal, where

Philippe had spent the last several months. On that subject, Philippe spoke cautiously, his eyes scanning the room as if wary of spies.

As soon as the presentation was over and the guests had departed, Eugène glared at Paul, seeming to say, if there is a spy here, it's *you*.

"I think the white boy should not be here," he said. "Our guests cannot speak freely."

"This is a republican circle," Alex said, coming to Paul's defense. "It's clear that our guest had no problem with his white neighbor being here. If you want an Africanist circle, Eugène, then perhaps this is not the one for you."

Most of the other students nodded agreement. "Our group should be open to all," Sophie said. "We are discussing the future of Martinique, not Africa. Not that it is unimportant, but we are French, oui?"

Eugène huffed, then shrugged, clearly defeated. It appeared he and his friend, Césaire, the two of them whispering in a corner, might leave. But they settled back down and remained silent for the rest of the meeting.

Even with the support of the group, Paul remained uncertain of his place here. But it pleased him that Philippe and Stéphanie had boosted his credibility among his friends.

EUGÈNE AND CÉSAIRE left the instant the meeting was over. Paul joined Armand, Alex, and the other young people in restoring the classroom to order before the boys escorted the two girls home.

"I am sorry that Eugène was so rude to you," Sophie said, as she walked beside Paul along Rue Victor Hugo. "There are differences among us, and I suppose they must come out, eventually. It is perhaps better they are exposed now, do you think?"

"Oui, it's just that I don't want to be the divisive one. I'm not sure I really belong in this group."

"Nonsense," said Alex, who walked behind them. "It's Eugène who is being divisive. We had agreed to something and he is not honoring the agreement."

"But that's the thing," Paul said. "You agreed to it. I wasn't part of that discussion."

"I know what you're saying," Alex said. "But there are issues among us that had to be worked out before we invited you to join the circle. Issues that a white boy might not understand."

That brought Paul up short. He stopped and turned around to face Alex. "Isn't that why I'm here? To learn about these things?"

"These are issues between people of color," Alex said. "We must work them out among ourselves. The question is, do we see ourselves as créole, and therefore in relation to France, or do we see ourselves as descendants of Africans, first."

"Are you not both?" Paul said, speaking a little too sharply. "Are you not also descendants of Europeans?"

"You see, it is a question of alliances and identity, oui? Many of the radicals of color believe we should identify primarily with our nègre brothers. Others think—"

Paul threw his hands in the air in frustration. "This is all impossible for me to take in."

"You are being defensive," Alex said, "This is exactly what I'm talking about."

The three of them fell into silence for a while, listening to the hushed giggles behind them from Armand and Désirée, who had missed the conversation entirely. Paul turned back around and Sophie brushed up against him. His heart palpitated as her perfume, like sandalwood and bois d'inde, left him half delirious.

"Don't be discouraged," she said in a quiet voice, nearly a whisper. "We all disagree. Even within my family, my brother is an Africanist, for instance. But he is also French. We need to speak to one another. That is what being a true republican is about, oui?"

Paul turned to gaze at Sophie's earnest face, wondering what it would be like to kiss this sweet girl. But then they reached the Pont Roche and the Fort district. The gossiping men and the washerwomen had gone home for the night, and the bridge was abandoned. The small group of friends stopped for a moment to contemplate the Roxelane on its way to the sea. Then they dropped Sophie off at her home on Rue Royale, Désirée a few houses away on Rue Levassor. Finally Alex and Armand turned off toward the séminaire, waving their bonne nuit, leaving Paul to walk home alone with a whole new world to think about.

THE STUDY CIRCLE continued into the summer without Armand, Alex, and Eugène, who had all returned home to Lamentin and Fort-de-France. Now there was only Césaire, Sophie, and Désirée and a few new students from the lycée. Paul tried to interest Mannie and their neighbor, Raoul Dufail, both a year older than him. Mannie thought the whole exercise was a waste of time, which didn't shock Paul. His brother steadfastly ignored political affairs. Raoul had just taken a job at the Dupouy distillery, where he was learning the cooper trade, and had no time to spare.

Nearly all the students lived in the fashionable Fort district, and Paul thought it would be more convenient if there was some place to meet in the neighborhood. Although, to tell the truth, he enjoyed the long walks with Sophie and Désirée, whom he had taken to regularly escorting to and from the meetings. Sophie informed him she was under strict orders and could only attend if Désirée accompanied her. Paul was a bit surprised either girl was permitted to go out at night, but her maman, Sophie explained, was outspoken about republican politics and the rights of women, and she wanted her daughter to be independent. Désirée's auntie had given up at the girl's strong-headedness, and no longer cared what she did. At least, according to Désirée.

Without Armand and Eugène to lead, the group floundered. They'd taken to reading and discussing articles in *Les Colonies* or *L'Opinion*. But it was hard for them to keep focus. Paul wondered if there was a reason not to suspend the circle until the other boys came back in the autumn. But when the meetings were over and he was walking back home in the moonlight with two charming girls, he knew he didn't want this to end.

Still, it wouldn't be fair, he thought, to keep the group going for his own private reasons. Not if the others thought it was a waste of time. So, one evening as they were walking home, he asked the girls what they thought.

"We shouldn't wait on those boys from down south," said Sophie, her pronouncement emphatic. Désirée grinned, and Paul sensed some veiled communication going on between the girls. "Paul, I liked the time you told us about that book by Monsieur Verne," said Sophie. "And I like some of those fanciful stories in *L'Opinion*. We never discuss those. Just the boring political essays."

Désirée smirked. "And then there are the walks home, oui?"

Paul felt himself blushing. He glanced sideways at Sophie and saw that she was self-consciously scanning the cobbles on Pont Roche, every bit as embarrassed as he.

Désirée laughed. "It's alright. I don't mind being your chaperone."

Paul clammed up the rest of the way to Sophie's house, both of them suddenly too shy to speak. Goodnights were more awkward than usual and he felt relief when Sophie disappeared behind her door. Afterward, he walked Désirée in silence up to her maman's apartment on Rue Levassor.

Just before they parted, she said severely, "Sophie is a good girl. You better treat her right."

Paul regarded Désirée in confusion for a moment before "Oui, of course" came tumbling out of his mouth. In fact, he hadn't really thought about any of this. But he knew how some men talked about the mulâtre girls, as though they existed for their own amusement and gratification. "I'd never behave toward Sophie like that."

Désirée looked skeptical, but this quickly became a friendly smile again as she turned toward her front porch with a wave and bonne nuit.

He was kept awake that night, thinking about what Désirée said. He thought about all the mixed relationships in his family, the Caminades and the Petits and even Uncle Edgard, not yet married but living for years in Fort-de-France with his amour, Idalie, and their daughter, Bernadette. He considered for a moment what a relationship with a mulâtre girl might mean.

But he was still young. How much thought does a fourteen-year-old give to such things? And what business did he have even thinking about a girl in this way? Father Edouard and Maman would not be pleased that he was so easily tempted. And then, of course there was the matter of his eternal soul. *I made a promise to God. What will become of me if I don't honor it?*

STÉPHANIE'S SALON

Stéphanie unfastened the jalousie, unhooked the shutters and opened them outward. As she was fastening the first shutter latch, she heard Paul Poncy call out his morning greeting from the street below on his way to séminaire. Alice Germaine, who had just turned five years old, was already on the balcony waving her little arms and calling out, "Bonjou, bonjou, Mesye Paul."

Stéphanie followed the boy as he disappeared up the street, but her mind was on Philippe. There was no use denying it any longer, a baby was on the way and it was as likely as not that Philippe would be in Africa when this child came into the world. His brief visit little over two months ago remained with her in the form of this flower unfolding in her belly that had made its presence known by the absence of her menses and a slight nausea that hovered over her mornings. Stéphanie still wondered how Philippe managed to leave the struggle and come home, but it must have had less to do with her and more to do with the students and workers who materialized out of the darkness by ones and twos and threes to fill her patio all summer. Paul and his friends were often among them. The day before Philippe left, a couple of men from Fort-de-France sat with him and talked so low she could not hear them over the cicadas' chatter as she put Alice to bed in the next room. She arranged the mosquito netting, checking to make sure there were no holes large enough for one to slip through.

Stéphanie didn't have to see gendarmes lurking about to know that what they were doing held an element of danger, but she felt as strongly as Philippe did, that workers deserved to be paid a fair wage for their labor—these men and women in the cane fields, in the sucreries, the distilleries, and on the docks, lugging barrels of sugar and rhum to boats that carried the fruits of all their labor out to ships waiting in the deep waters. And when that was done there were ships to unload, filled with all the things the island needed and could not produce itself. Goods to fill the warehouse shelves of the Caminades.

Then Philippe was gone again. Sailing off on a steamer bound for Senegal. On his way back to the struggle. Stéphanie worried Philippe would be found out and detained before he could return to his work in Dakar, where he and his comrades were organizing among the soldiers being sent to fight Touré, the Mandinka rebel, and put down the insurrection in Dahomey. She carried the dread about with her until she received his letter. He would not tell her where he was, just that he was okay and perhaps on his way soon to Saint-Louis, where the first leg of the new railroad neared completion. A second railway was being built to the Mandinka town of Tambacounda, railways which he feared were meant to hasten troops to the front.

One fear allayed, another arose. There were so many ways to die in this situation. It was not just his life she worried about. If Philippe was caught, what would it mean for her and Alice? Would the gendarmes come for her? It would likely be death for him. After all, he was no longer just a socialist organizing the workers, he faced the prospect of being a traitor to France. Still, what he was doing was important. What would happen to Africa if all its empires and people fell to Europe?

"Mandinka," she said, not meaning to speak aloud.

Alice Germaine stopped playing and tugged at her mother's dress.

Stéphanie absently stroked her daughter's back. *My little Alice,* she thought, *you barely know your papa. Perhaps that is a mercy.* The little girl did not miss him now that he was gone again.

THE PASSION that had ignited Stéphanie and Philippe when she was barely a woman and he a promising young intellectual headed for université in Bordeaux was not enough to carry her through his long absences. She remembered how disconsolate she was when Philippe stepped down from the pier into the lighter that would take him to the steamer anchored in deep water. She watched until the ship slipped the chain that connected it to Martinique and moved out of harbor bound for the Métropole.

Bordeaux. All that she knew of the city was what Philippe described to her in his letters and what she'd found in books, but she felt drawn to it and thought once again about how marvelous it would be to see it, walk its broad streets, attend its theaters and salons.

Martinique's ties to Bordeaux were deep. For centuries, the colony's products were barreled up, stamped with the planter's mark in case the ship made it through storm and becalm, past buccaneers and beyond the grasp of scurvy to dock at the wharves in the harbor of Bordeaux. Sugar, molasses, rhum; sweet things for rotting brain and tooth, exchanged for barely more — to hear the wealthy planters tell it — than what it would cost to import all the things the planters needed, including wives and — no longer! — slaves. Captains lifted their sextants to set their course by witless stars, always true in their orbits, never complicit. Don't blame the stars if you go off course. It's your own miscalculation, your own failure to recognize when you are sailing off the edge. Or sometimes it is the hurricane and broken mast. Only now, the masts are fewer, replaced by the black stacks of steamers that sail without sails, blowing smoke as black as the Saint-Pierre beach. They make the Atlantic crossing in less than two weeks' time, drawing the island ever closer to the Métropole. Perhaps one day, she would board a steamship bound for Bordeaux.

"YOU SHOULD START that salon you've always wanted, ma chère," Philippe told Stéphanie before he left for Africa, in response to her half-hearted—but fully felt—complaints of abandonment. "Invite those young people in that study circle. They are floundering and the group won't last the summer without some direction. And it would give you something to do with your time."

She'd laughed at him, a little anger creeping in around the edges. "You think I have nothing to do, Philippe? Huh? You think raising our daughter alone and sewing dresses for the neighbors isn't enough?" Philippe was properly chastened, but she knew he was right as well. If she didn't keep her mind busy, she would be thinking of him all the time, of the fighting in Africa, and of all the ways he could die over there.

Several weeks went by after Philippe left before she decided to take action. Uncertain she could organize an actual literary salon, like the ones in Paris, she decided upon a compromise.

She would offer to host the study group over the summer and then, if all went well, they could begin inviting speakers—Tata Rosa ran in those literary circles; Henry Marlet had been a writer from a family of writers. His father had been the editor of *La Liberté,* a journal of some note in the early days after slavery. They could grow the salon slowly, with the young people to help her spread the word. She had a few speakers in mind: Marcus Herrard, the editor of *Les Colonies,* and the industrialist Amedée Knight, who was prominent in the democratic left and related somehow to their neighbors, the Dufails. She didn't know the Dufails well, but one of the Poncy boys, Emmanuel, ran with Raoul Dufail. She'd seen them together on the street.

The next time young Paul came by with his morning greeting, she asked him what he thought of her idea. "Do you think the others might approve?"

"Oui," said Paul enthusiastically. "We have no place to meet now in the summer, and your home will be much closer for everyone."

"Would you be willing to let your friends know? And could you ask the Dufail boy about Amédée Knight?"

"Of course," he said. "When shall we meet next?"

Stéphanie hadn't really thought about that. "Why not next Sunday?" she proposed.

FOR THE FIRST FEW WEEKS, the only attendees at the planning meetings were Paul and the girls, Sophie and Désirée. The other boys had all abandoned muggy, hot Saint-Pierre and returned home for August to other, more reasonable, parts of the island. Alex and Eugène to Fort-de-France, Armand to Lamentin. Stéphanie, herself, had visions on these hot, summer days, of packing up Alice Germaine and taking a coach to the

Atlantic where they might bask in the cool wind from across the sea, from Europe and Africa, those faraway continents which had taken her Philippe. But a coach was expensive, and she lacked the resources, so it remained an unrealistic dream.

At the evening salons, the young people chatted and socialized, mostly. The meetings took place in Stéphanie's garden, around the big patio table on which she placed fruit and cookies and citronnade. They were waiting for the summer to be over and for their friends to return.

Now it was September and Armand and Alex and Eugène were back. Even Césaire was there, sitting with Eugène, their chairs pushed away from the table as though they were only disgruntled observers waiting for some expected misstep to occur. So they could… what? Prove a point? Stéphanie considered whether to say something when Désirée did it for her. "Are you two part of this group or not? If so, join us at the table."

Eugène snorted his adolescent disdain before he begrudgingly pulled his chair up to the table. Césaire moved his chair just enough to show solidarity with Eugène, while somehow not being any closer to the table at all. Désirée sighed.

"So," Stéphanie said, "we should create a list of speakers to invite. Does anyone have suggestions?"

"There is that new young writer, René Bonneville, who sometimes has pieces in *Les Colonies*." Sophie said, and Eugène sniggered. Césaire mumbled, "Sophie likes the white boys." Paul turned toward Césaire, wanting to punch him, but Sophie put her hand on his arm and Paul backed off.

"I will not have disrespect in my house," Stéphanie said, her eyes shooting arrows at Césaire.

"Let's leave," said Césaire to Eugène, rising from his chair with as much commotion as possible. Eugène was clearly reluctant to go, but he finally rose and followed Césaire out the door.

Once the two disgruntled boys were gone, Armand said, as

though nothing had just occurred, "I would like to go see the new Schoelcher Library in Fort-de-France. I hear it's amazing."

"I think that is a magnificent idea, Armand," Stéphanie said. "I would love to take Alice. I will see if I can arrange an excursion. Perhaps on a Wednesday when there is no school. Also, I think René Bonneville is a wonderful suggestion, Sophie. And Amedée Knight as well. Shall I see who might be willing to speak to us?"

"Oui," came the chorus. The young people seemed enthused, except Désirée, who looked skeptical. "But who will come?" she said.

"We will make broadsides," Stéphanie said. "We will post them at school and hand them out at le Pont Roche. I should think there will be some adults interested in this as well, not just students." Désirée still didn't look entirely convinced. "You'll see," Stéphanie assured her.

Discussion over, an agenda was set for the next week and tasks assigned. The young people left to return to their homes and dorms, the ones who boarded in a scurry to beat 9 pm curfew. Stéphanie extinguished the citronelle torches and cleaned up with the help of Alice, who had quietly entertained herself in the garden during the salon. Then Stéphanie tucked her daughter in and went herself to bed, thinking of how enjoyable the evening had been, and only briefly of Philippe and Africa.

THEY CHOSE a Wednesday in late September to visit the Schoelcher Library. Stéphanie found a boat to take them to Fort-de-France and back again for a reasonable price. The cost was not a problem for any of these middle-class kids, except Désirée, whose maman was not as well off as the others. Later, on the walk home, Paul offered to pay for her share, which led to some teasing. "Maman says to never take a gift from a boy, especially a white boy," said Désirée. "It is almost always a Trojan horse. An army of little men will come out in the middle of the night and have their way with me."

Sophie bent over laughing. "Girl, you're hilarious."

"Paul, is this a bribe to close my eyes while you fool around with Sophie?"

"I don't care if you look," Paul shot back, and they all laughed again, but then without warning Désirée's face dropped. "I really can't accept," she said.

"No, no," Paul insisted, "you must come. You are one of us."

Désirée shook her head firmly.

"I don't understand," Paul said, but Sophie stopped him from saying more by cutting in. "We should all contribute. All for one, vous savez? You would accept then, oui?"

"Okay," Désirée said, trying to sound humble, although she was obviously delighted by Sophie's solution.

Paul still didn't understand, but when he tried to ask, Sophie cut him off with a look that said, *we'll talk about this later.*

THERE WERE no required school activities on mercredi, leaving the students free to go to Fort-de-France. Alice didn't begin primary school for another year, but she was as thrilled as the others to see this marvel. "Books as far as you can see," Paul told her with dramatic gestures. "Books stacked up as high as the sky, I've heard. And the building is beautiful, like a castle."

Alice's eyes were huge as she imagined this.

"They built the library in Paris," he told the girl, "then they took it apart brick by brick and brought it over to Martinique."

"All the way from Paris?" she said. "On ships?"

"Oui, it's true. Can you believe that?"

After the library, which seemed truly grand, they visited the dry goods store owned by Eugène's family. The boy had quietly returned to the group the week before, sans Césaire. The Savane was just across the street, so they had a picnic lunch in the park before returning to Saint-Pierre. They even arrived home in time for the students to attend communion, although no one did.

Stéphanie was very pleased with herself. It had been a very good day and she realized how much she enjoyed organizing this salon. *Perhaps this is something I'm good at,* she thought with satisfaction.

~

THE FOLLOWING DAY, a letter arrived from Amédée Knight:

Bonjour Mlle. Grainau,

I have received your kind letter of invitation to your monthly salon. It would be my honor to speak to your group about my writing and the state of political and cultural matters in Martinique. You mentioned a Sunday evening. I am available on either the 15th or the 22nd of October. Please let me know your preference, and the location where the salon shall be held. Also let me know if there is anything specifically you would like me to address.

Please give my kind regards to Madame Marlet, should you see her.

Cordially yours,
Amédée Knight.

. . .

STÉPHANIE WAS THRILLED. Though she might not have been had she known then the kind of crowd the event would bring to her small home. On the following Sunday, she relayed the information to her small group of students, who were excited and ready to make broadsides. Stéphanie knew a printer who would print them gratis. He was an old acquaintance of her uncle, Henry Marlet, and a radical republican. The young students promised to circulate them, Sophie and Désirée at the girls' school and Paul would ask Mannie to take a few to the lycée. The other boys would help post them around Saint-Louis-de-Gonzague.

Soon, the broadsides were everywhere in Saint-Pierre. You would have to be in a coma to not know that Amedée Knight was speaking at Stéphanie Grainau's salon.

STÉPHANIE CHOSE the Sunday before the salon to announce her pregnancy. She couldn't hide it much longer and, well, now was as good a time as any, she thought. She was unhappy. It seemed to her as though her youth was rapidly diminishing while Philippe fought his wars in Africa. She would end up alone in Saint-Pierre with two children and no way to feed them. Philippe's parents might send around a few francs for their grandchildren now and again, but her small inheritance from the Grainau family and her hero father's pension would only last a few more years. Tata Rosa would always help her, of course, but even the Marlet fortune had been nearly depleted after two generations, as the sucreries began to fail, one after another.

Paul noticed the troubled eyes behind Stéphanie's smile as she lit the citronelle candles. He wanted to ask her what was wrong, but not now with the others around, fearing that might embarrass her. But then, after the last candle was lit, she sat at the table. "I want you all to know something," she said, trying to put on the smile of a proud mother-to-be. "I am pregnant. The baby is expected in early March." *Mars, the god of war,* she thought. *How fitting is that?*

They talked about the baby and about Philippe, then they talked about their progress with the broadsides for the salon. Armand was unusually quiet. Paul had been focused on Stéphanie and failed to see his friend's distress. Finally, at the end of the evening, a somber Armand rose and faced the group. "I have an announcement, as well," he said, his voice soft and dispirited. "I'm sorry to say, my father has become gravely ill, and I am needed to help with the family business."

Paul was shocked, as were all the rest. "You're quitting school, Armand?"

"Oui, my family can no longer afford the tuition, and they really need my help at the store. I have no choice."

"When are you leaving?" Eugène asked.

"I will be here next week for our first salon," he said. "Then perhaps the week following, before I leave for Lamentin."

STÉPHANIE FRETTED about the state of her apartment. She put out the flowers which Tata Rosa had brought by, divided them into three vases, placing them around the living room. Here. No, here. She stood back, moved them again, unable to decide. Meanwhile, Sophie and Désirée were in the kitchen with Alice Germaine preparing citronnade, and arranging plates of tartines and gâteaux secs for the guests. Paul and the other boys were in the jardín, being useless, as boys often were. Talking about the night's guest of honor, speculating about who among their friends might come, who would not.

Stéphanie gave up the arrangements, deciding that she was nervous and overthinking everything. *It will just have to be what it will be.* There were two plates of sandwiches, two plates of cookies, and two pitchers of citronnade. This should be enough for two dozen guests, she hoped. Surely there wouldn't be more than that. She put out a few bottles of Chardonnay. Perhaps there should be more, but it was all her budget could afford.

The guests, when they arrived, however, soon overwhelmed Stéphanie's small apartment. There were over forty already even before Monsieur Knight arrived, and he always came with a small entourage, she'd been told. There was a half hour yet before things began, and already the food was gone. Sophie and Désirée busied themselves preparing more citronnade. But they needed more wine.

"Sophie," she said, "will you go over to Madame Marlet's and see if she has more wine? And glasses? We're already out of everything."

"Oui, of course." Sophie left and returned fifteen minutes later with Tata Rosa in tow, the two of them carrying several bottles of wine and a mixed box of glasses.

When the guest of honor arrived, he indeed had an entourage, including a white boy, whom Stéphanie recognized as René Bonneville. Nearly fifty guests, now. She was excited, she was horrified, she didn't know which. *Calm down,* she told herself, repeatedly. *Everything will work out.*

The guests crowded into her courtyard. They were pressed all the way back between the banane and the magnolia. Stéphanie was certain her carefully cultivated roses and begonias would be trampled. She talked herself down, finally, but her nerves remained unsettled as she stepped before the gathered audience. "Bonsoir," she said, "welcome to our first salon. I didn't know there would be so many here tonight, and I'm afraid I am under-prepared. S'il-vous-plaît, pardonnez-moi."

People clapped and said, "It's wonderful." and "Such a lovely house." She didn't know whether to believe them. Many of these people, she realized, lived in far more lavish homes than hers.

The audience listened intently as Monsieur Knight talked about the future of Martinique. But Stéphanie heard almost none of it. She was thinking about how she would manage to clean up after everyone left. The girls would help her, and Paul, but the other boys would have to scurry to make curfew.

When she came back from her thoughts, Amedée Knight had finished with his talk and the guests were already leaving, except for the few who came to take part in the ensuing intellectual discussion. Monsieur Knight approached her and thanked her again for her invitation and complimented her on being a gracious host before cornering Madame Marlet. Stéphanie was fairly certain she didn't deserve the compliments.

A handful of people remained behind, including, to her surprise, René Bonneville, who was in the garden engaged in a discussion with Paul Poncy. With René was Valentine Surlemont, a young mulâtresse, introduced earlier as his fiancé, whom he planned to marry in a few weeks on Sainte Lucie, against his father's wishes. The other students were there as well, standing back, listening. René and Paul were talking about family, and being white, in Martinique.

"If there's to be a new Martinique," René was saying, "then the whites, especially the békés must shed their racial prejudices. We can't continue with these old patterns. The rich whites must understand the damage they've done."

"You mean slavery," said Paul. "Papa says it should have ended years before it did."

Stéphanie watched an agitated Eugène pace.

"That is admirable of him," said René. "My own father

refuses to admit any role or make any reconciliation, the stubborn old fool."

"I thought your father was a banker, not a planter," said Paul.

Eugène held his tongue until finally he couldn't any longer. "What about your grandfather, Paul? Was he only a négociant?" Eugène's words were sharp, cutting. "Was this only a *humble* business owner who had my ancestor hung at Place Bertin?"

What was Eugène talking about? Paul looked around for support. At Armand and Alex, at Sophie, at Désirée, finally at Stéphanie. They were looking at him as though waiting for an answer. What did they know that he didn't? "What has my grandfather to do with what happened at Place Bertin?"

"You should ask your father about that," said Alex, putting the question to rest. At least for the time being.

STÉPHANIE HAD LEARNED A LESSON. No more important personages. No more broadsides. It was too much work and her garden had been utterly destroyed by trampling feet. She was happy to have hosted Amedée Knight and in the course of the evening they'd met several of Saint-Pierre's artistic elite; that was a thrill, but one time was entirely enough, thank you. People knew about the salon now, so no handbills or broadsides should be needed. A poet or a professor to speak once a month. No one famous! Then, in January, she would retire until the baby was born.

It's too bad that Armand will no longer be with us, she thought. His moderating voice in the group would be missed, but perhaps the girls or Alex could fill that role. Maybe Eugène would tone down his rhetoric, now that he'd finally confronted

Paul, instead of just acting petulant around him. They were all still children. They had so much to learn.

The Poncy boy was very guileless, she thought, and clearly bewildered by Eugène's accusations. It was too bad he had to go through such an ordeal over his grandfather. Still, it was only discomfort and he needed to know the truth. He needed to know why Eugène and Césaire treated him so poorly. And he needed to know what it meant to be a white boy in Martinique, especially to be the grandson of someone like Jean Joseph Poncy, when so many people had long memories, had grandfathers of their own who were slaves, had ancestors who were treated so cruelly by the whites. What was an evening, a year, ten years of discomfort compared to such suffering?

The others teased Paul about being a béké boy, but his family was really petit blanc. They were not rich like the Plissonneaus or Hayots, even if they were cousins. Even if his father worked for the Soudon sucrerie, Anatole Poncy was an employee, not an owner. Not a bourgeois. Stéphanie knew there was nothing simple about social relations in Saint-Pierre. Not between rich and poor; not between white and mulâtre, or mulâtre and nègre; certainly not between nègre and blanc. And not between men and women. It was a constant struggle.

THE GHOST IN THE BASEMENT

After helping Stéphanie and his friends clean her apartment, Paul excused himself and, without waiting for Sophie and Désirée to join him, left for home. The two girls protested, but he didn't want to be in their company tonight, for them to see his despondency and anger on display. Or his shame at this thing that he couldn't really understand. They and Stéphanie and the rest had all tried to smooth it over, tried to convince him they weren't blaming him for the deeds of his ancestors, whatever those might have been, and yet their words felt evasive and untrue to him, as though in fact, a finger of guilt had been pointed his way.

When he arrived home, he went immediately to Papa, who sat behind his desk in his library, puffing on his pipe, adding up his columns on the ledger sheets. "Papa," he said, "may I have a few moments of your time?"

"Of course, son," said Anatole. "What may I do for you?"

Paul hesitated, and his father looked at him in that way that said, *hurry, I don't have all night for this.*

"It's about Grandpére Poncy," he said, faltering.

"What do you wish to know, son?"

"It's just that my friends mentioned him tonight, as if he was some kind of reprehensible man. I want to understand why."

Anatole gave a wave of dismissal. "There is nothing to know, son. My father was a hardworking and respected man. He was the man responsible for giving us all the good life we have."

"But, what is this about Place Bertin, Papa?"

His father scowled. "I don't have time for this, Paul. If you want my advice, find better friends." With that, the old man's concentration turned again to his books, but frown lines remained etched on his face. Paul received the message that the subject was now closed.

He retired immediately to his room and closed the door behind him. He dressed for bed and climbed in beneath the mosquito netting, but he lay there for a long time awake, unable to shake his low spirits.

If Eustase were still alive, he would know.

AS HE DRIFTED TOWARD SLEEP, Paul thought about his childhood and the Sablon house, trying to call forth those summer days with Mannie and Joseph and Eustase when there was little to distinguish the brothers from one another except their height and his own big ears, but all he could envision was a broken-down manse with faded carpets and weathered wood, cobwebs filling the corners, dust on the surfaces, a hollow emptiness in the hallways, much as it had been the last time he saw it. He tried to imagine the old house alive again, its rooms inhabited by his loved ones. Of course, there would be sad corners, horrific corners, in fact, but he would just have to avoid those. He walked along the halls, opening doors along the way, thinking about whose rooms were where. But in this unreliable house made of memory fragments, this dream house, there was no logic. A room that had been there a moment ago, if you turned around, would be there no longer.

When along the way he stumbled upon the kitchen, he could almost hear Euphrasie calling out to the children, announcing supper, clanging the lid down on the old coal-fired oven as she removed a loaf of manioc bread and a sweet pie. He could nearly smell the rumcake and the curried salt cod as she lay it out on the table.

When at last he came to the cellar door, he couldn't resist opening it. He could never go in there as a child, and the old basement had always held a mysterious lure. The door scraped when he pulled it open, and he stepped onto a rotting landing which smelled of fungus and mold. The stairs creaked and groaned and his heart pounded with each step into the musty darkness, lit only by dim light which shone through small windows too grimy to see through. He wondered what might be kept down here. Wine and tubers, perhaps. He thought he heard footsteps and doors rattling. He wondered what ghosts were here in this far corner of his mind.

At that moment, a man appeared in the light of one of those tiny basement windows. He recognized the face, much like Papa's, but more severe, scowling. He had never met his grandfather in life. He had died ten years before Paul was born. But there was a picture of the old man in the hall at the top of the stairs, near his bedroom door, hanging next to Granmé. Paul wasn't surprised to see him. He'd half expected to see him. Because the dead sought him out for reasons he could never understand. At least that's how it seemed to him.

Tell me about Place Bertin, Grandpé.

Why must we bring up this ancient history, Son? What's done is done.

It wasn't so long ago that others have forgotten.

Very well, then. They burned down our house on Rue Conso-

lation, as you know. They burned Maison Pecoul. They burned all of our neighbors out. Fourteen houses in all, burned to the ground in the '31 riots. Not to mention the murderous terror inflicted by those God-damned nègres and their allies. Your grandmother and your papa, who was seven years old, your Tata Elmire, just a little girl—all forced to flee to the harbor for their lives.

Yes, Grandpére, I know the stories of that rebellion.

Rebellion? Merde! It was a murderous insurrection. It was treason! You make it sound like a child's petulance. It killed your grandmother, you know. Your uncles never returned to Martinique from the Métropole.

Just then, the old woman appeared, standing on the other side of the window.

Nonsense, she said. *It was you who killed me, old man. One child after another for twenty-five years.*

It's not my fault if that's the lot of woman. I did not ordain the order of the heavens.

But you could have made it easier on your wife. You shouldn't lie to the young man. She turned to Paul. *It isn't all his fault, you know. Since our oldest three boys were swept to sea in Havre, on their way to school, may the Lord bless them, my husband has been in grief.*

Pish, said the old man.

But I want to know about Place Bertin.

Well, that was after my time, the old woman said. *I was in Paris, dying when that happened.*

The old man sniffled, and Paul couldn't tell if it was the dust, or some emotion surfacing. *Does it have to do with those who were hanged, Grandfather?*

The old man scowled. *As I said, there is no need to stir up all of that ancient shit.*

~

WHEN HE AWOKE the next morning, Paul decided it must be so, that his grandfather must have played some role in the hangings at Place Bertin, when two dozen insurrectionists were executed for their part in the uprising of February 1831. If Papa wouldn't talk to him about it, then he must research the subject himself.

He'd given no thought to those old family stories before. Now he wondered if there had been some reason la maison Poncy had been torched. Had it been targeted? Or was it the action of a mob setting fire to whatever was in their path? In any case, how could you blame those enslaved people for wanting to be free? Had the loss of a house and a night of terror been an excessive price for his ancestors to pay for justice? Had a little embarrassment been too much for him to pay?

He didn't think so. But he worried about what all of this antagonism meant for the future of Martinique. And even at such a very young age he could see that change would not be an easy thing.

CARNAVAL

From his bedroom window on Rue Castelnau, from just a certain angle, Paul could see the tall masts of barques and schooners in Saint-Pierre harbor. He thought of these vessels as vestiges of the old world. In a few more decades, there would be no more tall ships, only steamships. In a few more years, it would be the twentieth century. His century. This old era of kings and tyrants would be vanquished to history. But today, as he watched the ships, he wasn't concerned about these things. He was thinking about Sophie and the salons at Stéphanie's house. His mind had been reeling for the past two weeks, since that night Sophie kissed him and invited him to Carnival with her. Now it was Mardi Gras, and tonight he would meet Sophie at le Pont Roche.

He feared it was all because of Stéphanie. And Sophie's jealousy. He didn't want to choose between Sophie and his friendship with Stéphanie. Admittedly, he often eyed Stéphanie across the room, where he sat with Sophie and Désirée and the others each dimanche discussing the latest book or listening to the evening speaker. He couldn't explain why he was drawn to this young pregnant mother, ten years his senior, but he thought about her at the oddest moments. Thinking about how beautiful she looked with Philippe's baby growing in her. Paul was unsettled by these random thoughts, which were sometimes not as chaste as he pretended.

One night a few weeks ago, on the way home, Sophie had revealed, with a jealous pique, that she'd noticed how his attention kept sliding over toward Stéphanie. "You can't keep your eyes off of her, Paul. How am I supposed to feel about that?"

Paul felt the flush in his face. "Non," he protested. "Stéphanie is a maman... she has a baby coming... she's like an auntie to me. I'm not attracted to her in that way. How could you think that?"

"Uh huh," Sophie said, "Tata Stéphanie, may I help you take off your dress?"

Désirée snorted loudly. "Men," she said. "You're all alike."

Both girls laughed raucously and Paul was mortified. He was ready to take off, leave them to walk home alone when Sophie noticed his discomfort and put her hand on his shoulder. "It's alright, Paul," she reassured him. "Stéphanie is very pretty. Just remember who you are sitting beside, oui?"

But, it's not like that, he wanted to protest again. He sensed that to say this would be a mistake, so he let it hang in the air.

Later at home he thought about it some more, but only for a brief time. He liked Stéphanie, it was true. She'd been a good friend and neighbor. He admired her for her courage and perseverance. Certainly, what he felt was only that.

Sophie's face was somber in the moonlight when Paul and the girls walked home together the following week. The full moon had risen above the peaks of the rooftops and its light glistened on the cobbles of Rue Levassor. Paul wished he knew what Sophie was thinking. As always, Désirée followed a few steps behind, playing her self-appointed role of chaperone. Paul was certain she was listening to every word he was thinking.

At last Sophie said, "Stéphanie's baby will arrive soon."

"Oui," said Paul.

"Another month, she told me," Désirée chimed in.

There was another long pause in the conversation. Then Sophie said, "I saw you looking at her tonight."

Not this again, thought Paul. He didn't know what to say, so he said nothing, just let it sit there between them.

Finally, Sophie said, "Would you like to go to Vaval with me?" Paul was mystified. Was she angry with him, or not?

"Oui, I would love to go to Carnival with you. I've only been with my brothers as a child."

"It would be fun to go on our own, oui?" Sophie said.

"I will be in Fort-de-France with family on dimanche gras," Désirée complained. "But perhaps on lundi."

"I was thinking Mardi Gras," Sophie said. She flashed Paul her shy smile, but there was a mischievous twinkle in her eyes. "In the evening, after the children have all gone home. Just Paul and I. Maybe we'll stay over until la Fête des Diablesses."

Désirée stopped cold in the middle of the street. "Sophie! Your manman will kill you."

Paul and Sophie halted and turned to face her. "I'm fifteen now," Sophie said, her voice edging on anger. "I'm old enough to go out on my own."

Désirée looked at Paul, who shrugged, then back at her friend. "All night? On Mardi Gras? Are you sure about this, Sophie?"

"Désirée, you go around wherever you like, whenever you like. Why can't I?"

"I just want you to be sure is all," Désirée said.

"I don't need a second manman," snapped Sophie. Paul stepped back, not wishing to be involved in this row. Truth be told, he wasn't so sure about this all night thing, either. Sophie's maman would not be the only one seeing red if he staggered in on Lent, after a night on the town. And what would this mean for them, for Sophie and him?

"Fine," said Désirée, anger flashing in her eyes. "Bonne nuit." She spun around and marched toward home, leaving Sophie and Paul standing alone on the street. Perplexed, Paul looked at Sophie, who glared back at him, daring him. He should say something, but he was afraid anything he said would be wrong.

They silently resumed the journey to Sophie's house and after a while she said, "I think we should make costumes for the parade."

"But it's only two weeks away."

"Don't worry," she said. "I can finish them on time."

They were now standing in front of her house. Paul wanted to back out of this crazy scheme, make up some excuse, but Sophie leaned in without warning and kissed him full on the lips, drawing him into an embrace. He put his arms awkwardly around her and they lingered like that for a long moment. "You don't really want to become a priest, n'est-ce pas?" she whispered in his ear, before she turned away and disappeared inside.

What could he do now? He was uncertain until this moment, with Sophie's voice in his ear. But no, he really didn't think he any longer wanted to be a priest.

MARDI GRAS HAD ARRIVED. In her room, Sophie finished the two costumes in the black and white style of la Fête des diablesses. She had also made two red masks for the night. Carnival was the time of opposites, she reasoned, so Paul would wear the darker, but more feminine. She, herself, would wear the lighter, masculine one. Paul hadn't seen them yet, and she hoped he would approve. She'd sewn them secretly, because, if her manman saw them, she would realize they planned to stay out all night.

At first Manman was very cross with Sophie's plan to go at all, until it was plain the girl wouldn't budge. "You know, cher, this béké boy is only going to use you. That's how they are. He'll get you pregnant and leave you, and where will you be, then? You'll have a little one to feed on your own. You'll have to leave school and find some way to support yourself. And you know children who aren't sanctified—"

"—Manman," Sophie rolled her eyes, "do you hear yourself? You are always saying, a woman should be able to do this and a woman should be allowed to do that, and a woman should be free to make her own choices. And you, yourself, did these very things. Where is my sanctified Papa? Huh?" Sophie took a curl of her hair and wrapped it around her forefinger. "Besides, Paul is not one of those rich béké boys. He is sweet and innocent. He cares about me."

Manman clearly was having nothing of it. Sophie could see it in the set of her head, the way she squinted her eye. Then, Manman sighed audibly and let down her guard. "You're right," she said at last. "I'm perhaps being a little hypocritical. But you are my only daughter, and I want you to not be caught in the same trap as your manman. Do you understand?"

Sophie hugged her mother. "I will be careful, Manman. Paul will be my guardian angel."

It was Manman's turn to roll her eyes.

When it was time to leave, Sophie waited impatiently for Manman to be distracted, and when all was clear, with costumes under her arm, she slipped from the house.

The drums of Carnival filled the streets of Saint-Pierre, as they had for three days now. Throngs of people everywhere strolled along the cobbled streets and hung out on balconies on Quai Paynier with their drinks and their smokes, some in costume, some not. Some of those on the street were early revelers, some were families trying to get the children home from the parade before the wild party began. Sophie headed toward her rendezvous with Paul, trying to get into the spirit of the music, trying to convince herself that this was right, that this wasn't a desperate move for a boy she thought she might lose. A boy she thought she loved.

Perhaps she should have listened to her manman, *but I am fifteen, a woman. Manman has forgotten what this means.* She forged ahead to meet her boy at le Pont Roche. And there he was, hands in his pockets, leaning against the railing. He turned and spotted her, waved, smiled shyly. She could see his lingering reluctance about this adventure. But she had been certain since she kissed him that night under the full moon she could win him over.

She reached out her hand as she sidled up to him, said, "Come, let's change into costume at my cousine's house on Rue du Centre." Paul resisted a little as Sophie pulled him away from his perch. "I won't have to drag you everywhere tonight, will I?"

"Non," said Paul, allowing himself to be led away at last into the dark, moonless night, with a pout on his face.

PAUL WAS NEARLY PARALYZED with fear. He had a nervous feeling about this night. Sophie had transformed from a schoolgirl into a wild woman, someone he barely recognized. There was something exciting in this wildness, something that made him feel alive like he'd never felt before. But he was afraid of it too. Afraid of being pulled across a threshold into another world from which there was no return.

Despite his fear, he let himself be pulled along behind her

as she practically ran through the street, weaving in and out among the throngs along Rue Victor Hugo toward the Rue du Centre.

Despite his resistance, he was soon part of the big dance that was Carnival. He had only ever been an observer, except for one year when he was small and Eustase took him and Mannie to be part of the children's parade. Papa and Maman were too conservative. To them, Carnival was a nuisance they must put up with every year. The children's parade had been filled with wonder for him. But nothing like this.

From a side street wound a parade of human-size birds adorned in red feathers, feet dancing to the complicated rhythms of the ka drum, punctuated with the mocking call and response of trombone and French horn. They called this music beguine, which meant béké girl. People moved aside and applauded as the dancers snaked their way through the crowds, led by a slender young man in a white mask, hips swaying, coconut breasts bobbing as he wove sinuously to the beat. "Hey baby," the trombone calling. "Oh, better watch out, white girl," the horn responding. The night and the color and the music cast their mesmerizing spell, the air full of incense and spice and tobacco. If you breathed too deeply, there was also the foul odor of alcohol and vomit from the gutters, so the trick he learned was to take shallow breaths as Sophie led him on, into the unknown.

Soon they turned up Rue du Centre where more people were hanging from balconies of the maisons de ville and pieds-à-terres, everywhere leaning over the rails, children with their noisemakers and adults with their drinks splashing down on the partiers below.

"This way." Sophie led him by the hand through a narrow doorway, up a flight of stairs. Without knocking, she opened her cousine's door. "Maryse," she called. No one answered and Paul shrank back, suddenly feeling like an intruder.

"Maryse!" Sophie called again, louder this time.

"We're out on the balcony," came a reply, barely audible over the sound of the revelry.

"Wait here," said Sophie, disappearing into an adjoining room.

Paul felt like he was drunk, although he'd consumed no rum. It was only the hypnotizing rhythms of the night, his youthful vigor and the turmoil of yearning, of love, another kind of intoxicant that left him dazed and tilting.

He took in the room, its white plaster walls and planked floor. A nice modern sofa rested against one wall where Sophie had thrown the costumes, and a side table on another wall with family photos above it. On the table was a vase with red and orange roses and a bottle of agricole, a sugar bowl, spoons and glasses for making ti punch. On the sofa, a rag doll draped her little arm over the edge of the cushion. A few other toys were scattered on the floor.

Sophie returned with a young woman about Stéphanie's age. Beside her, a little girl tugged on her mother's arm and said in Matinik, "Who is that white boy?"

The woman reprimanded her in French, "Don't be rude, Margot." Then to Paul, "Please excuse my daughter. She has no manners."

Paul smiled and shrugged. "No problem, Madame," he said, although he again felt like an interloper.

"This is my ami, Paul," said Sophie. "Paul, this is Maryse, my cousine, and her daughter, Margot."

"Pleased to meet you, Madame and Mamzel," managed Paul, sounding a little too stiffly formal than he meant.

"Is he your doudou?" asked Margot.

"Margot, that's not appropriate," Maryse took Margot by the

shoulder and turned her around. "Go back out on the balcony with Jerome." Margot stood her ground until Maryse added, "Now," in a sharp voice. The little girl snorted and stomped away.

"Children," said Maryse after Margot was gone, "they can be so annoying."

"It's no problem, really," said Paul, sounding nervous, feeling nervous. Maryse returned a look which said, *oui, it really is a problem.*

"We would like to change into our costumes," said Sophie, seeing Paul's discomfort, steering the conversation in a new direction.

"Of course," said Maryse. "You're welcome to use our room."

Sophie quickly gathered up the costumes and grabbed Paul's hand, dragging him into the couple's bedroom.

IF THE EVENING so far had been filled with anxiety for Paul, now he was on the edge of panic as Sophie began to remove her clothes. She turned to see him red faced, immobilized, and she became suddenly self-conscious. But here she was, down to her underwear, alone with the boy she loved, and, well, she just couldn't help herself. She smiled and walked over to the semi-paralyzed Paul and unbuttoned his shirt. "Shall I undress you?" she asked, trying to be the seductress. Succeeding.

Paul stepped back, aghast, afraid this had all gone too far. What would Maman think if she saw him now? "Maybe," he said, pointing to the door, "I should wait out there for you to finish dressing."

"Silly boy," she said, "I won't embarrass you any more. I promise. I can turn my back and you can turn yours, and we can dress in private." She tossed him the black costume with the skirt, and the red she-devil mask.

"What's this?" he said.

"That's your costume."

"But—"

"I am the bourgeois gentlemen. And you are my doudou." She winked at him.

Was she making fun of him? Was she being deliberately cruel? He couldn't tell. "You said you wouldn't embarrass me anymore."

"This is Carnival, Paul," Sophie said, sounding like a teacher trying to get through to a small child. "It's all in fun. And no one will know you behind the mask, oui?"

"I suppose you're right," he said as he turned around to change. But he wasn't so sure.

She turned too. "No peeking," she said with a sly little laugh.

THE THING ABOUT MASQUERADE, the mask is everything. Once Paul put it over his face, his discomfiture faded. He wasn't yet fully ready to play the part, but he could now see the possibilities. "You look stunning, mon doudou," said Sophie as she adjusted her white paper top hat, her voice deep and melodramatic. "So much more lovely than that twittering femme blanche Française I married for her family fortune."

"Why, merci, ma chère," Paul replied, completely surprising himself.

"Come," Sophie said, "Let's show our costumes to Margot."

Paul paused in front of a vanity mirror and saw himself in Sophie's black muslin skirt. He thought about what his school friends would think if they saw him tonight, and the merciless teasing he would receive from his cousins. He lost his confidence again, but before he could object, Sophie grabbed his hand and dragged him from the room into another which opened out into the balcony where Maryse and Jerome hoisted their glasses of ti punch and little Margot, on the verge of sleep, sat listlessly playing with wooden blocks.

Margot looked up when they come into view and made a squeaky exclamation of surprise. "What do you think, Margot?" Sophie said. "Do you like our costumes?"

"Why are you a boy?" asked Margot.

"Because it's Carnival," Sophie said. Explanation enough.

Jérôme harumphed and turned back to the street, but Maryse looked them over with a big grin on her face. "Perfect," she said. "Can I get you two a ti punch?

"Oui, merci," said Sophie. "Would you like one also, ma doudou?" Sophie prodded when Paul failed to respond.

"Oui," Paul said reluctantly. Much may be forgiven at Carnival, but Papa and Maman would be displeased if he came home tonight reeking of rhum.

Margot tugged at her maman's skirt, and Maryse picked up the little girl. "I think I better put her to bed first. Help yourself to the rhum."

Sophie and Paul returned to the living room and downed a ti punch as Maryse lugged the exhausted Margot to bed. Then they drank another. Paul was feeling a little woozy. Maryse returned to the balcony, and Paul heard Jerome say, resentment in his voice, "Has Sophie and her white boy gone yet?"

Maryse said, "She is my cousine, Jerome. Treat her with respect."

"Oui, oui," Jérôme grumbled, his voice a little mocking. It was not quite a fight, but Paul felt uncomfortable. "I think we should go," he said to Sophie, tugging her toward the door.

"Good night, Maryse," Sophie called out, then they were through the door and back in the Rivière du Carnaval.

ON THE STREET, the ka drums again asserted their primacy, and Paul allowed the night and the dance and Sophie to pull him into the stream. "Come, ma doudou!" she exclaimed. "Let's find the fire jugglers." Because there were always fire jugglers, and every kind of theater. Sophie and Paul were part of the theater. "Shall I buy you something pretty for your hair, cher?" asked the bourgeois gentleman. "Some pearls for le Grand Ball, perhaps?"

"Why, Monsieur, you do not need to buy my love with trinkets."

"But I want you to be the finest jewel of Saint-Pierre, ma doudou."

"Am I not already?"

"But of course, of course, ma chérie."

Laughing they danced their way into the night, stopping for sweets and accras and ti punch offered freely by the vendors on the beach, where they crossed paths with stilted mokozombis and touloulous. Coming toward them, Karolyn zyé Kokli carried her drunken husband on her back, weaving skillfully among the revelers on the beach. Paul and Sophie looked at each other and laughed again, becoming more and more drunk on the love and the rhum and the music of Carnival until they were nearly at the edge of town, beyond even the Dupouy rhumerie, where the crowds had thinned to almost nothing. Where the forests of the Carbet reached down into the sea. They found a hidden grove there. It might even have been one of those painted by Gauguin a few years before. They heard the midnight bells of Notre Dame ring out across Saint-Pierre, somberly proclaiming Ash

Wednesday, but the party was still in its infancy as they fell down together in the sand and pushed off their masks.

"Do you love me, doudou?" said Sophie, breathless.

"Of course," said Paul, suddenly serious now, although he was not really certain if the masquerade had ended. He kissed Sophie, and she returned his kiss with a hungry fervor. His hand found her soft breast and he caressed it, his own fever rising.

"Is it real?" asked Sophie. "Do you really love me?"

He paused for a moment. "Oui," he said and leaned in to kiss her again. But she turned her face, rebuffing him.

"You aren't going to be like they say about those béké boys, are you? You won't make love to me and treat me like one of the girls on Rue Bouille? I need to know, Paul, before we continue with this."

PERHAPS, he thought so many years later, *that was where you should have stopped to think a little about what she was actually asking from you.* But that would have meant pausing for a moment. Was that too much to ask from a fifteen-year-old boy drunk on alcohol and hormones? To stop and think? Instead he said, without considering his words at all, "I would never treat you that way, ma chère," as his hand moved back to her breast, his eager mouth toward hers. And she gave in, allowing him to explore her body, to have her body.

And afterward they lay side by side, each having offered their virginity for love—something much easier for a boy than for a young woman. And, of course, that was when he thought about what Sophie wanted. Was she asking for a commitment? What sort of commitment was she looking for? Was he ready to make promises to her?

An honest Saint-Pierre négociant knows it is too late to pull out once you have sealed the deal. Ah, but the wild west of love and conquest. The two of them entwined now on that hidden beach, arms and legs wrapped around one another like some sea creature from Monsieur Verne's adventure novels, and already, in his thoughts, Paul had begun to extract himself.

HE PULLED his leg back into the shade, away from the hot sun where it had been cooking. Beside him, Sophie stirred. He remembered the evening as though a blurry dream, his head throbbing from the rhum and sugar.

Voices from far off called out, "Vaval est mort!" On the road above, a small parade of women dressed completely in black and white, with high, mismatched socks, one of each color, faces white with ash, paraded solemnly toward the center of the city. "Arise, Pierrotins! King Carnival is dead!"

He suddenly realized that the sun was in the far west and it was early evening. The widows of Vaval were already gathering the mourners to the funeral pyre. He couldn't believe they'd slept all day. Sophie pulled away from him, freeing her arms and legs from his. She rose to her feet, naked, and brushed away the sand and detritus from her bare skin and then retrieved the crumpled costume from the ground where it was discarded in the heat of the night. "Get up, Paul," she said. "It's time to burn Vaval."

For a long moment, he didn't move. He wasn't thinking about King Carnival or Sophie. He was thinking about the fact that the sun was going down, it was Ash Wednesday, and how disappointed Maman would be that he'd spent the night debauching himself and had missed Lent services.

"Come, get dressed," said Sophie, a little sharper than last time, anger or frustration creeping into her voice.

He held back for another beat, an irrational impulse to defy her that came and left in an instant. He looked at her naked body as she pulled on her costume. *Who is this seductress who's lured me away into this devil's night?* But he knew that thought too was wrong. Sophie was just a girl. A sweet girl he thought he loved. And why was he thinking of that love in the past tense? *Don't you still love her? Don't you want to take her home to Maman, and say, "Maman, this is the one for me?"*

"Fine," she said, fastening her last button. "I will go on by myself." She was visibly angry now. But what had he done?

"Wait," he said. He rose hurriedly and grabbed his clothes to shield himself, suddenly embarrassed by his own nakedness. He brushed off the sand and stumbled into his costume. Sophie was already walking away. "Wait," he said again, running to catch up to her, his costume still only half fastened.

Just as he reached her, securing his final button, she stopped and crouched. Someone had built a fire on the beach last night, and she took a handful of white ash and rubbed it on her face. "Go ahead," she said, indicating the ash, so he bent over and took some in his hand, rubbed it into his own face too. On the road above, more widows of Vaval advanced in solemn procession toward the site of the funeral pyre.

A half dozen Frigate birds circled high over the harbor, far out near where the sun was perhaps an hour above the sea. He heard the mourners now, wailing for King Carnival, and accompanying them were the ever-present ka drums. He had to run again to catch up with Sophie who marched ahead, unheeding. He was out of breath and his head hurt when he finally caught up with her. "Slow down, Sophie," he pleaded, but she didn't seem to hear. She kept pacing ahead.

Around him now the beach had become an endless barren desert, as grim as any he could imagine. The Gobi, the Sahara, the great Mojave of the North American Southwest, all were nothing compared to this desolation he felt. Sophie led him onward, but to what destination? And these weeping women, who were they weeping for?

The desert whispered, *They weep for you, for themselves, for everyone who is alive, but one day will not be, for all who were once alive, but are no longer. They weep for the end of Carnival, the last of the good times. They cry for the lost times of abundant harvests and maman's warm breast. They wail for the final days of childhood and the coming of the long fast of Lent.*

Paul's eyes were suddenly wet with tears as he struggled to keep up with Sophie. "Sophie wait, s'il-te-plaît."

Ahead, men dragged brush, branches, planks, broken rhum barrels, anything that could burn, piling it high beneath Vaval's funeral pyre. The crowd let out a cheer as another group of widows arrived. Bottles of agricole were lifted to dry lips and passed around.

Sophie halted suddenly and he stopped beside her. Beneath her ghostly ashen face, her eyes flashed anger, disappointment, resolve, something he couldn't identify. The crowd cheered again as a funeral procession carried the effigy of the dead Vaval and hoisted it onto the pyre. He turned to say something to her, but no words came forth. The crowd became wilder as the rhum flowed and the drums beat out their incessant rhythm.

Chants of "Viv' Vaval, Viv' Vaval!" broke out. Someone gave an oratory before the pyre, the words lost to him in the cacophony. Every now and again the crowd cheered, and playing their part, the widows wailed an eerie counterpoint. Sophie stood silent beside him.

"Sophie, please speak to me," he pled.

"I have nothing to say, béké boy." She spat the words. Her face was cold in a way he'd never seen it before. "You are going to leave me. I thought you were different. Go cry to your Stéphanie. Go marry your white cousine. I don't care."

Just then a huge cry arose as a flame was touched to the pyre, and the fire caught, exploded, sent sparks up into the air and onto the crowd, which edged back away from the heat and embers, pushing Paul along with it. Through his misty eyes, it looked like the end of the world.

He turned back to Sophie, where she had been standing before, and she was no longer there. He panicked and ran through the crowd looking into every ash covered face, looking for the girl he'd let down, wanting to apologize, ready to plead and promise his undying love, if only she would tell him what he had done wrong. But every face looked back at him with the same uncaring eyes. Some part of him knew how hollow that promise would be. He wasn't ready for love. Sophie isn't ready for love, either, he thought. Not the kind of love she believes she wants.

He didn't want it to end like this, but it was too late to change it. What was done, was done. He stepped away from the crush of people and collapsed to his knees on the beach. Tears streaked the ash on his cheeks. Sobs tore from his throat, he cried until there was nothing left, and then he watched the last embers of Vaval paint red streaks across the night sky.

IN THE MORNING, the ship, which was called the *Liberté*, set sail. Yvonne woke before sunrise, as she often did, and she watched through her window as her home of Saint-Pierre, nestled in the arms of Montagne Pelée, receded in the distance.

Yvonne missed the crowing roosters. In their place, she now heard voices of sailors, shouting to one another above whipping sails, and the sound of waves lapping at the sides of the ship.

The *Liberté* rocked gently back and forth, and Yvonne hoped she wouldn't get sick like the pirates in Auntie Rosa's book. She wouldn't be drinking any rhum, that was for sure.

The ship sailed north, past the island of Dominica, before it turned toward the morning sun and the open Atlantique.

Shortly after sunrise, Captain Marie called through the cabin door.

"Children," said the captain, "it is time to eat some breakfast and go to work."

Yesterday André had been so excited to be part of the crew until he'd learned that his job would be swabbing the deck.

"Do I have to?" he groaned.

The door to their cabin swung open fiercely, as though caught in a hurricane, and slammed against the wall, causing the whole cabin to shudder. Yvonne's eyes grew wide, and she backed up until she was flat against the cabin wall. Captain Marie's face was a storm of rage bearing down upon André.

"Would you prefer to feed the sharks and barracudas?" she shrieked. "I'm sure they would find you quite tasty."

André turned green, and Yvonne thought he might throw up. He shook his head and in a tiny voice, said, "Non, Madame."

Captain Marie must not have heard him, because she roared, "What did you say?"

"Non, Madame," André said again, this time loudly through his tears.

Yvonne trembled and tried as hard as she could not to cry as she finished putting on her clothes and brushing the ash from her hair. She was still tying her shoes when André hurried from the cabin on his way to the mess.

Yvonne supposed the place where they ate was called the mess because it was hard to hold on to your food with the ship rocking back and forth so. That would create a mess for sure. She didn't envy André because he had to mop it up after meals.

Captain Marie had finally calmed down and she smiled at Yvonne. "Little boys are such a bother," the captain said, in a pleasant but slightly put out tone like Maman sometimes used.

Normally, Yvonne would have agreed with her, but she

didn't want André fed to the sharks. He wasn't *that* much of a bother. And besides, he was her brother.

Captain Marie reached out and took Yvonne by the hand. "Shall we go up to the bridge and figure out which direction we're going, my dear?" she said, smiling sweetly.

Yvonne was glad that Captain Marie wasn't mad at her, too. But one thing was certain, she didn't trust that smile.

ON THE BRIDGE, Yvonne saw various instruments made of brass and polished wood and a large table with a map laid out on it. The helmsman, an ancient sailor with a long gray beard and faded tattoos on his bare arms, hummed an off-key tune, which Yvonne decided must be a sea shanty.

Another sailor looked through an instrument Yvonne knew was called a sextant, although she didn't know how it worked.

"Lieutenant," said Captain Marie to the man with the sextant, "I would like you to meet Yvonne. She will be helping to keep the charts in order. Yvonne, this is Marcus. He is chief navigator of the *Liberté.*"

Marcus, who was a young man about Papa's age, turned and grinned warmly at her.

"I'm very glad to meet you, Mademoiselle," he said, in fine Métropole French.

"Please show the young lady around the bridge," said Captain Marie. "I must go to the galley and check in on the new cook. Petit-déjeuner was entirely unsuitable this morning. For one thing, there were no croissants on the Captain's Table."

Yvonne knew Captain Marie was talking about Maman, and she watched her leave with trepidation. Yvonne thought breakfast had been fine, as always. She preferred Maman's butter brioche to croissants, anyway. She hoped Maman didn't get in too much trouble.

Chief Navigator Marcus yawned. Then he took Yvonne by the hand and showed her the map closet, which contained big, flat drawers with dozens and dozens of sea charts.

"You must memorize the numbers at the top of these sea charts," said the Chief Navigator. "And then you must learn to keep them in order and pull out the correct one when it is needed."

The Chief Navigator yawned again. "I must get some sleep," he mumbled to himself.

Seeing how sleepy the Chief Navigator was, Yvonne asked, "Are you the only navigator?"

Chief Navigator Marcus gave a sad smile. "I used to have two Assistant Navigators," he said, "but now I have only one left, so I must work twice as long."

"What happened to the other one?" asked Yvonne.

The Chief Navigator looked even more sad. "He used the wrong sea chart, and Captain Marie missed an important meeting in Barbados."

"Did he get a scolding?" said Yvonne, hoping it wasn't like the one André got this morning.

"Much worse than that," said the Chief Navigator, now looking positively morose. "Captain Marie made him walk the plank."

"Oh, dear," was all that Yvonne could manage to say.

She frowned and grew very quiet for a long time. Finally, she decided what she wanted to say.

"Excuse me, Sir," said Yvonne. "But I don't know whether I should call you Lieutenant or Chief Navigator."

"You may call me Marcus," he said. "That is, unless Captain Marie is around. Then you should probably call me Chief Navigator."

"Marcus," said Yvonne, "Do you think I could learn to be a navigator?"

Marcus looked at Yvonne and smiled that warm smile. "You must be a very brave girl. Just the sort of girl I need to be Assistant Navigator."

PART 3
LA FAMILLE

A VISIT TO STÉPHANIE

There came a knock on his bedroom door. Sandrine had brought him buttered toast and mango. "Are you not feeling well, Monsieur Paul?" she inquired.

"Non," he said. "Merci, Sandrine."

"Let me know if you need anything." She departed, quietly closing the door behind her.

For the rest of the day, Maman left him alone with his thoughts. She must have known something was up, because she prudently held back, not once coming to his door. Or perhaps it was because she was still angry about his late return from the festival, when he came in, still in that ridiculous costume, grimy with soot and ash, and without a word slipped upstairs to his room.

At Sandrine's urging, Paul attended dinner with his family that evening but he was sullen and quiet and left immediately afterward without engaging in the usual conversation that took place around meals, avoiding a confrontation with Papa. Papa's broad forehead seemed bonier, his sunken eyes were black stones that saw straight through him whenever the old man was forced to look his way. It was one thing for Papa to be unhappy, but to show it was unexpected. The old man's anger had power. Best to give him a wide berth.

For the next few days, neither Papa nor Maman said a word about Paul's absence from the family's Ash Wednesday activities. Nor did they inquire about his continuing failure to attend school. But he knew from Maman's clipped phrases how much he had hurt and disappointed her. Even Mannie left him alone.

He attended mass on Sunday, sitting dutifully with Mannie and Papa and Maman, but he was not interested in the sacraments or the priest's boring Latin soliloquies. Stéphanie's salon would be that evening, and he wondered if either Sophie or Désirée would be there, or any of the few other students who remained in the group. He wanted to see Stéphanie, whose new baby would be born soon. But it would be too painful to attend the salon, too embarrassing. Surely, all that happened between him and Sophie was common knowledge now. Would they all think he was a brute?

He'd stop by and talk to her tomorrow.

Or the next day.

Or maybe Wednesday, when there was no school. Not that it made much difference. He may never return to school. What point is there, when your whole life is ending?

~

MONDAY MORNING BROUGHT another knock on his bedroom door. Instead of the expected Sandrine with his breakfast, it was Papa. He braced himself. He put down Jules Verne and sat up straight in bed. He hoped the talk, when it came, would be with Maman. No such luck.

"You know, Paul," Papa said, looming over his bed with his walking cane. "I have put up a considerable sum in order for you to attend séminaire. The family is experiencing hard times just now, and I think you owe it to us all to finish out the school year."

Paul's sigh was perhaps more deep than necessary.

"I can't, Papa. What's the point?" Of course, he knew all the answers his father would give him. They did not need to be spoken. Which was probably why Papa didn't speak them, but only stood there, angry. He studied his son until Paul was forced to look away from his dour face. Then he said, "So, who is this girl who's making such a fool of you?"

How could Papa possibly know about Sophie? He'd never mentioned her to the family. Not even to Mannie.

"I can't talk about it," he said and turned away.

"I will not be dismissed by you, son." His father banged the floor with his cane. "You will listen to me. You are fifteen years old and these girls, they mean néant! Do you understand? *Néant!* Young girls come and go. Fall for as many of them as you like, but when it is over, it's over. Do you understand?"

"Oui," he said, not entirely sure that he did. This is not what the Fathers had taught him.

"Paul, you are much too young to say, c'est la bonne. The right one will be the one who will serve as your life partner, who will help you make your fortune in this difficult world."

Papa paused for a moment, no longer so angry, considering his next words. "I know your generation has a different idea than mine about marriage. You read these romances and you think love is some fluttering butterfly you must chase after. I knew by your age that I would eventually ally myself with the Fauvé-Sablons or one of the other old créole families, because it was in the family interest to do so. You reject our attempts to help you in finding someone who is suitable for you and for the family. I can't say I understand this. But I will give you some fatherly advice, whether or not you choose to heed it.

"This thing will pass, son. There are many young ladies out there in the world. Some are suitable to bed, and some are suitable to marry. But you are much too young to throw away your future moping over a frivolous romance."

Paul wanted to object. Sophie was no frivolité, and love was not some business arrangement. But he had no desire to argue with the old man. So he didn't. His father left, having spoken the words he needed to speak, closing the door firmly behind him.

Perhaps Papa is right in some of his points, Paul thought. *Maybe it is foolish to quit school because of Sophie.* But right now... right now he couldn't consider that. He could only deal with this horrible sadness inside.

Perhaps Stéphanie would console his broken heart. Stéphanie, who was alone with Alice Germaine waiting for her new baby to come. Stéphanie, who had held a constant place in his thoughts, even after all that had happened in his life.

The next day, he slipped quietly out the front door and trekked slowly up the hill to Stéphanie's house. It was a February midmorning, the dry season of carême, and the air was as cool as it ever became in tropical Martinique. In the groves, they were harvesting the mangues. The markets were filled with the fruit, and vendors were selling it from their carts. The air was sweet with the fragrance of fruit and blossoms. He stopped and purchased a ripe mango from Alexandrine, a gift for Alice Germaine.

Alice was playing on the balcony as he approached the house. "Bonjou, Mesye Poncy," she called cheerfully.

"Hello, Alice. How are you this morning?"

"I'm fine thank you, Mesye Paul."

"Is your Maman home?"

"Oui, Mesye."

∼

WHEN THE KNOCK CAME, Stéphanie was too exhausted to move, so Alice Germaine ran down the stairs and eagerly answered the door. Paul Poncy's voice drifted through the open door. "I brought this mango especially for you, Mamzel," he said. "I thought perhaps your maman cannot get out much with the new baby coming."

"Merci," said Alice. "Tata Rosa has been helping, but Tata's gone to Fort-de-France today."

"Come in, Paul," Stéphanie called out. "I'm on the patio."

Stéphanie heard Paul's steps approaching down the hall, through the kitchen. She was sprawled in a rattan chair, her fully pregnant belly protruding immodestly from her loose cotton clothing. She could see the boy was abashed at the sight of her, but it was too much effort to cover herself.

"I apologize for coming unannounced," he said, hesitating, trying to not look directly at her, but toward the garden as though admiring it.

"You are welcome anytime, Paul," said Stéphanie. "It's good to have a visitor. What brings you by today?"

"I've come to ask about the salon the other night. I wasn't well, so I missed it."

Stéphanie gave a small laugh, wondering what the truth was. "You are not the only one. The girls missed it as well."

"I'm not surprised," he said, unsuccessfully trying to swallow his tell.

"Oh?" said Stéphanie, "has something happened between you and Sophie?"

Paul sighed heavily. "It's nothing."

Stéphanie shrugged. "You can talk to me about it if you'd like."

Paul was embarrassed by her offer. "Maybe another time."

He couldn't possibly tell Stéphanie it was because of her, although this was surely the case.

"Would you care to sit down? I can have Alice bring you a citronnade."

"Merci," he said, claiming the other rattan across from Stéphanie.

"I will bring Mesye Paul a drink," said Alice, scurrying off to the kitchen like a good host, not waiting for her mother's instruction.

"So, Paul," said Stéphanie, "I have decided that I must disband the salon. It is becoming too much with the baby arriving soon."

She could see the disappointment in his eyes, although surely he realized the difficulty. "I'm sorry to hear that. I've enjoyed them very much."

"If you'd like, you can still come by when you don't have school, and we can talk about books or politics or whatever you like. I would enjoy that."

Paul was floundering with his thoughts when Alice returned, balancing a tall citronnade which splashed over the edges of the glass. "Merci, Alice." His hand trembled as he set the glass on the table beside him.

"I may not return to school," he said.

"Oh, Paul, you mustn't do that," Stéphanie said. "Pourquoi?"

He didn't want to answer her question, so he shrugged and said, "Is there anything I can do to help you out, Madame?"

Stéphanie smiled. "Non, sweet boy. Aunt Rosa is here for me. But thank you for your thoughtfulness."

There was a moment of recognition between Stéphanie and Paul, a mirror of one another's loneliness and pain. A moment of clairvoyance maybe, when each of them saw into the future, sensing this thing that would grow between them. Stéphanie turned quickly away from these thoughts. He was fifteen, after all. Little more than a child.

"I have to leave," Paul said, springing from his chair in a panic.

Stéphanie's smile broadened, but the sadness remained in her eyes. "I meant what I said about talking. Anytime you feel the need."

"Merci," he said.

"And Paul, please rethink school. Few are so fortunate to have the opportunity you have."

"I will," he said. "I promise."

And he was gone.

WHAT WAS this sadness inside of her? And this secret she held so closely, afraid to allow its escape into the world — this news that she will have a baby in a few weeks, and that its father has left to die a hero on the battlefield of l'Afrique. Like her own policeman Papa, who died in the line of duty on the streets of Fort-de-France, leaving her without a father. Like Philippe had left Alice Germaine and the new baby, whom she was certain would be a boy. She would call him Germain Georges Adrien after his father, Germain Georges Philippe Guillaume.

Stéphanie was not so much lonely — she'd grown used to Philippe's long absences — as sad that a dream had died. A dream that someday he would come home to her and take them all away to Bordeaux where he had gone off to school. A bourgeois dream to be sure. Not one that the socialist Philippe would approve. But it was her dream, nonetheless.

And now she would have another baby and no more dreams of the Métropole. No more dreams of escape from this poor island she'd known her entire life.

No, Stéphanie was not poor herself, but the poverty was all around her, just outside her door. And it was obvious to anyone who should look that everyone she knew was just a death or a job away from devastation. Even the Poncys with their rich relatives and nice house and white skin lived on the verge of the abyss.

She hoped young Paul would take her up on her offer. She would love to spend time with him in intellectual conversation, and he was growing into a fine, handsome young man, still sweet in his adolescent shyness.

It would help her perhaps to forget this loss for a few hours a week. Because now, as the baby approached, it was all she thought about.

SHE RECEIVED Philippe's first letter, his second letter, third, a whole packet of them. Where had they been residing? Since he went back to Africa, the letters had come like this in bunches with strange bits of life and soil clinging to the creases where the envelopes were glued together and sifting inside to settle on the sheets, grainy punctuations that confused her eyes. He was deeper into the continent now. *Africa is vast,* he wrote. *Look out at the sea, my Stephanie. Imagine it is grass. That is Africa. I think this is Africa until I see the dunes. A dry sea, wave upon wave.*

He had nothing to say about where he was going, what he was doing. It was all landscape. So that she had to think hard, hard, stare into the Caribbean, clutching the shape her baby made in its ocean, and walk out on the gritty black sand until it became gold-yellow like her arms. She sank between tall palms, dipped her hand into cool pure water and drank. *Ah, Philippe,* she said as he knelt beside her, calling to his companions. She touched his cheek and for a moment, he leaned against her palm. His face reflected in the pool until it broke in her hand, rippled. Beneath her knees, the ground was solid. Dogs barked, and the bells of Our Lady of Bon Porte rang out the hour. It wasn't cold. It's never cold in Martinique, but she knew Philippe existed in a kind of heat she couldn't imagine. Only part of it burning his body, the greater heat was inside him.

Since the letters came in batches weeks apart, she didn't notice until so much time — two months? more? — passed without a bundle of carefully pasted envelopes or even a single thin sealed paper to unfold. She pulled open the drawer in her desk where she kept them. Was there a soft layer of mold? She reached in just as the baby kicked against her rib. The baby occupied her mind, pushing out the ghosts of memory. It wouldn't be long before the little one came. How could she miss Philippe? How much had he been here since he first cast off for Bordeaux? Stéphanie had grown more and more like Alice, forgetting to think about Philippe, to search for him, to see his Africa, to imagine the dunes and savannas, the rivers and forests. When she thought of him, he was gripping a rifle, his cheek against the stock, sighting down the barrel, not seeing her standing in front of him. And it had been two months. It had been over two months since the last bundle of letters.

GERMAIN GEORGES ADRIEN GRAINAU *was born at home on Rue Montnoël in the Fort District at six in the morning, on Monday, 5 Mars, with the assistance of midwife, Pauline Décord, who registered the birth.* The father was not listed in the record.

No letter ever came from Africa bearing regrets. Not to

Stéphanie, nor to Monsieur Guillaume. Perhaps Philippe had forgotten her.

When Philippe's father came to see his new grandchild, his face was heavily creased, he leaned on the cane he once only carried. "I have lost my son," he said, "to those communards. Africa! Of all things. What does he think he is doing? Keep this one alive for me." Monsieur Guillaume traced a finger along Adrien's cheek. "He is my hope now."

It settled into Stéphanie that Philippe was likely dead or imprisoned. She woke one morning feeling suddenly alone. Alice cried when Stéphanie told her she didn't think her father would be coming home again.

"Why? What happened to him?"

"How can I know for certain? No one knows, do they? They would write to us. If your papa could send us a letter, he would." Stéphanie rubbed Alice's back, kissed her forehead, murmured tenderly meaningless assurances. Alice recovered. She was not heartbroken. She was only missing possibility. Still, it was several days before her natural gaiety returned, prompted by a visit from Paul Poncy.

Stéphanie was grateful that the somberness had lifted. "Bonjour, Paul." She kissed his cheek. "Bonjour," she said again, softer. "Thank you for coming."

FAMILY TROUBLES

THE FAMILY TROUBLES began the year Paul turned sixteen. Martinique had always lived and died by the vagaries of the sugar market, matters of weather, and all the hundreds of things that bubbled up and burst, disturbing the economy. Lean times and fat times. Until that year, such things had not concerned him. But now Paul was old enough to remember when things were different and how they had changed. Three years after the hurricane, closed businesses still dotted Rue Victor Hugo. The wealthiest planters stretched their reserves to buy failed plantations that had not seen a new crop since the storm. And in families like the Poncys, times were especially lean. All summer, whenever Papa and Joseph were home from Lamentin, the patio filled with Dupuoys and Caminades, drinking dusty bottles of rhum, measured with conservative care, as they talked about the sugar market. It was such a day when Paul sat on a wicker stool near the garden edge of the patio. Samuel passed him a glass and no one objected.

"Beets," Samuel Dupouy sighed. "They are flooding the market. I don't see an end to it. Sugar from beets is cheaper. It can be grown almost anywhere in Europe, any temperate zone.

It makes no difference if your pastry is frosted with beet sugar or cane sugar. If it's cheaper, bakers will use it and there it is." He threw up his hands.

"There we are," Papa said and gave a brittle laugh.

Paul felt a shock at the fragile sound, wondering how long his father had looked this tired and small.

"Maybe we should invest more in the rhum business," Mannie said.

"We are in rhum," Papa replied. "Sugar pays Joseph and I, but our money works in rhum, coffee, and imports."

Joseph spoke up, "Emmanuel, where do you think rhum would be if the cane plantations fail? The rhumeries have always depended on a good supply of sugar cane, but they don't buy enough to keep plantations from folding if sugar prices keep dropping."

Papa's eyes were closed. He looked as if he was sleeping. Samuel stood up. "What do you say, gentlemen? Should we leave Anatole and Joseph to enjoy their time at home?"

On cue, Raphaël and Gustav rose. Paul and his brothers stood to say their goodbyes, kiss their uncle and cousins' cheeks. Anatole remained seated, eyes still closed, lost, it would seem, in the aches and pains of swollen joints and exhaustion.

It was a full week before Anatole was well enough to return to his job, looking after the Soudon sucrerie's finances in Lamentin.

ALTHOUGH THERE HAD ALWAYS BEEN downturns in the lives of the Poncy family, it was a little different this time. Mannie found a job at the end of the school year, working as a clerk's assistant at the Plissonneau shipping company. His pay was poor, but it helped a little to make up for the times Papa missed work. Joseph had begun work as Papa's assistant in Lamentin, preserving Papa's position there and helping to keep it in the family. Paul had offered to work also, but Maman insisted, "You are the youngest of my sons. Times are changing, and an education is very important." She didn't mention the priesthood, somehow knowing how far from that ambition he had strayed.

In late July, shortly before the Saint-Louis-de-Gonzague August break, Papa called the family together. Paul stood with Joseph, Mannie, and Maman around Papa's desk in his study with its mahogany wainscoting and towering bookshelves, his ledger books open on the walnut desk. Papa sat in his big chair, his pipe stuffed with spiced tobacco from Macouba, its distinctive aroma filling the air of the study. His face was very somber.

"As you know," Papa began, "I've been ill for the past several months. My doctor has advised me I must discontinue work soon. Too much strain on my heart. I'd hoped by now to have a considerable sum put away for something like this, but these past few years have been very hard on our family, and our investments have left us short." Mannie began to say something, but Papa put up his hand, cutting him short. "Your maman and I have discussed contingencies. This may come as a shock to you, but we see no alternative.

"First, we must let Sandrine go. We can no longer afford to pay her." Paul and his brothers all moaned and Papa put up his hand again. "Second, we may have to move into a smaller house. There is pie- à-terre on Rue Saint-Denis, owned by the Petits, which will be available in a few months. Jean-Claude has kept very good care of it, and I'm sure it will be adequate for us, should it be necessary." Another moan.

Jean-Claude was Maman's cousin in Morne Rouge who owned several properties in Saint-Pierre, so they would probably get a family deal on it. "If we need to move," Papa said, "we shall move before Christmas, but we will have a few months to prepare."

The boys remained in shock at the prospect of losing Sandrine. Paul and Emmanuel had lived in this house on Rue Castelnau since they were born, and Sandrine had lived with them their entire lives. "But Sandrine," Paul said, "what will she do?"

"We have talked with her," Maman said. "She will live with her sister in Fort-de-France. We will give her a recommendation to take to a new employer. There are always housekeeping jobs."

Paul wasn't so sure about that. It was one of the things they talked about at the salon. When people like Paul's family were doing poorly, the mulâtre shopkeepers were doing much worse, to say nothing of the workers.

"I could get a job," he blurted out. "I've said it before and it's true." His brothers looked at him and nodded agreement. They believed Paul was the spoiled one who didn't pull his weight.

"Non," Maman repeated, adamantly. "You will not quit school, Paul. That would be short-sighted. Someone in this family must be looking toward the future."

Everything is changing, Paul thought. Maman had twice invoked the future within the last month. Maman, who always brought up tradition whenever he strayed from her path. The irony didn't escape him. But in this she is right, he thought. We must be looking toward the future.

THE OLD CENTURY was already slipping into the past even before it officially ended. Paul knew keenly that Martinique needed workers skilled in certain trades. Electricians, machinists, and mechanics would modernize the rhum and sugar factories, move agricultural products like cane from plantations to sucreries and rhumeries or move bananas and coffee to the harbor for shipping to ports all over the world. He was convinced that he must learn a trade to help his family and Martinique move toward prosperity — for how can one extricate the family's fortunes from the island's? Before Martinique could progress, railroads must be built, and highways for the new automobiles, and factories that would supply more of the island's own needs, independent of the Métropole and the ships that came to port from the United States and Canada and Brazil.

Saint-Louis-de-Gonzague, between Latin, God, and a thinly disguised nostalgia for the monarchy, also taught economics. Paul had awareness of economic scale. He knew that small islands, by nature, can never be truly independent — Martinique would always be a lesser appendage of France. If not France, then another colonial power would rush in to fill the vacuum. And who wanted that? Well, some, perhaps, but it would be a mistake. They were French, after all, despite England's occasional interference.

His thoughts constantly returned to the railroad and how things would be so much different if there was rail to carry the sugar cane into Saint-Pierre from the Atlantic. And not just sugar, but passengers as well. *Are there plans for passenger trains? Wouldn't that be something? To ride the train to La-Trinité? To the beaches of Sainte-Anne?*

Whenever he had a chance, he mentioned the railroad to Samuel or to his Plissonneau cousins. "It's coming, Paul," they assured him. "In a few years, we will build a railroad into Saint-Pierre. It is essential for the rhumeries." As to passengers? *Well, perhaps in time.* Paul was determined to be part of this future. He explored the advertisements for workers in newspapers from France. He applied his limited knowledge of English to the occasional paper from New York City that he found draped over a dowel among other foreign newspapers at Madame Gemeau's, the tobacconist on quai Peynier. Engineers, machinists, mechanics and laborers. He could imagine what the laborers did. The hard physical work of laying and repairing tracks and coupling the cars. Dangerous work, he could see by the sensational stories of men crushed in the course of their work in the rail yards.

But what of the machinists and engineers? A railroad doesn't run without them and he felt sure he could learn such work. There were machine shops in the distilleries. It would give him a taste of it. The best thing would be to go abroad and apprentice at an actual railroad shop.

Yet, Papa could no longer be expected to send him to the Métropole or America or Canada for school or an apprenticeship. Even if the family could afford it, it would be a burden, and he didn't dare to ask that of them. The only thing he could do was prove himself and maybe one of the relatives would help. Samuel or Georges could surely afford a stipend, he reasoned. An investment, really.

"It's too much to expect Papa to support my school," Paul said later to Stéphanie, after he'd told her about the family meeting. He wasn't sure he ought to be confiding family business to her—Papa wouldn't approve—but who else could he talk to about these daily troubles on his mind? Stéphanie always understood and sympathized. "I've been talking to Raphaël," he said, "and I'll take him up on his offer of a job at the rhumerie. I can start next week."

"But your maman will be so unhappy if you leave school," Stéphanie said. "What will you say to her?"

Paul's academic interests were now unapologetically focused on applied science and math. His theology studies were an unwelcome interruption. Cousin Raphaël had been right—his religious instructors were all hopelessly conservative. He sometimes regretted the motivations that brought him to Saint-Louis-de-Gonzague. His loyalty to a childish vow made in despair when Eustase died and Maman's determination to make him into a priest. And what of Papa? Educating his youngest child with the sons of the powerful, assuming that Paul could carry the family forward on the shoulders of that prestige alone. Was that it? But how could he possibly face Maman with this revelation that becoming a priest was no longer something he could do? That he wanted to learn a trade? If only he had gone to the lycée, he could have studied engineering and mechanics full time.

"I have to be firm," he said. "I'm a grown man, and I've made my decision. Maman will be disappointed, but I'm still her son, oui? What will she do?"

"I suppose you're right." Stéphanie had nodded support at all the right places, but Paul knew she was disappointed in him, too. And that hurt more than Maman's disapproval.

"This may be for the best," he argued. "We're entering a new era of industry. There will be a need for electricians and machinists and engineers soon in Martinique. Everywhere in the world, in fact. And they'll earn much more than a clerk at the sucrerie." He could see the "but..." remaining in her eyes; it didn't sway the confidence he felt in his opinion. Stéphanie comes from a family of intellectuals, he reasoned. She thinks all young people should want to go to school.

CLÉMENCE EXAMINED her son for a protracted moment after he announced Raphaël's offer of a position at the rhumerie. The boy was becoming a man. He already had that high, wide Poncy forehead and alert intelligent eyes. He was taller now than both his parents. Now he was saying that he had accepted the position and would begin on Monday. Feeling a little sadness creeping into her eyes, she pressed her palm against his cheek before turning away. She was not looking forward to the work that would be hers to do when Sandrine was gone. Just now, she had not the energy to argue with her youngest son. He would do what he was going to do and she could not change that. Like Eustase leaving the safety off his rifle, like Anatole growing old and sick and Joseph losing... losing what? That easy way he had before the hunting accident. Now his face was always pinched into a frown. And now Paul. Well, she would just have to make another bargain with God.

Anatole put off the move to Rue Saint-Denis for another year. "We can see how it goes," he said. He was relieved that Paul was working. More money coming in and less going out. "The economy will improve and our investments will grow," he often repeated like a spell that if said enough times might come true.

Sandrine was sent on her way with a thank you and kisses and little else. "We will keep in touch," Maman said. One of those things people say but don't really mean. Sandrine made no such promise in turn, although Paul knew the fondness in her smile was genuine. So was the bitterness in her eyes. *Maman may forget Sandrine,* Paul told himself, *but one day I will go to Fort-de-France and visit her, say hello and see how she's doing.*

One doesn't fault Sandrine—or us—for not believing it.

THE RHUMERIE

Paul's first job at the rhumerie required taking inventory and inspecting the oak barrels before they were laid out in rows between the bay shore and the warehouse, prior to being transported to the mouillage. Once at the mouillage, he'd audit the barrels as they were loaded onto the flat boats that would carry them out to the steamers anchored in deep water. He also audited the incoming inventory when a newly arrived ship was unloaded. On these days, he was often left ample opportunity to be out and about in Saint-Pierre, making acquaintances among the sailors, gabariers and stevedores, and the petit proprietors of the Mouillage district. This gave him a certain sense of satisfaction he knew he would miss sitting in an office all day like Papa. Let brother Joseph be Papa's successor in the business world, Paul had always been happier outdoors doing physical work. Not that happiness had anything to do with making your way in this world. There was time to be happy once you were earning a living.

With the exception of the short Saturday, Paul arrived home after working ten hours or more. Beginning work at five in the morning, he seldom left before 3:30 in the afternoon. He often could do little more than eat supper with his family and go to sleep.

He hadn't seen Stéphanie for weeks, and he terribly missed their Wednesday afternoon conversations. But he expected Papa to soon announce the move to Rue Saint-Denis. After that he could find a new routine and reconnect with her somehow.

"PAUL PONCY." The voice rang out across the storeroom floor, where the rhum barrels were stacked, waiting for orders to be loaded onto wagons or rolled down to the docks at Place Bertin. Most were bound for the mouillage to be shipped overseas to Bordeaux; a few would end up in Fort-de-France to be bottled on the island. Paul paused in his task of counting barrels and turned to see his neighbor, Raoul Dufail, his muscled, sunbrown arms bulging, as he cautiously maneuvered a 230 kilo cask of rhum. Paul was impressed at Raoul's strength, knowing he could never do the same. He seldom saw Raoul, who, as an assistant in the cooper's shop, built and repaired the oak barrels. Most of the barrels came new and unassembled from Hamlen House in North America, but some arrived damaged and there was always a need for more than could be ordered from the U.S. manufacturer.

"Antoine has you rolling barrels today?" Paul asked.

"Oui. Clovis didn't come in, so we are shorthanded. They'll have some new boys this afternoon, but for now..." Raoul stood and shrugged.

"It's been a while since we've talked," said Paul. Even though the Dufail family lived in the Quartier du Fort, Paul had seen little of his childhood friend since entering séminaire. "Do you have time for a tartine at Noëlly's? I'll buy."

"Just a few more barrels and I'll be more than ready for

déjeuner," said Raoul. Raoul had flexible time when not needed in the shop. In a few years, he would be a full-fledged cooper, one of an elite group of skilled artisans in the industry who, along with millwrights, electricians, and carpenters, had a degree of independence from the carefully supervised routine of the warehouse workers. Paul, too, had this sort of flexibility in his job—a job which would lead to middle management and eventually upper management. But he envied Raoul, who worked with his hands, as well as his mind.

After Raoul had finished rolling in the remaining rhum barrels, the two young men shed their aprons and cleaned themselves before ambling up to the Noëlly Décomis boulangerie on Rue Victor Hugo. There was a small line at the bakery, but it moved quickly.

"Good morning, Noëlly," said Paul when their turn came. "How are things today?"

"Travail, travail," said Noëlly, a good-natured young mulâtre with a round, smiling face.

"Oui, I know how that goes," Raoul said. "So, how are the young ones?"

"In school, fortunately," said Noëlly with a wink.

They laughed amiably and ordered their tartines and coffee. Paul paid and they found a table outside in the shade of the awning, where they could relax and catch up on each other's lives.

"Have you heard, my brother Alcide has moved to North America?" said Raoul. Alcide was a few years older than Raoul and in their younger days had often let Paul, Raoul, and Mannie follow him on expeditions up Morne d'Orange. Alcide would frighten them with tales of the fer-de-lance, pointing up at snaky vines, any of which could come to life and drop on the boys with its deadly bite. From the height of the morne they could look down upon the harbor crowded with toy-like ships.

Paul shook his head. "I hadn't heard."

"Oui. He's in Maine and engaged. They're to be married next year."

"Send my congratulations," Paul said. "I would love to hear about America. I would go if I could, just to see it. But I need to improve my English first."

"There are places — some of the textile towns — where nearly everyone speaks French, according to Alcide. There are many Québécois in New England."

"I would want to see more than a few textile towns."

"Oui. Alcide says it is amazing how big everything is there. There are forests many times the size of this little island. In fact, bigger than all the Métropole. Which reminds me, my uncle Paul has recently returned from France—I suppose you've already heard this. He's been studying medicine in Paris. He's a doctor at the hospital now."

"We always need more doctors." Paul knew this story already, because such tales spread rapidly in Saint-Pierre, especially among the comfortable classes of the Fort District. "Tell me about his new wife, Marie. Is she as lovely as they say?"

"Oui," Raoul declared enthusiastically. "A sophisticated Parisian woman. Quite a catch. And she is amiable as well." There is a brief pause in the conversation as the two young men silently contemplated the subject of desirable female qualities.

"So, tell me, what is happening in the Poncy family?"

Paul struggled to think of something to say. He didn't really want to talk about family troubles, but it appeared everything led back to that uncomfortable subject. "Joseph has been working with Papa in Lamentin. Papa's been ill a lot lately. He hardly works anymore, and I think he would like to turn his job over to his eldest."

Raoul nodded gravely. His own father died just before Raoul's birth. His mother remarried, but there was still that knowledge that someone else had fathered you and died, like so many, at an early age.

"Maman is busy with the church and keeping the house up now that Sandrine is gone," Paul said.

"You've lost your housekeeper?"

"Oui," Paul said without elaboration. He wanted to say, *She was so much more than a housekeeper,* but he didn't. Even as he thought it, he wasn't sure it was true. You don't send a member of your family out into the world with nothing, do you? "It's been quite hard on Maman. Mannie is working at the Plissonneau shipping office. That's about it."

"So, what are your plans, Paul?" asked Raoul. "Are you going to be a house manager like Anatole?"

Paul shrugged. *That's the track I'm on, isn't it?* "I'd like to work for the new railroad when it comes. I want to do something with my hands. Like you. Perhaps a machinist or an engineer."

"Manual labor is hard," Raoul said. "I often wonder what I'll do when I'm too old."

"You'll run the tonnelier's shop, with many strong young assistants to assemble the barrels."

"I can only hope."

Unmentioned between them was the reality of Martinique. So much depended upon the economy. Or sometimes the very ground you stood upon. Or fire. Pierrotins, indeed all Martiniquais, argue among themselves and with each other whether it is better to build with stone or wood. Stone is abundant and fireproof, but crushes the life out of you, while wood will sway instead of fall in an earthquake but blow down in a storm and burn down around you if a fire starts and spreads — as it did a few years before in Fort-de-France — until everything is ashes.

AFTER BIDDING FAREWELL TO RAOUL, Paul continued to the docks, his inventory lists in his hand. Frigate birds circled high in the afternoon sky above the harbor. Gulls squabbled over a dropped fish. The gabariers called back and forth to one another as they pushed their loaded barges out to the waiting ships. A part of him cursed his inability to shut out all of this beauty, push it away into a compartment, just as the family, along with most of the comfortable classes of Saint-Pierre, so easily denied the existence of these working men and women who made their middle-class lives so comfortable. These invisible black laborers of Saint-Pierre who sent his family's rhum off to Europe, under the watchful eyes of their mulâtre supervisors, who themselves were watched over by Paul's rich cousins who returned home each evening to the finest French wines, paid for by the sweat and blood of their workers.

Were these men just numbers in a ledger book? Like casks of rhum? Had his Papa taught him that? It was only a year ago when he sat with the others in Stéphanie's garden and talked with his prosperous mulâtre friends about a new Martinique, a more equitable Martinique, a Martinique of black and white together. And now here he walked along this wooden dock, counting the toll of other people's lives. He twinged, just a little, as he recorded those numbers.

He dodged the busy workers who saw him only as an obstacle to be avoided. He found the place on the dock where the barrels were marked, "Dupouy, Cie," and checked them off one by one. Fifteen casks ready for shipping to Bordeaux this afternoon. Verified. He signed and carried the shipping order to the dock supervisor. Then he moved back to the area of the mouillage dedicated to the Dupouy company, where the barrels were taken from that small storeroom at the plant and placed here in the open air with hundreds of barrels of rhum and sugar bound mostly for Europe. Not only from Saint-Pierre's twenty-two rhumeries, but from sucreries and rhumeries all over the island.

A young black man sat on a barrel of Dupouy rhum as though waiting for him. He was perhaps a year or two older than Paul, who wanted to shoo him away. *Take your break somewhere else.* Instead, he said, "May I help you?"

"That depends," the man said in Matanik, insolently patting the side of the oak barrel. "You have any of this ready to drink?"

Paul smiled at his little joke. A nervous smile because he was being too flippant to someone who might be a superior, for all he knew. But the young man smiled back at him and said, "Just taking a breath. I can move if you wish."

"Non," Paul said. "You're not in the way. I just have to count these."

"Do you work for these people?" the young man asked, again patting the barrel.

"Oui," Paul said. He was wondering why the man's supervisor allowed him to lie around harassing people during work hours. Paul turned away to begin his barrel count.

"Do you mind if I ask you something, Mesye?" the man said, interrupting, causing Paul to lose the sum he'd carefully added up in his head. He wanted to yell, *get lost,* but something, maybe it was his conscience or his liberal tolerance or just plain curiosity caused him to look at the man instead. He saw for the first time the young man's black face, scarred where some blade had cut it open, the hard set of his mouth, the twinkle in his eye. He waited.

"I am Ludger," the young man said, extending his hand.

"Paul," he replied, reluctantly taking the offering.

"You're one of those Saint-Louis-de-Gonzague boys, aren't you?" *How does he know that?*

"Oui, but—"

He cut Paul off by answering the unspoken question. "It's

that priestly je ne sais quoi." Paul was surprised at the flawless French from the mouth of this working class fellow. Then he was abashed at his own prejudices.

"Oh," he said, "quite astute."

"Oui," Ludger replied, as though it was a matter of common knowledge. "I could show you some things."

"I have no doubt," Paul said.

"The question is, do you wish to see them?" Ludger asked, his face very serious.

It was a challenge. Paul wondered if he would take him up on it, surprising himself for even considering it. *But there is nothing in this world that should make me want to close my eyes to its existence.* That's what he believed.

While he was thinking it over, Ludger said, "I will be drinking tonight at *Lonbraj ble*, should you wish to join me."

With that, young Ludger pushed himself up from the oak barrel and strolled off toward the dock.

WHEN PAUL FINISHED his count and was walking back toward the rhumerie, the scene with the young dock worker remained stuck in his mind. *I am world-wise,* he told himself, offended by the man's insinuation that he was naïf. *I am a republican. I believe in a better world for all of humanity. Why would I not want to know all there is to know?* But soon there was another voice in his head. One that said, *you are just a sheltered child. You do not know how dark the world can be; the world of the guillotine and the hangman's noose; the world of the battlefield; of slaughtered innocents; the ghettoes of the starving; the alleyways full of murderers and thieves. You know nothing of these worlds, young Monsieur Poncy, outside the novels of Victor*

Hugo and Emile Zola. And what's more, you do not want to know them.

But how can this be true, that he doesn't want to know the world as it is? *Non!* he protests, because he has a story of himself, the story of a young man forging his way into the modern world, and how can you make your way if you don't know the landscape? If you are wearing a blindfold over your eyes?

Non. The challenge could not be avoided. This evening he'd go to that working man's bar on Rue Bouille, the Lonbraj Ble, and have a beer with young Ludger.

SYLBARIS

THE WANING MOON, nearly full, rose above the houses of Saint-Pierre, casting anxious shadows across the cobbles of Rue Petit Versailles. It was Saturday night and the music of a honky tonk piano drifted up the street from the brothel on the corner of Rue Bouille. Paul had second thoughts. The Lonbraj Ble would be filled with big burly nègres from the mouillage, letting off steam at the end of a hard week. And what business did a white boy from the Fort have there? He'd heard several stories about knife fights and brawls—of murders even —in these notorious establishments along the waterfront. Would he let some silly sense of pride put him in mortal danger?

I will not be afraid of the world, he told himself, screwing up his courage. *I can have a beer with my friend, can I not? Who is going to stop me? It's my right!*

So, this Ludger is now your friend? Well, by all means let's go have a beer with our good friend Ludger.

He rounded the corner in front of the brothel, and there it was, two doors down. Lonbraj Ble. Two men stood outside smoking in the dim blue light of the bar. From inside came voices, laughter, challenges. Paul turned away, but then he steeled himself and resumed his trajectory.

"Are you lost, white boy?" said one of the men, blowing smoke in his face.

"Pardonnez-moi," he said, "I'm meeting my friend."

"He's meeting his friend," the man said to his companion with an inclination of his head. The other man spit on the ground at Paul's feet. The men parted for him, bowing slightly, in a mocking display of respect.

Inside, a pale, flickering light coming through the blue glass of an oil lamp illuminated the bar. Eyes turned toward him. They were not friendly eyes, but they lingered only a moment before turning away again, having assessed the threat and found it wanting. But the atmosphere, it seemed, had changed. It was not as boisterous as it had been before he came through the door. He looked around for Ludger and didn't see him, so he made his way through a smoky haze toward the patio at the back of the bar where shadowy figures sat around tables lit by citronnelle torches. Someone pushed a stool out in front of him, tripping him. He somehow avoided falling. He wanted to run. On the edge of panic, his eyes searched the shadows for Ludger. He must be here somewhere.

"White boy," someone said and he turned around to see the man who had tripped him with the stool, now standing, a cigarette hanging from his lips, challenging. "The béké bars are up there," he said, his thumb pointing up the hill toward Rue Victor Hugo.

"Leave my friend be, Marius," a voice said from the patio. He recognized the voice. The man called Marius turned away, clearly not wanting to fight with Ludger. Paul looked into the dim light of the patio and saw him at last. Ludger beckoned him to the table where he sat with his arm draped over the shoulder of an attractive young woman.

"I thought for a moment I had misjudged you."

"My bravery," Paul asked, "or my foolishness?"

"Oui," Ludger said. "Come meet Charlise, ma chérie. Join us."

Paul obeyed. There was already a glass of rhum waiting for him, with a bottle beside it. "Charlise, my dear," Ludger said, "this is my good friend Paul. He's studied to be a priest, you know."

Paul turned red with embarrassment. Charlise bore down on him with a frankly sexual gaze and, without taking her eyes off of him, said, "He's a good boy. I can see."

"I'm certain of it," said Ludger. "It is in his face... but mostly it's the skin."

There was the slightest touch of danger in his voice, barely noticeable. Thoroughly uncomfortable now, Paul wondered what he'd gotten himself into. But for the moment, he felt safer here with Ludger and Charlise than returning through that gauntlet that stretched between him and the door out to Rue Bouille.

"Pardon me, my friend," Ludger said, his tone once again amiable. "but I'm afraid I've forgotten your family name."

"I don't believe I have said. It's Poncy. Paul Poncy." Charlise raised a finely sculpted eyebrow, but said nothing.

"Monsieur Poncy, I am Ludger Sylbaris. I am pleased to make your acquaintance."

"Likewise," Paul said, unconvincing, even to himself. His gaze turned briefly to Charlise, but when no attempt was made to include her in this exchange of niceties, he said to Ludger, "I have heard that name, I'm sure."

"Probably one of your neighbor's housekeepers, no doubt," said Ludger. "My name has a certain cachet, especially among the ladies. Would you like to hear an interesting story about my surname?"

Paul nodded. Ludger had been leading him here. What else could he do?

"My granmé's manman," Ludger began, "was from Africa. Her masters at the l'habitation Donneau did not allow her to keep the name she was born with and so they gave her only the prénom, Reine—yes, I know, ironies abound. In those days, a slave wasn't allowed to have a surname. Without a surname, you are not a real person, you know. You are just a dog."

He watched Paul's reaction before continuing.

"But Granmé Reine has this idea. Since she is permitted to name her own children, she gives each of them the second prénom, Sylbaris—Euphrasie Sylbaris, Robertine Sylbaris, and so on—so that if they are sold or orphaned or separated, they will always know one another. And each of her daughters do the same. So when slavery ends and they may choose a real surname, every one of them takes the name Sylbaris. It is a surname which comes from mothers, not fathers.

"Although, in my case," he said, grinning, "it is my father, Eucher, who is the son of Robertine. Interesting, is it not?"

Yes, it was interesting. Paul nodded and knocked back the rhum that had been put in front of him to replace the one he'd already consumed. As soon as it was gone, Sylbaris tipped up the bottle and poured him another.

"So, Monsieur, do you have any little stories to share about your own family?"

Paul was embarrassed and a little irked perhaps, to be put on the spot. What could he say? At that moment, he only wanted to leave. He shrugged and shook his head slightly, considered standing and... what? Return down that hostile gangway? He flashed his anger at Ludger, but remained seated.

"But I don't suppose you wish to share them with the likes of us," Ludger Sylbaris said. The menacing edge had returned to his voice. "What do you think, Charlise? I have invited my good friend here to join us for a little imbibing. I have protected him from a big, scary black man who would like to beat him up. I have introduced him to my love of loves," he put his arm around Charlise and gave her a wink and a lascivious look, which she returned. "I have even told him the sacred story of the Sylbaris name. And what do I get from him in return? I see only murder in his eyes."

Paul's fear turned to fury. *But why?* he asked himself. Sylbaris had done nothing to him, he was playing with him. He turned his eyes away, calming himself. Telling himself all this intimidation and anger was only imagined.

"Murder?" said Charlise. "Surely not this nice white Catholic boy?"

"Non, non," he protested. "I would never."

"He would never," said Sylbaris, mocking, sharing a secret look with Charlise. Sylbaris took a knife from his belt, its curved blade about three inches long, and laid it on the table where it shimmered in the flickering torchlight. "I will wager, before this evening is over, this white boy will cut someone with this knife?"

"Oh, surely not, Ludger," said Charlise.

"Five francs," he said. "What do you say, Charlise?"

"I say," said Charlise, plucking a five franc note from her brassiere, "I'm with the white boy."

"Wait," Paul protested, "I've made no bet."

"This is between Charlise and I," Sylbaris said. "But if you would like a stake in this little wager, how about this? If Charlise is right and you do not cut someone tonight, you can take the wench home with you." Charlise looked at Paul and licked her lips. Then she scooted her chair over beside him and threaded her arm around his in a show of solidarity.

"And if you are right, Monsieur?" Paul asked Sylbaris, downing another rum. The question was ridiculous. How could

Sylbaris possibly make him do something against his will; against his very own nature?

"Then, priest," said Sylbaris, "you must live knowing that you are not the man you think you are. And that you are no better than this no-good rogue, Ludger Sylbaris."

"But that's not my belief," he said.

Sylbaris gave him a penetrating stare that said, *oh, isn't it?*

Paul, eyeing the knife on the table, shook his head.

Ridiculous.

THE NIGHT CONTINUED in a blue haze. Paul quaffed his rhum beneath the flicker of citronnelle flames. Sylbaris rolled a cigarette, handed him one, and he became immersed in the cacophony of the cicadas as the smoke curled insolently from his lip. Charlise whispered something in his ear. He couldn't understand the words but was lost in the sensuality of their sound, of the warm breath on his neck, the perfume, an expensive perfume, he thought, a perfume from the Métropole. For a moment he was in a café in Bordeaux or Paris and the voices of the insects had become the conversation of the streetcars and the passersby on the blue cobbled streets, glimmering in a softly falling rain. Then Sylbaris cleared his throat and Paul was suddenly snatched back to this world of Saint-Pierre, devastated in his disappointment.

"It is a fine night," Sylbaris said. And Paul said, "Oui," despite this not being Bordeaux, despite this sense of danger hanging in the air of the Lonbraj Ble. He looked at this young son of a slave from the Donneau plantation. He was only Paul's age, or close, barely a man, and yet he had the worldliness and the hard weathered face of a much older person. It was not pity Paul felt for him, but something akin to pity, and it alarmed him, because he realized this feeling came from a place of someone above looking down. It troubled his comfortable sense of republican égalité. In this new awareness, he attempted to shift his perspective, to look at Sylbaris as an equal. But he was unsure whether he had succeeded, or could succeed, and he wondered if perhaps Sylbaris was right. Maybe this was impossible.

Another rhum, another cigarette, that exotic perfume, the blue smoke of forgetfulness, all conspired to lull him into a complacency, a sort of self-satisfaction. Until he looked again at the table and saw that blade waiting there, its shiny surface reflecting the colors of the night. Reflecting an anxiety in his being, an abyss between worlds. *Ridiculous, to think that I would use this knife on another person.* But there it sat, a sign of something, a gulf between him and these dark-skinned people he shared the table with. *What do they want from me?* he asked himself.

Paul stood suddenly; he could no longer bear this torn feeling. "I must go home," he declared. He turned to leave, suddenly remembering those men he would have to pass at the bar.

"Don't you want to take Charlise with you, Monsieur?" said Sylbaris, his voice challenging.

He turned to say goodnight to Charlise, who had clearly consumed too much rhum, who winked at him. The evening, through the haze of rum, pressed his mind and without warning, he was in a rage. "To hell with you and your games, Ludger!"

Before he could turn again, Sylbaris was on his feet. "Had enough of these nègres, have you?" He was in Paul's face now, Ludger's large, muscled body intimidating as it towered over him. Paul stared down at the knife. *Non. This is what he wants. For you to take that knife.*

"Go ahead, pick it up," Sylbaris dared.

"Non, I'm not playing your game, Ludger."

"You think it's a game, white man? You think I won't beat the shit out of you?" *Slit your throat*, Paul heard him say, although he didn't actually say it. Paul's eyes darted to the knife on the table, thinking, *he's going to grab the knife.* So he reached out and took it before the black man had a chance, holding it up between them, fire in his eyes. "I said, *non.*"

A triumphant grin emerged from Sylbaris' anger. He grabbed Paul's wrist in an iron grip. And the two of them stood like that for an eternity, staring at the hatred in each other's eyes. Two men wrestling over a deadly weapon, fighting for their lives. He wanted to cut Sylbaris, now, but he was helpless beneath the man's vastly superior strength. Paul pushed toward him and Sylbaris relaxed his hand, allowing that knife to move toward his face, steady, so Paul could neither pull back nor thrust, until the blade pressed against his black skin and a line of blood formed there, seeping around its edges.

As Paul pulled away, Sylbaris suddenly let go, and he staggered back, putting distance between himself and this madman. "I guess Charlise is mine, after all." Sylbaris expelled the words between bursts of laughter. He scooped up the two five Franc notes from the table and stuffed them in his pocket.

Paul protested, "I didn't cut you, Ludger. You forced the knife."

"Perhaps, but it was in your hand, Priest. And you wanted to. You wanted to cut this black man. Did you not?"

IT WAS late summer of '95 when Papa finally announced that the family would be moving to the house on Rue Saint-Denis. Maman wrapped dishes and precious knick-knacks in old issues of *Les Antilles* and *Les Colonies,* which she had been saving for the purpose, and packed them away in chests. The house was so big and there were so many things that needed to be moved: tables, sofas, settees, lamps, chairs of various sorts, family heirlooms, such as her mother's vanity, photographs and paintings, rugs, clothing, garden furniture. She couldn't keep track of it all, and there was no chance all of this accumulation of the years would fit into the smaller house. She must give much of it away, what she couldn't sell. The only close family left in Saint-Pierre were the Dupouys and the Plissonneaus and a few Assiers, and she couldn't imagine any of them wanting this old stuff. There were Petits around, of course, and she convinced Jean-Claude to take some of the furniture for his rental properties. She set aside a few small things of her maman's she thought her brother Edgard might wish to pass on to Bernadette someday. The rest, what wasn't spoken for, or bound for the new house, she had the boys take to a secondhand shop.

The move went slowly because Papa was sick much of the time and did not wish to be disturbed in his rest. At these times, Maman busied herself in the garden preparing for the sale. They'd engaged Sandrine's brother, Théo, to haul the furniture they were keeping to the new residence at the end of September. This would be done over a period of a day or two, and then Maman could begin arranging their new home. Or rather, the boys would arrange it under Maman's direction.

But until then Paul returned from work each day to a house turned upside down, transformed from his home into a place he was abandoning, bare walls marked only with broken outlines where pictures had hung and furniture had pressed for his whole life against them. Maman usually retired for the afternoon to rest until dinnertime. She looked exhausted most days, more exhausted than Paul felt, and she was not interested in conversation. And there was nowhere to sit. He tried turning in early a few times and reading a book in bed until the sun was down, but it was no good, he felt as though he was in some interminable purgatory. He wanted to go out somewhere social, but he'd sworn off bars and rhum for the foreseeable future.

He hadn't been around to see Stéphanie for several weeks, not since Papa announced the move, and now he wondered what she would think if he showed up unannounced. The last time he had done that, when she was pregnant with Adrien, she hadn't seemed to mind. In fact, she had asked him to come again and talk, and he did weekly for a few months. He missed those late afternoon conversations in her garden.

One evening, he came to a decision and changed from his work clothes into something more comfortable. "I'm going out for a while," he called to Maman. He left through the front door and down the steps to Rue Castelnau, thinking how there were only a few more weeks of walking down these steps; only a few more nights sleeping in his familiar bedroom; of eating meals on the patio where his family had always eaten; thinking this world was slowly ending; that it could no longer be sustained without change. Papa would soon pass away and Maman would rely on her boys. Saint-Pierre would survive, march on, though changing in a thousand subtle ways, would always be Saint-Pierre. And he must march on into the future with it.

~

STÉPHANIE GREETED him at her door, baby Adrien on her hip. "Paul," she said, smiling, "how nice to see you."

"I hope you don't mind my showing up on your doorstep like this after so much time."

"No, no. Of course not. May I offer you a citronnade?"

"Merci, I would love that."

"Go on back to the garden and I'll bring it out to you." She beamed at him again and his heart raced. He smiled back self-consciously and made his way through the kitchen to the garden patio, where he found his favorite wicker chair and put his feet up on its matching footstool. He felt so comfortable here with Stéphanie and her children. *I could live here with her.* It was a casual thought, rueful.

"Where is Alice?" he asked when Stéphanie emerged with a glass of citronnade in her free hand. He had half expected the little girl to greet him.

"She's playing with her new friends from school." Stéphanie placed the full glass on the table with expertise, as she shifted the baby on her hip. "It is so good for her to have new friends. And to be honest, it is good for me also to have her out of the house."

It must be hard to raise two children on your own, he thought. It was a grownup thought. And that thought, itself, surprised him.

"You will be seventeen soon," Stéphanie said, as if reading his mind, which grew suddenly dark at the thought of Eustase, who died this time of the year, a few weeks before his birthday. There was no avoiding these thoughts, it seemed. They came every year with the Autumn equinox.

"Oui," he replied.

She must have seen the solemnity on his face, because she said, "Eustase?"

"Oui." *She understands me,* he thought. *Like no one in my family. Not even Mannie.*

He sipped the cool citronnade. "How have you been, Stéphanie? Have you heard yet from Philippe?"

"Non," she said. She looked off into the distance, but it wasn't sadness in her eyes. Not like the last time he asked about Philippe. "I don't think he's coming back."

This surprised Paul. All these months, when they met in this garden to talk about politics and books and school—and to console one another—she had presented an unshakeable faith in Philippe.

"Perhaps he just hasn't had time to write," he said in consolation.

"Nearly eight months, Paul. He is dead in Africa. Or he's found another woman. Or he's decided to marry his god damned revolution. I don't know. I think I no longer care. I must continue with my life. I have children to raise, you know. Enough of this," she said. "Tell me how the move is going."

AT HER INSISTENCE, Paul returned to Stéphanie's nearly every afternoon to talk and daydream and avoid the mess at home. Then one day, just before it was time for the family to move to the new house, she asked him to stay for dinner. "I have been to the market today and purchased potatoes and Colombo spices and some wine from Bordeaux. And I have been soaking the salt cod since yesterday morning. My curry is very amazing, if I may say so. My Maman's recipe. And Alice will be disappointed if you say no."

How could he possibly turn down such an offer? What sort of chenapan would disappoint Alice? Of course he said oui. What choice did he have?

He sipped her citronnade, and the aroma of Colombo spices wafting from the kitchen sent him into a rêverie as he recalled Sandrine's meals at the Poncy home, meals he no longer tasted these days because Maman did not know how to cook them, or preferred to try out new recipes from the Métropole, or for some other reason he couldn't fathom.

Alice played in the garden nearby, occasionally calling out to him, pulling him back from his dreams into the world, a nearly seamless transition, he thought, because the real world in this garden was so much like his dreams.

And the meal was as amazing as Stéphanie promised. The dry white wine a perfect complement to the fish curry. Alice, being very ladylike, put down her fork and smiled up at him. Adrien slept nearby in his crib. "This is very delicious," Paul said, and Stéphanie smiled, too. A deep smile that came from her eyes. "Merci," she said. "It's my pleasure."

I could live here with this family, he thought again. This time he knew he meant it.

ONCE THEY SETTLED IN, the new house felt cramped. Still, it was a relief to not be tripping over half-moved furniture. Paul supposed he'd become used to the diminutive size, but the garden was too small, with a patio that took up most of the space; there was a tiny balcony overlooking the street; and downstairs there was only a small entry hall with a coat room, the kitchen, and the parlor, which was really a living room, although Maman insisted on calling it the parlor, because Papa had always had a parlor where he could talk business with his associates. It was the *idea* of a parlor that seemed to be important to Maman.

Joseph moved into his own apartment in the Quartier du Centre, which eased the space situation a little, but diminished their finances. Maman would not hear of Paul or Mannie moving out. "You're young still," she said in full lecture mode, "you need to save money to invest before setting out on your own."

Of course, Maman was right. With his wages from the rhumerie, he was still too poor to afford a place of his own, but he could help with the family's expenses. Samuel had promised Paul his wage would increase as he assumed more responsibilities. For now, he must be frugal.

Now that they were established in the new house, he had no convenient excuse to visit Stéphanie every day. He wasn't sure that she would object, but he didn't want her to think he had no life, that he was needy for her companionship. And at seventeen he still didn't have his feet in the world, as Maman had so often pointed out. So he waited a few days before he visited her again.

"Paul, how good of you to come over," she said when he arrived at her door. "Are you all settled into the house on Saint-Denis?"

"Everything is unpacked and in its place. Maman is still fussing with the decorations."

"Have a seat in the garden, Paul. I imagine you have been busy between work and helping your maman." He nodded and made his way to the courtyard. Stéphanie soon appeared with a citronnade. No need to ask anymore. It had become a ritual.

"I miss our conversations," he said. "Your home is so…" He paused and felt a blush riding up his face. It was so what? Like home? Better than home? Paul rushed past these thoughts and stammered out, "My friends are more interested in rhum than important things." He was thinking about Sylbaris, who was not his friend. He realized that aside from his cousins and Raoul, he didn't really have many friends anymore. Not since he left school. Not since the salon ended and he messed things up with Sophie.

"Then let us agree you will visit regularly. Perhaps twice a week?" Adrian began fussing, calling Stéphanie back into the house.

Paul was relieved and happy that she seemed to want his company as much as he wanted hers. It would be easier for her if she knew what days he was visiting. And unlike him, Stéphanie had friends. He had often seen them as he passed by, women mostly in long white dresses, their hair wrapped in yellow and red madrases, sitting on her balcony. He heard their voices and laughter, hoping that they were not laughing at him—that Stéphanie had given them no reason to.

She brought Adrian with her when she came back out. Without thinking, Paul held out his hands to take the infant. She gave Adrian to him and sat down.

"Perhaps Wednesday and Saturday," she suggested.

"Oui, just right." They agreed that on Wednesday he could come after work. Saturday, he should come in the evening because he can sleep in the next day. "I would love for you to stay for dinner, occasionally, if you would like."

Oui, he would like, and so every few weeks through the long autumn, before leaving to spend Saturday evening at Stéphanie's, he tells Maman, "I will not be home for dinner this evening." Maman looks at him with curiosity, clearly wanting to ask, but says nothing, smiles—her son is becoming a man. And he sits down at Stéphanie's table with Stéphanie and Alice Germaine. Sometimes he holds Adrien until the baby falls asleep, then places him gently into his crib.

~

ONE EVENING after leaving the Graineau house, Paul wandered along Rue Montnoël to le Pont Roche, savoring the moonlit night and a sharp longing that had overcome him at the door as he bid bonne nuit to Stéphanie. He could no longer pretend to himself that his feelings for her were purely those of a young friend. The emotion that came rushed over him. He desperately wanted to be more than a friend. He knew how utterly foolish he was being, still there were moments when her hand brushed against his or when she lightly kissed his cheeks in greeting that he thought he could hear her heart beating.

Paul's mind was racing and he couldn't decide if he wanted to cry or shout. He was already on the bridge when he saw the young man whose broad shoulders and muscled arms seemed to so easily carry full barrels of rhum out of the warehouse. Paul hesitated, but Sylbaris already knew he was there.

"Priest," he said, "how is our lovely Stéphanie tonight?"

Paul was filled with rage. How dare this man confront him again? How dare he speak of Stéphanie in such a way? So familiar, as if he laid claim to her in a way Paul could not. Paul was acutely aware of Sylbaris' superior strength and that the man was baiting him. He let the breath he had been holding out of his lungs and turned away. The evening was ruined.

Behind him, Sylbaris laughed softly, "Well, my friend, so you are not such a fool, perhaps, after all."

~

IT WAS SATURDAY, a few weeks before Christmas, Alice had been tucked into bed; Stéphanie poured Paul another glass of wine. It was one more glass of wine than he usually consumed. She placed the bottle on the table and sat beside him on the patio settee, close enough to make him slightly uncomfortable. This was new. No words were exchanged between them. They sat in that awkward proximity, not talking but listening to the cicadas and the gentle rain on the roof. It was near the end of the rainy season, still a month before carême, and the rain had been a nightly occurrence for the past several days, leaving the ground wet and pungent. The night was beautiful.

The uneasy feeling fell away, replaced by something else: contentment. Paul gazed at Stéphanie, her profile soft and lovely in the lamplight. He extended a hand and took hers in his own. She leaned into him and sighed quietly. It felt as though it had always been this way. This being together.

She turned her face toward him and they kissed. She stood and gently pulled his hand. He needed little encouragement to follow her to her bed. And then they were fumbling to remove each other's clothing. And when they finished making love, they lay entwined, listening to the night sounds. And it was as natural as the rain. This love.

SHE'D MISSED two cycles before she decided she was pregnant. It was early May and Paul had been with her every other weekend for the past five months. She had known it was risky and she'd been refuting the evidence, but her denials would no longer do. *I'm not ready for this,* she told herself. *For another baby to come along without a father.* Not that she had any doubt that the father was her young Paul. It was just that he was so young and — let's face it — he was a white boy from a well-to-do family with all of those pressures: to make a career; to marry into wealth; to carry on the family traditions.

And who is she really, when it comes down to it? She is the daughter of a police hero who has left a small inheritance, it's true. And the granddaughter of a successful entrepreneur. Also true. She is a shirt-tail niece of the Marlet family. She has these family connections, but they're fleeting; they seem as if they're nothing in reality. She is an older woman with two children already. She is mulâtre, he is white. Her relatives are not Plissonneaus or Dupouys or Caminades.

Of course, Paul would deny that he cared about any of that, but that wasn't the point. His family would care. So she can't count on him and she can't tell him, because he thinks he is in love with her.

She was between the rocky shoals and the deep blue sea. And to make matters worse, the economy had been hard, not only on the Poncy family. Last year's drought devastated the Marlet fortune and that of the Guillaume's as well, making it more and more difficult to maintain the Grainau household on her small stipends and investments. It would ease her plight considerably to move into a smaller apartment, but with a new baby coming, how could she possibly do that?

Weeks passed by and it became harder and harder to keep the truth from Paul. Stéphanie began avoiding him, pleading work, even though requests for her sewing had dried up along with the drought. When no one has enough money, they put aside unnecessary things, like new dresses. They wear the old frayed ones or buy inexpensive readymades from North America.

The late summer rainy season had begun, and things looked slightly better for this year, so she remained hopeful that business would pick up eventually. But there is always a lag before the economy recovers from a bad year, and things wouldn't improve before the winter harvest. Maybe by the time the new baby arrived.

Paul, of course, did not know what was going on. He feared Stéphanie had grown tired of him, that she was trying to separate herself from him. He didn't really believe her excuses about new clients, new commissions. He was as aware of the economy as anyone. His brother, Joseph, had been let go at l'ursine Soudon as management positions were eliminated or consolidated, and had moved back to Saint-Pierre. "I never had a chance of replacing Papa," he complained. Although, in better times, they would have found another position for him. Cousin Samuel was now advising family members to avoid investing money in Martinique until the end of the season, when it would become clear whether there was a recovery.

One Wednesday, after she'd put off another Saturday night together, Paul confronted Stéphanie about his suspicions. "Do you wish to stop seeing me, Stéphanie? Is that what this is all about?"

"Of course not, my love," she protested, caressing his face tenderly. Not ready to speak her uncertainty.

"Then why are you avoiding me?"

"It's just that..." She paused, considering her words. "I've been thinking about Philippe. It's that time of year, you know?" The lie sat there a moment in the silence of a late September afternoon.

"Yes, I know," he said, a distant look in his eyes, and she knew he was thinking about Eustase again. She did not mean to bring up that ghost, only her own. But now it was done. She pulled him to her and held him in a fierce embrace.

"Come over on Saturday," she said. "I will prepare a special dinner. We will celebrate Philippe and Eustase. Oui?"

IT'S TIME, she thought, as she prepared the broth for fish stew —the pregnancy was showing, and she couldn't keep it from him much longer. *We'll celebrate our ghosts, and we'll celebrate the coming birth. And then?*

She rehearsed the words she would tell him, repeating them over and over in her mind. The problem was, she didn't know what she wanted to say, so as soon as one response was practiced, she moved on to another.

I am pregnant, mon cher, and I'm afraid you will leave me.
No, too desperate.
I am pregnant, love. But I think you will disappoint me.
Too whiny?
I will have your child in the spring. Will you still be there?
That left the decision to him. No, no, no, it will never do. She must make this decision herself. But she couldn't. And perhaps it was too late to make a difference, anyway. Mon Dieu. She was pregnant. She would have a child and there would be three to raise, whether or not Paul was still there to help.

She wiped the tears from her face. She was lonely. There was no shame in admitting that. And if she were to hold on to him as long as he was willing, then who did it harm?

STÉPHANIE WANTED to shake the look of horror from Paul's face when she told him the news. "What did you think, my love? That you were safe from making babies? That it couldn't happen to you?"

"But what are we going to do, Stéphanie?"

"I am going to have a baby. Your baby. What you do... I don't know. That's up to you." Or maybe not, she thought, because she still hadn't decided about him, about her future.

"Non," he protested. "It's our baby. I will never abandon you."

"Paul, you are seventeen years old. Do you even know what you want? What I want? What a baby will want? Do you know the pressures your family will put on you when they find out?"

"I won't tell them. Not until we know," he said. She noted the We — the assumption that there will continue indefinitely to be a We. She sighed, but she didn't contradict him. She would wait for him to suggest that We live together, that We make plans for Our family, that the realities of the world bend to Our will. And what would she do then when that day comes? Would she fall into his arms? Would she reject him?

"Maybe," he said, after they had eaten and settled into their chairs in the garden, "after I have learned the rhum trade, Samuel will post me in Bordeaux, and we can move there. Oui?"

And maybe pigs can fly, she was thinking. But Paul's mention of Bordeaux brought her thoughts back to Philippe, and a certain reverie overcame her. Sensing this, understanding, Paul raised his glass. "Here's to Philippe and Eustase," he said.

Stéphanie lifted her glass and they toasted the lost young men. Then, with a wistful smile, she raised her glass once more. "To Bordeaux," she said, "and to the new baby on its way."

NOËL, 1896

Paul didn't speak to his family about the pregnancy. But Stéphanie continued to grow until it was no longer a secret in the neighborhood. And of course Maman and Madame Marlet attended the same mass on dimanche. No one had to tell her it was her son who had been spending time with Stéphanie Grainau every weekend. She never mentioned it to him of course. And so he had no inkling that she knew.

"It's just a passing thing," Anatole said when Clémence told him her suspicion. "His fancy woman. She has two bastard children already. It's nothing for us to worry about."

"Still," Clémence said, "I think it's time for him to meet some *suitable* woman."

"What are you thinking, Clémence?"

"There are cousins," she said, "with daughters the proper age to marry. Perhaps we can arrange an introduction."

"Do you think that's too old-fashioned for our Paul? He has these modern romantic notions in his head."

Clémence sighed. "Oui. But it's worth a try. Christmas," she said. "Perhaps we will have a special dinner guest for Noël." She had just the girl in mind for her Paul.

~

CHRISTMAS for the Poncy family was traditionally celebrated with a huge feast at the Dupouy home, with relatives often arriving from Basse-Pointe, Marigot, Trinité, Robert, and Fort-de-France, wherever there are Fauvé-Sablons or Petits or Caminades or Blondels or Billiotis; often a token Plissonneau would arrive; occasionally a Rousseau from the north, although that hadn't happened for several years now. On the table would be roasted pig and a precious Christmas goose, sweet potatoes, mangoes, pineapple, sweet manioc bread, tarts and pies and pastries of all kinds, and, of course, the foie gras. There would be no French Noël without foie gras, imported from the Métropole by Caminade Brothers.

Té, Edith, and Maman busied themselves with flower arrangements and preparing hors d'oeuvres for the arriving guests while the men attended the meat out back, where a pit had been excavated in the Dupouy's huge garden. This was also a tradition for family members to prepare the feast, including the digging of a pit, and to give servants the day off to spend with their own families.

Mémé Jeanine supervised the kitchen. The old woman was still the Matron of the family, and Maman backed off when faced with her mother's insistence. There were plenty of younger women and girls to do the more exhausting tasks.

Nearly twelve, Rachel Dupouy was old enough to take over the supervision of the children this year, although Léonie, who loved the responsibility and resisted letting go, helped her young cousine keep them all rounded up and out of the way of the adults.

Trying to avoid Papa and the other men, Paul hovered near cousine Léonie, a thin and tall girl with deep-set eyes and long blonde hair, which she wore in a single plait to the middle of her back. While most of the Poncys were dark-haired and dark-complected, the Billioti children had come out fair and light-skinned. Paul had no memory of Léonie's father, Edith's husband, who died over a decade earlier. Léonie was not quite a year younger than him, so the girl essentially grew up without a father, a role which her uncle Samuel happily performed for his sister's children.

"The Ballys are coming by," Léonie said. The Ballys were cousins through the Assiers. "Simon Hayot, as well. I think they've come to talk rhum business with uncle Raphaël. Josephine is pregnant, Maman says."

"It looks as though it will be a good sized gathering this year," Paul said, wishing Stéphanie and the children could be there, and feeling a little sour about it.

"I heard there are going to be Petit cousins here from Sainte Marie, as well," Léonie said.

"Oui," Paul said. "Maman invited them, although I don't know why. We haven't spoken to them in years." The Petits were related to both sides of his family, Anatole and Clémence being cousins, and there were dozens of them spread around the island.

"Are you quite serious, Paul? You don't know why?" Léonie gave a little laugh. Of course, he knew why. Amelie Martineau, who was the same age as Léonie, was approaching marriageable age. And, well, there were three unmarried Poncy boys. It was just embarrassing that everyone in the family was talking about this, and no one even knew that he would have a new baby in the spring.

He recalled Sophie, so long ago. *Go marry your béké cousine,* she'd said, breaking his heart. *Non,* he'd often told himself, *I will never marry some boring cousine.*

"It has nothing to do with me," he said to Léonie. *Surely, this*

Amelie will make a fine wife for Joseph, who is far more ready to marry.

Léonie laughed again. "It has everything to do with you, cousin. Maman says Tata Clémence is worried about you and Stéphanie Grainau, who is quite obviously pregnant." Léonie spoke in a whisper, because one didn't speak such things aloud for the world to hear, even if the world already knew.

Paul sighed heavily and turned bright red. So they all would fix him up with a 'proper' wife. He felt a little sick and made excuses to Léonie, disappearing into the house, where he sought a quiet corner to be alone.

THE MARTINEAU FAMILY landed in a fancy two-horse coupe, which arrived at the Dupouy's door in the early afternoon, disgorging the well-fed Pierre Martineau, his flowery wife, Ophelia Petit, and their daughter, Amelie, all dressed in ostentatious Christmas finery. It was a display at which even Maman must roll her eyes. Nevertheless, the Martineaus were an upstanding family from the east, where Monsieur Pierre had a small sugar factory and rhum distillery. *And isn't Amelie just lovely in all of that splendor?* Clémence hoped the Martineaus would not look down upon their humble family.

Paul watched the spectacle from the window of the upstairs hall as Maman greeted the new arrivals. Already he was angry and a little disgusted that his family would select people like this for potential in-laws. All this pomposity, as if there was not already enough self-satisfied smugness in this family.

Maman led the Martineaus inside and already her eyes were searching for him, wanting to be certain that her youngest son hadn't fled. Which was exactly what he wished to do—to flee to his beautiful, pregnant Stéphanie and her children. To hide in the comfort and simplicity of their lives. But the Grainaus were celebrating Noël at Tata Rosa's with her brother and her cousins, and it would be rude to show up uninvited.

He retreated to the balcony where Mannie was hanging out with Fernand Billioti. "Hey, Paul," teased Mannie, "your new sweetie has just arrived." If looks were fatal, Mannie would have been long ago deceased, but he had become impervious to them.

"Maman is so old-fashioned," he said, as Paul's pique turned to sadness. He pushed a glass and the bottle of rhum on the table toward his little brother . "No one arranges marriages these days. Just those fancy country bumpkins." Mannie twirled the end of the mustache he'd begun to grow.

Paul snorted. "I would never marry a cousin." He tipped up the bottle without bothering to pour it into the glass.

"Not even Léonie?" said Mannie.

Paul scowled. "Léonie is like a sister. Would I marry my sister?"

"If you were one of those Atlantic coast békés and she had enough money," quipped Fernand. Everyone laughed but Paul. It was a great sport among these city boys to make fun of their country cousins. But there was a certain sad truth that gave him pause.

"Oh well," said Paul in resignation. "I guess I should go face the music. Get this whole charade over with."

DESCENDING THE STAIRS, Paul felt as though suddenly he lived in another time, making an entrance into some grand ballroom with expensive crystal chandeliers above his head and fine Italian marble below his feet. He imagined Stéphanie on his arm dressed in a fairytale gown, lace and silk and flowing skirts, a tiara in her coiffed hair crowning her exquisitely fabricated face, and a string quartet playing *La Valse Viennoise*, le grand maréchal announcing, "Sieur Joseph Paul Poncy et la duchesse, Dame Stéphanie Grainau," as they step elegantly onto the ballroom floor.

It is the eyes of Maman, Papa, and Joseph which see this vision. Not his own. He attempted to adjust his point of view, but it was no use. The only part of this scene that he claimed was Stéphanie. It certainly did not contain pasty-skinned cousine Amélie.

He could never make Stéphanie a duchesse or the rich white wife they wanted for him. He had to make his family understand this. The past was gone, and good riddance. He didn't care about the money or the influence or any of this aristocratic merde. He only cared about this family he wanted to make with Stéphanie.

And there on the floor they all stood, this older generation, mingling and chatting in the parlor, lost in their illusions and their old world prejudices. Through them came Maman, her guests in tow, the portly little man in his tails and tophat, his fleshy wife, and the daughter in a frilly blue gown with bows and bustle, cheeks pink with blush. She was comely, with light auburn hair and sparkling eyes which demurred beneath his gaze. He hoped he wasn't being rude.

"Paul," said Maman, "I would like you to meet the Martineaus, our cousins from Sainte Marie."

Maman moved aside as her guests stepped forward. "This is our youngest son, Paul. Paul, this is Monsieur Martineau and his wife, Ophélia Petit, who is the daughter of your grandmother Jeanine's cousin, Jean-Baptiste."

Paul nodded and smiled weakly. He felt no kinship with these people. "Nice to meet you Monsieur, Madame."

Maman paused in her introduction, building up the

suspense. "And this," she said, hesitating an instant longer, "is their daughter, Amélie."

Amélie tried to smile, but Paul could see she was just as embarrassed as he was. "Pleased to meet you, Mademoiselle," said Paul, bowing and taking her offered hand in his own.

"Why don't you two young people get to know one another," chirped Madame Martineau, as she disappeared into the kitchen with her husband and Maman.

"Well, that was nicely choreographed," said Amélie. "So I guess we are to be wed next week. Is that the plan?"

Paul laughed. He thought perhaps he could like this cousine under different circumstances.

"Oui, a few weeks ago, if Maman had her way."

Amélie sighed. "So, you're the wayward son, or what? Why is she so eager to marry you off when you have two older, unmarried brothers?"

"My family believes I should be... dissuaded from a bad choice?"

"I understand," she said. "But I dare say, we women have even less choice in these matters. My papa will disinherit me if I don't marry a respectable Martinican." *Meaning well-connected and white,* Paul thought. Plantation békés are even more prejudiced and exclusive than the petit blancs of the city, but Paul was not about to say so to his country cousine.

"We should be free to marry whom we please," said Paul. "Men and women, alike." Amelie's eyes darted away toward the kitchen, then she looked at the floor, suddenly silent and embarrassed by the direction of the conversation. Paul was caught short by his faux pas. This guiding principle of French republicanism should not be so difficult to express. But it seemed so radical, socialist even, to express these thoughts openly. No matter how liberal and progressive his family believed itself, they were all products of another—more conventional—era. And proper decorum dictated not speaking of uncomfortable things at Christmas dinner.

He sighed. Amélie mirrored him. They both smiled awkwardly.

"It was nice meeting you, Monsieur Poncy. I must go mingle, but I hope we talk again before we depart in the morning."

"It's been my pleasure, Amélie." This time his smile was confident and genuine as he kissed the hand of his new cousine. Amélie disappeared through the kitchen.

ON THE BALCONY, Mannie poured Paul another glass of rhum agricole, which the young men preferred to the dark, molasses-based rhum that was so popular among Europeans and North Americans and the old men of Saint-Pierre. The clear agricultural rum was both cheaper and smoother, in the boys' opinion, and it's what was required to make a decent ti punch. The older men scoffed at their juvenile 'native' taste. "But it gets you drunk," Mannie was fond of saying. "And quicker, because you can actually drink the damned stuff."

Paul stirred a little sugar into his rum, but he didn't like his ti punch too sweet. The Biliotti boy had left to join the older men in the garden, and Paul was alone with Mannie. He was on his third glass of ti punch, hoping that dinner would be soon, before he fell over.

"I will make an announcement this evening," he said, not really thinking about his words, just his need to say them.

Emmanuel, who had a pretty good idea of what Paul planned to announce, leaned into his brother, inches from his ear and said, "Paul, perhaps you should wait until you're sober before making announcements that might affect the rest of your life."

"I have to stand up to them, Mannie. I am having a child and I want Stéphanie for my wife. They need to accept that."

Mannie backed away and studied his young sibling. "But Christmas, Paul? Think about it. They've invited Amelie here, all the way from Sainte Marie, just to meet you. Maman will never forgive such rudeness."

"That's ridiculous, Mannie. Maman will be angry for a few days, but she'll get over it."

"Can't it wait until the Martineau family is gone

No, Paul thought, *it can't wait.* "It's the only way they will listen," he said. "If I do it now, Mannie, while the whole family is here. It will be an official pronouncement."

Mannie shook his head. "This is not the office of the mayor, Paul. It's your family."

"I've decided." There, it was final now.

"Alright, Paul. It's your funeral, brother." Mannie stood up and left Paul alone, stewing in his angry thoughts.

"THE LORD HAS GENEROUSLY BLESSED this family," Anatole said, his voice cracking, his champagne glass shaking in his arthritic hand, as Clémence stood at his elbow steadying her husband while he made the annual Christmas toast. "And even though this year has been difficult for us all, we are here once again, together, sons and daughters, nieces, nephews, cousins come to celebrate the Holy Birth. And to celebrate one another. À la famille." Papa, now breathless, lifted his glass, champagne splashing over the rim. Around the long makeshift dinner table there was a cheer as everyone's glass was raised in salute.

Aided by Maman, Papa took his seat and it was Samuel's

turn to stand and toast, followed by Uncle Edgard and Pierre Martineau. Paul was listening to none of it. He was too lost in his own thoughts. He looked up to see Mannie across the table staring at him, and glared back defiantly. He didn't yet have the courage to stand and make his announcement. Maybe it would be better to wait until everyone had eaten. There would be another round of speeches and toasts and compliments before the men all adjourned to the parlor for cigars and brandy. And the women to the kitchen to clean up the mess.

Paul downed his champagne and pushed the food around on his plate, not really hungry. He drank a glass of wine, then another, allowing the alcohol to fill the void in his gut. *Why can't they be reasonable? Why don't they understand times have changed, will change even more? The evidence is here daily. And yet they all continue on this road to disaster.*

He poured another glass of wine and was about to pull it back when he heard his name across the table. It was Joseph, who was talking to Louis Billioti. Joseph noticed Paul staring and warned him in a fierce whisper, "Brother, you're becoming embarrassingly drunk."

"Is that all anyone in this family thinks about?" he said much too loudly. "Being embarrassed?"

"Paul, you need to calm down."

"No brother," said Paul, practically shouting now. "What I need is for you all to treat me with respect."

Little Josephine Dupouy dropped a fork and it rang across the suddenly silent dining room. Paul's head was spinning as he stood. "I am going to have a child in a few months," he proclaimed to the shocked room, "as you all know. And that child will carry the family name. I refuse to be a hypocrite, like the rest of you."

Paul was wobbling, about to be sick now. Joseph and Mannie had come around the table to prop him up and lead him from the room. As they were leaving, Joseph hissed between his teeth. "Go back to your whore, little brother. But no little pickaninny is going to have this good family name."

Mannie suddenly stopped short and faced Joseph, angry. "Big brother, I think you should return to dinner. I'll take Paul home. And, Joseph, you need to take a good look in the mirror before giving the rest of us advice."

THE SEA TREMBLED VIOLENTLY, tossing him like a leaf in a storm, and his head seemed about to explode. He hung on, wondering how he came to be here, gripping this piece of flotsam for dear life. Then he awoke and it was his pillow, soaked in sweat, and it was his body that was trembling. And his head. His pitiful head.

He sat up in bed too quickly and the pain wrenched, the throbbing nearly unbearable. He willed himself still until the pulsations settled and became regular, then he took a towel from his bedside, left there last night by Mannie, along with a pan for his vomit, and he carefully wiped off his drenched forehead.

Christmas returned like a ghost, slowly and with a chill. He looked out the window at the shadows and realized it was afternoon again. He'd been passed out all night and more than half the day. He'd missed the goodbyes to the Martineaus. Although, he couldn't imagine why they would want to see him again in this lifetime.

There was a knock on the door. Much too loud. Much too insistent. It was Maman and he didn't want to see her. He put his hands over his ears. "Go away."

Miraculously, the knocking stopped. He couldn't believe his own rudeness toward his mother.

He needed water, but was unsure if he could make his way

to the kitchen to pour himself a glass. And even if he could, he couldn't face Maman and Papa. If only Sandrine was here. She would bring him juice and pastry and a cup of café. She would have kind, non-judgemental words for him. A warm cloth to soothe his throbbing head.

With no warning, his bedroom door opened and Papa stood there stiffly, his gnarled, blue-veined hands clapped one over the other, gripping his cane. Anatole's hands were steady for the first time in years, no longer shaking with age. Paul's eyes focused on them, as he tried to hold back this throbbing pain in his head.

"Your behavior was inexcusable," said the old man. "You have brought dishonor to this family."

Anatole's face was white with anger. When Paul peered up at him, the throbbing returned with a vengeance. He wanted to object to his father's admonishments, but the old man held up a hand. "You will listen to me," he said.

"I was forty-five years old before I married your mother. I earned my fortune first so I could support my spouse and children in comfort. I married a woman chosen by my father, a woman whose family was successful and could contribute to our own success. This is what families do. They work together to survive in the world."

"Times have changed, Papa." Paul winced at the pain.

"This is an illusion, Paul. There are things which never change. And bringing dishonor to your family's name—"

"—dishonor the family's good name, Papa? How can I bring more dishonor to this family than my grandfather did? He is the man responsible for the hangings in Place Bertin in '32. How more dishonored can we be?"

Anatole was taken aback, wondering what brought this ancient history to light. "My father was only a paragraph in that sad story," he said. "That's the past and you are advised to let it lie."

"But you would have us all live in the past, Papa."

"Those black men burned down our house and the houses of many neighbors," said Anatole. "They would have murdered us all. 'Kill the whites,' they were chanting. 'Kill the whites.'"

"And you think they had no reason, Papa?"

"I was seven years old when those nègres came with their torches, declaring murder. I was a small child. And your tata Elmire only a year older, and oncle Louis not yet eleven. You have no idea what it was like to flee that murderous mob. To be ferried to a ship in the middle of the night while Saint-Pierre burned. Your grand-mère never recovered from it, and she died in Paris two years later. My brothers Eustase and Raphaël never returned to Martinique."

"Oui, Papa. But I don't know what it is like to live a slave, either, and to want and not have the liberté and égalité which is my birthright. To have my family torn apart and sold like cattle. So we Français can have our rhum."

Anatole furrowed his brows, his old eyes narrowed like deadly darts. "So we could survive," he spat. "You children are ignorant. You and your brothers were born into a world of comfort and plenty. But our ancestors couldn't afford this romantic notion of égalité." The word hissed derisively from the old man's lips. "This is a world of wolves. It has always been so, and will always be."

"Papa," said Paul, the throbbing not gone, but now relegated to some isolated portion of his mind, "this world is ruled by men. Men and women who choose how to behave toward one another. Who choose their laws and whom they will love and engage in commerce with."

The old man shook his head and glared at his son for a long time before saying, "You will apologize to your family. Especially your Maman. And you will send a letter of apology to Monsieur Martineau."

"Oui, Papa," he said. "I will apologize for my bad behavior, but not for my sentiment."

Anatole struck the door with his cane but said nothing more before he turned and left.

YVONNE LEARNS ABOUT NAVIGATION
THE ADVENTURES OF YVONNE

Chief Navigator Marcus introduced Yvonne to Étienne, the old helmsman who steered the ship. Étienne turned to greet Yvonne with a big toothless grin. Deep wrinkles etched his black forehead.

"Pleased to meet you, young lady," said Étienne. His words made a whistling sound through his missing teeth.

Yvonne thought he must be ancient. She didn't know if it was polite to ask him how old he was, but she was curious, so she decided to ask, anyway.

It must have been acceptable, because Étienne answered her with no hint of irritation.

"I'm older than I can remember," he said, scratching his grizzled beard. "I was born a slave, so it was at least that long ago. I was nearly a young man when we won our freedom."

Yvonne thought about that for a few moments. She knew the slaves had been freed in 1848, over fifty years ago. That meant that Étienne must be really old!

"How did you learn to be a helmsman?" asked Yvonne.

"Well, jèn dam," said Étienne, "I work on the docks loading rhum barrels since I was yon ti gason. I always love these big ships, and wondered where they might take me if I work on one of them."

"So, did Captain Marie give you a job?" asked Yvonne.

Étienne laughed from his belly. "Captain Marie wasn't even born yet," he said. "In them days, only France white men could be captain of a ship like this. Certainly not a black Kréyole woman like Captain Marie. They didn't need a black helmsman like me, either, they say."

"So what did you do?" asked Yvonne.

"I find a job on a small fishing boat," said Étienne. "That's where I learn my trade. I worked on fishing boats for many years, until Captain Marie came and hired me."

"Do you like working for Captain Marie?" asked Yvonne. She couldn't help whispering, "I think she's kind of mean."

Étienne gave a sly smile.

"It is amazing that a Matinik Kréyole woman can be captain of a big ship, yes? But I learn an important lesson in my life," he said. "A captain is a captain. Never forget that, young lady. Black or white or other, man or woman, they are all the same. Marie *le Méchant,* indeed!"

∼

BY AFTERNOON, Yvonne had memorized the numbers on all the sea charts and had sorted them into proper drawers so they would be easy to find.

Marcus was clearly impressed.

"You have done very well, Yvonne," he said. "Now I'll show you how to use the sextant."

Marcus crossed the bridge and picked up the shiny brass instrument Yvonne had seen earlier.

"It is a very simple instrument, really," said Marcus. "You look in this telescope, here."

He pointed to an eyepiece. Yvonne put her eye to the telescope, but she only saw blue sky. So, Marcus showed her how to line it up with the horizon, and how to find the sun at its zenith.

The zenith, Marcus explained, is the highest point of the sun as it crosses the sky.

"It is highest at noon," Marcus said. "That's when we want to take our reading."

Yvonne nodded.

"So, if you make an imaginary line from the noon sun, straight down to the sea," said Marcus, "that is called the azimuth. That's where you want to look at the horizon."

Yvonne nodded again and hoped that she would not forget. It was an awful lot to remember.

"Now, there are two mirrors on the sextant," said Marcus.

He pointed to one mirror, across from the telescope. "This one is called the horizon mirror. You can see through it, so you can find the horizon."

Yvonne looked through the telescope again. She was clumsy at first, but she soon found the horizon, where the sea met the sky.

"The other mirror at the top," said Marcus, "is called the index mirror. You adjust it by moving the index bar, here. It reflects the sun onto the first mirror when you get it just right."

Yvonne moved the index bar, and just as Marcus said, she could now see the sun through the telescope.

"I see the sun!" exclaimed Yvonne, excited.

"Bon tifi," said Marcus. "Now move the bar again until the sun is right there on the horizon."

Yvonne moved the mirror again until it looked as though the sun was setting.

"I think I've got it," said Yvonne.

"Now," said Marcus, "we must look at the number the index bar points to on the arc."

Yvonne was becoming confused. What was the arc?

"I don't think I can do this," said Yvonne. "I'm becoming dizzy."

Marcus laughed. "I think I'm trying to show you too much at one time. Let's rest and we can come back to it later. You are doing very well, Yvonne."

"This is hard work," said Yvonne.

Marcus laughed again.

"This is the easy part," he said.

AFTER DINNER, Yvonne went to the cabin and waited for Maman and André. She was excited to share all the things she had learned on the bridge.

André came in first. When Yvonne tried to tell him about her day, he became very cross.

"I don't care about your stupid day," snapped André, "just leave me alone."

André laid down on his bed and sulked. Yvonne felt like yelling at him, but she decided maybe that wasn't such a good idea.

Yvonne lit a lamp and tried to read one of the books that Tata Rosa had given her for the trip. But she soon fell asleep.

When she awakened, it was late, and Maman still hadn't returned to the cabin. Yvonne decided to put on her nightgown and climb into bed. She had just blown out the lamp when the door rattled and suddenly creaked open.

Yvonne jumped, but it was only Maman.

"Are you still up, mon ange?" said Maman.

"I was just going to bed, Maman," said Yvonne.

Yvonne still wanted to tell Maman about her day, but she could see that Maman was very tired and sad. She gave Maman a kiss and climbed into bed.

"Bonne nuit, Maman," said Yvonne.

Maman said nothing. So Yvonne turned over and tried to sleep, herself. But she couldn't.

Yvonne felt bad because Maman and André were so cranky and tired. But all she could think about was how very exciting her day had been.

PART 4
AU REVOIR, MADANINA

RENÉ ANDRÉ PAUL

It was never really a question for Paul. He'd brought a child into the world and it was his responsibility. So, of course he would give the boy his name. Not that Stéphanie cared one way or another—as far as he knew—or that society expected it of him. Contrary to all the pious proclamations, it was common for men in those days to abandon their children, or to refuse them legitimacy, which was the same thing in reality, but Paul refused to be one of those men. Even if Stéphanie was not yet prepared to marry him.

His brother, Joseph, continued a relentless campaign to dissuade him from bestowing the boy with the family name, as did Papa, who traded his anger for something he liked to call Reason.

"All men sow seeds in their youth," Papa said, in one of their many conversations on the subject. One-sided conversations, because Paul had no intention of changing his mind. "You must not fall in love with the first little wasp that attracts your eye, son."

Paul wanted to laugh at the old man's use of that popular

phrase, wondering where he could have possibly picked it up. But he held his tongue. Instead, he said, "My feelings for Stéphanie are my business, Papa. But taking responsibility for a life I've helped to create, that's something I must do."

Anatole was having none of it and the argument devolved into another heated exchange until Paul stormed from the room where his father lay ill in bed. He wanted to be a good son, but he was tired of this argument. How many times must he justify himself?

Joseph's anger with Paul was visible, but Mannie, while sympathetic, always dropped back, not willing to argue with either Papa or Joseph. In private, though, he supported Paul and spoke kindly of Stéphanie and of Paul's desire to build a mutual life around their children.

Maman, the good Catholic she was, hadn't disputed Paul's logic, even if she couldn't entirely accept her son cavorting with a mulâtre woman. Especially one who already had two children outside of holy wedlock. She fretted about Paul's future, as always, but the scene at Christmas cast a shadow over any desire she might have about interfering in the matters of his heart. Part of her admired his clarity, even as she found it foolish. She loved Anatole because they had been married so long and she loved the children they had together. She chose not to consider if Anatole had always been faithful to her, and certainly she could not be concerned about the women who passed through his life before they wed. *This girl will break Paul's heart,* Clémence thought. *Then he will get over it.*

Even Stéphanie tried to dissuade him in the beginning. "You don't need to do this, Paul. I am a free woman. I'm capable of raising these children on my own."

"That's not the point," he insisted. "This decision is for me, ma chère. To take responsibility for myself as a man. And for the child, so he knows his father loves him."

Finally, she shrugged, acquiescing to his argument. Or possibly she was simply too exhausted from the act of giving birth to fight with him.

"Good," he said. "It's settled."

Still, a full five weeks passed before he found the courage to visit the registrar's office at the Ville de Saint-Pierre with his friend, Raoul Dufail, and Joseph Ceïde, a carpenter at the rhumerie, as his witnesses.

PONCY, *René André Paul.* It was the name he and Stéphanie had decided upon. Their son. His son. They would call him André Paul to distinguish him from his father. Paul signed his name, followed by the witnesses, and finally, Clavius Marius, the registrar.

"Now, mes amis," said Raoul, as they left the office, "we must go by Madame Gemeau's and purchase some cigars. A son is not truly christened without tobacco. Oui?"

The men all agreed. Of course, it is a true, time-honored tradition. Paul strutted proudly through the streets of Saint-Pierre as the trio made its way to Julie Gemeau's cigar store on Quai Peynier.

Like most of the small businesses along the quai, there were no signs on the storefronts. If you lived here, you knew where things were, and who did what business. A small bell jingled as they walked through Julie's door, and a pert little girl, about Alice's age, stepped from a back room. She beamed at the sight of Raoul. "Messya Dufail," she said, very professional and lady-like, "bon après-midi."

Raoul smiled. "Bon après-midi, Marguerite. How are you today?"

"Mwen byen, Messya. What can I do for you?"

"Messya Paul, here, is the proud Papa of a new son."

"Konpliman, Mesya," said Marguerite, then turned and called out, "*Manman.*"

Julie Gemeau appeared in the doorway. She was a small, thin mulâtre woman with weathered skin, who looked as though she'd lived an especially hard life. She smiled at Raoul, a regular, and then her eyes settled on Paul. "Has Stéphanie named the new child yet?"

He had waited too long and it niggled at his conscience. He didn't know Julie well, but he had purchased pipe tobacco from her for Papa, and for himself. Of course, Saint-Pierre was a small enough town that everyone knew everyone. Or so it seemed.

"Oui. René André Paul Poncy," he said proudly. "We have chosen it together."

Julie raised a surprised eyebrow. "Congratulations," she said. She retreated to the back room and returned with three cigars. "My best cigar," she said, handing Paul a fine, fat specimen. "It is on the house." She looked at Raoul and winked. "You two must pay for your own."

Raoul laughed and handed her enough money to cover the cost of all three. "You keep the change, Madame." Turning to his friends, he said, "Someday, Madame Gemeau will be my mother-in-law, you know." Raoul winked at the grinning Marguerite, who was clearly taken by his charm, and the three men left, laughing.

Now it is done. There is nothing more Papa can say about the matter.

PAPA'S DEATH

PAUL IS to be forgiven for not knowing that his papa would pass from this life just three months to the day after the birth of his new son; for not patching things up with the old man before he died; for not helping him to understand that the new Martinique is going to be different from the old. And better. Better for him and for his children. Better for the people of color who built this land, and who had never been treated as equals. Better for the blancs who were so reluctant to embrace this future.

Papa had been ill, unable to work since last summer, so he knew the old man's time on earth was limited. That came to be one more regret, that they had never come to an understanding about Stéphanie. About his child to whom she had given birth.

Had his Papa died still angry?

Paul often recalled sitting with him at his deathbed, awkwardly attempting to talk to him, his resolve, the stubborn old man's equal resolve, butting heads like two bulls in a pasture. "It is the good family name, Paul."

"Oui, Papa, but it's my name, as well."

"I'm your father. I'm still the head of this family."

"Non, Papa, I have my own family now, with Stéphanie and my new baby. I'm no longer under your roof."

He'd been unable to hold his tongue. He had blurted out, without thinking, "You are the old Martinique, you stubborn old man. Your time has come and gone." What a thing to say to your papa on his deathbed. And when he was gone, there was no taking back the words. Words that would circulate over and over in his mind. Words that would influence his relationships with his own sons.

It was over now, and Maman was weeping as Papa's body was carefully prepared for the wake, and for tomorrow's funeral.

C'est la vie, as Papa would say.

THE COUSINS and the friends of the old man began to arrive in the afternoon with their sympathy and their offerings. Paul stood in the parlor with Joseph and Emmanuel, greeting guests. The Dupouys and the Caminades had arrived and given their condolences. Simon Hayot was there also with his spouse, Josephine Bally. There was no one here yet from the Plissonneau family, but Georges was expected to appear before sunset. Maman's brother, Edgard, had come up from le Robert, along with Idalie and Bernadette. Possibly her brother, Louis, would come as well from Trinité.

The men of the family would remain overnight for the wake. The wives of the out-of-town guests would spend the night at the Dupouy house. Paul was expected to stay also with the men and, being a good son, of course he would. Stéphanie promised to stop by for a few moments with their son, and Paul was apprehensive about this, although it was he who'd insisted.

"Your father did not approve of our relationship," said

Stéphanie. "I'm not sure it's entirely appropriate for me to come."

"Whether or not the church has blessed us, André Paul is my son," he said, maybe a little too pointedly. "And my father never disowned me, as much as he groused. That isn't our way. Besides, Léonie and Alix and the other young cousins will love to see him."

"If you insist," said Stéphanie, "but only briefly. I don't want to cause disharmony at your father's wake."

Despite her arguments, Paul saw the pride in Stéphanie's eyes. She would love to show off her new son, to assert his place in the family, even if her own was in doubt.

STÉPHANIE ARRIVED before sunset with André Paul on one hip, an offering of flowers and salt fish embraced in her free arm, and Alice Germaine behind, clutching the hand of little brother Adrien. Eight-year-old Alice heard the voices of children from the courtyard and tugged at her mother's skirt. "May I go play, Manman?"

"Non," said Stéphanie in her no-nonsense voice, handing André Paul over to the girl while she took her gifts into the kitchen. "Hold your baby brother, Alice."

"Please, Manman," insisted Alice, standing in the doorway with André Paul now on her little hip, a mirror of her mother.

"We are only staying a few moments, cher."

Paul came to greet them and took André Paul from Alice, lifting the baby gently, as though afraid of breaking him. "Let her go outside for a few moments with the other children," he said. "I will hold André Paul." Stéphanie scowled, but nodded her head when Alice looked at her, pleading. Before Stéphanie could say the words still on her tongue, Alice was already through the kitchen and out the back, with Adrien close behind.

Stéphanie offered Clémence her condolences and turned her attention to Cousine Té. Paul returned to the parlor with the baby in his arms. Did he mean to rub his illegitimate relationship in the face of his conservative brother? Who knows? Least of all, Paul. But his brother, Joseph, glared at him with something resembling hatred. The kind of hatred that only a brother can feel toward another brother.

The others, of course, smiled at the new father. Offered their congratulations if they hadn't already. "What a handsome boy you have there in your arms, Paul. He looks just like you."

WAS THIS WHEN MAMAN, adorned in her black mourning clothes, slipped into the parlor and called away Uncle Edgard? To talk to him about her son, of course. Her youngest son, who had broken her heart; who had given up his religious studies to live in sin with the mother of his child; who was squandering his Papa's heritage for a future Martinique that no sane white person wanted. This, despite her best efforts to interest him in a nice Catholic girl to substitute for her lost hope of a priest in the family.

Of course, she didn't express this to her brother, who had himself been living in sin for years with a mulâtre "girl" and their young daughter, Bernadette. At least Edgard would marry Idalie in a few weeks, making them all legitimate in the eyes of God. Perhaps Paul would do the same, eventually. But for the moment his mortal soul was endangered, not to mention those of Stéphanie and their unfortunate child.

Instead, she spoke to her brother in terms of Paul's education, his future earning potential, his father's wishes for him.

"What can we do for his betterment, Edgard?" asked Clémence. "He's such a bright boy, and he's not thinking straight. There's more to life than raising children on a poor man's wages."

Edgard's eyebrow almost went up at that statement. Maybe it did go up a little. But he knew she was speaking of men. *Men's* lives should be more than raising children. That's how it was and should be, he thought, perhaps seeing the irony in her words. Or not.

And Clémence? Did she see this irony as well? Who knows?

"Paul would like nothing more than to be part of this new railroad," said Edgard, after a moment. "I will speak with Georges. I'm sure we can find a role for him somewhere. Perhaps Samuel can raise a fund for his education."

"But where would he get this education, Edgard? There aren't schools like this in Martinique."

"The Métropole, perhaps," said Uncle Edgard. "More likely, the United States or Canada where they are building modern railroads across the American West."

This sent her down an unexpected path. She now imagined Paul at school in France, meeting some nice French woman in Paris, or perhaps in North America with a Catholic girl from Québec. Someone to take his mind away from this Stéphanie — she chastised herself for thinking it, but *harlot* is the word her mind brought up for her to chew on.

She had tried to accept Stéphanie. The girl was from a good family and the daughter of a hero, Paul assured her, a policeman who died in the line of duty, protecting Martinicans. Stéphanie was a good mother to her children, he said, and Clémence saw no reason to doubt it. And the girl was very light skinned, as well, this was true. She could almost pass for a blanc if it wasn't for that hair. Much lighter skinned than her first two children, whose father was that black activist. The one who disappeared in Africa. The one some say is a traitor to France. So there was that as well. Paul already had unfortunate ideas. What sort of influence was Stéphanie having on him? This was not what she wanted for her son. Radicals and bohemians. And what else? she wondered. Where can this lead?

PAUL TOOK his baby son back into the kitchen, surprised that the women hadn't come to retrieve him yet. Stéphanie remained by the bread table with Thérèse Dupouy and Idalie Dupeyrat. Stéphanie took the baby from Paul, and cousine Té immediately started cooing over him. Cousine Edith was chatting to Adèle Blondel and the very pregnant Josephine Bally by the door to the terrace. Maman had gone off somewhere, probably still discussing something or other with Uncle Edgard. Or perhaps her grief had overcome her once again.

Stéphanie seemed to be holding her own, and Paul was pleased that Idalie was here. She was someone Stéphanie could identify with, make herself feel part of the family.

The women passed little André Paul around until Idalie said, "We must introduce him to the other children." Té, who was holding him now, said, "Oui. Of course," and together the three women migrated toward the terrace. Within seconds, the young children were all gathered around greeting their new cousin. "Look, a baby!" "He's so cute."

"Hello, André Paul. Very pleased to meet you." That last from six-year-old Bernadette.

Paul couldn't help but notice that the mixed-race children predominated in his parent's own backyard. How could Maman and Joseph not see the way even their own private Martinique had changed? It was no longer a béké world, and it would never be again. And that was a good thing.

Ah, but the béké world still had a tight grip. It would not let go of power so easily. A little here, a little there, out in the open where everyone could cheer, while in the back room the old white men continued to roll their dice. You'd be mistaken to think they were gamblers.

STÉPHANIE WAS FINALLY ready to leave with the children. She assured Paul that she had a pleasant time, but Adrien was now cranky, and the other women and children were about to depart for the Dupouy house with Adèle. All but Maman, who would stay here with her departed husband and mourn.

Paul bent over and kissed Alice Germaine on the cheek. "Did you have a good time with your new cousins, Alice?"

"Oui," Alice said, "I would like to play with them again, sometime."

"We can probably arrange that," Paul said. "There will always be family gatherings."

Stéphanie smiled at him. "Bonne nuit. Don't allow the bad spirits in." She said this with a wink and a sly grin.

"Bonne nuit, love," Paul said. Stéphanie gave him air kisses and herded the young ones through the door.

Back in the parlor, Paul settled into a chair next to Mannie, who leaned into him and, in a quiet voice, confided, "You have a fine, sweet family, Brother. Don't let Maman and Joseph get to you."

"Don't worry, they will change in time. I'm certain of it."

"Maman, maybe, because you are her favorite son." Mannie scowled. "But I don't know about Joseph. He's hard. And it's for the same reason, you know."

"What do you mean?"

"Because you are Maman's favorite."

Paul scoffed and gave Mannie a look, but inside he knew there was truth there. Joseph resented the extra attention given to Paul since the death of Eustase. If Paul had been more like Mannie, Joseph believed, he would put his chin up and accept the world as it is. But Maman chose to pamper her little baby and now look at what he's done: he's passed the family name to some little negrillon. And when he marries that harlot, he will give away their name again to the little black children of a traitor.

Maman may have chastised herself for using that particular epithet, harlot, in reference to Stéphanie, but not Joseph. In his mind, Stéphanie was no different than the whores he often paid for services on Rue Bouille.

AS USUAL WHEN these men of the family came together, the evening discussions revolved around the economy, the sugar markets, the cane harvests, the stock prices. But this time the '91 hurricane went unmentioned, its affects no longer evident on the streets of Saint-Pierre. Although the Poncys had not fully recovered from it, the Plissonneau fortunes were soaring and, according to Samuel, the takings from his stock investments had improved. The family businesses were thriving, again, and the Poncy sons would do well to apply themselves now while the markets were good.

It was true, Paul had let his life slide. This was Maman's real objection to Stéphanie. Poncy men had always put their fortune first before they considered raising a family. Maybe he'd made a mistake. Becoming entangled with a woman at such a young age put unnecessary obstacles in his way.

"Paul, I understand you are still interested in the railroad."

The voice of Georges Plissonneau pulled Paul from a deep rêverie.

"Oui. It's still my dream."

"Some funding proposals will be put forward soon in Saint-Pierre. I'm hoping for money to train local Pierrotins. It may require study overseas, however."

Paul remained silent. Yes, he would love this more than anything, but there was Stéphanie and his new baby to think about. It seemed like a monumental decision to make so soon.

"It's still a year or two away, of course," said Georges. "No need to answer at this moment, but think about it, young man. It may be a way for you to make your future and build wealth for the Poncy family. Not to mention a little adventure, oui?"

A PROMOTION

Stéphanie and Paul had waited until after Papa died to move in together permanently. Paul had been shifting back and forth between the family home on Rue Saint-Denis to Stéphanie's new apartment. Maman made certain the door was always open for him, silently hoping he might change his mind and come home again.

Shortly after Papa's wake, Paul took some of his belongings to Stéphanie's. Not everything, he also wanted to keep a room in Maman's home. But he took enough with him to the new apartment to feel at home there with Stéphanie and the children.

With the new baby, the apartment was too cramped. It wasn't what he was used to. If the move from their family home on Rue Castelnau to Rue Saint-Denis was a step down, then this move to the old parish housing across from Eglise Saint-Pierre was yet another step toward poverty. It was not what Stéphanie was used to either, and sometimes it caused friction as they rubbed against one other at unexpected turns. But before long it felt like home, and Paul enjoyed waking up with Stéphanie beside him in the morning, to the sounds of children's laughter.

He delighted in the children most of all. Alice Germaine, with her quick wit and charm, had started calling him Papa regularly. She knew so little of her real Papa. Paul encouraged her, calling her ma chère. Three-year-old Adrien was full of curiosity and chatter. He followed his big sister around like a shadow, and, according to Stéphanie, sometimes cried or complained loudly when Alice left for school.

It was not yet sunrise when Paul looked in on his new baby son before kissing Stéphanie and Alice and Adrien goodbye. Alice said, "Bonne journée, Papa," as he stepped out the door to make his way along the familiar streets to the Dupouy rhumerie.

At midday, Paul shared some bread and salt fish with Raoul, and the two finished déjeuner with a smoke as they chatted about work and politics. Politics was an inescapable fact of life in 1897 Saint-Pierre. It had been a decade of economic tumult and worker agitation. Whether you were on one side or the other, everyone knew.

Before they parted, Raoul informed him he would be leaving in April for a new cooper's position in Cayenne. Surprised at the news, Paul wished his friend well and promised to write often. But a despondence at this turn of events remained unspoken. Whom would he now take his lunches with? It appeared many of his friends were abandoning Saint-Pierre, and a few, like Raoul, leaving Martinique altogether. The hard times had left them sour.

On his way home after work, he stopped at the Pont Roche for the day's gossip. He carried home a bottle of rhum and a copy of *Les Colonies* under his arm, and in his pocket were sweets for Alice and Adrien. When he opened his front door, he was met with the fresh aroma of fish and spice and warm bread baking in the oven. His spirit was lifted as he realized that life had been extraordinarily kind to him.

~

IN JUNE, Raphaël informed Paul of new positions at the rhumerie. They were to build a modern distillery room with updated equipment and he thought Paul should apply to be the millwright's assistant. "This is an opportunity," he said, "to learn mechanical and electrical skills. This is the future you've been wanting, oui?"

"Merci, cousin! Merci, merci, merci!" Paul hugged Raphaël, who was a little embarrassed by his young cousin's effusive display of gratitude. Paul stepped back, suddenly aware that he was in his workplace, not a family gathering.

"Not to curb your enthusiasm," said Raphaël, "But we are on a tight timeframe. You must learn quickly. And it will be longer hours. But it will be more pay. It is yours if you want it. We still have to go through the paperwork."

"Whatever it takes," said Paul. He couldn't wait to run home and tell Stéphanie. To go to Maman's house and brag to her and Mannie about his new fortune. For the first time in years, it appeared the economy was truly improving, business expanding, the future once again possible. Should the railroad schemes not pan out, he would still have skills that would be in high demand. One thing was for certain, full electrification would soon come to Saint-Pierre. It wouldn't be just the distilleries and sucreries and richer neighborhoods that had power. He could even start his own business wiring homes and shops if he wished.

~

PAUL QUICKLY ADAPTED to his new position and within six months, he had earned his electrician's license and picked up the basics of metal working, including operating the machining mills. Impressed, Lucien, the mécanicien de chantier, increased his wages and placed him in charge of the machine shop, which was equipped with the latest foundry and machining equipment from North America.

The new distillery contained two of the latest copper vat stills, and there was a new tank in the fermentation room to handle an expected increase in production. This equipment, as well as the older stills and tanks, needed constant repair and maintenance. Paul's job required him to fashion new parts as necessary, and to keep the coal-fired electrical generators running.

Much of the increased production would be shipped and aged in Bordeaux where the cooler European climate meant less evaporation loss. Five-year rhum aged on the island could expect to lose 35 percent of its weight "to the angels," as the phrase went. A small portion of the distilled liquor, though, would be held back and aged in Saint-Pierre to satisfy the connoisseurs, a small minority willing to pay a higher price for "genuine" Martinican rhum. And then some would be distilled from pure cane juice for the local market. Paul believed that this agricole rhum, which many of his young friends preferred, should be marketed more vigorously abroad.

"You could save a lot of money if you didn't have to import molasses from Brazil," he told Raphaël one day, "Oui?"

"You're right, Paul," Raphaël said. "And it's true, tastes are changing. One day this may be viable. But right now the buyers want molasses rhum, so we make them what they want."

Paul had to admit he didn't really know much about product marketing and the metropolitan tastes. He was satisfied with keeping the equipment running and leaving the business decisions for his cousin.

~

STÉPHANIE WAS THRILLED at the news of another income raise. With the uneven economic recovery, her sewing business languished. Her best clients were friends of Tata Rosa, wives of successful business owners, both mulâtre and white. Many of these businesses failed after the drought, leaving hard working Pierrotins behind in the destruction. She had faith that some would eventually return, but the marketplace had changed and Caminade Brothers were now importing fancy readymade dresses from Paris and New York, so alterations and repairs might be all she could hope for.

Between the two boys, she was often exhausted by the time Paul arrived home, so thoughts of her little business were pushed to the back of her mind most days. Since the arrival of André Paul, little time remained for herself. He'd been a difficult baby, prone to prolonged periods of unhappiness, but fortunately, for Paul's sake, he wasn't a night crier, and usually wore himself out before darkness fell. She filled in her precious quiet hours, reading and sewing clothes for the children. It could be a worse life, she thought at these times. And she could have a less satisfying partner than Paul who adored the children and seemed happy to give her a break most days, even after a hard day at work. And that was the downside of his new position at the firm: longer work hours, including many late evenings repairing a leaking fermentation tank or some broken down masher that couldn't wait until the next day. Alice Germaine helped after school as well. At nearly ten years old, she'd become quite competent with the little ones, keeping them entertained while Stéphanie prepared supper. Most days Alice couldn't wait for her Papa to come home, and she protested at these longer days when she had to go to bed with no nighttime story, and must reluctantly agree to one from Manman, a clearly inferior substitute. But Stéphanie was happy that her daughter had someone to call Papa.

As for Paul, the children were everything. "Vous êtes notre avenir, mes amours," he intoned like a prayer as he tucked them in at night. He had faith in this one thing above all. The children were the future. It was difficult having so little time for them, but how would they grow up, how would they have a start in life, if he didn't work hard now while he was young and strong?

MAMAN HAS A PROPOSITION

OF COURSE PAUL must have Christmas dinner with the Dupouy family. They were family and Raphaël was his cousin as well as his boss. And he'd avoided them last Christmas by going with Stéphanie and the children to Tata Rosa's. Mama frowned at him for weeks afterward. He couldn't do that for two years in a row.

Stéphanie was agreeable. "You promised Alice that she would have more opportunities to play with her new cousins," she said. "And so far, that has not happened." It was true, he had been evading family events. He'd forgotten his promise to Alice.

He thought about her word, *cousins?* Did this mean Stéphanie now viewed herself as part of the family? He would be proud to claim her beautiful children as his own when they married... if they married. He realized he'd been looking for signs that Stéphanie shared this plan of his, one which she constantly argued against. "I do not need a bourgeois ceremony, Monsieur," she would tell him teasingly, "just your company in my bed." She avoided any further conversation on this subject by kissing him passionately until all was forgotten, if only temporarily.

So it was that their small family bundled up its gifts and trekked up Rue des Bons Enfants for dîner de Noël with the cousins and the aunts and uncles. They placed their gifts beneath a beautiful and strange fir tree imported all the way from Amérique du Nord on the steamship Madiana, decorated with baubles and handmade ornaments and colorful tinsel that glittered in the light of little candle-lanterns.

And here was Maman, hugging Alice and Adrien and cooing over André Paul. Embracing Stéphanie and leading them out to the garden where the Dupouy and Caminade children were playing. There was Bernadette. And there was Amélie and Paul Plissonneau. Their father must be around somewhere.

Paul looked upon this little Christmas miracle in wonder. He needn't have worried at all.

IT WAS LATE WINTER, shortly after André Paul's second birthday when Stéphanie informed him she was once more pregnant. The news was not as unexpected this time. Or as unwelcome. With his increased wages, he had made some small but profitable investments under Samuel's tutelage. The mayor had just announced a plan to electrify all of Saint-Pierre in the next few years, and with his electrician's license, Paul would be guaranteed work for the foreseeable future, not just in Saint-Pierre, but throughout the island. "I can go anywhere," he told Stéphanie. "I won't need to rely on the health of the rhumerie anymore."

The new baby was due in August, and the young couple began looking for a larger apartment in the Fort district, near Maman and Tata Rosa. They talked about hiring a maid, and Paul wondered silently if Sandrine might be available. They'd decided to take their time with the search and make sure they found the right place. But Maman put an end to that when she arrived unannounced one day to visit Stéphanie.

"Why Madame, so nice to see you," Stéphanie said, more than a little surprised to see Paul's mother on her doorstep. "To what do I owe the pleasure?"

"I just came around to see my grandchild. And to have a little visit. To see how you are doing." Stéphanie harbored a slight suspicion about Maman's motives, but wisely decided to keep them to herself.

"The truth is," Clémence said, seeing Stéphanie's hesitance, "I am in that big house all alone. Mannie has left to live with Joseph. I have only myself and empty rooms. My sons are good to me, they stop in often. And the Dupouys, of course, come see me and invite me to their home after early mass for a late Petit-déjeuner. But it's not the same, is it? I go to bed in an empty house and when I awake, I am still alone. I miss the daily presence of others—of conversations and laughter and tears. Even tears. How long it has been since I have heard feet rustling on the stairs and someone asking if there is coffee?" Clémence sighed. "I have never been alone, Stéphanie. I have always been surrounded by family. It's just too quiet. True, it is not as large as the house on Rue Castelnau, but..." Here, she paused and searched Stéphanie's face for a sign she could take to know how her narrative is going. Did she have to say it out?

Stéphanie gave her no hint. Her face was as smooth as a painting, though her eyes watched intently.

"But," Clémence continued, "It is large enough for myself and my son's family, if you wish to, that is. Alice could even have her own room."

Stéphanie gave Clémence a warm smile. "Maman, it is so kind of you. I will speak to Paul about it." *I won't be a substitute for Sandrine, though,* she thought. *I refuse to be a servant for this white lady whose investments keep her in all her necessities except for a live-in servant.* She knew Clémence had hired someone to clean once or twice a week and to cook an occasional meal when she wished to entertain. Maybe, if they moved in, they could afford to have the woman come in more often to clean.

Stéphanie was wise to be cautious, but Maman had accepted her as Paul's choice, as her daughter-not-quite-in-law. And this was Saint-Pierre, after all. So what was Maman's *other* motive? Well, Clémence knew that Georges Plissonneau would visit Paul soon with a proposition of his own. One she hoped he would accept. And having his family safe in her house might make a favorable decision easier for him.

THE SAME DAY Maman paid a visit to Stéphanie, Paul had a visitor as well. It was late morning and he was just about to take a break for déjeuner when Georges popped into the machine shop. Paul was shocked to see him. Georges may be his cousin, but he was a very busy and important man whose face was rarely seen outside of family functions. Paul put down the tap and die he'd been using to repair an offline tank cladding with a stripped out bolt.

"Monsieur Plissonneau," he said, holding up his greasy hands as a way of explanation for not embracing his cousin. "What brings you to Dupouy and company?"

"I would like to buy you lunch, Paul, if you have time. I have some news which might interest you."

"Of course. Let me clean up a bit here. It will only take a moment."

Paul cleaned the grease from his hands with kerosene and detergent while Georges examined the machine shop. "You are doing very well here," he said. "Raphaël has only good things to report."

"I think it's my calling. Shall we go?" Paul said as he hung his heavy work apron on a hook by the door.

Georges led him to a small café on Rue Bouille, one preferred by the Saint-Pierre négociants, where the atmosphere was subdued and properly bourgeois. They sat at a table fronting the bay and ordered chicken colombo and white wine. While waiting, they chatted about family. Émile and Thérèse had a new baby daughter, Georges reported, and Joseph's and Eugénie's youngest son Robert just turned two. Their daughter Louise has been ill. How is Paul's family? I understand there is a new little one on the way.

Paul told him about his family. André has just uttered his first words, and Alice will be eleven this year. Adrien is a quiet boy who still cries when his sister leaves for school. Stéphanie is well.

"And what is your news, Georges?" Paul asked when he could wait no longer.

"Ah, oui, the news," Georges said, drawing out the suspense a little. "We have just received a key piece of funding for the railway from the Atlantic to Saint-Pierre. It's enough that we can now set a date to begin."

Paul wanted to jump up and shout in his excitement. But of course he was not a child anymore. "This is good news," he said, grinning ear to ear.

"The precise route has yet to be decided. There is discussion of Trinité or perhaps le Robert."

What Paul understood, but was left unsaid, was that this political decision was actually an economic battle between sugar interests. "Work will probably begin in 1902 or 1903."

And what does this have to do with me? Paul was impatient for an answer, but he knew Georges would get to it in his own time. "I'm excited," he said, but he was much more excited than those words could convey.

"The reason I'm talking to you," Georges said, "is that Martinique lacks the skilled people needed to operate a full-scale railroad, as you know. There is an opportunity here for well-trained engineers and machinists. There is training available in North America."

Paul's mood suddenly sank. He had a family. He had another baby on the way. How could he leave Stéphanie alone with four children? Alice was old enough now to help her mother. Yet....

"How long will it take?" he asked, hoping his apprehension wasn't too obvious.

"It will take a few years, Paul. You must be willing to leave your family while you become settled in America. Perhaps you might send for them after a few months." Georges shrugged. "I expect you will be three or four years gone, altogether."

A MEETING IN MORNE ROUGE

"Your Maman came by today," Stéphanie said when he arrived home.

"Oh?" The news surprised him.

"She thinks we should move into the Poncy house and live with her. But I haven't decided if it's a good idea or not. We would have to discuss some things, I think."

He knew what Stéphanie meant, about her issues with the family, and now it was suddenly clear to him that Georges and Maman had already discussed his fate. He told Stéphanie the news about the railroad and she didn't hesitate. "You must go."

"But the children. I don't know."

"We don't know what will happen in life, cher. You must take advantage of the opportunities that come."

Paul knew what Maman thought he should do. He knew what Stéphanie thought he should do—or what she *said* she thought he should do, which might not be the same thing. He would certainly not be the first young man to leave his family, his children, to make his fortune in the world. In fact, it was the expected thing to do. But Georges' suggestion that he send for them once in America was a pipedream. It would be beyond his means. He would miss the early years of his children's lives if he left them behind in Martinique. He knew this was sentimentality. He was soft and he'd grown up in easy times, even if they had not always felt so easy. And yet the world was changing, and maybe this softness was the way we should be. Was it selfishness to care more about your family than about the progress of the world? Or were they the same thing, as his papa often told him?

"I will have to think about it," he said. "And I will talk to Maman about moving into her house."

There was no point in delay. He went to see Maman the next day. And when he was satisfied that this was really what Maman wanted, and after she promised to treat Stéphanie with the respect of a daughter-in-law, then he agreed.

Stéphanie's hesitation remained, but they soon began to pack their belongings. Alice was excited about the prospect of her own room, and how could her maman deny that to her?

A FEW DAYS after moving back to Maman's, Paul received a letter postmarked Cayenne, from his friend Raoul, whose opinion he had solicited about America:

MY DEAR PAUL,

So, there is another little one on the way. Please pass along my congratulations to Stéphanie. Are you actually going to move back home with your maman? It seems like a sensible thing to do for all of you, I suppose. I'm just surprised.

It is exciting to hear the news about the railroad and about America. I definitely think you should go. You should contact my brother Alcide in Maine. He works in the cotton mills. The pay is very good there, compared to Martinique. He has married an American girl, Louise Lamarque, and they have a baby boy who is my namesake. You should look them up when you arrive.

The heat and humidity is horrible in Cayenne, much worse than Martinique. And nothing much grows here but cane and mosquitoes. But I am making good money as a cooper, so I think I will stick it out for a while.

Take care, my friend. And think about America.

Ton ami,

Raoul Dufail

PAUL SET aside Raoul's letter. Small doubts lingered, but he believed he knew what he wanted now. He'd looked at all the angles, examined his mixed feelings, had endless night-time conversations with Stéphanie and with Maman and with Mannie. He'd even talked about it with Léonie, who was excited for him. And the more he talked, the more he realized this was what he really wanted to do, deep down, to go on this adventure of a lifetime. Yet, the guilt lingered, this idea that he would be abandoning his family, the suspicion that he had gained this opportunity at others' expense.

And of course it was true, if he was going to be philosophical about it: the well-off always live at the expense of others. All one can do is promise to make it up to the world. To balance things out in the long run. To give more than you get.

Easy enough said, eh?

When he spoke to Raphaël, his cousin nodded. "Of course, Samuel has already told me about this. We will hire someone to take your place right away. You will train them." It was not a question and Paul could see that Raphaël was resigned, but not particularly pleased about losing one of his best workers.

Later in the morning, a young boy appeared in the doorway

of the machine shop where Paul was hammering a piece of metal into a band. "Monsieur Poncy? I have a message for you." When Paul beckoned, the boy ran to him and handed him a folded paper. It had the weight and texture of expense.

"I'm to wait for your answer."

It was an invitation. A meeting in Morne Rouge at the Caminade country house. Uncle Edgard wrote that besides Gustav and himself, Georges and Samuel would be there, as well as the chief of the Department of Roads and Bridges, an Assier de Pompignan cousin. He looked at the boy patiently waiting. Paul took a pencil from the bench behind him and wrote on the back of the invitation that yes, he can come next Saturday and will accept their offer of a carriage. It was only a little over six kilometers, and he had walked the road before many times, but it was a steep climb and slow.

IT HAD BEEN a long time since Paul had been in a carriage. There was little need in Saint-Pierre for anyone with strength to travel by carriage. After all, if one's legs became weary walking from one end of town to the other, one could catch the horse-drawn tram on Bouille. The family rode in carriages to visit l'habitation Sablon when he was a child. And the occasional excursions to the Atlantic coast. He also remembered a carriage in Bordeaux that first took them from the wharf to their lodgings and then about the city whenever they needed. His memories of Bordeaux had become vague. He recalled the street they lived on for a short time in a multi-storied building that seemed to go on endlessly. Sainte Catherine. Rue Sainte-Catherine, number 13.

The carriage belonged to one of the Petits. Paul's attempts to engage the driver in conversation were met with oui mesye and non mesye. He was clearly not interested in entertaining the young white gentleman. Paul recalled the salon and the uneasy, confusing discussions often pointed his way as the presumptive representative of béké culture, and it gave him pause.

Many of the families of the Quartier du Fort had country homes in Morne Rouge, while families like the Fauvé-Sablon who lived in Basse-Pointe on the Atlantic Ocean side of the island maintained such houses in Ajoupa Bouillon. Places where they tried to escape yellow fever, places where they could relax away from their warehouses and rhumeries, from the sulfur stink of the sucreries.

The steep mountain road was well-used and the carriage passed many people on foot. Some were barefoot, some were women with the large bundles of wares balanced on their heads, goods that they peddled up and down the mountain, legendary in their strength and endurance. Mostly, they avoided his eyes, talked and laughed among themselves, greeted the taciturn driver, but never his passenger.

Paul was very glad to arrive at the Caminade country estate, where he was greeted by Papa Tav himself. "Paul, come, come. We are enjoying the view of Saint-Pierre from the terrace. For once, it is not raining. What will you have to drink, young man?" Papa Tav asked as he ushered Paul through the large house. All the shutters were open and Paul could see into the rooms as they passed; a room where children on the floor played with dolls and some kind of game involving a small ball; the kitchen where several women were busy at the stove and around a table spread with flour for kneading dough; and a library full of shelved books where he glimpsed a stereopticon and a large wire-haired dog who half rose to watch them pass. And then they were at the rear of the house, poised on the edge of a ridge overlooking the city.

"Tea, merci," he said. Gustav left to fetch it.

The spectacular view awed Paul. He had seldom been to Morne Rouge this time of year when there was no curtain of mist or pouring rain in the afternoon, the sea glinting below, the red-tiled roofs and white plastered walls of Saint-Pierre glowing in the early afternoon light.

"Well, here we are, Paul. We are so very pleased you could join us today," Uncle Edgard said and swept his arm, encompassing Georges and Samuel where they sat at a large round glass-topped table. Behind them, folding doors along the back wall of the house were open to the generous Caribbean breeze.

Paul accepted the glass of cold tea Gustav held out to him, bowed his head toward the group of men as he took his place among them. *My place among them*, he thought, heady, disorienting, and thrilling.

The men took their time. They asked about his family, he asked about theirs. Time slowed with talk of the market, the shifting economy, they glided past worker unrest with a flick of the hand, *there are no socialists in Martinique, eh Paul?*

Paul's eyes narrowed, but he held his tongue. They know whatever they know. He isn't here to champion the cause of workers or denounce them.

At last, the matter at hand. Georges leaned forward, "You have been asked here because we believe we can rely on you, and you are as eager to see the railroad in Martinique as we are."

Paul nodded vigorously.

Georges settled back. "If only I were your age, it would be me going off to America." It wasn't true, but no one contradicted him. He cleared his throat. "You are a bright young man. Samuel and Raphael have only good to say. We admire your sense of responsibility and it appears you've put behind the brashness of your youth."

Paul couldn't help but blush at this finger pointing to that disastrous, drunken Noël when Maman tried to marry him off to his cousine.

Samuel spoke up. "We'd like to see you in America within six months. Three, if possible. We expect you to become fluent in English and learn as much about the railroad business as possible. We know nothing here. The planters' short-lines have about as much to do with a real railroad as a cart has to do with an automobile—which are also coming to Martinique, mind you."

"We won't be idle," Georges interjected. "We'll be studying, as well. But you will be there on the ground, learning the business firsthand. When you return to Martinique, you will be in an excellent position to run the new enterprise."

"I am very honored that you have chosen me. You know I have a family. I support three children and their mother. I will have to find work immediately," Paul said firmly, not mentioning the fourth child on the way.

"Of course, of course. We'll get you there," Georges said. "I will arrange passage. We are the agents for the Québec Steamship Line, as you know. We will see you settled as well, then you can find work while you are becoming fluent in English. If you are to find work in the industry immediately, that would be most ideal."

The afternoon progressed, the sun fell into the sea. The breeze picked up again. It was comfortable in the shadow of the house and the mountains. Gustav invited him to spend the night, but Paul declined, "Merci, Papa Tav, I am expected at home."

"I will have the carriage brought for you then."

Paul shook his head. "I would very much like to walk. It will give me time to settle my mind."

Was this when he said his first farewell to his island home? As he walked down the slope, between the towering palmiste, ausubo, and guava trees, past ferns taller than himself, the gingery scent of alpinia blossoms mingled with the always present, faintly fetid, smell of decaying vegetation.

Gustav had given him a torch, which he lit when night came. The air around him was alive with insect noise. The torch he held was steeped in citronnelle to keep the mosquitos at bay. Now, he is the one who walks as carriages pass and men on horseback or mule, as well as an occasional group of two or three women. He thinks one of them is Désirée. She does not spare him a glance. But it is dark and he can't be sure, and everyone is picking up their pace, because the night road brings out the snakes.

AU REVOIR

THERE WERE STILL, of course, all the details to be worked out. Where would he land, precisely? He remembered what Raoul said, that there were forests in America larger than Martinique. So many cities and people. The next day after work he sat with Mannie at the patio table, which had just been cleared of dishes and wiped clean from a late afternoon meal. He had only a couple of hours of good light left in the day. Mannie unfolded a map Paul brought from work of the eastern seaboard of the United States and Canada. He found Manchester, New Hampshire.

"The Manchester Locomotive Company is here," Paul said. "They build many of the steam engines. That's where I should go."

"With your English? I don't think so, brother. You need to work in a place where they will hire a French speaker, but still be able to learn English so you can go to work in... Man... however you say it. Maybe you should go to Montréal."

"But almost everyone speaks French in Montréal. How will I learn English there?" And besides, he thought, he'd never seen an advertisement calling for electricians or machinists to come to Montreal. He scanned down the map, tracing the coastline, reading the unfamiliar names of towns and cities. Until he came to Boston and New York. A rush of excitement overwhelmed him. These were places he had read about. New York was not Paris. No Frenchman would ever say it was so great a city as Paris, and yet the city had a magnetic pull.

Paul looked up when he heard Stéphanie call to Alice, "Take this letter to your papa." Alice appeared in the open door.

"Look Papa, a letter from America."

"Maybe someone had heard you are looking for work and is offering you a job already," Mannie laughed.

Paul took the letter.

"It's from Alcide Dufail," he said. "Raoul has written to him about my plans."

Stéphanie came from the house into the garden and stood beside him.

"Wait," she said. "Alice, go and bring Granmére. Papa is going to read the letter."

When Clémence and Stéphanie were settled in chairs, André on his mémé's lap, Adrian leaning against Paul, holding his sister's hand, Paul read:

BONJOUR, *Paul,*

I hope your family is well. Please give my best to them all, to your brothers and your maman, as well as Stéphanie and the children. Tell Joseph he owes me five francs for the bet we made before I left. He will know what I'm talking about.

My condolences on the passing of Anatole. He was a true pillar of Saint-Pierre.

Raoul has informed me you will be coming to America and have not decided where to settle. I will offer my humble advice. There are many mill towns in New England, but the one I would choose is Woonsocket in Rhode Island. My new bride, Louise, has family there. You will have no trouble finding work, as the mills are constantly hiring. You must have seen the advertisements in Les Colonies. Many Québécois have gone there because the mills pay so much better than farming. The mills hire French speakers. I have heard there are thousands living there and not just French-Canadians, also some from the Métropole. The largest number of French speakers in one city in the United States, it is said. Still, you could learn English, I think. According to my neighbor who lived in Woonsocket until recently, there are many public schools, all English, and many children attend until they are four-teen. You should have no trouble finding a tutor.

This is a very large country, but if you should ever come through Lewiston, my wife and I would be most happy to welcome you into our home.

Your friend,
Alcide Dufail

THE BABY KICKED. Stéphanie stood abruptly, turned to leave, her foot tangled in her chair, it fell back, but she did not pause. "Stéphanie!" Paul called as he hurried after her.

Tears were running down her cheeks when Paul caught up with her in their bedroom. "How can you think of leaving us now?" She sobbed.

"I thought this was settled," he said. "I thought you wanted me to go." He held her as she continued to sob, the curve of her belly more than filling the hollow beneath his ribs. He couldn't remember ever seeing this strong woman cry before. He tried to soothe her as he would one of the children.

"I will stay," Paul said.

"No, no, you must go. I am being foolish. It is only being so close to the baby coming." She lifted the lap of her dress and wiped her cheeks. "See, I am okay." She smiled and gave him a quick kiss, pushed him toward the door. "Let's return before they think we've gone to bed."

CLÉMENCE CONFERRED WITH FATHER EDOUARD, who assured her that there were churches serving the French parishes in Woonsocket. Maman was happy about this. "Can you write to them, Father? Paul must find a room with a good Catholic family."

"Have your son come around, Madame," said Father Edouard. "I must make certain the young man is someone I can recommend. I have seen little of Paul for several years now. Will he and Stéphanie Grainau marry before he leaves for America? That would be a consideration. Of course, I remember the boy's conviction that he wanted to be a priest."

"His brother's death had affected him so, Father," Clémence responded.

"Yes. Everyone loved Eustase, did they not? Handsome, good-natured. Already a well respected man. He was learning about the work of the Bourse with Samuel Dupouy, was he not? And if I remember, before that, he worked with Gustav Caminade. There were rumors he liked to gamble, but there are always rumors."

When Paul came to see him, Father Edouard saw he was not unlike his brother Eustase, good looking in that almost swarthy way. He had the high broad forehead all the Poncy men seemed to have, the Father thought, and it was common knowledge that they were every bit as intelligent as they appeared.

"Please sit," Father Edouard invited Paul. They regarded each other for a moment across Father's cluttered desk. "I don't remember seeing you at mass on dimanche last."

"You would not have seen me, Father." Paul did not look uncomfortable. He was matter of fact. He had not been to the church since Papa's funeral mass.

"Your mother has asked me to recommend you to Father Napoleon of Saint Anne in Woonsocket, Rhode Island."

"I would be most grateful, Father. It would be a relief for Maman. The church is a safe harbor for her."

"And you, Paul? Is the church not a place of safety for you, as well?" He was chiding the young man and hadn't meant to. "It can at least be a comfort to us when we are far from home. Perhaps you will find your way back to God."

It wasn't something Paul considered. Had he lost his way from God? Why would Father Edouard think this of him? He frowned and studied the Father's face in the silence between them. Of course, he hadn't confessed for years. He remembered how Maman's eyes reproached him as he remained seated while the rest of the family, even Stéphanie, took communion. Paul thought, I wonder what Stéphanie confessed before the funeral mass that she calmly accepted the bread and wine, body, and blood. *Forgive me, Father, for I have sinned. I've had carnal knowledge of the dead man's son for many years.* And when he gave her penance and urged her to sin no more, she came home and wrapped him in her arms. Paul smiled. Stéphanie would not have confessed to something she did not consider a sin.

Father Edouard saw the smile lighting up Paul's eyes and pulled a sheet of paper embossed with the parish insignia. "Very well, I shall write a letter of recommendation."

LOUISE VIRGINIE YVONNE PONCY IS BORN *on 19 August 1899 at home on Rue Saint-Denis in Saint-Pierre at four o'clock in the morning.* Paul wasted no time registering Yvonne with the Poncy name. This time there were no family arguments to delay him, and there was so little time before he must leave.

And there is Yvonne, herself, who has become part of his story. And his regrets. Alice was delighted to have a sister and he was relieved to see her so happy. She had been despondent since learning he would be leaving for work in America. But Yvonne. He would miss knowing her in these first few formative years, and the thought made him incredibly sad.

Looking back, now, Paul saw himself standing at the rail of the *Madiana*. The Caribbean calm, an achingly beautiful blue. He turned away from the endless sea to take a last look at the island of Martinique. It was an exceptionally clear morning. Saint-Pierre had disappeared from view, but Mount Pelée was visible, ringed with a transparent collar of mist. When he had stepped from the pier onto the lighter, he couldn't decide if he should sit facing his family or outward to the steamship anchored in deep water. He longed to face the open sea, but he sat with his back to it and waved to his family. Joseph and Emmanuel behind Maman and Stéphanie and the children. Samuel of course, and Léonie off to the side, the sunlight glowing through her blond hair. He had been surprised to see Joseph. His brother had gripped his arms just below his shoulders and kissed him on both cheeks. As he pulled back and turned away, Paul saw Joseph's eyes were wet.

He could still see little Alice Germaine hugging her mother, Adrien clinging to Alice. Stéphanie holding Yvonne and Maman lifting André Paul up high so he could see his papa disappear. Paul's feelings were confused and he couldn't decide if he was a man exiled or a prisoner escaping. Was this the beginning of an exciting adventure, or simply some mundane future unfolding before him?

The other thing he remembered that turned over uneasily in

his mind was Ludger Sylbaris in the lighter, his hand on the tiller. How he guided the boat to the steamship's plank, tossed the ropes easily and accurately to the sailor standing by. He did not seem to notice Paul until it was his turn to leave the boat. Ludger tapped the tiny scar on his cheek and smiled, "Bon voyage, Priest."

PAUL HAD three letters locked in his trunk. One Father Edouard wrote introducing him to both Father Napoléon of Saint Ann and the Tambois family, who would be his hosts; one signed by both Raphael and Samuel Dupouy; and the third from Georges Plissonneau. These last recommended him as a skilled man of moral character from an exemplary, long-established Martiniquais family. The previous day he'd met Samuel Dupouy in his office at the Bourse, where he exchanged the francs provided for his journey for United States dollars and coins. Samuel explained the value of each coin. As a well-traveled man, he admonished Paul to be wary of pickpockets and men or women who pretend to be helpful, but are only about to rob you of your money.

"New York City," Samuel had said, "is not a place for which you can prepare. It is most important that you monitor your trunk at all times. Do not allow a cab driver to cheat you too much, just enough to make him happy." Samuel spread a map out on the table on his desk and pointed out Pier 47 where the *Madiana* would berth and drew a line with a pencil to show the way from the pier to the Grand Central terminal where the New Haven line would carry him to Providence. "There is a hotel across the street from Grand Central. You will want to stay there for a night. You can rent a room for $1, if the price has not changed since last I was there. They will transport your trunk from the station for no charge, but it is customary to give the porter a one cent coin. The hotel will have a safe where you can leave your money and letters. It is most important that you are discreet when you ask the clerk to lock your things away and be sure to keep your receipt on you at all times."

By the time he'd left Samuel's office, he'd harbored doubts about this America, so filled with caprice and thievery. But most likely, Samuel was just being overly cautious about his young cousin's welfare. Even in Saint-Pierre, one had to be careful, after all.

Paul began his first letter to Stéphanie on his second night aboard ship and added a little to it each night. Most of what he recorded was about fellow passengers and the seabirds which followed the ship and dove for trash thrown overboard. He also wrote of his longing for her and the children. *Each day that passes is one that brings me closer to returning. That is how I ease the loneliness that comes on me most suddenly as I lay in bed listening to the engines and the slap, slap of waves.* Still, he didn't neglect the excitement he felt. *What will it be like, my love, to live in North America? I feel certain that I will be changed. I will always be your Paul, but more, I will be a man of the world.*

The *Madiana* made good time, even with stops in Sainte-Lucie, Guadeloupe, Puerto Rico, and Bermuda, before heading to Brunswick, Georgia in the United States. It was the first American city he saw and it looked like a quaint village, only half the size of Saint-Pierre. Perhaps much about this country had been exaggerated. He soon came to realize that there might be a hundred sleepy villages like Brunswick or a thousand, but this was just one face of this country where, unbeknown to him then, he would live for most of the remainder of his life.

Even before the steamship entered New York harbor, he was awed by the enormity of the city. He had been standing at the forward rail with, it seemed, most of his fellow passengers tightly packed beside and behind him. At first, what he saw was like a jagged mountain, which slowly resolved into towering buildings that caught his breath. He'd seen pictures, of course, but so many structures of great height left his mouth hanging open. And the closer they came, the more stupendous it was.

"There she is," someone shouted, pointing ahead.

"That is our statue," someone else proclaimed in French. "Our gift. She is the biggest statue. Vive la liberté."

"Vive la France!" a few French travelers around him shouted. They clapped their hands and each other's backs.

He heard some laughter from other passengers whose English was too rapid for him to understand more than a word or two. This was a cruise for them and this was their home they were greeting after a holiday in the exotic Caribbean.

A HURRICANE BLOWS THE LIBERTÉ OFF COURSE

THE ADVENTURES OF YVONNE

Yvonne woke up feeling sad. She missed Auntie Rosa and Uncle Louis. She missed her friends at school. She missed Adrien and Alice Germaine, who had been inexplicably left behind. She missed the roosters in the morning and Auntie Rosa's stories at night. She missed her home in Saint-Pierre.

But, most of all, she missed Maman's smiling face at Petit-déjeuner, as she served André and Yvonne poached eggs on buttered brioche.

Living on a pirate ship was exciting, but it wasn't home.

She wanted to stay in bed and sleep, but she was afraid Captain Marie might make shark food out of her if she did.

When Yvonne arrived at the mess for breakfast, she looked for André and Maman, but they were nowhere in sight.

She picked at her food and tried to wish it away. But it did no good. So she forced down her breakfast and reported for duty on the bridge.

Marcus had taught her many things, such as how to use a sextant and a ship's chronometer, and how to figure out the latitude and longitude by looking up the tables in the maritime almanacs.

She also learned about wind speed and direction and how to determine course corrections. It was a lot to remember, but Yvonne had always been good at mathématiques in school. This helped because there was a lot of maths involved.

"You are a quick learner, Mademoiselle," said Marcus. Like Captain Marie, Marcus spoke French most of the time. But he spoke Matinik to the crew.

Yvonne knew both languages, because Papa spoke French and Maman insisted it was the language they must speak in the house.

"French is the language that is spoken in Bordeaux," Maman said. "They do not know Matinik there."

Yvonne was glad she knew both languages, because her teachers and most of her friends at school spoke Matinik, their native Créole.

Yvonne thanked Marcus for his compliment, but she was too sad to smile. Instead, she looked down at her shoes.

"Is something the matter, Mademoiselle?" asked Marcus, in his kindest voice.

"I miss my home and my friends," said Yvonne. "And I never have time to talk to Maman anymore."

"Yes, I understand," said Marcus. "Living at sea can be very lonely."

"Will we be in Bordeaux soon?" asked Yvonne, with a frown on her face.

"I am sorry to inform you, Yvonne," said Marcus. "There is a big storm to our south, and we must go around it. This may add an extra week or two to our journey."

"I don't think I can stand it," said Yvonne, dramatically.

Marcus was moved and saddened to find Yvonne in such distress.

"Don't worry, young lady," he said. "I shall take the *Liberté* as fast as she can go."

THE WIND PICKED up in the afternoon, and by the end of the day, the *Liberté* was tossing back and forth on the sea swells. Yvonne felt as if her stomach was turning somersaults.

Marcus looked anxious as he attempted to steer the ship around the storm, which had turned unexpectedly into the path of the *Liberté*.

"We must go to the north of the storm and outrace her," said Marcus. "The winds are much too strong to sail against them. If the hurricane comes too close, we shall have to lower the sails and ride her out. Otherwise, she will sink us."

Yvonne became very alarmed. *But if anyone could get us out of this unfortunate situation,* she thought, *it is Chief Navigator Marcus.*

Captain Marie burst suddenly out of her office, which was at the aft of the bridge. She frowned at Marcus.

"Do you think we can win this race, Chief Navigator?" asked Captain Marie.

"Yes, Ma'am," said Marcus. "It is too late to turn back now."

Captain Marie looked very cross. "How did you let us get so close to the storm?"

"The storm turned into us unexpectedly, Ma'am," said Marcus. "I thought she was well to the south."

"You thought? You thought?" Captain Marie yelled, her face turning red. "It is your job to *know*. You better get us out of this alive, Chief Navigator, or you will be walking the plank."

Captain Marie stormed back into her office, slamming the door. Yvonne might have giggled, if she had dared.

Then a horrible thought came to her. Yvonne wondered if it might be *her* fault the ship was in grave danger. She had begged Marcus to go quickly to Bordeaux, but maybe he should have been more cautious.

"Mesye Étienne," Yvonne said, when she and the helmsman were alone on the deck, "may I ask you something?"

"Natirelman, Mamzel," Étienne said in Matinik.

Yvonne told Étienne about the promise Marcus made to her to go quickly to Bordeaux.

"Do you think I'm to blame?" asked Yvonne.

"No, no, Mamzel," Étienne said. "You must not think that. The Chief Navigator would not risk the ship unnecessarily. Storms are very unpredictable."

Yvonne was very relieved to hear Étienne say this. But still she felt guilty. She wanted to talk to Maman, but she was needed on the bridge, and there was no use in going to the cabin, in any case. Maman wouldn't be there, and Yvonne wouldn't be able to sleep with the ship tossing so.

THE STORM CONTINUED TO WORSEN. The huge waves soon reached as high as the bridge, soaking everyone. At times, the ship listed nearly over on its side, and Yvonne had to hang on for her life.

The First Mate burst onto the bridge suddenly and talked excitedly to Captain Marie, who then turned to Marcus.

"We must bring down the sails," the captain yelled over the roar of the storm.

"Yes," said Marcus. "I agree."

The First Mate hurried from the bridge. Marcus and Captain Marie followed to help them lower the *Liberté's* many sails.

Yvonne felt sick to her stomach. Without the sails, the ship would bob up and down like a cork in the tempest, with only the keel to steer them away from rocks.

"You should go below, Mamzel," Étienne shouted.

"But I don't want to leave you all alone, Étienne," Yvonne said.

"Don't you worry about me, Mamzel," Étienne said. "Go find your Manman. Make sure she is safe in her cabin."

Yvonne had forgotten all about Maman and André in the excitement. She must go make sure they are okay.

Just as she was about to go below, a huge wave hit the side of the *Liberté*. Yvonne hung on to the railing with all of her strength. Then there came a loud crash of lightning, and a second wave hit the ship. Yvonne felt her grip on the rail slip.

A third wave hit. The last thing she knew, she was over the rail and sailing through the air.

PART 5
LE NOUVEAU SIÈCLE

COIN DE SOCIAL

Social Village, a district of Woonsocket, Rhode Island when Paul arrived in 1899, was primarily inhabited by French Canadian immigrants who worked in the numerous textile mills along the Blackstone River. Seventy-five percent French speaking, the district was an ideal place for him to land on his feet in Amérique du Nord, a place where people spoke his language and where he could find a job while becoming fluent in English. The letters of recommendation he carried buoyed his confidence. Especially Raphaël Dupouy's, which was generous, practically fawning over Paul's exemplary performance. But that's what cousins were for. Oui? Also in his possession was the address of a good Catholic family from France, passed along by Father Edouard of Saint-Pierre who knew Father Napoléon of Saint Ann Parish. François Tambois, a weaver at the Nourse Mill, lived with his family on Rathbun Street, across from the Precious Blood Cemetery. They took boarders.

The carriage Paul hired at the train station took him up the hill to Social Village. He was relieved that the driver spoke French, although his accent made him difficult to understand.

The man informed him the Tambois home was "practically in Massachusetts — right on the border."

The train passed many row houses on the way up from New York and he'd assumed he would be rooming in one of those. But the Tambois house was unlike any of his previous dwellings. It sat alone, unconnected to others, yard on all sides, more like the country homes of Morne Rouge or Ajoupa Bouillon than a city apartment, yet it was smaller, made entirely of wood and far less substantial than those grand country manors, and little about it made him think of l'habitation Sablon. Yet it amazed him that a humble factory worker could afford to own a home like this, something that would have been impossible in Saint-Pierre.

The family was expecting Paul, curious about their new tenant from the exotic island of Martinique. Francine Tambois greeted him at the door. Her husband — Frank, she called him — was at the mill, where he worked ten-hour days, and wouldn't arrive home until 4:30 pm.

"Shall I show you to your room, Monsieur?" she asked, inviting him inside with a smile. To his relief, Madame Tambois' French was only slightly different from his own.

The carriage driver grabbed one handle of his small trunk, while Paul grabbed the other, his overstuffed duffel bag over his shoulder, and together they carried it inside. These two unassuming pieces of luggage contained his books, his letters of introduction and a small collection of personal letters he'd found on his first night onboard ship, which Alice had written and slipped inside his trunk. One for each day of his journey. He had read them all now. The trunk also contained all the memorabilia he possessed. A few family photographs, a jasmine flower Maman had pressed, wrapped in tissue paper and inserted into his favorite novel, where he would be sure to find it.

Paul gave the driver a gratuity, still not at ease with this odd American custom, and Francine Tambois led him into the interior of the house. It felt comfortably lived-in. Several area rugs of various sizes and shapes covered wooden plank flooring. An overstuffed couch in good condition sat beneath a window overlooking the street, bracketed by two chairs, one a walnut rocking chair, the other a dusty green fabric matching the couch. A small bookcase had been built into the living room on one side of the fireplace — where he was grateful to see a fire lit — and contained a smattering of books. Family photos adorned the mantle. There was a dining room and he could make out a kitchen and a hall beyond.

"Frank and I sleep down here," she said. "You will be upstairs with Lea. Lea works nights and doesn't arrive home until after six, so you shouldn't be bothered when she comes in."

Francine Tambois hefted one end of his trunk and together they carried it up the narrow staircase with its polished oak banister. "It's a small room," she said apologetically, "there is a bath between your room and Lea's, so you have your privacy."

She indicated Lea's room at the top of the stairs, and took him past it to the bathroom, pointing out its modern facilities. Just beyond was Paul's room. It was small, but not so much smaller than his room growing up. Room enough. There was a window overlooking Rathbun Street and the cemetery. Beneath the window stood a small writing desk with an electric lamp.

He placed his duffel bag on his trunk as Francine asked if he would like tea or coffee. "Or would you prefer to rest from your long journey?"

"Oui, merci," he said. "I will clean up and take a nap, if you don't mind."

"I'll call you for dinner at about 6 pm," she said. "You can meet Frank and Lea then. Lea is looking forward to tutoring you in English."

Francine Tambois smiled and closed the door behind her.

~

FOURTEEN-YEAR-OLD LEA TAMBOIS worked the night shift in the spinning room at the Nourse Mill. She was an ordinary looking girl with unruly hair, cut short, a spirited girl, not yet worn down by the long hours of the cotton mill. Her father, Frank Tambois, was a big man in his forties with a chronic cough. He wore a blue chamois work shirt to the dinner table. Francine had on the simple blouse she had been cooking in with a scarf tied around her hair. Paul had put on a clean white dinner shirt, wanting to make a good impression on his first day with this family. But now he felt uncomfortably formal.

Seeing his unease, Francine complimented him. "Is your shirt from New York? It's a very fine weave."

"Non," he said. "It's from Bordeaux. My cousin's husband, Gustav, imports them to Saint-Pierre."

"Does Gustav have a clothing store?" said Frank.

"He's in the import and export business," Paul said. Quiet descended on the dinner table, and he wondered what it was he said. Frank, who had been shoveling his food away while Paul was talking, pushed his chair roughly from the table. "Excusez moi," he said and took his plate to the kitchen.

Francine looked after her husband, her jaw clenched, but she remained seated.

Lea smiled at Paul, shyly. "Papa is tired," she said, breaking the silence. "We can study votre Anglais after dinner, if you'd like."

"Oui," he said, glad that the young girl had intervened, leaving him not quite so unsettled.

~

PAUL'S FIRST ENGLISH LESSON — well, not the first, because he could already read and write competently — took place in the living room of the Tambois home. While Francine washed the dishes, Lea tutored him, using a simple illustrated children's book to begin. She had him repeat the words until the difficult sounds came out presentably. The girl had a knack for teaching and encouraged him when he'd mastered a word. But English was difficult. Too many words spelled the same way, but pronounced differently, spelled differently but pronounced the same.

"Very good, Mr. Poncy," she said in English as she closed the children's book. "I must prepare for work now." She smiled at him. It was a complicated, sweet-sad smile full of unspoken questions and dreams that put him on guard as he returned it.

He pulled a quarter from his pocket, their agreed upon exchange, and handed it to her. "Thank you, Lea," he said in halting English.

"Thank you," she said and started up the stairs to her room. "Good night, Paul."

"Good night, Mademoiselle."

⌒

29 OCTOBRE 1899

My dearest Stéphanie,

I'm about to lie down for the night, so I will keep this letter brief. I have settled into my new room in the United States. The Tambois family has been very kind, and their daughter, Lea, has provided my first English lesson. I am afraid Frank Tambois and I got off on the wrong foot when he took umbrage at our class differences. Even so, I am excited to be here, although I already miss you. I hope you are all well. Please give my love to Maman and the children.

New York is an incredible city, immense in a way that is hard to describe. Many buildings are taller than I would have thought possible. And there are so many people! I wish I had spent some time there, but I stayed only one night and had to be at the station very early to catch my train to Blackstone, where a carriage brought me to my new home in Woonsocket, Rhode Island.

These are industrial cities. The bricks are black with coal dust, and the river, they say, is too poisoned to provide drinking water. Instead, it is used to power the turbines and steam engines of the factories.

It is very cold here. I haven't been so cold since that winter my family spent in Bordeaux when I was a child. I am glad to have found Papa's wool coat from those times. I hung it out in the cabin, as you suggested airing it out. The smell of naphthalene is nearly gone. The Tambois family has told me it will get much colder yet in the months to come, so I fear I must shop for some warmer clothes, including a good hat.

That's all for now, my dear. Give my love to the children. I promise to write again soon.

With all my affection,
Paul

YOU WALK through the rain forest along a familiar trace of black volcanic stone, one of several paths you've walked as a child along the slope of Montagne Pelée. There is a muscular black man on the path, familiar in some way you can't name, and you steer your course around him, close to the incline that drops away into the mist, when your foot catches on something. You slip over the edge, grabbing at the lianas. You catch one, but when you climb back up, you slip again. In the deep pit below is a nest of snakes. Fer-de-lance below you, waiting. Above you is the black man, his hand extended. You've seen him before, somewhere, a ghost from your past. "Let go, Priest, and grab my hand," he says. "I will catch you."

"Why should I trust you, Ludger?" you say, suddenly recognizing the young dock worker from the mouillage. "You've taken advantage of me once."

"What choice do you have, my friend?" He laughs. A demon laugh. A wind has come up and it's bitterly cold, colder than you've ever felt. You shiver. You grip the liana tighter. The snakes or the black man?

Then snow falls. A curiously black snow.

PAUL AWAKENED FROM THE DREAM, everything around him unfamiliar. Wondering why it was so cold and so quiet. He'd tossed off his blankets in his uneasy sleep. He heard only the tick of a grandfather clock in the hall. In all his life, it had never been so quiet at night. On the ship, there was the noise of the engines and the sea. In New York, the constant clatter of automobiles and carriages in the street below. At home, the cicadas would be singing their noisy lullaby. He rose, shivering, and went to the window, opened it. The cold made him gasp. Somewhere in the distance a dog barked. Then all was quiet again. In the morning, he would find out the insects had all gone underground for the winter, like the birds and the leaves on the trees. Now he closed the window, hurried back to bed, and pulled the blankets up over his head. It was a long time before he felt warm and could drift back to sleep.

THE TAMBOIS FAMILY invited him to Sunday mass. He had mixed feelings about this, but he'd made a promise to Father Edouard that he would try to be a better Catholic, and it was a chance for him to meet some of his new neighbors. Lea, who was charming and almost pretty in her fashionable hat and Sunday dress, insisted on walking beside him to church, to her maman's consternation. "I think my daughter wants to show off our new boarder," said Francine with a nervous laugh. "Don't get any notions, Lea," she barked at her daughter a little too loudly. Paul was shocked to hear a mother chastising her daughter so publicly. He couldn't help but think it was meant for his ears as well.

"Oh, Mama, you're embarrassing me."

"I'm sure Monsieur Poncy is a gentleman, but there is still propriety."

He felt he should say something reassuring to Madame Tambois, but he was tongue-tied. These Americans seemed so brash and prim at the same time. There were the pious in Saint-Pierre, also, of course. But it was different in some undefinable way.

Father Napoléon's theology was not so different from Father Edouard's. Conservative and narrow. His Québécois French, like the driver's, was sometimes hard for Paul to understand. He'd noticed some of the same curious Québécois phrasing when Lea had spoken, although not so much from Frank and Francine, who immigrated from France when Lea was a baby, and so maintained a better grasp of the mother tongue. Father Napoléon's sermon at the end of Latin mass was filled with references to the protection of French culture and language from "English" influence. *La Survivance,* they call this philosophy. Paul found this curious and decided he must ask more about it.

Parishioners gathered in the vestibule after mass. Francine

introduced him to several people whose names he quickly forgot. Then she spied a young couple with an infant emerging from the chapel and nudged him in their direction. "You must meet our neighbors, the Bouleys. Albert," she hailed, waving her hand. The young couple stopped and veered toward them. "Albert, Annie, I would like you to meet our new tenant, Paul Poncy. Paul, this is Albert and Annie Bouley, and their little Olivia." Francine reached out to let Olivia grab her finger. Cooed at her.

"Pleased to meet you, Monsieur, Madame," Paul said. He was unused to this American familiarity toward strangers.

"Monsieur Poncy is an electrician," Francine said. "Albert is a carpenter, Paul. I thought you might have some common interests. The Bouleys live just up the street from us."

"Pleased to meet you, Monsieur," Albert said.

"Likewise," he replied, happy to make the acquaintance of another trade worker. Albert was closer to his own age than Frank Tambois. He would guess no more than thirty. And Annie, not much older than Paul, himself.

"Monsieur Poncy is from Martinique," Francine said.

"Oh, is that so?" said Annie Bouley. "You must tell us sometime what it is like there."

"I would love to tell you about my home and family, Madame."

"We must have you over for dinner, then," Annie said, looking at her husband, who smiled and added, "certainly."

"We will talk it over and I will let Francine know," Annie said.

"Very good," Paul said. "I will look forward to it. It is nice to meet you Monsieur, Madame."

Although the conversation was in that curious Quebec French, English was Albert and Annie's first language, and he thought this a good thing. It seemed a good sign for his own prospects of learning to speak English that most of the people here in Social Corner were bilingual.

8 NOVEMBRE, 1899

My Dear Paul

I was so happy to receive your letter and know that you have made it safely to North America. Your maman says to send her love and she will write soon. We are all well and miss you. Alice especially, who says nearly every evening at bedtime, "I wish Papa was here to read me a story." I read to the children, of course, but it seems you are the storyteller they want at their bedside.

Your maman gave us a fright when she became ill, but it turned out to be only a passing cold. Dr Dufail called on her and gave her something to take, and he prescribed plenty of rest.

The political situation in Saint-Pierre continues to be volatile. There have been several small strikes, including a brief one at the Dupouy rhumerie. Most of the unrest has been in Fort-de-France, and the newspapers from the Métropole claim it is the work of "socialist agitators." It is so disingenuous of them. I don't think many here would see it that way, except perhaps the békés who would like to defeat Senator Knight and the radicals in the next election.

Take care my love and write again soon.

Your Stéphanie

HE SET the letter on his bedside table next to the photograph taken nearly a year before Yvonne was born. In the photo, Stéphanie sat with André Paul on her lap, Alice and Adrien standing on either side. He turned off the lamp, thinking about his children, wanting to be there to tuck them in and read them a story about pirates or adventurers, to wake in the morning next to Stéphanie, to greet Maman in the kitchen as she handed him his morning coffee. At least, perhaps, they would be in his dreams.

In the next day's mail he received a reply from the Nourse Mill to his job application. The job involved maintaining the mill's electrical generators and the big 1200 horsepower Corliss steam turbine, which powered the shop's 40,000 spinners and other modern equipment. They wanted to interview him on Monday.

Things were going well. But all of that still didn't ease his terrible homesickness for Saint-Pierre.

OF COURSE, Paul immediately noticed the cemetery opposite the Tambois' house when he'd first arrived. It was impossible to miss. And when Francine had left him to settle into his room, he went first to look out the glass window to see what view it afforded him. The Cimetière de Sang Précieux, he read aloud. For an instant, he felt connected to Saint-Pierre, as if the land of the dead were one country and that one merely had to touch the soil of the cimetière here to reach the beloved souls waiting patiently in their tombs in Martinique. The tombs here varied in size, from ones barely larger than the single coffin they contained, to mausoleums accommodating several family members. Scattered among these were more humble graves simply marked by headstones. Statues of angels and saints climbed a gentle slope along with the graves and tombs as if they were all on a heavenward journey, though individually they had made no progress. For as long as he remained at the Tambois house, *Precious Blood* would be his anchor. Whenever he was restless and longing for home, he wandered along its paths and among the graves.

Sometimes he might stop for a conversation with his dead brother or Tata Elmire. He would have liked to have a talk with his Papa, but he stopped short of imagining the old man. He didn't know if he could bear those judgmental eyes.

Occasionally, he might sit on a low tomb and write in his journal or, as he did that evening, write to Stéphanie with the stylographic pen Maman had given him for bon voyage, along with a jar of ink and eyedropper for filling the pen. He would refill that original small bottle of ink several times by the time he left Woonsocket.

≈

17 DÉCEMBRE 1899

Dear Stéphanie,

I am here again among the silent ones, mostly undisturbed by the sounds of the city. If I look to the south, I can see Woonsocket, if I take a few steps to the north, I find myself in Blackstone, Massachusetts. I can stand with one foot in each state and not belong to either. I know it may seem strange, but here in this cemetery I feel close to Eustase and the Cimetiere du Eglise de le Fort, which brings me closer to you and the children. I do not try to make sense of it. My longing for you is a wound in me I keep raw by touching. In this way, I keep you and the children close. What would I be without my wound?

I must tell you that America is often unpleasant. It is cold and drab. The trees these long months have been barren of leaves. The Tambois family assures me that in the spring they will sprout new leaves. I cannot believe that these skeletons will ever be green again. I yearn for color! Even the clothes we all wear are dark grays or brown, if not the black of mourning.

Ah, my love, I shall write more later when I am not so sad. I am not always sad. It is just today. Imagine, it is only 4 o'clock and the sun is already dying in the west. A bitter wind has come up. My fingers are stiff and I must go back into the warmth of Francine and Frank's parlor. It will cheer me to sit by the wood-fired stove and warm up.

With all my love for you and the children.
Paul

A BUZZ of voices emerged from the living room as Paul re-entered the house. He would not be warming himself by the wood stove after all, it seemed. A meeting was in progress involving Francine and several of her friends who had formed a committee to ensure the voices of women were present in the Société Saint Jean-Baptiste d'Amérique that would soon have its first official meeting. He sat in the kitchen instead, where the cookstove radiated warmth, grateful that Francine had food baking in the oven.

Now and then he would hear one or another woman's voice, deeper or higher, louder than the rest through the door. From these, he gathered that the establishment of a national benefit society for the French in America was not the sole — or even the main — purpose for the meeting in the parlor. The door swung open as Francine came through to check on the cassoulet.

"Suffragettes put their immortal lives at risk!" rang out a voice behind her.

Francine stopped midway through the door. She stared at the woman who had spoken. "Are women slaves?" Francine asked, "Are we slaves? Have we no right to be human? Do we not have souls?"

Her voice was steady, but when she turned around, Paul

saw fury in her eyes. The door fell closed behind her. "Do you think God is cruel, Monsieur Poncy?"

"I don't know," he answered honestly. "Certainly, sometimes, such seems to be the case."

"I don't," Francine said firmly. "God is not cruel, men are, and women suffer for it." She pulled the cassoulet out of the oven and set it on the stovetop, turned around and paused before the swinging door to square her shoulders and march back into the fray in her parlor.

NOURSE MILL

At the intersection of Adams and Rathbun Street was a large house perched even closer to the Massachusetts state line than the Tambois residence. As he showed Paul around his home before dinner, Albert Bouley explained that the upstairs apartment was inhabited by the Lanois family, who were away for the weekend. Dolphus Lanois was a forty-two-year-old woolen weaver from Québec. His wife, Clara, was thirty-seven, and the couple had a four-year-old daughter named Florida. The Lanois family had lived in the United States for eighteen years. The Bouleys, who owned the house, lived on the main floor. The house had a single kitchen and dining room, where meals were shared by the families. Albert was a native of Rhode Island, and had inherited the house from his father, who migrated to the state from Canada earlier in the mid-1800s to find work in the mills. The Bouleys were a respected family in the community, and there were uncles and aunts and cousins scattered throughout New England and Quebec, some working in textiles, some farmers, and others, like Albert, in the skilled trades. Some spelled the name "Boulay" or "Boulet" or "Boulé" and some of the later generations spelled it "Bullet." But they were all the same extended family descended from early Québec pioneers who had originally settled in Montagny, on the Isle d'Orléans. The family maintained strong ties by meeting every few years — alternating between Montréal and Isle d'Orléans — for a huge family gathering.

Albert paused in his narrative and after a moment said, "So, what brings you to this country, Paul?"

"I've come to learn about the railroad industry," Paul said. "But first I must converse better in English. Lea Tambois has been giving me lessons."

"She is a bright girl," Albert said. "It's too bad she's trapped in that horrible job at the Nourse Mill, breathing that dust all night long."

"I know what you mean," Paul said, choosing not to mention his pending interview. "Everyone coughs. Frank comes home and hacks all night long as well."

Annie shook her head. "I hear unkind things about Nourse Mill. I think it's a disgrace, especially for children like Lea. They work ten-hour days, and six on Saturday, the same as an adult."

"I agree, Madame," Paul said, "but it's true everywhere. The hours are the same or worse in the rhum distilleries back home." He thought of the young black men manipulating 200 kilo drums at the mouillage.

"We are fortunate, you and I," Albert said. "So what is your next step, Paul?"

"First I will find work here in Woonsocket, but I'm expected to attend the Pan American Exposition next year for the family businesses. I may leave early for Buffalo, I hear they are paying well there."

"What businesses would those be?" Albert said, "If you don't mind my asking."

Paul paused, wondering how much to reveal about himself to strangers. But he'd taken a liking to Albert and his family, and it was really harmless knowledge. "There is rhum and sugar, of course. My cousin, Georges Plissonneau, is in the shipping business. He is trying to arrange some training for me. I'm interested in learning about the railroad. There may be a new locomotive manufacturing company forming in Manchester, New Hampshire in the next year if the American Locomotive Company merger goes through."

"Why the railroad?"

"A new railroad will be built in Martinique in a few years to transport the cane to Saint-Pierre from the Atlantic coast. And there are few skilled workers with the knowledge needed to make it a success. I've been interested in railroads since my school days, and so my cousins decided I should come here to learn and make business connections."

"So you plan to return?" said Annie.

Paul thought about this for a moment. Of course, he planned to return. But here he was in this huge country with its untamed West, opportunities and adventures waiting for him. He felt a sudden stab of guilt for thinking this. But of course he planned to return. It was his duty to his family. To his country, but mostly to his family who had sent him here. And to Stéphanie and his children. "Oui," he said, "my children are waiting for their Papa."

"So you are married," Annie said.

"Oui," he replied without hesitation. He considered himself married, even if there was no paper but his name on the birth certificate of his children. "I have two children and Stéphanie has two more. It's quite a ménagerie."

"You are so young for such a large family."

"That's what people keep telling me." It had never really occurred to him it might be a remarkable fact, although the men in his family like Papa had tended to marry much later in life to much younger women.

"You are thinking you will work at the Expo?" Albert said.

"Oui, the Expo is very important to Martinique. There will be businessmen from throughout North and South America gathered there. You should come, Albert. There will be plenty of carpentry work."

Annie glared at Paul but said nothing.

"I'll certainly consider that," Albert said, as his wife's daggers slid from Paul to her husband. "It sounds like an opportunity too good to miss."

THE NOURSE MILL was a massive three storey brick building between Social Street and the Social Mill pond. It was about a twenty-minute walk from Paul's house. The office door was distinct from the guarded mill entrance where the workers came and left. A young man greeted him, and when Paul told him his business, he was led to an empty office. "Mr. Jencks should be with you in a few moments," the young man said and offered him coffee, which he politely refused. He doubted that the cotton workers were offered refreshment. It was likely a distinction, a privilege reserved for skilled professionals.

After about ten minutes, a middle-aged man entered. He wore a dark blue sack suit with a matching vest and a high-collared white shirt. He was clearly not someone who walked the factory floor. "Bonjour, Monsieur Poncy," he said in American-accented French. "I am Arthur Jencks."

"Bonjour, Monsieur Jencks." Paul recalled from dinner conversation at the Tambois house that the Jencks family was one of the mill's consort of owners. "Pleased to meet you, sir."

"I am very impressed with your letters of recommendation, Paul. May I call you Paul?" He nodded assent, not feeling it was actually a question, but a statement of intent. "I see you have experience in a factory setting. Have you worked with a Corliss engine before?"

"Non," Paul replied, "but I have worked with a variety of steam engines and know the principles well."

"Very well," he said, "we will start you out under the master mechanic, who can assess your knowledge. Standard electrician's wages, $2.00 per day."

Was that all there was to it?

"Merci. When do I start?"

"Tomorrow morning, 6 am sharp. Now I will have Roger introduce you to the master mechanic."

THE YOUNG MAN who had met him at the door now led him to the millwright's office. On the way, they passed through a massive room where dozens of young women stood at machines, moving back and forth in monotonous repetition, guiding spindles of combed thread. The sound was the loud thrum, thrum, thrum of the turbine, the whirring and clatter of the machines, the hacking coughs of the girls as their spindles of coarse material were fed to the machinery to be spit out somewhere, eventually, as finely spun thread for the weavers. Paul could not see how the magic was done. He was on his way to what he knew to be the heart of the factory, the huge Corliss engine that powered everything in the shop.

They arrived at a room near the center of the factory where the thrumming of the turbine became nearly deafening. The room was greasy, with tools scattered everywhere. A short but beefy fellow sat at a small desk, his head bowed over a ledger of some sort. He looked up as Paul and his escort entered.

"This is your new man, Owen," said Roger in English. Then in French: "Paul Poncy, this is Owen Rouse. He's the millwright and master mechanic."

"Thank you, Roger," Owen said, and the young man left.

"Glad to meet you, Paul. I gather you don't speak English."

"Not well," Paul said.

"All right. French it is then. For now."

Owen showed him around the factory, pointing out electrical issues and connections that needed to be fixed or might become a problem. He showed Paul which conduits fed which machines, which row of lighting. Everywhere on their tour, Paul saw children working dangerous machines, amid a cacophony of hacking. Most of the workers in the weaving room were adult men and women. They too coughed in the dusty, fiber laden air.

Thankfully, he thought, *I won't stay here long.* But this job would get him through until he learned English. Until word arrived from Georges, and he could move on to something better.

The first few weeks exhausted him as he adjusted to the long hours, leaving well before dawn, arriving home as the sun was setting. It had been nearly two months since he'd worked a full shift anywhere, and never in his life had he worked in such miserable cold. The engine room of course was the warmest part of the mill, but most of his actual work was performed in the cold rooms where the spinners and the spindle girls toiled in the icy air, or in the weaving rooms, which were no warmer.

Like Frank and Lea, Paul found himself coughing after work some days when his lungs filled up with phlegm, trying to expel the foreign fibers from his body. He knew it would only become worse the longer he stayed, but for now, it was what he must do.

At night he would often rather go straight to bed after dinner, but Lea was insistent, dragging him to his lessons. He was happy that she was so dogged about keeping him focused. Frank was slowly coming around after their rough start, and occasionally they engaged in earnest conversation at the dinner table. Mostly rants about politics or working conditions. He seemed to have forgiven Paul his bourgeois family. Frank was a hard-working man, and he respected other hard-working men. And their views were more similar than different, it seemed.

As the end of the year approached, Lea began to throw out hints about going to see the fireworks in Providence for New Years Eve. "It is the fin de siècle," she insisted, "it will only come around once in my lifetime."

Frank was having none of it. "Non. It is going to be a big drunken brawl, not fit for a young girl."

"Besides," Paul said with a wink, "the real fin de siècle is not for another year."

Lea huffed. "Everyone is celebrating *this* year. You are all a bunch of wet blankets."

Funny how a fourteen-year-old can make you feel like an old man, Paul thought. But Frank nudged him and said, "Good one, Paul."

PAUL MEETS Lea coming off shift most mornings as he's going on, looking haggard and spent. She greets him with a weak smile, not enough energy for words. He smiles back and punches in his time. He passes by the young girls at their spindles, hacking and coughing in the dirty air on his way to the shop where Owen Rouse assigns him his daily duties. Then he goes about his work, stringing new conduit, replacing frayed cables, repairing a circuit, an electric motor. Occasionally, he is allowed to help with repairs to the Corliss, but not today.

His erratically timed break for lunch coincided with that of the spinners, as it did every so often. He made his way outside to the yard where a few of the girls shivered in the November cold, smoking cigarettes. One of them, an older girl who had flirted with him a few times, approached him for a cigarette. Paul couldn't remember her name, Rachel or Michelle or something. He handed her the pack of French cigarettes and lighted one for her. She passed the pack of cigarettes back and smiled. "Merci," she said. He lit one for himself, and the two stood smoking, silent for a while, before she spoke.

"Will you be taking over the lead's place?" she said, as he bent close, straining to understand her Québec French. She was talking about Ben, the lead electrician, who was leaving at the end of the year. "Non," he said. "I have no seniority."

"Seniority," she snorted, "doesn't mean anything 'round here." She sounded bitter.

"Well, I'm not interested really, in any case," he said.

"I don't blame you. This is no place to stay if you've got skills."

"Oui," he said, "I suppose not. Why do you stay?" He wished he could remember her name, but it was still not coming to him.

"I've got a little one to feed," she said, "and Maman is sick — consumption — so she can't work anymore."

"I'm sorry to hear that."

"Yeah, ain't we both?" she said, throwing down her cigarette and shuffling back inside.

He finished his own cigarette, feeling bad for the girls here, feeling just a little ashamed at his own privileged position. He'd no more earned it really than these poor girls earned their lot.

The more he thought about it, the more he convinced himself he should leave this job as soon as possible.

An adventure in Buffalo sounded like just the thing to bring him out of his doldrums.

⁓

PREMIER JANVIER 1900

My Dear Stéphanie,

I hope the new year finds everyone well in Saint-Pierre. I finally have warm clothing and I am becoming accustomed to this cold weather, although, to tell you the truth, I would rather be home with you in Saint-Pierre and never see snow again. You can't go outside without bundling up. For Christmas, Francine knitted a nice scarf to keep my neck warm.

The Tambois family dragged me to midnight mass at Saint Ann on Christmas morning. I have to say I was reluctant, but it turned out to be a pleasant walk and there was only a Latin mass, no sermon from Father Napoléon, thank God. We had a nice Christmas dinner with ham and potatoes and something called a green bean casserole. Francine made an English bread pudding. Christmas in North America is very different. It is too cold to sit outdoors as we do at home, so everyone gathers around a fireplace with a roaring fire. They had an evergreen tree, much larger than those little ones that are imported to Saint-Pierre, and it was very extravagantly decorated with candles and tinsel and little carved figures of angels.

Did you receive the gifts I sent for the children? Please give my love to them, and to Maman.

As Always,
Your Paul

. . .

PAUL SET his pen aside and, after the ink had dried, carefully folded the letter and placed it into the envelope addressed to *Mme Stéphanie Grainau, Rue Saint-Denis, No 7, Saint-Pierre, Martinique.* He would leave it for Francine to post in the morning. He put out the light on his small desk and sat in the dark.

He thought about work in the morning and the girls shivering at their spindles in the brutal cold as he warmed up in the engine room with a cup of coffee in his hand, going over the day's routine with Owen and the other men. Many of those girls were not much more than children, some underage, he was certain. Some might even be as young as Alice. The state required children under fourteen to be in school, but many poor families ignored this, sending their children to the factories, and the factory owners willingly took them, knowing they were breaking the law, certain the value of the work they extracted outweighed the penalty of getting caught.

There had been union talk, but when a half-dozen girls were let go after being overheard by a supervisor, complaints died down on the floor. But Paul sensed an uneasiness when he talked to the girls on their machines, a bitterness in their hardened faces at the unfairness of the world.

And he thought about his own children at home in their bourgeois comfort. Alice at eleven didn't need to worry about life in a factory. He never wanted her or little Yvonne to have such worries. And he wanted the same for these girls, but there was nothing he could do about it, was there?

HE DREAMS AGAIN, nearly every night, that he is clinging for his life over a bouillon of writhing snakes, and a dark hand reaches for him from above as the black snow falls, settling in his hair and on his face. *You must let go, Priest. Grab my hand,* calls the voice above him.

Instead, he clings tighter.

Non, he says. Emphatic.

It's your funeral, Monsieur.

Sylbaris laughs.

The laughter echoes in his mind as he wakens to find himself clinging to a liana of twisted bed linen, sweating in the cold night.

LEA

Each night Lea faithfully sat with Paul for English lessons between his shift at the mill and her own. He was very grateful for her dedication and worried a little that it was too much for her to tutor him and then work for ten hours. But her enthusiasm for the lessons never wavered. She sat beside him as they read the English newspaper from Providence until one day he became aware she had brought her chair much closer to his and their thighs were nearly touching. He was dismayed by how this affected him and that his first thought was, *she is sweet on me.* She was a fairly attractive young woman, not so plain as he first thought. Not exactly pretty, perhaps, but there are other qualities which make a woman attractive. And he was a young man, attractive enough himself, he supposed. And each evening the two of them sat alone together while Francine was in the kitchen and Frank not yet home from work. The more he thought about it, the more he noticed the way Lea smiled at him, the coquettish way her eyes fell to the floor when she noticed him looking at her. Couldn't he have predicted this? She was just a girl. He did not want to hurt her or cause trouble.

Maybe if he brought up his family, reminded her he was not

available. Just in case that was what she was thinking. Then, before he knew it, it was time for her to go to work and she was closing up the books and putting them on the shelf. She smiled at him apologetically, and gave him a little wave. "Bonsoir, Paul," and she was gone.

The next evening he brought down the new photograph that Stéphanie had sent him to their session. It was taken in the parlor of the Poncy home, and there was his Stéphanie with Maman and the children before a white plaster wall with a portrait of Papa behind them. Before Lea was about to leave, he removed it from his pocket. "I thought you might like to see a photograph of Stéphanie and our children. That's Maman," he said, pointing her out. "And these are Alice, eleven, and Adrien, six. André Paul is three and our little baby girl is Yvonne."

Lea had a funny look on her face. "They're negroes," she said.

He was taken aback by her response. mulâtre, he wanted to correct, but he had already learned that North Americans had no subtlety about these things. "Oui," he said instead, "Most Martiniquais are, you know."

"Oh," she said, looking embarrassed. "I don't mean... it's just... you would not want to show these to people around here. People in this country are very prejudiced." She seemed to exclude herself from that category.

"But how is it possible you have an eleven-year-old daughter?" she said, abruptly changing the subject.

"Alice and Adrien are not really mine. Not by blood. Mine are the youngest two."

"Stéphanie seems older than you." She said it matter-of-factly, as though assessing what this might mean. Then she stood suddenly. "I must get ready for work." She rushed out the door without saying goodnight.

~

LEA CANCELED the next few English lessons, giving flimsy excuses, and Paul became dismayed. Surely the girl hadn't really fallen for him. But she was fourteen and he remembered a bit about being young and full of romantic notions. He winced as the memory of Sophie arose. Maybe he should have brought up his family earlier, but he was so intent on learning English that it really hadn't occurred to him.

When Lea called off their lessons for the third day at the dinner table, Francine took him aside after dinner. "She just has a temporary infatuation with you, I'm afraid. She was disappointed to learn you are married. Give her a few days." Francine gave him an intense look, not quite disapproving, but concerned. "You do not wear a wedding ring?" It was a question.

Suddenly Paul was embarrassed. No, he had no ring. He was suddenly aware of the cultural differences between North America and Martinique, how much easier it was there to have an easy, unsanctioned relationship. He didn't know what to say.

"Are you not married?" asked Francine. "Is she your paramour?"

"Oui, our relationship is not officially sanctioned by the Church," he admitted. Stéphanie was more than a paramour, he wanted to add, but didn't. She was his wife, married or not.

Francine nodded. "Forgive a young girl for having her hopes. She will get over it."

"Oui," he said. But now he had something more to think about. Something more to tease his Catholic guilt when he was enticed by an attractive young woman while far from home. He was not married, after all. Not civilly and, perhaps more important to these Catholic Americans, not in the eyes of the Church.

LEA HADN'T ENTIRELY GIVEN up. When her maman told her that Stéphanie was Paul's paramour, it rekindled her hopes a little. Although she was not sure what she thought about the whole mistress thing. And a colored mistress at that. She might have been born in libertine France, but she had lived in the USA almost all of her life. Rich people do that kind of thing, especially in metropolitan France where it isn't even particularly frowned upon, but a good Catholic girl who worked in the mills of Woonsocket cannot be so laissez-faire about her reputation.

The thing that most attracted her to Paul was that he was a man with a future. That he was thoughtful and intelligent only made him that much more desirable.

And her maman seemed to encourage her.

We can forgive Francine for being both an outspoken Suffragette and, at the same time, a mother whose daughter was destined for the textile mills. It was a difficult place for a mother to be. And who was this colored girl waiting for Paul on his tropical island? Surely he wasn't serious about that, was he?

When Lea resumed Paul's English lessons, she had a plan of sorts to spend more time with him. Paul would soon need to try out his English in the real world, in a place where most people speak the language. Unlike their Québécois friends, who seemed stuck in their cloistered little world, mingling only with like-minded, French-speaking neighbors, the Tambois family had been more venturesome in their lives, striving to learn English and associate with English-speakers as well. Lea's father and mother had immigrated to America to become citizens, and they rejected the conservative Catholic philosophy of La Survivance, so important to the Québécois. Not that they wished to lose their Frenchness, but they saw a future in their Americanness.

So, one day Lea took a deep breath to calm her racing heart and said to Paul, "I think we should go into Providence next Saturday and practice your English." *It will be a little like a date,* she thought, wondering if Maman would insist on a chaperone. They would need to be back by 8 pm for work, but on Saturday Paul left work at noon so there was all afternoon. "We could take the train and return in time for dinner," she said.

"Oui, I would enjoy that."

"I will talk to Maman," Lea was already imagining the two of them together, walking the romantic avenues of the city, eating at some quaint little café, his hand in hers as they strolled along a riverside promenade.

Now she just had to get this plan by Maman.

NOW THAT HE had straightened out Lea's misconception about his availability, Paul, too, was excited about going into Providence to practice his English and to see the city. He couldn't imagine Frank going along, but he envisioned a nice afternoon with Francine and Lea. He would like to see the famous Rhode Island School of Design and visit its galleries.

"Maman said a week from Saturday would be fine," Lea reported at their next meeting. "The weather is often beautiful in mid-May. I think Maman wants to talk to you about it first though."

"Of course. I would expect nothing less. I will speak to her after our lesson."

Francine stood at the kitchen sink scrubbing the dirty dishes when Paul sought her out. He remained in the kitchen doorway for a moment, watching her systematically wash, rinse, stack, repeat. Like the women at the factory, he thought.

"Lea says you want to talk to me about our outing to Providence?" he said at last.

"Oui." She put aside her dish cloth and, turning to face him, searched his face for a time before speaking. "You are a fine young man," she said, being careful and deliberate with her words. "I know you're honorable and a gentleman. I just want to give you a reminder. You will be alone in the city with my daughter, and as much as she believes she knows the world, she is still a vulnerable young girl. So I am counting on you to take care of her."

"Are you not going with us, Madame?" said Paul.

"I have a women's meeting that day. Lea knows her way around Providence. You do not need me."

He didn't know what to say. Wouldn't the straight-laced Christians of Providence be shocked at a young man and woman together, unmarried, unescorted? It would be a scandal among the fine families of Saint-Pierre, but this was a working class family and even back home that made a difference. It hadn't been his plan to be alone with this headstrong girl who clearly fancied him. Sophie and Saint-Pierre sat there on his mind again and he had a sudden flash of longing. Like Lea, she had been a strong-willed girl with a suffragist mother wanting her daughter to be self-assured and independent. Look at what trouble that had gotten him into.

Why am I even thinking about these things? I was only a boy back then. I am more mature now and in control of my desires, he thought. But it had been so long since he'd put them to the test.

"Oui, Madame," he said, assurance in his voice, if not his thoughts. "You have nothing to worry about. I will protect her with my life."

And, of course, he would.

~

ON SATURDAY, Paul arrived home to find Lea waiting and ready. She'd donned a pretty, rose patterned spring dress he'd never seen before. It looked new, as though she had just pulled it from the store rack. She was very fetching in an almost adult way. Her eagerness made him uneasy.

Of course, he'd just arrived from the shop where he'd been repairing an electrical motor. He must bathe and put on a change of clothing.

"I've just prepared your bath, Paul," said Lea. "And Mama will have lunch waiting for us when you come out."

"Oui, merci," said Paul, then in English: "Thank you, Lea. You look very nice, by the way."

"Thank you," she said in English with a little whirl to show off her dress.

The steaming tub felt wonderfully relaxing. How nice it was to come home to a bath already prepared and lunch waiting. He thought about the afternoon ahead of him and wondered what Stéphanie would think if she knew he was going out on the town with a young woman. Would she be jealous? Would she be expecting it? Would she laugh and tell him how bourgeois his concerns were?

Then it occurred to him he was making a big deal of nothing. Lea was a nice girl, his host's daughter, who was giving him English lessons, and if she was sweet on him, that was just because she was learning to be a woman, and it was kind of delightful to have a young girl swooning over you. As long as he was vigilant and didn't let his longings rule his behavior.

He put on his nice white dress shirt and his best jacket, and descended the stairs to the kitchen, where Francine had set out sandwiches and lemonade. Lea smiled at him sweetly and held out the sandwich plate.

~

IT WAS a beautiful sunny May afternoon in Providence, a little on the warm side, when Paul and Lea stepped off the train. The new Union Station, a majestic yellow brick building barely two years old, stood on Railroad Terrace. Behind it rose the State Capitol building. Just to the east were Market Square and the Providence River. On the other side of the river was the Rhode Island School of Design and the Charles Pendleton House, which was sponsoring a student exhibit. This was the direction they strolled, Lea on his arm, the two of them gawking like the tourists they were.

Market Square bustled with commerce on Saturday afternoon. Some vendors with horse-drawn wagons had set up on the edge of the square. People were everywhere, strolling in the sunshine and along the east bank of the narrow river inlet to the south where the river emerged from underneath the pavement. A tram climbed slowly up College Hill to Brown University. The dirty river carried the effluent of factories and sewers, like all the rivers he'd seen in America. On most days, the Roxelane was clean enough for the washerwomen of Saint-Pierre to clean clothes and linens in it. He couldn't imagine anyone washing anything in this river. Along the west bank, he saw slips and concrete quays where steamboats unloaded coal, freight, and industrial cargoes. Everything was black with coal dust.

Despite the filth and the noxious odor of the river, Paul was awestruck by Providence. It was a real city. A place with so many people you could lose yourself among them. Not a town like Saint-Pierre or Woonsocket.

"Mon Dieu," he exclaimed and Lea gently squeezed his arm. "We only speak English today," reminding him of their previous agreement.

He laughed and leaned in close to her. "Surely, I can be surprised in French, Mademoiselle."

"Well, I suppose." She grinned. "But it's my job to keep you honest, Mister Poncy."

The mock formality heightened a sense of intimacy between them, and Paul dwelt on the young woman on his arm. He was too much of a gentleman to take advantage of a lovesick young girl, but containing his thoughts was another matter altogether, and soon they were troubling him. Maybe coming to the city with Lea hadn't been such a good idea.

AFTER VISITING the museum and gallery, Lea led him to a café for pastry, a place where she had once eaten with her mother. She sat much too close to him at the table like a wife or an amour, he thought, not an English tutor. She leaned in close to his ear and whispered, "You must order for us. And no help with the English."

He turned to reply, but she didn't retreat, and he suddenly found her lips a few inches from his own. Her breath on his. Paul pivoted back to the menu. "I will try," he said, embarrassed. "Please tell me what you would like."

"You choose," she said.

He looked at the menu in confusion, trying to remember Lea's preferences. Finally, he gave up trying to make sense of the menu and when the waiter came around ordered coffee and fig and almond galettes.

"Galettes, my favorite," Lea said, leaning into him again. "This has been a wonderful day, Paul." Her breath in his ear was making him crazy. He wished to move away, put just a little more distance between them. But that would be even more awkward. He was thankful when the food finally came and her focus shifted from him to her plate.

After the café, she took him to a park across from the train station. She saved some crumbs for the pigeons and they sat on a park bench like lovers tossing offerings out to the birds and soon he was forgetting who this enticing young woman next to him was when she laid her hand on his chest and bent her face up to his, inviting his kiss. And without thinking, he leaned in until his lips were almost touching hers before he realized what he was doing.

He straightened up.

"Non," he said, reverting to French. "Je ne peux pas. This is not right, Lea."

"But it's what I want," she said, pouting her lips.

"You are only a child." He regretted the words immediately when he saw the hurt on her face. He added, "You're a lovely girl, Lea, but I have a family back home."

On the train trip back to Woonsocket, Lea attempted to hide her disappointment, but he could tell it wouldn't be the same between them any longer. He wanted to say some magic words to put things back the way they were, but he didn't know any.

PAUL AND ALBERT MAKE PLANS

Annie Bouley ladled another serving of thick beef stew onto the plate Paul Poncy held up to the heavy cast-iron pot. She had mixed feelings about this young Martiniquais. He was charming and well-mannered. You couldn't help but like him, yet he was French in a way they were not and this made her wonder why they had clung to the French culture and language, because they were Americans weren't they? But more than that, it was how his very presence had encouraged Albert to go from merely thinking and talking about the Pan American Expo to making actual plans. Albert was caught up in the excitement and novelty of the exposition. Annie didn't want to be one of those bitter, resentful wives, but she couldn't help being unhappy when she thought about Albert in Buffalo for the better part of a year. And that was another thing about Paul, he'd left his family behind. Didn't Albert say just the other night when she told him she didn't like the idea of him being gone so long, that "it will be less than a year and I will be home again. Many men, like Paul, must leave their families for much longer to make a better future for them."

It would be one thing if the money was as good as they

claimed, but how many times had men been lured away from their homes on such promises only to find their expenses far greater than any gain? How much of that money would be spent carousing in Buffalo before it even came home? There was plenty of work around Woonsocket for a carpenter. Annie would keep her silence in front of their dinner guest. It was bad enough airing their laundry with the Lanois family at the table. She would ladle out the beef stew and be proud there was plenty of it to share with company.

"I can't leave before July," Paul said. "And I need to explore living arrangements in Manchester before I go."

"So," Dolphus Lanois said, "you are moving up to New Hampshire after this?"

"It's uncertain. But they manufacture locomotives there, and it's my goal to work in the railroad industry."

"So, you will be... what? An engineer? A foundry man?"

"I hope to become a machinist. I have some experience in that area already."

"That will be good pay," Dolphus said. "Many of those shops are union. I wish the woolen weavers here would wake up. There's a lot of union talk, but there are not enough members yet to take on management."

"Same at the Nourse Mill, according to Frank," said Paul. "A lot of the weavers and spinners have union cards, but they're afraid to talk on the floor. Some girls were fired there several weeks ago."

"And the damned priests, Dolphus," Albert said, "are doing everything they can to keep you from challenging the bosses."

Paul had the impression this has been a longstanding conversation between Albert and Dolphus.

Clara Lanois gave Albert a look. "You shouldn't be blaspheming the priests, young man. They're only trying to defend our French culture."

"Nonsense, Clara," said Albert. "They're only defending the bosses. Did you hear what Father Napoléon said this morning? 'The socialists are doing the devil's work.' Foutaise."

"Albert," rebuked Annie, "There's no need to be impolite at the dinner table."

"Pardon my language, Madame," Albert said. "But I stand by my opinion."

ALBERT AND PAUL decided to leave in late October, before the snowy season arrived. They would winter in Buffalo, where much indoor carpentry and electrical work was promised, putting in place the final touches for the Pan American Expo.

Paul bided his time at the Nourse Mill until August, when two more girls were fired for union talk on the shop floor. Angered, Paul gave his notice earlier than planned. When Owen Rouse handed him a letter of recommendation the next day, he felt a small stab of regret that he didn't speak up for those girls. He didn't really need that letter from his supervisor when he had better ones from home in his trunk. But what was done was done and his protest was unlikely to mean anything to those girls now.

Albert found him a few odd jobs to tide him over for the weeks until they left, mostly small piecework jobs installing and repairing wiring in homes and apartment buildings for the Elliott Gas and Electric Company. This was the same work he would have likely been doing in Saint-Pierre had he stayed. The pay averaged about $2 a day, a little less than his pay at the mill, but more than adequate for his needs. Enough to continue sending home $30 each month to Stéphanie.

He would like to send home more, and once they were in Buffalo, he'd be able to do that. Electricians there made at least

$2.50 to start. And he would be living in inexpensive worker's accommodations during his stay for pennies a day.

Paul took to meeting Albert after work at the Monument Hotel billiards room for a beer and a game. The hotel was just around the corner from the Elliott Company and right on the Social Street tramway. They were gone only an hour or two longer than if they'd come home straight from work, but Annie didn't like it and Paul feared she had started to view him as a bad influence on her husband.

"Damn it, Paul," Albert complained when Paul expressed his concern, "I work fifty-six hours a week to buy food and coal for the winter, and to pay for the roof over her head. I think I deserve to go out and have a beer after work with my neighbor. It's not like I'm staying out all night every night getting myself snockered like some of these men do."

Paul gave him a sympathetic nod. "I don't want to cause any trouble with Annie."

"You're not the cause, and she knows it," Albert said, his eyes on the backside of the young woman who brought their beer and was now waiting on another table across the room. "It's just that she thinks if you weren't here I'd not have anyone to run off to Buffalo with. That's how she sees it. That I'm running off."

Is that what Stéphanie thought? Paul wondered. *That I ran off? Is that what I did?*

"Maybe I am," Albert said, as though reading his mind. "I mean, not really, but I become so tired of listening to Father Napoléon's pious sermons every damned Sunday. And all this talk of La Survivance this and La Survivance that, and how the unions are our enemy, trying to Americanize us and strip us of our Frenchness. Week after week, he serves that shit. And everyone else just eats it up."

"So you understand why I don't attend mass often?" Paul offered Albert a wry smile.

"Oui."

When the time finally arrived to go, Francine agreed to store his trunk until he returned from Buffalo. "It will be no problem, really. I have a closet with some free space."

"Merci," he said. "I am not sure what I will do when I return, I'm afraid. I know you must rent out the room. Please don't hold it for me."

"I'm sorry that you are leaving, Paul," said Francine. "You have been such a good tenant. If your room is available when you return, you will always be welcome in my house."

BUFFALO GALS

THE PRETTY YOUNG woman at the bar in The White Lion had been flirting with Albert for most of the past hour. Paul was impatient to leave, tired of his friend's divided attention. Finally he stood, signaling his intent.

"We're here alone, Paul. It's Saturday night in the city. Why don't we have some fun?" Albert leaned toward Paul and whispered, "I'll wager she has a friend."

What about Annie? Paul wanted to ask, but just shook his head and let the occasion pass. He didn't want his companion to see him as prudish, because he wasn't. Paul had been deflecting Albert almost since they stepped on the train in Woonsocket three weeks ago. Albert, it seemed, viewed their time in Buffalo as a chance to sow some wild oats. "Sorry, Albert, but I must go home. I'm tired."

"Father Napoléon would be proud," Albert groused.

Paul chafed, remembering his brothers and cousins teasing him in his school days. Calling him *Father Paul.* He conjured up an image of Sylbaris for an uncomfortable moment. "Priest," Ludger had called him. Was he really that pious person they all made him out to be?

"Go on home." Albert dismissed him with a flap of his hand, "I can manage on my own."

Paul threw some change on the table and turned to leave as Albert ordered another dram of whiskey. He ambled up Main Street toward the Elmwood Street Tram stop. He and Albert shared a room at a boarding house called The Millard Fillmore, at Virginia and Park Street in the Allentown neighborhood. There wasn't a curfew, but no women were permitted in the rooms, which mostly housed skilled itinerant workers in town for the Expo construction. He wondered when or if Albert would turn up tonight. It was still early, not yet 8 pm, and the well-lit sidewalks in the city center were busy with pedestrians on their way home after a beer or some shopping. Motor cabs and horse-drawn carriages plied the streets around the hotels. The bars were still mostly quiet, but they'd become rowdy in a few hours when the hard-working young laborers had a few more under the belt. Paul didn't really want to be out then.

He arrived at the tram stop just as the car pulled up. He climbed on board and tossed his nickel in the hopper. A young woman climbed aboard behind him, out of breath from running. Paul began to sit in the only available seat, then decided to do the gentlemanly thing and offer it to her. "Please," he said, gesturing with a sweep of his hand. The woman, he noticed, was very attractive, with dark, wavy hair, cropped in a short modern style. She wore a blue wool overcoat and a colorful scarf. With her hoop earrings she looked tastefully bohemian. A career girl, he guessed.

She sat down and smiled at him. "Thank you."

"Je vous en prie, Mademoiselle," he said, forgetting his English.

"You are French," she said. This surprised him. People usually asked if he was Canadian, unable to distinguish one accent from another.

"Oui," he said.

"Mais vous n'êtes pas de la Métropole," she said in perfect French. *But you are not from the Métropole.*

"Non," he said. "Martinique."

"Les Antilles," she said. "How interesting. Are you here for the Expo?"

"In a way," he said. "I am an electrician."

"Ah, a working man." She put her hand out. "Amanda Laviolette. Magazine writer."

He took her hand. "Pleased to meet you, Amanda. I am Paul Poncy."

"Nice meeting you as well, Paul." She fished in her bag, removed a calling card, and handed it to him. "I would love to interview you for an article I'm working on. The Expo."

He was about to ask her why she would want to interview *him* when he realized he'd gone past his stop. He vaguely recalled the streetcar turning onto Virginia Street, but he didn't remember it turning again onto Elmwood at all. But now they were approaching Allen Street. "I must get off here, Mademoiselle—I've passed my stop," he said, flustered by the broken conversation and his broken English. Not to mention the confusion he was feeling about this young woman.

"Goodbye, Paul," she said, smiling at him again. "Please call me."

HE WAS NOT TROUBLED about missing his stop. He was not really in a hurry to return to his dark room. He was more troubled by his reaction to this lovely young woman and her smile, which reached all the way up into those lovely sparkling eyes. His heart raced. He'd nearly decided to remain on the streetcar and ride it to wherever she got off. Now she must think he was a fool for forgetting his stop.

As he made his way back down Elmwood to Virginia Street, Paul examined the card he still held in his hand. It read: *Amanda Laviolette, Independent Writer,* followed by a telephone number. Was there a telephone at the boarding house? He realized he didn't know. He wanted to call her right away. Explain his absent-mindedness. *"I'm not usually like this, Miss Laviolette. I rarely stumble all over myself when confronted by a pretty face."*

Just like that, he'd forgotten where and who he was. *Does it really take so little for me to forget Stéphanie and our beautiful children waiting for me in Saint-Pierre? What kind of man am I?* Even so, he knew Stéphanie would not fault him his oeil errant. She might be jealous, but she'd shrug at his meaningless bourgeois scruples, which, after all, are only meant to apply to wives and daughters. And mistresses. And the poor, of course. But these qualms were ingrained in him in a way he couldn't explain. Even before he attended seminary he possessed a keen sense about the hypocrisies in the world around him and the fact that well-to-do men like his father were permitted to do as they pleased, while their wives and children and mistresses must obey God's will. *I am not them. I will not be a hypocrite.* If to be faithful is God's will, then shouldn't he be held to the same standard? And even if he didn't believe in God's immutable will, and even if Stéphanie herself rejected that suspect dogma, Paul felt the guilt. The Fathers and the Sisters of the Church had done a fine job.

There was no telephone in the boarding house lobby, and he knew he wouldn't have picked it up and called even if there had been one. In his room, he removed his boots and trousers and turned back his bed covers. He switched on the bedside lamp, climbed under the blankets, and picked up his tattered copy of

La Fortune des Rougon, which he was reading for the third time. When he tries to picture the fiery young Myette, marching at the head of the peasant rebels, he sees the face of Amanda Laviolette, and it is this image that lingers in his mind as he drifts off to sleep.

IN HIS DREAM he finds himself once more clinging to a liana, and below, instead of the snake pit, stands Amanda Laviolette, smiling at him through the mist. Above, he makes out the faces of the children, Alice Germaine and Adrien and André Paul and Yvonne, who is older in his dream and looks just like Alice, all gripping the liana as if it is a rope to keep him from falling.

"Hang on, Papa," cries Yvonne. "We will rescue you."

Standing beside Yvonne is Stéphanie, her face painted in grim fear, as they all try unsuccessfully to pull him to safety.

And behind them all stands Sylbaris, laughing. "It's no use, Priest," he says between guffaws, "you should have taken the hand I offered. You are lost now."

11 NOVEMBRE, *1900*

My Dearest Stéphanie,

It has been two weeks since last I wrote to you. I am in Buffalo, where I am working for the Pan American Exposition. As I wrote earlier, it is well-paying work and I will increase the amount I am sending to you monthly to 40 Francs, at least for the time I am here in Buffalo. I trust this is adequate for your needs. Please let me know if it is not.

Albert and I have found lodging at a worker's boardinghouse, which is conveniently near the tramway. There are trams every-

where in Buffalo and much of the city has electric lighting. It's amazing to see in the evening, when buildings and streets are alight.

Buffalo is a rowdy town, much like Saint-Pierre in that way, although many times larger. The Expo, as they call it, has brought hundreds of temporary workers, skilled and unskilled, and many are young and uneducated men. On weekends, the bars and brothels fill up with these men, who spend the little they earn on gambling and debauchery. Fights frequently break out on the streets, and there are strikes here and there almost every week. The police can be very brutal in America, but I guess that is not really all that different from Martinique.

I attended Mass this morning, something I rarely do anymore. The sermon was in Polish, so I did not stay after the liturgy. My English is getting better, but, ironically, everyone in this town seems to speak a different language.

Please give kisses to my beautiful children, my love.

Always,

Your Paul

AMANDA LAVIOLETTE REMAINED on his mind the following Saturday after work. He'd misplaced the card she'd given him, and he'd turned his belongings inside out trying to find it. But it was truly and irrevocably gone, it seemed. And now he was consumed with finding her again. He didn't dare share this with Albert, not after their recent conversations and his unkind thoughts about Albert's philandering. Although, he didn't know if Albert had actually followed through with that young woman last Saturday. He came back late and quite drunk. But he came back.

Now, all Paul could think about was repeating his steps

from the previous Saturday hoping to meet her again on the streetcar. But he quickly realized the futility of that course of action. He admonished himself for losing her card.

He and Albert sat in the building lobby considering their evening out, when Albert said, "I think we ought to go up to that tavern on Bryant Street for a drink tonight. What do you think?"

They had noticed the place, just off the tram line, soon after they'd arrived in Buffalo. It was called the Commonweal Tavern. The two of them agreed to go there sometime and see what it was like. Not that there was a shortage of taverns in Buffalo, not even along the Elmwood line, but the Commonweal seemed different, a converted house, freshly painted in bright colors. Boho. A slightly more fashionable neighborhood than the working class tenements of lower Allentown.

Now it seemed to him, this was the kind of place a girl like Amanda might go. And, even if not, it would be a different world from the sawdust and beer-stained floors of the down-town saloons, or the quiet hotel bars they were used to, such as The White Lion.

"I'm game," he said. "I'm sick of those hotel bars, anyway."

"Yes," Albert said, too readily.

"You embarrassed yourself with the young lady last week?" Paul guessed.

"Non, I never got up the gumption to do more than flirt a little. Some carouser I am, huh?"

Paul laughed.

THE COMMONWEAL TAVERN met Paul's expectations. Its wooden floors were covered in oriental rugs and colorful tapestries hung from its walls. One wall was covered with flyers for seances and salons and workers' gatherings. A gypsy band, comprising a fiddler and an accordionist, played lively dance music, and a few young couples whirled on the small dance floor. They were dressed in the colorful rags of vagabonds, but they seemed well fed, not poor. The bartender was a woman of mixed race, about Stéphanie's age, and he was reminded for a moment of Saint-Pierre.

"This is quite a place," Albert said, as they edged up to the bar.

"Oui," Paul agreed, and turning to the bartender said, "I would like a beer, s'il-vous-plaît. And one for my friend."

"Vous êtes français," she replied.

"Oui. Je suis de la Martinique."

"Really," she said in English. "My maman came here from Guadeloupe. I'm Celeste Montagne. I am a co-owner of this establishment."

"Pleased to meet you, Mademoiselle Montagne," he said. "I am Paul Poncy. This is quite a place."

"Are you new in town? I don't believe I've seen you here before."

"Oui," he said. "Albert and I work at the Expo. I am an electrician."

"So," she said, handing them their beers, "a bringer of light. Welcome to Buffalo."

"Merci." He paid for the drinks and tossed a tip on the bar.

They found a table in the back, away from the music, where they could talk, but Paul wasn't really in the mood for conversation. He couldn't take his mind off Amanda Laviolette, so he listened to the gypsy music, his head turning toward the door each time someone arrived. He knew this obsession was silly, but he couldn't focus on anything else.

Soon, Albert noticed his distraction. "Do you have something on your mind, my friend?"

"Non," Paul said, turning his head toward the door when another patron walked in.

"Are you expecting someone? Perhaps someone more entertaining than your boring friend, Albert?"

"Désolé," Paul said, "I am just distracted."

"What is her name?" Albert winked.

Paul expelled a deep sigh. He'd been caught.

"No one, really," he said.

"If you say. But you've been mopey all week."

"Her name is Amanda," Paul admitted. "I met her on the streetcar last Saturday."

A stupid grin crossed Albert's face. "I believe Father Paul is in love."

He should never have told Albert that story. Embarrassed, Paul rose without responding and sauntered over to the bar. He rarely had more than a beer or two, but tonight he was determined to drink this woman out of his head. He perched on a bar stool, ignoring his friend at the table.

"Another one?" Celeste Montagne asked.

"Oui. And one more for my friend. May I ask you a question?"

"Of course. I may not answer it, but you can always ask."

"Do you know a magazine writer named Amanda Laviolette?"

"Of course. Amanda is here often with the Rubaiyat Club. Sometimes she comes to listen to music or dance, as well."

"The Rubaiyat Club?"

"It's a literary salon," she said. "They meet here about once a month on a Sunday. There is often a speaker."

"That sounds interesting." With a twinge of guilt, he was again reminded of Saint-Pierre and Stéphanie's salon. Everything led back home.

"How do you know Amanda?" Celeste asked.

"I met her last week. She gave me her card, but I lost it. She wanted to interview me about my job at the Expo."

"I will mention that you asked after her. Is there a way for her to contact you?" He thought about that. He had no telephone, and women were not allowed in the Millard, as they called it.

"Non," he said. "But this place is on my way from work, so perhaps I can stop by now and again, if you wouldn't mind being a go-between."

"Sure," Celeste said. "I'll let her know."

So much, he thought, for forgetting about Amanda Laviolette in drink.

ON WEDNESDAY, a powerful storm blew down the War Cyclorama exhibit hall on the west edge of the Expo grounds. The storm arose quickly about noon, and within a short time winds reached 80 mph. Several dozen men, mostly carpenters and laborers, narrowly avoided serious injury when the unfinished building collapsed, scattering wind-tossed lumber and debris across the fairgrounds.

Paul was working inside the electrical building, listening to the howling wind as he cut a length of conduit, wondering if the contractors would suspend construction until the storm passed. Without warning, the structure shook violently and a horrible clamor ensued outside as debris slammed the side of the building. He ran to the doorway and threw open the door. He knew better than to go outside in a strong storm, but the building was unfinished and he worried about the integrity of its structure as it strained against the gale. The ferocious wind reminded him of the '91 hurricane in Saint-Pierre, which had been a disaster for his family and Martinique. Except this wind coming off Lake

Erie was cold and bitter. And to think, just a few days before, they had been working in shirtsleeves.

He was only outside for a few brief moments, but it was enough time to see the collapsed Cyclorama to the west. Men ran for shelter, a few headed in his direction. "You should get back inside. It's dangerous out here," one shouted at him. He knew only too well how dangerous it was. He ducked back inside, followed by the fleeing men, thinking for a moment about Albert, building scaffolding next door for the Electrical Tower, which was behind schedule. But mostly he was a frightened twelve-year-old once more, helping Sandrine and his brothers secure the storm shutters before they all huddled in a hallway with Maman, listening to the shrieking wind shaking the rafters and tearing slate tiles from the roof.

Albert had just begun work for Smith and Eastman, the contractors. His small crew had been up on the top, but fortunately, because they were behind schedule, the top wasn't that high yet. Before they were ordered down by the supervisor, they too witnessed the Cyclorama collapse. It shook up the entire crew of union men. "I'm not paid enough to work in this *merde*," Albert complained. The other men nodded agreement. He started to say something more, but the supervisor gave Albert a sharp look, and he quickly shut up. The men continued to grumble among themselves as they were sent to punch out for the day. No one could really afford to go an afternoon without pay.

Paul, too, was sent home early. The wind had died down somewhat by the time they caught the streetcar, and Albert insisted on stopping for a beer at the Commonweal. It had been a harrowing day for both of them.

～

THE TRAM COULD ONLY GO AS FAR as Breckinridge, where a tree had fallen across the street. Crews were busy cleaning up, but the wait, the driver said, "Could be a half hour or more." The two men decided to walk the remaining six blocks. The wind, though still brisk, had died down considerably. Torn away roofing and other debris, as well as whole trees pulled up by their roots, lay everywhere along the residential streets. When they arrived at the Commonweal Tavern, it was packed inside with mostly neighborhood men come out to discuss this anomalous phenomenon which had struck their city.

"The wife says it's the punishment of God," a man snorted. The men around him laughed. "Wicked city, building the devil's playground."

"Is she one of them temperance types?" asked a companion.

"Nah. She don't mind a beer or two. But she'd have a cat fit if she knew I was down here at this house of sin with you fellas." He laughed again, nervously, and the men nodded their heads.

Paul and Albert pushed their way up to the bar, where Celeste smiled a greeting. "What can I get for you gentlemen?"

"A couple of beers, Celeste," said Paul.

"You are already on first names with Mademoiselle Montagne," said Albert when she left to fetch the drinks.

Paul gave a slight nod.

"Fast mover," quipped Albert. Paul laughed.

Celeste brought them their beers and when Albert left to find a table, Paul hung back.

"I passed your message on to Miss Laviolette," Celeste said with a smile.

"Merci," said Paul. "Did she say anything?"

"Non," said Celeste. "But she seemed pleased, if that's any consolation."

He wondered if his motives were really that transparent.

Albert seemed to think so. "Merci," Paul said again and followed Albert to a table near the front windows, where they could look out on the gusty windblown streets.

THE NEXT WEEK was Thanksgiving and the men had the feast day off. They ate dinner at de Lourdes, a new French-speaking church on Best Street, a short walk from The Millard. Father Henri encouraged them to attend mass on Sunday, and both Paul and Albert promised to try their best, although neither man had any intention of doing so. Albert's crew at Smith and Eastman had voted to go on strike on Friday, and short of the company meeting the men's demands for higher wages, he planned to luxuriate in idleness all weekend.

As for Paul, he still had those troubling thoughts of Amanda Laviolette. Guilty thoughts, admittedly, but he wasn't ready to atone for them just yet. He put Stéphanie and his family safely away in a corner of his mind, a sort of room of their own, part of him, but apart. Their existence in Saint-Pierre did not need to intercept his life here. He invited them out occasionally so he didn't forget them, so he didn't forget his children and Maman and Saint-Pierre, because he was afraid that he might lose them amid the crazy excitement of this America.

Perhaps he would spend his evenings at the Commonweal Tavern for the next few days. Perhaps Amanda would show up there. He didn't want to watch this excitement from afar. He wanted to be right there in the middle of it all.

AMANDA LAVIOLETTE

The moon's a gong, hung in the wild,
Whose song the fays hold dear.
Of course you do not hear it, child.
It takes a fairy ear.
— Vachel Lindsay

Saturday night at the Commonweal was bustling. Several young people crowded around the small dance floor in the dress of glorious gypsies. The women wearing either no makeup or an abundance of it, beads around their necks and oversized earrings dangling from their ears. The men's garb, Paul noticed, was nearly as colorful as the women's. Their embroidered shirts, loose trousers—one man had tied a scarlet sash about his waist, ends draping to his knees—reminded Paul of pictures he'd seen of actual gypsies. He felt drab in his stained workingman's clothing. Conversation filled the tavern, the volume rising as more people came in calling out to their friends, but the tone of it all seemed serious, almost somber.

Celeste made her way down the bar and Paul ordered his usual beer. "What is the occasion?" he asked her.

"Haven't you heard?" she said. "Oscar Wilde passed away today."

"You mean the English playwright? This is a celebration?"

"Oui."

"I'm surprised to see so many out for that," said Paul, putting his money on the bar. "Oscar Wilde is considered something of a degenerate, isn't he?"

Celeste scrutinized him, wondering if she'd misjudged him. "Oui," she said, picking up the money from the bar. "Among the self-appointed guardians of morality, at least. I hope you aren't one of those, Monsieur."

"Non," said Paul, backing away from this faux pas. "I try not to be critical. My own life leaves much to be desired. I'm just surprised. Americans seem so priggish."

"Welcome to the big city," Celeste shrugged. "Not everyone in Buffalo holds those tired bourgeois values. Although most certainly do."

Paul suspected Albert would not approve and was relieved his friend was occupied for the evening with a union meeting.

The music, if there was to be any tonight, hadn't yet begun. Paul took his beer and ambled out across the floor, where people stood about in small clusters. He felt very much the outsider. He counted himself lucky to find a small table and a single chair next to a window near the door. He soon understood why the seat was available as it was constantly brushed and bumped by people entering and leaving. He held his pint to avoid wearing it. After a while, a tall, thin man in a fez and collarless shirt strolled in and took over the bar from Celeste, who grabbed a rag and circulated among the tables.

When she arrived at his table, Paul ordered another beer, and when she arrived with it, she said, "Miss Laviolette is expected this evening."

"Merci," he said, throwing her a smile. "I will look for her."

Ten minutes later Amanda strolled in, going directly to the bar where she chatted for some time with the gentleman in the fez. She was dressed with the same flair as the others in the tavern, but she wore a green felt workers' cap and a plain woolen scarf around her neck, looking like one of the working-class radicals you might see around the shop floor. Paul kept his eyes on her, hoping to catch her attention, but she didn't look around until Celeste whispered something in her ear. Amanda turned and glanced at him, her look brief and ambiguous. Paul's spirit sank a little as he wondered if she'd lost her interest in him.

When Celeste came around again, Paul ordered a third beer. He was nearly finished with it when Amanda plopped down across from him.

"Hey cowboy," she said with a wink, "buy a girl a beer?"

Paul laughed at the Wild West reference. "Of course, Ma'am," he said in a terrible imitation of a burlesque show he'd once seen. He guessed the effect must have been quite comic judging by Amanda's groan. He waved Celeste over. "One for Emma Goldman here," he said with a wink.

"Another one for you as well?"

"Non. I think I'll nurse the dregs for a while. Merci, Celeste."

"Your tip will be thanks enough." She smiled and sauntered off.

"I understand this crowd has something to do with Oscar Wilde," he said to Amanda.

"We're planning for a party next week, if you would like to come."

"This bunch?".

"Nah," she said. "Most of these kids are just hangers-on. *The Rubaiyat Club*. We're organizing a bash at the Michael

House next week. Invitation only. To keep out the morally self-righteous and their hawkshaws."

"The Michael House?"

Amanda pointed toward the bar and the man in the fez. "That's Cameron Michael. He's co-owner of this place with Celeste. He lives on Millionaires' Row." This last part was whispered.

"Are he and Celeste married?"

"Not in the way you mean." She spoke barely above a whisper. "Cameron is... well, he's different."

"Oh," Paul said. Not sure what she meant, he didn't want to sound naïve. Paul felt a bit like a fraud in fact. Amanda must believe he was something he was not. But he didn't want her to think he was just off the boat, either. "I would love to come to your party. I've been thinking I would like to know more about this *Rubaiyat Club*."

There was a salon in Saint-Pierre, he considered telling her, but that led to thoughts about Stéphanie, and for just a moment Stéphanie stuck her head out of the room he'd put her into. *At least this Amanda has a brain in her head,* she taunted. *And she likes to read. But she's not the mother of your children.*

Stop being so bourgeois, Paul said, and Stéphanie retreated inside her room.

"What?" said Amanda.

Paul was embarrassed. He didn't say that out loud, did he?

AMANDA WORE THE SAME WORKERS' cap she'd sported the previous weekend, but the night of the Rubaiyat Club party it was adorned with a dyed purple feather pinned to the felt with a brooch. Her green sweater and scarf set off her unadorned face in a way Paul found very enchanting. He wore his nicest clothes, including the classy fedora he purchased in New York, yet he still felt anxiously ordinary amidst all of this theatricality. If it didn't concern Amanda, he figured he must be acceptable.

The Michael estate sat on a few wooded acres fronting Delaware Avenue. Far from the street, the large colonial-style mansion was concealed among the trees, the nearest neighbors enough distance away to maintain privacy. Leading up to the house was a long gravel roadway lined with old silver maples. A few automobiles were parked in front of the house. Paul felt suddenly disoriented, his stomach tensed. He should be used to all of this by now, but he was certain that he was about to make an ass of himself, to do or say something rude or to misunderstand what he heard or forget how to speak English. He realized he was exhausted from the effort of it all.

"Now, I should warn you," Amanda said as they walked along the driveway, "Cameron's parties can be a bit crazy, if you're not used to them."

Crazy, he understood. Carnival in Saint-Pierre, filled with wonder and magic, that wild night with Sophie. He didn't believe he would find Cameron Michael's party so very shocking.

"But don't worry," Amanda continued, "they're all peacherine."

"Je ne comprends pas," said Paul, apologetically. "My English..."

"Sorry for the slang. I spend too much time among these bohos. Peacherine. Peachy. Outstanding. Anyway, I'm just saying that it might not be what you expect but they're on the up-and-up." She stopped and looked at him with the slightest smile, examining his face before stepping back and taking in the whole. "Don't worry. You'll be alright. Although we might need to find you a dashing scarf to go with that killer fedora."

He picked up the end of the scarf Francine had knitted for him last Noël, running it through his fingers. He liked it, actually. But he said nothing. *Ce n'est rien.*

CAMERON MICHAEL GREETED them at the door, kissing Amanda on both cheeks, shaking hands with Paul. "Welcome to my not-so-humble abode," he said with a snicker.

Music and voices emanated from somewhere deep inside the house and butterflies fluttered in Paul's stomach. Michael was wearing a fez, this one much more colorful and elaborate than the one he'd sported at the tavern, and his shimmering silk jacket was adorned with multicolored peacocks. It looked vaguely oriental, but Paul couldn't say from where. Michael seemed effeminate tonight, what the boys on the job would call a pansy. *Maybe he is a fairy.* Is that what Amanda meant? It didn't really bother Paul, but those working men would lay into someone like Cameron Michael if they came across him on a dark street.

Michael was taking a considerable risk by hosting this party in honor of someone as controversial as Oscar Wilde. Paul knew something of the eccentricities of the rich, which are often tolerated among their own kind as long as discretion is observed. Money, after all, rules the world. But, of course, those same fine people would crucify Cameron Michael in a minute if his peccadillos ever became public. And there would always be some who would go to lengths to uncover them.

So, why, he wondered, had Amanda Laviolette invited him, a virtual stranger, to this "bash," as she called it?

Cameron took his guests' overcoats and led them into a small hall where a few dozen celebrants gathered, drinks in hand. There was an upright piano across the room, and the walls were adorned with paintings in various styles. Numerous Queen Anne style chairs had been placed around the room. A few musicians with their instruments gathered around a small riser in one corner.

"Amanda knows her way around. Pour your friend a drink, honey," Cameron said, kissing her cheek again before sashaying away through the crowd.

"What would you like?" said Amanda. Paul wanted to say agricole and sugar — he would like a ti punch right now more than anything. But he remembered where he was. "Perhaps a whiskey."

While Amanda fetched drinks, Paul spied Celeste Montagne across the room conversing with two middle-aged men dressed in ruffled Victorian style finery, one about ten years older than the other. The three stood beneath a painting of a man in a top hat, a dapper scarf wrapped around his collar. Whomever the gentleman in the painting was, it looked more like a caricature than an actual portrait, something from *The Atlantic,* or *Harpers,* perhaps, rendered large.

"Monsieur Poncy," Celeste said as he approached. "So good to see you here tonight. Amanda said she was going to rope you in."

"Hello, Mademoiselle Montagne." He smiled at her as he attempted to translate her meaning—recalling Amanda's cowboy reference last week — but the reference was beyond him. "She thought I should experience — how did she say it? — another side."

Celeste laughed. "I think she really wants to show off her new Martiniquais. Paul, you must meet Count Venetti — he's not a real Count — and his, uhm, nephew, Charles." She bent toward his ear and whispered, too loudly to be a confidence, "he's not really his nephew."

Count Venetti roared with laughter. "Please to meet you, Monsure."

"Likewise," Charles said.

"Monsieur Poncy is from Martinique."

"Is that so." Charles leaned toward Paul flirtatiously. "I would so like to hear about that lovely island. I've read Mister Hearn's accounts, and I must say, are those big muscled black men really as gorgeous as he says?"

Seeing Paul's obvious discomfort, Celeste intervened. "Back off, Charles. Amanda has dibs."

"Speaking of the lady..." Amanda had arrived with Paul's drink, and he let out a silent sigh of relief.

"Are you talking about me, again, Count?" said Amanda with a wink.

"Honey," said Charles, "why would we be talking about anyone else?"

THE MUSIC BEGAN. The same gypsy band which played the first night he and Albert had visited the Commonweal Tavern, but tonight a guitarist and a tambourine player accompanied the lilting gypsy violin. Amanda led Paul around the room from conversation to conversation, plying him with whiskey, until he was quite drunk and had danced with nearly everyone. And he now understood the term, "social butterfly." It was created for Amanda Laviolette.

Amanda introduced him to a few Buffalo artists and poets, and a young art student named Vachel Lindsay, who'd taken the train from Chicago for the evening. "Vachel," Amanda said, "is experimenting with the most interesting sort of poetry. He calls it singing poetry."

The young man, who was about Paul's age, waved away the

compliment. "It's just something I'm playing with. Not very well developed, yet. I'm more an artist than a poet, although I believe one certainly informs the other."

"I hope you will perform for us tonight," Amanda said.

"Maybe one or two," Vachel said. "I have this little piece I wrote after hearing the Buddy Bolden Jass Band in New Orleans. Someday that negro music will be a big item, mark my word. Give it fifteen or twenty years."

"I would be interested in hearing it," Paul said. "Your poem as well."

"We'll see," Vachel said.

"You may as well get it over with," put in Cameron Michael, who had arrived from somewhere, "One doesn't deny Amanda." He winked and was gone again.

So Vachel Lindsay stood before the stage and recited—or rather, rhythmically chanted—a poem, while the gypsy violinist played softly behind, and everyone in the room listened and made polite applause at this strange new art form. Paul was moved by the exotic rhythm of the words, although he didn't understand half of them.

Later, Paul chatted with the poet about Saint-Pierre. Everyone, it seemed, wanted to know about Le Petit Paris des Caraïbes, and while he enjoyed the attention, he wearied of the repetition.

After they were done with the social dance, Amanda led him into a back room where hashish was being smoked from a hookah. While she modestly imbibed, he demurred, afraid of losing more control than he already had. Afraid of losing himself in the degeneracy of the night, this wildness reminding him again of Carnival, but Carnival was always followed by Lent, and the return to the mundane world of struggle and sorrow. He feared that here—in America—there may be no Lent, only endless Carnival, if you were to allow it, if you fell into that trap.

But he was far too drunk to deny *all* of his desires. And when Amanda led him into a vacant bedchamber, he forgot all about Lent. He forgot about Stéphanie and his family and Saint-Pierre. He forgot his dead, Eustase, kind Tata Elmire, Papa, with whom he'd never resolved his differences. He forgot his own troubled childhood. His loves and all his sadness vanished in Amanda's sweet embrace.

GUILTY? Of course, he felt guilty. He was a good Catholic boy. Even if Paul didn't still believe all of those things he'd been taught, he carried the guilt of the world around with him on his shoulders. Wasn't this true?

"Why feel guilt?" said Amanda, as she turned over to face him in the bed of her strange apartment at Elmwood Heights Flats, where she had surreptitiously slipped him past the night manager, explaining in her inebriated state, "I don't care if we get caught, a few simoleons will take care of *that*," and he thought about a day's wages. And, of course, Amanda. He was definitely thinking about Amanda.

While that night he thought about Amanda, in the morning, as he contemplated the colorful menagerie of tapestries hanging from the walls and draped over every available surface, he was thinking about Stéphanie and the children and his disloyalty.

"You're far away from home," said Amanda, when he confessed his discomfort, "and what harm is done, really, Paul?"

And he thought about that. There were a thousand answers to that question. Most of them begin with, "Father So-and-so says," or "the Pope says," or "Maman says," and he knew how childish they would sound to the libertine Amanda. How childish they sounded to his very own ears, even. "It's about betrayal," he said. "I feel as though I'm betraying them."

"Haven't you told me that Stéphanie thinks much the same as I? That we are Sisters in Thought."

Yes, it was true. He told Amanda that. But it was not just about Stéphanie. It was about so much more than that. It was about family and his relationship with his family. And Martinique, because he felt as though he was losing touch with his purpose in life. "Most of all, I need to be true to myself."

"Our lives, you know," said Amanda, "are just the stories we tell about ourselves. I don't mean you should be untrue to yourself, but you are a young man, and young men have adventures. Young women do, too. It's natural. It's our time of life to explore."

He watched her, naked, slip from the bed, stroll to her dressing table, and retrieve a news clip from *The Courier*, which she handed to him. "Girl Will Write of Her Romances," read the headline. The tagline beneath said, "Will Make Herself the Heroine of Her Travels in Male Attire."

"This article is about a young woman named Susan Shelly, who refuses to accept the limited expectations of her sex. You see, you too, Monsieur, can write your own story."

This was a new idea to him, but immediately he had doubts. Write stories? He was not a writer. And doesn't God write your story? If there is a God, of course. *Yes, we all make choices,* he thought, *but how do we choose to not feel guilty about them?*

"Perhaps," he said.

HOW EASILY DID Amanda become his story — for a time. He wrote home to Stéphanie at Noël, but he was in Amanda's arms when the bells rang in the New Century. It was her lips that kissed his as the fireworks exploded over the City of Light in those first exciting minutes of 1901. And for a while he was fine with his own authorship—as long as he could keep both worlds and keep them apart. If he didn't look too far into the future. As long as he could write his way back into the familiar. It wasn't too much was it? He could have this adventure. What risk was there, after all?

Martinique was so very far away. Long periods of time went by with Stéphanie and the children barely in his thoughts. His letters home became sporadic. Their letters came, or didn't come, for weeks at a time. Each month he visited Western Union and sent the better part of his paycheck. But Saint-Pierre and everyone there belonged to a fantastical Verne-like world of the imagination. Paul felt his connection drawing thin. Even Papa's words, and his promises to take care of the family, receded like an echo. When he attended to his responsibilities — almost out of habit — the thoughts he had pushed away would return. He assured himself that the family was not his alone to perpetuate. Mannie and Joseph would marry one day, surely. It was not all on his shoulders to carry the family forward into the future. *Who are we Poncys anyway?* he asked himself. *It is not like we have any great wealth. We are useful cousins of the powerful elite. Trusted only because we are family.*

Paul thought increasingly about Amanda. About sweeping her away down his chemin de fer, to Oklahoma or California or some place where the rails could take you. Into the pages of some Western romance.

But some place where he could acquire a return ticket. Because you never know.

IT WAS a crazy cold and wet spring. Not unusual, he was told. But miserable just the same for a man from the Caribbean tropics. The wind from Lake Erie remained bitter, even when the sun shone through a clear sky. Amanda helped to keep him warm, and he began to think that he might be in love with her.

He wanted to be with her all the time when he wasn't working. He had random thoughts of proposing, which were then quashed by the sudden intrusion of Stéphanie. And Amanda, herself, who put him off whenever he attempted to steer the conversation toward their relationship. He wondered why he was attracted to these independent women who avoided conventional ideas like marriage.

As the weather improved, Amanda grew more distant. He stopped suggesting activities more than a week in the future, because the mere suggestion, it seemed, made her grow solemn. He wondered if maybe her reluctance had to do with his guilt about his family. Because it couldn't possibly be about her own aspirations. All women really want the same thing, don't they? Once you break through all the doubts and the daydreams? The fears and apprehensions? Wasn't that why he tolerated Stéphanie's protestations about marriage? Because he suspected she didn't really mean it? It didn't occur to him that after two children she really meant what she said.

"Amanda, I want to marry you," he blurted out suddenly, with no forethought. It was early April and the two of them were sitting at a table at the Commonweal, nursing beers, discussing the Expo, set to open in three weeks.

She stared at him, first with exasperation, then fury. "Don't you ever listen to me, Paul? Do you think my words are just a game? I don't believe in marriage. I will never believe in that bourgeois institution. it is religious dogma meant to subjugate women."

"But I love you," he protested, knowing her reaction as he

said it, knowing that this is the phrase that will break them. "I want to be with you. I want you to have my children."

"I can't do this." Her face locked in determination, a tear forming in the corner of her eye. A tear of anger or regret? He had no way of knowing. "I just can't."

Amanda stood and downed the remainder of her beer. She put the glass on the table, gently, as though she didn't want to leave a trail of anger behind her.

"Goodbye, Paul," she said and strolled out the door.

THE PAN-AMERICAN EXPO

Early July weather was miserable. Photographer Arthur Mandeville had planned to take outdoor portraits for a few days, while his mother and two eldest daughters took in the sights. If things went well, he might come back in August or September for a longer stay. Now he wasn't so sure. He'd paid good money for a permit to set up his equipment on the Midway, but a fierce thunderstorm, complete with howling wind and rain, greeted their arrival Saturday morning. Much of the Midway turned into a muddy mess, and most of the attendees fled to the exhibition buildings or evacuated the expo for shelter elsewhere. The worst thing, the vendor fees cost an arm and a leg and, so far, he'd not made enough to break even.

The bad weather hadn't let up, but on Monday he finagled a spot in the Ethnology Building, which was mostly empty and struggling to attract visitors. So far there was only a mediocre display of arrowheads and Indian artifacts. But, on the plus side, a long-awaited exhibit from the French Antilles had just arrived, and they were putting finishing touches on their displays as Arthur dragged his equipment into the building with the help of his hired driver.

He found his spot nearby the exhibit and began unpacking his backdrops. He unfurled the one that had secured him this prime spot near the new Antilles display, a tropical island backdrop. He always used original backdrops, it was a point of pride which set him apart from many competitors. He'd traded services with an artist friend to buy it, and this was his first opportunity to use it. Still, he was disappointed in the entire affair. He suspected visitors would prefer their portraits taken with the Expo, itself, as their backdrop. He'd just have to wait and see.

He fixed the canvas to its stanchions, then unpacked the tripod. It took him about an hour to set up all of his equipment. He'd brought his Gennert 5x8, which was more portable than the Scovill and Adams 8x10 he used in his studio, but it took almost as long to set up as the studio camera would have, because he was fussy about getting everything precisely right. An annoying glare on his backdrop, caused by the electric lighting, remained a problem no matter how he positioned his setup, and he had forgotten to bring side curtains. He needed to talk to the young electrician who'd come by earlier to check on the Antilles display.

His two girls had gone off that morning with their grandmother. Both were excited to take in the sights and the rides. The oldest, Clara, had won a contest, full railway fare and admission to the Expo for herself and a companion. She had chosen her younger sister, Berthe, to accompany her. His wife, Clarinda, stayed home in Labelle with the youngest girls, four of them, including a newborn. He'd been hesitant to take the older ones away with him, knowing how much their mother relied on them, but his maman insisted. "You will regret it if those girls miss this opportunity of a lifetime, Arthur."

In the end, he relented. "Of course, Maman," he said. "You

are probably right. And I'll never hear the end of it from those girls if I leave them."

WHEN THE ELECTRICIAN returned to the French West Indies exhibit, Arthur walked toward the booth to talk to him. The electrician was engaged in conversation with an apparent acquaintance, a young black man, about the fellow's same age. Arthur stood back and waited, intrigued by the drama of old friends meeting.

"Eugène Legeay, this is certainly a surprise," the young electrician said in French.

"Well, if it isn't the béké boy, Paul Poncy," Eugène said.

Paul laughed, briefly. "Are you on the crew?"

Eugéne sneered. "Of course, the colored man is always the laborer, is he not?"

Abashed, Paul said, "Excuse-moi. I just thought—"

Eugène didn't allow him to finish. "I am a graduate student in archeology, Monsieur," he said. "In Paris. At the Sorbonne. I am doing field work back home on indigenous artifacts. I've received a sabbatical to accompany Dr. Pichevin here for this opening." Eugène paused for a dramatic moment. "So I see you have a new career as an electrician?"

It sounded like a snark to Arthur, but Paul seemed unoffended. "I'm actually in America to learn about the railroad," he said.

"Yes, of course," Eugéne said. "The Plissonneau empire. We must get the sugar cane to the rhumeries."

"A railroad is important for the island, oui? But my vision is more than just transporting products. People travel on trains as well."

"Oui," Eugène said. "But there are other things important

for Martinique. You address the needs of the white planter class, but what of the rest of us? We are the vast majority. Your republican sentiments do not go far enough, I'm afraid."

"I agree, Eugène. But a railroad will make everyone's life easier. And it won't just help the planters. It will also be valuable to the Caminades and other mulâtre business owners."

"My ancestors have walked the width and breadth of Martinique for centuries. It has kept us strong. When you are in charge of the railroad, will my old granpé be able to afford your fare? Sorry my friend, but all of you only think about one thing. And that thing is money. How much money can be made off the backs of the black man. And your Caminade cousins are no different."

"You are wrong, Eugène. After all these years, hasn't a pause for new thought occurred in this old argument of ours?"

At that point, Eugène noticed Arthur on the sidelines and waved Paul off. "I have work to do, my friend. And you have someone waiting to speak with you." He nodded toward Arthur and turned back to his partially assembled display case.

Arthur observed this frank discussion between a white man and a negro with interest. He did not know what race relations were like in the French islands, but such a thing seldom, if ever, happened in the US or in Canada. He thought the two must have been students together. But that, in itself, would be surprising.

When the electrician approached him, he stepped forward and offered his hand. "Monsieur, Paul, is it?"

"Oui," the young man said. "Paul Poncy. How may I help you?"

"I'm Arthur Mandeville. I am the photographer next door. I'm wondering if you can help me with the light glare."

"Let's see what we can do."

Arthur led the young electrician back to his exhibitor's stall.

"Do you see the reflection on my backdrop?" He pointed out the light hanging a few feet from his backdrop. Most of the lighting in the open beam structure was strung on cords suspended from the ceiling.

"Of course," Paul said. "I could simply shift the light over a few feet. It should take only a moment. I'll go find a ladder."

Arthur watched the agreeable young man hurry away to fetch a ladder. He was very pleased to be receiving such prompt attention without the necessity of going through a half-dozen committees. Already, early morning visitors were filtering into the building to see the new exhibits. Maybe some of them could be persuaded to have their photograph taken.

IT WAS SO amazing to see someone from school thousands of miles from home. Even if it was Eugène, who was his same old antagonistic self. But just the same it brought back memories of Armand, Sophie, Désirée, trips to Fort-de-France and Lamentin. Even the Holy Fathers who gave him no end of grief. *Home.* It had been so long since Paul had thought of Saint-Pierre as home. Now his old nemesis made him think of home again. And Stéphanie, mon Dieu. He hadn't written to Stéphanie and the children for three weeks. What would the children think of him? Would the little ones forget him? For the first time since his arrival in America, he thought about attending Confession. How could this be that he had just forgotten his loved ones? Truly, what kind of man was he?

By the time he found a ladder and returned to Monsieur Mandeville's photography stall, he was tormented with that old familiar guilt. But the grateful photographer soon took Paul's mind off of his misery.

"So Monsieur," said Arthur, "you are from the Antilles?"

"Oui," said Paul, adjusting his ladder beneath the offending light. "Martinique. My family lives in Saint-Pierre."

"I overheard some of your conversation with that negro. A school acquaintance, I presume?"

"Oui. Eugène and I attended Saint-Louis-de-Gonzague together several years ago. We have—shall we say—certain philosophical differences. But he's a good man."

"He seems to have done well for himself if he's an advanced student at the Sorbonne. Pardon my saying so, but I do not understand many of these negroes. Even when they benefit from the universities and are doing well, they are still dissatisfied with their lot."

Paul thought about what to say to this as he removed the hook holding the light cord. He'd felt this same way but he realized the situation was more complex. "It has only been a half century since the end of slavery in Martinique, Monsieur. The large majority of my country is negro or mulâtre, but still there is so much discrimination and poverty. It breeds discontent. Rightfully, I think."

"I apologize, sir," Arthur said. "I don't wish to speak of things I know so little about."

"No need to apologize." Paul moved the light cord to the other side of the ladder, away from the artist's stall, and refastened the hook. "I haven't thought about these things for several months and it's good to remember where you come from, non?"

"What does your family do, Paul?"

Ah, there was the question he was so uncomfortable answering. "Papa was a business manager when he was alive. My brothers work in businesses owned by my cousins. Rum and shipping."

"Did I hear mention of Plissonneau and company?"

Paul sighed.

"Pardon me, Monsieur. I don't mean to pry."

"Non. Non. The Plissonneau-Duquenes are my cousins. Do you know them?"

"Only by name. They have something to do with the Quebec Steamship Line, I believe."

"Oui. They are agents for the line. I believe they own some portion of shares, but I couldn't really say. What about you, Monsieur?" Paul said, deflecting the subject as he descended the ladder. "Where might I find your studio?"

"My studio is in Montreal, Rue Saint-Ferdinand." He handed Paul a card. "Look me up if you are ever in the city. I will give you a good deal on a portrait to send home to your family, perhaps."

"Merci." Paul put the card in his pocket and folded the ladder. "There, Monsieur, that should solve your problem."

PAUL AND ALBERT met for lunch later near the Children's Building on the midway. It was the nearest eatery to be found between the Ethnology Building and the still unfinished Albright Gallery, where Albert was now working. They ate lunch here every Monday when possible. Today was a quiet day in the restaurant. Much of the midway remained muddy from the recent rains, discouraging families with small children.

"I met an old school friend today."

"Is that so? From Martinique?"

"Oui," said Paul. "Small world, yes? He is assisting with the Antilles exhibit. You must come by with me and see the exhibit."

"Of course. Perhaps there will be time tomorrow."

"Let me know and I will join you there. We can eat our lunches on the esplanade."

"Oui, let's do that."

"I also met an interesting photographer from Montreal. His name is Arthur Mandeville."

"Arthur Mandeville?" Albert said with a look of astonishment.

"Yes. Do you know him? He gave me his card and offered me a discount if I'm ever in Montreal." Paul fished the card from his pocket and handed it to Albert who laughed a deep belly laugh.

"That's my cousin," he said. "He's not close, a third cousin or something like that, but I've met him at family reunions. His mother is a Boulet."

Paul laughed and slapped his friend on the back. "What did I say. A small world, mon ami."

~

8 JUILLET *1901*

My Dearest Stéphanie,

Please forgive my neglect of failing to write for so long, my love. I trust you and the children are doing well.

My days are busy and the hours long. I must be on the job when the Expo opens and usually cannot leave until after dark. But the extra hours mean I can send you and Maman a little extra for the next few months.

You will never guess whom I met at the Expo. Eugène Legeay! He is now a student at the Sorbonne, although he is presently studying archeology in Martinique. He is in Buffalo to present artifacts from the indigene. I can't say how much meeting him made me miss home and think of you and the children.

I am taking Albert to see the exhibit tomorrow during our break for Petit-déjeuner. In another one of those strange coincidences that happen, his cousin from Montreal has a photography booth nearby in the same hall.

I promise, I will write a more detailed letter on the weekend.
My love, always,
Your Paul

ALBERT MET him on the esplanade in his carpenter's overalls and knit worker's cap, Paul was still draped in his grimy electrician's apron. Neither man had time enough to change clothes for their brief lunch break. They planned to pick up something at one of the stands on the midway.

The unpaved areas of the Expo were still muddy. As a result, the midday crowd was again thin. It was a little more lively inside the Ethnology building, which had benefited from publicity for the new exhibits, but it was a modest turnout.

As they crossed the floor, Albert waved to his cousin, who was standing near his tripod and camera. An older woman and two fetching young girls in summer dresses stood next to Arthur. "My cousins, the Mandevilles," said Albert. "Come meet them."

"Albert Bouley," Arthur Mandeville exclaimed. The two shook hands and Arthur eyed Paul. "You two know each other?"

"Paul and I came to Buffalo together. We are neighbors in Woonsocket."

"Incroyable," Arthur said. "It is very good to see you, Albert. And you again, Monsieur Poncy. Please let me introduce my family." He turned to the elegant, gray-haired woman behind him. She was striking, though small in stature, perhaps in her sixties, and wore a simple felt boater hat with a silk scarf and fashionable pearl earrings. "This is my mother, Madame Mandeville née Boulet. Mother, this is Paul Poncy."

"Madame," Paul said.

"Enchantée," Madame said.

"And my two eldest daughters, Clara and Berthe." Berthe

curtsied. Clara was no taller than Berthe, and he guessed the girls to be about the same age. Clara did not curtsey, just nodded her head and smiled.

"Pleased to meet you, Mesdemoiselles."

"Enchantée," the girls said together, beaming broad smiles at him. Charming children, he thought, before turning his attention to the men.

"How is business, Arthur?" asked Albert.

"It is another disappointing day." Arthur scowled. "I may as well pack up and go home."

"But Papa," Berthe said, "I haven't even ridden in the gondola, yet."

"Papa doesn't mean that literally," scolded Clara like a mother hen. She looked at her father. "Do you, Papa?"

"Non, we will stay long enough for you girls to see your sights." Berthe gave a dramatic sigh of relief.

Clara rolled her eyes and sidled over near Paul. He noticed she walked with a limp and wondered if she'd injured herself, but he was too polite to inquire.

"Papa says you are from Martinique, Monsieur," she said.

He was surprised to hear Arthur had talked about him to his family. "Oui," he said. "My family is from Saint-Pierre."

"That's so fascinating," she said, her eyes sparkling with a child's curiosity. "I've met no one from the Antilles. You must tell me what it's like."

"I wish I had the time, but I'm afraid Albert and I must return to work."

She looked momentarily crestfallen. Then an idea lit up her face and she said, "Perhaps I could correspond with you. I need to practice my letter writing. I'm really very curious about it."

Paul smiled at her enthusiasm. It would be delightful to correspond with this bright young girl who lived in a world so very different from his own. "I would love to, if it's alright with your papa."

CLARA TUCKED Paul Poncy's address into her small hand purse. Berthe grinned at her in that little-sister-has-something-to-tease-you-about-now way. Clara smiled back smugly. But she couldn't believe the handsome young man agreed so readily to her impulsive suggestion. She couldn't wait to write her first letter. She wondered if he found her attractive, not that she was old enough to expect anything to come from that. It was just a childish flirtation. In fact, he probably saw her as a child to indulge. She would have to work on that image.

Clara didn't think of herself as a child. As the eldest girl, growing up in Montréal with five younger siblings, and a mother who bore one child after another, mostly boys who miscarried or died in infancy, she'd too often been required to play the role of grownup, taking care of Maman and her little sisters. Adding to all of that unhappiness was her own misfortune, the polio she'd contracted during the Montreal epidemic of '94, which left her with one leg more than an inch shorter than the other and required she wear specially made shoes.

But in the face of all that, Clara kept her head up, refusing to be defeated by an unfortunate disease, the effects of which she must deal with for the rest of her life. Who had time for feeling sorry for oneself?

Of course, her childhood hadn't been all struggle and responsibility. There had been good times, too. She'd spent lovely summers at her Charlebois grandparents' second home on Lake Champlain in Vermont, or with the Mandeville grandparents in Labelle. Papa had only just moved the whole family to Labelle this year, saying he wanted the little ones to grow up near their grandparents. Grandpa François Mandeville was the notary for the village of Mont-Laurier. Like many comfortable Montreal families, the elder Mandevilles had once maintained a residence in both the city and the country, but they had given up the home in Montréal's Mile-End some time ago to live in Labelle full time.

Clara harbored mixed feelings about life in Labelle where the family home with its white picket fence perched on the main street, a few blocks from the stinky lumber mill and hillsides covered in ugly tree stumps. She had to admit to herself the village held a certain charm, despite the mill, but she missed the excitement and bustle of the city, with its libraries and universities and theaters.

At least now she had something new and interesting to look forward to.

WHERE IS HOME?

JULY BECAME August and the Mandevilles and Eugène Legeay faded from Paul's thoughts. With only a few months left of the Expo, he thought about the connections he had failed to make with the businessmen from Martinique, his purpose for being here. Most of them were now gone back to the island. And he thought about his other purpose, employment with the railroad industry. He'd passed the booth for the American Locomotive Company several times now on his tour through the Machinery and Transportation Building. ALCO, as it was called, was the new company formed by the merger of seven steam locomotive manufacturers, among them the one he wished to apply to in Manchester, New Hampshire. He wasn't sure why he had waited so long to talk to them, but maybe it was because he wasn't ready to be uprooted again.

Finally, he could put it off no longer, and his visit to the ALCO exhibit was not nearly as intimidating as he had feared. When he showed the company representative his letter from Georges Plissonneau, it seemed to him as though they had been waiting for him, that they would have hired him on the spot if only the paperwork had been ready. *A letter will soon be on its way,* they assured him.

In September, President William McKinley was assassinated while touring the Pan-American Exposition by a lone anarchist and a shockwave was sent through the ranks of labor as the federal government and its hired Pinkerton detectives ran roughshod through the Expo workforce. Everyone was on edge. To the Pinkertons, if you worked for wages, you were a potential anarchist, and very little attention was paid to the difference between skilled workers and ditch diggers, except for not-very-subtle efforts to turn one against the other.

Paul had been far away from the Music Hall when the shooting took place. But word circulated quickly through the crowds from the site of the shooting to the expo boundaries. When the news finally reached him, he wasn't sure how he should feel about it. He was horrified, surely. Yet McKinley was not well liked among many of the workers he'd talked to, particularly immigrants and unionists who believed him to be a tool of Imperial America. But a political assassination was always a serious event that often affected the lives of ordinary people, almost always in a bad way. And it seldom changed anything.

It was several days before McKinley died, but when he did the mood in Buffalo soured even more. After the assassination, foreigners — no matter from where, Poland or Germany or Italy or even French Canada — were treated with suspicion, hostility and even violence by the citizens of Buffalo. Never mind that the gunman, Leon Czolgosz was a second generation American, an Indiana farm boy. He had a Polish name, after all. Paul found he was suddenly being treated differently in the cafes and markets, and he no longer felt safe in the streets after dark. The only thing that made the city even bearable now was that a huge portion of the population were also fellow immigrants.

Now, with this anger against foreigners he experienced a

short stabbing fear that he might be put on a boat back to Martinique before he could accomplish his dream. Or before he decided if returning to his Saint-Pierre was even the course he wanted to take. That now ALCO might not hire him because he was a potential anarchist. It was a thought that came and left in an instant. Of course, they would not do that. He knew how the world worked. He was a white man with family connections.

BY THE END OF SEPTEMBER, Paul was happy at the thought that his Expo job would soon end and he could return home. Except that now he was no longer sure where home was.

The expected letter had arrived a few days earlier from the new American Locomotive Company, promising him a job in Manchester, beginning in April. The letter he knew would come because of his relationship with Georges Plissonneau-Duquêne. A part of him wanted to go immediately and adjust to a new city. But Albert was trying to persuade him to return to Woonsocket for the winter, and he had left his trunk there with Francine, so it made a kind of sense. And it would be comfortable to spend the holidays with the Tambois family and with the Bouleys. And maybe what he needed now was comfort more than anything. When he thought about it, he knew that retracing his journey from Buffalo to Woonsocket would be a kind of unraveling, an undoing of his affair with the bohemian girl. He imagined emerging from the train a new man, Buffalo safely tucked away, Stéphanie and the children once more in their rightful place.

Yet, it had been two years since he had seen his family in Saint-Pierre. If asked, he would tell people he thought of them daily, and maybe in some back room of his mind he did, but in actuality he thought about them less and less. Stéphanie,

Maman, Mannie, Alice Germaine, all of them, even his own flesh and blood children, had become ghost-like. Was there something wrong with him? Confession had done him no good —the priests had no salve for his guilt.

He should be homesick, but as hard as he tried he couldn't convince himself that this lost feeling was homesickness, rather than unrelieved guilt. Guilt because in another back-room hid his growing desire to stay, to go out west maybe and explore this new land. To find a new adventure and a new life. Leave behind the harsh future that was Martinique, where life and livelihood were so tied to the vagaries of rhum and sugar and its legacy of poison and resentment. He didn't want to think these things, but the thoughts came unbidden.

HE ARRIVED BACK at the Millard one evening to find a letter from young Clara Mandeville, whom he had forgotten would be writing to him. The return address said, simply, *Miss Clarinda Mandeville, Labelle, Canada*. He was happy to have something to take his mind off of his pending decisions. He found his letter opener and cut open the envelope. It read:

24 SEPTEMBRE *1901*

Labelle, Quebec, Canada

Dear Monsieur Poncy,

I hope you are well.

It was so shocking to hear news of President McKinley at the Pan American Exposition. My thoughts immediately went to you and Monsieur Bouley. I hope you are both alright. Were you there at the time? If so, it must have been a frightening experience.

Papa was impressed by you as he kept mentioning your name for some time in dinner conversation.

As for me, I am still very interested to hear of life in Martinique, what it is like there, what the people are like and so on. Has your family been there long? What do they do? Did you go to school in Saint-Pierre? Do you have brothers and sisters?

Pardon all the questions. I would love to hear stories about the island and your family, but you don't need to answer all of them at once. I will probably think of more questions later, but I'm certain this is more than enough for now.

I'm so happy you've graciously agreed to correspond with me. There is no need for an address more than Labelle, Quebec, Canada, as the postal carrier knows everyone in the village.

Merci.

Best Regards,

Clara Mandeville

~

HE THOUGHT about Clara's letter for some time before sitting with his pen to reply. He didn't know how much he wanted to say about his family's history in Martinique. He was embarrassed by them, by his grandfather and his slave-owning planter ancestors. He could talk about Maman and Mannie. He could talk about Stéphanie and the children, but was reluctant to do so. And if he talked about his extended family, Dupouy or Plissonneau or Fauvé-Sablon, then how would he explain that these people, some whom he loved deeply, had grown rich from the misery of others?

Maybe there was a way to just avoid all of that.

MADEMOISELLE CLARA,

It is so nice to receive your letter. I enjoyed meeting your lovely family very much. Please give them my regards.

Yes, President McKinley's assassination was a shock to us all. We are still trying to understand what it means and to get on with our work as best we can. It is not the same in Buffalo as it was before this terrible act, and I am looking forward to this Expo ending and returning to a quieter life.

Martinique is a beautiful island. We lived there for several years, including some of my school years. We came there from Bordeaux when I was young, as my late father had business ties in Saint-Pierre.

I have two brothers, Joseph and Emmanuel. They both work as clerks in the shipping industry in Saint-Pierre. I went to Séminaire-Collège Saint-Louis-de-Gonzague, which is near our home in the Quartier du Fort. The College gave me a good education and I have many fond memories of my school days.

If you want to know about anything in particular, please let me know. I can tell you many things about the island, as I've been nearly everywhere. The entire island is only 40 kilometers wide. Although the roads over the mountains are steep and sometimes impassable, it is usually only a half day's journey by carriage from one side to the other.

I would love to hear about your life in Quebec, as well.

Yours in Correspondence,

Paul Poncy

HE CRINGED ONLY a little at the half-truths, but some things he had written were actual lies, although he tried to convince himself that they were not. It is a thing that everyone does. Is it not? He didn't bother to ask himself why he was ashamed.

~

IN THE END, he decided to return to Woonsocket. Francine's warm fireplace, dinner at the Bouley's, nightly walks in the cimetiere where he could talk again with his ghosts. These won out over the cold loneliness of a new city.

Francine, it turned out, had his old room available, the most recent boarder having moved out at the end of October. She was delighted to have him back. Paul settled quickly into his familiar and comfortable life in the Tambois home. Even Lea seemed happy to see him, having made peace with her disappointment. And Annie forgave him the theft of her husband, it seemed. All would be well if not for a certain unnamed sadness, which he could not shake. Maybe it was the long nights of approaching winter. Maybe it was the growing distance between him and Saint-Pierre.

The cemetery continued to be his solace. He strolled nightly among the graves of the French diaspora, talking to his lost brother, Eustase, to Tata Elmire, to Papa. These graves were threads that kept him tied to Martinique. If not for the spirits of his dead, and the letters from home, he would be in danger of losing it entirely.

He'd nearly thrown it all away, but he'd made promises to people. He had a duty to his family. *If you can't honor your family, then you are truly lost.* He believed this in the deepest part of his soul. It was not just the promises to Maman and Stéphanie. Samuel and Georges had placed their faith in him, too. Martinique needed him to follow through on those promises. It needed a railroad, not just to carry the lucrative sugar as Eugène had charged, but because the island must become part of the modern world. The wheels of progress. Maybe he was wrong, mistaken about it all. But he didn't think so.

In the spring, he moved on to Manchester with many hugs and goodbyes and well wishes and he settled into a shabby westside tenement to begin his new job for ALCO, the next phase of his life, machining parts for the ever-expanding railroad industry.

Like Woonsocket, Manchester was an industrial city, big and lonely and dirty, but there were French speaking Québécois here, too, and his apartment was only a few blocks from Sainte Marie Cathedral, in case he needed to take solace in the confessional.

He had just moved in, hardly long enough to look around and get his bearings, when the first letters from home arrived at his new address, reminding him of his commitments, reminding him how far away he was from home.

His dreams were often of the snake pit and liana. Ashes falling like snow; the smell of sulfur bubbling up from the cauldron below, a bouillon of snakes. Sometimes it is Maman who stands above urging him to hang on for dear life. Sometimes it is Stéphanie or Alice Germaine. The children shriek in terror, "Papa, hang on. Please don't fall."

And always it is Ludger Sylbaris extending his black hand. "Let that vine go, Priest, and take my hand. It is your salvation."

And then he wakes up thinking about home.

Where is home? Will he ever find it again? Or is this his life now, to be a wanderer in a foreign land? But his bed is comfortable and warm despite the cold outside. He feels safe here during the long North American night. And it is a betrayal, isn't it, to feel these things?

SHIPWRECKED

THE ADVENTURES OF YVONNE

WHEN SHE WOKE UP, Yvonne thought she must be in the land of the dead. She couldn't see a thing, and all around her, the dark world was as still as a graveyard. The only thing she could hear was the gentle sound of waves on the shore.

The world smelled of fish and salt. Not even the slightest breeze touched her face.

Yvonne reached up to her eyes, fearing that she had gone blind. She found no eyes there at all. Where her eyes should be, her new skin felt wet and slimy.

A sense of relief filled her when she realized what had happened.

"Yuck," Yvonne said, as she peeled a huge glob of seaweed

away from her face. She could see again. But what she saw did not make her happy.

It was daylight. Yvonne was lying on a sandy beach, and all around her, pieces of the *Liberté*, and possibly other ships as well, were strewn across the beach and nearby rocks.

There was the ship's sextant half buried in the sand. And the map cabinet, shattered on the rocks.

"O non, que s'est il passé ?" Yvonne said. That means, "Oh no, what has happened?"

And then she remembered Maman and André, and she cried.

A little girl can only be so brave at times like these. Yvonne put her head back down on the sand and wailed for Maman and André, certain that she would never see them again.

AFTER SOME TIME, Yvonne lifted her head from her sandy pillow. Although dire circumstances had overcome her, she knew she must be brave and try to go on.

Even though her knees were shaking, she stood up on her feet and once again surveyed the island around her. It was tiny, no larger than the town of Saint-Pierre.

A small hill stood at the center of the island. The hill was not as high as the one at le Morne Rouge, which Yvonne could see from the terrace of her home.

The thought of home made her sad. Then she remembered Maman and André again, and she had another cry.

When her crying was finished, she wiped her eyes and began to climb the hill. She was determined to go to the top, hoping to see the *Liberté*, or what was left of it.

As she clambered over the slippery rocks, Yvonne was very careful to avoid snakes. The fierce fer-de-lance of Martinique is very dangerous, and Yvonne had grown up with many sad stories about poisonous snakes. But fortunately she saw no snakes here at all.

As Yvonne climbed, she wondered what she would eat on this barren island. There were no fruit trees or familiar plants she could see. She knew a little about fishing. At least Auntie Rosa had read a book to her once about a boy who fished. It couldn't be too difficult.

When she finally reached the top of the hill, she could see all around the island, and there on the far end lay the *Liberté*, leaning on its side, stuck in some rocks on a spit. The waves pushed and tugged at the ship, trying to pull her apart.

Yvonne's heart soared. Maman and André, perhaps they were saved, after all.

But how was she going to get out to the ship? It was so far from the shore, and she didn't know how to swim very well. She must get there before the *Liberté* was washed to sea.

YVONNE RAN down the far side of the hill, no longer thinking about snakes or food or anything but saving Maman and André.

There was no beach on that side of the island, just sea-worn rocks and crashing waves. She climbed out as far as she dared on a slippery outcropping.

"Ahoy!" shouted Yvonne—that was what the pirates always yelled in Auntie Rosa's book.

She hoped she might be heard above the roaring of the sea. But no answer came back to her. The sea was just too noisy and the ship too far for her small voice to carry all that distance.

Yvonne looked around for some driftwood or ropes or anything she could use to make a raft and paddle out to the *Liberté*. But nothing was big enough.

She had seen larger pieces of driftwood and detritus back on the other side of the island, but were there enough to build a raft? What was she going to do?

Yvonne climbed over the slippery rocks until she made it back to the beach. She walked along the shore to see what she could find. You never know what might have washed up on the shore. Maman and André needed her. She mustn't give up now!

YVONNE SOON GATHERED a large collection of driftwood, broken planks, including a door with hinges still attached, and she found a few fairly large pieces of rope. The wood would float, and the rope could hold it all together. She could make a raft, after all.

Étienne had showed her how to tie some knots, so she went to work pulling her raft together, wrapping and tying, until she had something that she was pretty certain could carry her out to the ship. But she did not know how she would get it out beyond the dangerous surf, and, once it was out there, how was she going to steer it and avoid crashing into the rocks.

Yvonne thought about the gaberiers in the harbor of Saint-Pierre. How they often steered their flat boats out to the big ships by jumping into the water and pushing the boats along with their feet. She didn't know if she could do this, but she had to try. She couldn't leave Maman and André and the others out on that ship to drown.

Mustering all of her strength, she dragged her raft down to the water, and pushed it out into the surf. The waves washed over her feet. She pushed and pushed and the waves just pushed back. But with each push her raft went out a bit further, until she found herself up to her waist, then up to her shoulders, and then her feet could no longer touch the seafloor. She feared again that she couldn't do this. She was just a little girl, after all.

Yvonne let herself float in the water, her legs trailing behind her, like when Uncle Louis tried to teach her to swim, and she kicked as she'd seen the gaberiers do, pushing their boats along. Soon she found her raft was slowly inching forward.

Before Yvonne knew it, she was almost out as far as the *Liberté*. She looked back at the shore where she had started and she froze. *Mon Dieu,* she thought. She was so far away from the safety of land. And the waves around the *Liberté* batted the ship back and forth like a toy, crashing it against the rocks. What was she going to do now?

There was no turning back. She must get to Maman and André and Chief Navigator Marcus and Étienne, the helmsman. She must help them get to shore, because if she didn't do it, who would?

So she began paddling again, as hard as she could. A few times a large wave tried to tear the raft away from her, but she hung on with all of her might, until, at last, she arrived at the ship.

"Maman," she called, and she heard a voice call back. "Yvonne! My precious Yvonne. You are alright. André and I have been looking everywhere for you."

"I'm here to save you, Maman," she called. She couldn't believe she had done it. She had made it all the way to the *Liberté*. And she felt so happy. Maman and André were safe!

PART 6
OÙ EST LE COEUR?

MADAME PELÉE AWAKENS

In Saint-Pierre, Stéphanie sits at her writing desk just inside their bedroom, hers and Paul's, though he's been away for over two years — can it have been so long? She longs for him to return home. The foul air has forced her to close and shutter the doors and windows so that the room is dark and she has no view of the flowers she and Maman Clémence have cultivated. The bad air seeps in through spaces and cracks along with slivers of light. How much to tell Paul? Should she tell him how closed in, how claustrophobic Saint-Pierre has become? Going to the market is unpleasant. There is also that undercurrent of tension, laughter that is too loud and sudden outbursts between shopkeeper and customer, husband and wife, child and mother. There is an edge and yet everything seems to keep ticking along at only a slightly elevated pace. After all, the heat has not left. The papers are full of the impending election and the governor's plan to support his party's candidates with a visit to Saint-Pierre. He'll come with his wife to show how safe it is and how important it is to ensure the election isn't affected by Madame Pelée's temper.

The earth trembles as she writes and her pen wants to

careen across the page. She doesn't take out a clean sheet of paper. She could go through a lot of precious paper if she pulled a new sheet every time the earth moved and caused her pen to strike off on its own.

∾

26 *Avril* 1902

My Dearest Paul,

I hope that all is well at your new job, mon cher. I am glad that you are comfortably settled in your apartment. We can't wait to hear your tales of Manchester. Alice says we should move to America, and I can only laugh. But I tell her if she studies her English at school, perhaps someday.

The mountain woke up yesterday. It was quite frightening for several moments. There came a loud explosion, the ground shaking beneath us, and the air was filled with the smell of sulphur. The children were terrified. It's reported that stones showered down upon people along the road to Morne Rouge.

This morning the streets are covered in a fine layer of ash, and the smell is horrible. Alice and Adrien wore kerchiefs over their mouths as they left for school. I am glad it is Saturday, and they will be home early. I feel so helpless when they are not by my side.

They say it is nothing, that it happens every so often, but they would say that, wouldn't they? The elections are coming soon and no one wants to rock the boat. I must agree, this election is very important for our island. It may decide the future for Martinique. But no one asks what Madame Pelée has to say. I have said prayers with the children, but I worry we pray to the wrong god.

This is blasphemous, isn't it? Now I must ask for forgiveness as well.

We all send our love. Keep us in your thoughts, mon amour.
Your Stéphanie

~

Monday, 5 May 1902

Mannie stands in the doorway of the family home on Rue Saint-Denis. Having removed his panama hat, he turns it absentmindedly in his hands. His once-white linen trousers, already turned gray from days of ashfall, are ruined from the muddy water covering Rue Bouille, where every building below Rue Victor Hugo has been flooded. He is still in shock. Nothing has been normal since Pelée began throwing out ash and stinking gasses. It had been a quiet morning until suddenly it wasn't.

He recalled glancing from the window of his office on the second floor that morning, just as a high wave rose out of the bay and rushed toward shore. *Jesus, Joseph, and Mary.* He crossed himself and rushed downstairs to the ground floor. Water covered everything less than three meters above the sea, it roiled around and flowed out the open windows. His fellow workers, the few who hadn't yet fled home to their loved ones, clung to shutters and window sills, whatever support they could find against the current.

He waited until the water calmed before he entered the vast warehouse. Careless of his now hopeless suit, struggling against waist-deep water, he reached the open door. The bay was quiet, waves with their little white crests rolled gently in and the floodwaters flowed backward, as if recalled. They sucked at his legs and he held the door frame to steady himself. Pierrotins had all seen far worse. This was nothing compared to a hurricane. Yet, it disturbed him more than finding half the roof tiles of their house on Rue Castelnau blown off and shattered on the street, along with those of all their neighbors, after the hurricane of '91.

Everyone at the distillerie set to work cleaning up. Later in the afternoon Raphaël brought them the news about the Guerin sucrerie on the Rivière Blanche. That is when they first knew the cause of the wave. "A wall of mud," Raphael said. "People who saw it say they've seen nothing move so fast. They didn't have a chance. They are looking for bodies, but—" Raphael's voice broke at that moment. He didn't continue, only shook his head.

Now home, Maman says, "Bonjour, Emmanuel. Look at your suit! You've been in the floodwater. Mannie, you must be careful. What brings you here? Is there a problem at the distillerie?" She takes in his demeanor, the hat turning. His mouth is a grim line. He stares at her without speaking.

"Joseph? Has something happened to Joseph?"

"Ah no, Maman. It is not Joseph. It is the Guerin Factories. All gone, Maman. The mountain has destroyed them and all the people swept away." He pulls his mother into his arms and holds onto her, collapsing into her embrace.

IN MANCHESTER, a cold fear gripped Paul, not borne of some prescience about what was to come, but of his complete lack of control over events, that he was two thousand miles from Saint-Pierre. It's nothing, he told himself. Madame Pelée huffing. It's happened before, the last time only fifty years ago. But it was not like Stéphanie to complain. This, more than anything, infused his sense of urgency. After reading her letter, he set off immediately for Western Union and sent a telegram urging her to leave: *Take the children and Maman to Fort-de-France.*

He received her brief reply from Western Union the next

day. *"Soldiers guarding the roads. Berths to Fort-de-France all booked. No way out. Joseph thinks Plissonneau might help."*

Later that evening, Paul attempted to send a telegram to Georges Plissonneau, but Western Union told him that the cable was damaged. No telegrams could be sent out of or into Martinique.

Paul hurried to a newsstand to purchase the evening paper, but he could find nothing about Martinique. What might cause the telegraph cable to break? In his heart, he knew it must be the mountain. But surely, if things were desperate, Georges would help his family leave. He returned to his tenement, feeling a little sick, unable to sleep, unable to take his mind off of his family, thinking about the shower of rocks on the road to Morne Rouge and the children attending school with cloth over their faces so they could avoid breathing the filthy air.

As soon as the newsstands opened in the morning, he was there, scouring the front pages. But again there was nothing. About to leave in defeat, he scanned one final paper, *The St Albans Daily Messenger,* and a small article on the front page caught his eye. "Lava Destroys Factories," read the headline. "150 Persons on the Island of Martinique Disappear."

The Guerin Factories. A few kilometers north of the Fort District. His heart sank, the paper shook in his hands. It was so much worse than he had allowed himself to believe.

UNBEARABLE NIGHTS

On Friday morning, 9 May, Paul was up, ready for work, and eating breakfast. Beside his plate rested three letters, one for Stéphanie, one for Maman, and one for Samuel Dupouy. He'd found the time and quiet finally, last night, to answer letters from each of them. There was a postcard, too, among the letters, for the children. He'd put all their names on it. Alice first, because she was the oldest, then Adrian and André, and he ran out of room so Yvonne was written above and to the side. The address was Auguste Graineau's home in Fort-de-France. By the time the letters arrived in Martinique, Stéphanie and the children would surely all be there at her brother's house. Tomorrow, he would write to Mannie and Joseph. He couldn't imagine that any of them would remain in Saint-Pierre after the 5th of May. But he recalled Stéphanie's telegram. *Berths to Fort-de-France all booked. No way out.* Surely, the Plissonneaus had come through. You come through for family, don't you? He must remember to write to Georges, thanking him.

On his lunch break, he took his letters to the post office and stood in line to buy postage. He waited impatiently, taking his watch out of his pocket to make sure there was plenty of time to get back to work. Early days on a new job, it was especially important to not be late. He set the letters on the counter, the postcard on top. I need postage, he said, three first class and one postcard to Martinique.

The clerk looked at him, cleared his throat, "Where?"

My English, he thought. "Fort-de-France, Martinique," he said, taking care to pronounce the "t" in Fort, though which city or village made no difference in the amount of postage.

The clerk nodded. "It's very terrible," he said, sliding the stamps across the counter.

Preoccupied with paying for the stamps, it wasn't until Paul took a few steps from the counter that he wondered what the clerk meant.

"What?" he asked, but the clerk was already helping the next person in line and didn't hear him. *Perhaps he is referring to the news of the Guerin factory workers.*

He hurried from the post office, no time to lose if he was going to have any lunch before returning to work. A few blocks up the street on the way to his favorite lunch counter, the newsboy was at his usual corner, shouting in almost incomprehensible English. Paul has no clue what headline the boy is yelling until he sees it as he passes by. He drops two cents into the boy's box and rips the paper from his hands.

"Hey mister," the boy starts, but doesn't finish. *The tall, dark-haired man hasn't moved. He's staring at the paper as if he can't read, his eyebrows drawn together, lips moving over the foreign words, the alien language. Then he pushes the paper back at the boy's chest and says something in French that sounds like "prawnla". The paper falls into the gutter. The man walks away. Crazy Quebecers!* The newsboy turns back to his business, shouting out the news, "25,000 Killed!" The words ricochet off the Frenchman's back. "Saint-Pierre destroyed."

Paul had forgotten lunch, he was looking for a French

language paper. *Impossible! You can't trust these American papers. They sensationalize to sell their feuilles de chou. What a relief that Stéphanie has taken everyone safely to Auguste's home.* His heart jerks. Everyone? What about Mannie and Joseph? Surely not Samuel or Raphael! Nor Léonie... he couldn't go on naming them. *Mais non, ce n'est pas vrai. Ce n'est pas possible.* He takes a deep breath. For a moment, he thinks he might faint.

Non. He refuses to believe it. *It's all a big mistake. Surely Stéphanie will write from Fort-de-France and explain it all.*

He returned to work in a daze, retracing his steps in the unfamiliar city, his eyes on the sidewalk, all of his thoughts focused inside. 25,000 *killed.*

But how many, really? he thought. *That can't be right.*

He stepped up to punch in, but his supervisor stood in front of the time clock, holding Paul's card in one hand, *The Boston Globe* in the other. That headline shouting at him. 25,000 *killed.*

"My sincere condolences, Paul," he said. "Take the afternoon off. If I'd known, I would never have asked you to come in this morning."

"Non," he said, angry at the implication. "I can work." What would he possibly do all afternoon if he had it off?

The supervisor looked him in the eye with an intense gaze. "I don't think so, son. Take tomorrow off, as well. It will be in no one's interest if you lose a hand or an eye."

"I'm sure I will be fine."

"Go home, Paul." The words are final.

But how can he go home? How is that possible?

～

HIS FIRST UNBEARABLE nights alone in Manchester were filled with whiskey and haunted by his ghosts. What would he do with all of these memories? All of these revenants walking through his dreams? He found himself traipsing through the dusty halls of l'habitation Sablon, peering into empty rooms, searching for forgotten artifacts to remind himself of happier days, only to be heckled by Maman and Joseph and Mannie at every turn. Little hands tugged at his shirt and said things like, *Papa, what are we to do now?* and he had no answer to their questions.

With that sad thought, he put away his whiskey and retired to bed. He must sleep. Work in the morning. Then he remembered, there would be no work for awhile.

He hadn't been in Manchester long enough to make friends. There were people who cared about him, but in his pain Paul had forgotten them. In Woonsocket, Albert and Annie Bouley read the news of Saint-Pierre, and thought about Paul, their friend. Annie wrote to him because Albert was not so good with these emotions. She offered him support, urged him to attend mass. *"Take some comfort in Mother Church,"* she wrote. But he didn't know if there was any comfort to be found inside those cold stone cathedrals, or anything left in his heart to feel at all but rage at the god who betrayed him. The god to whom he once had been willing to give his life.

But that anger couldn't hold for more than a few days and he soon discovered a desperate need to talk to someone. Not Annie or Albert, but someone who shared the pain he was going through. He thought about Alcide Dufail in Maine. Much of the Dufail family, too, must have been lost in Saint-Pierre. Certainly Dr. Paul Dufail and his beautiful Parisian wife, and Alcide's mother, Lucie Berne.

After some searching, he located Alcide's address in his

trunk and sat down at his tiny desk, where he maintained his convenient pen and a small stack of stationery.

"My Dear Alcide," he began, "I hope this letter is not an unwanted intrusion into your life at this terrible time. I am afraid I am at a loss for words. The news from home is so horrible, I can't bear to think about it, and yet, forgive me, I feel a strong need to reach out to you, my fellow Pierrotin, that I may share my grief. As kind as my neighbors are, they are strangers to me now. I move as though through a different world. Perhaps you have felt this estrangement too and we may console one another and in doing so, find our way again."

He finished the letter, signed it, and mailed it the following morning on his way to work. Within the week he received a reply from Alcide, who expressed his own sadness at the news from Martinique. He had lost his mother and brother, Félix, and aunts and uncles, as well as many cousins and friends. At least he had heard no news of them and had resigned himself to their deaths. He wrote,

There will be a mass at Saints Peter and Paul on the first of June for the victims. Please come, if you can, and we will share our sorrow and reminisce about our childhood in the Quartier du Fort. Mary, my wife, and our son, Raoul, are pleased by the possibility of meeting a friend from Martinique, even on this tragic occasion.

COMFORT

Paul boarded the train Friday evening. It was his intention to sleep for most of the journey. The car was nearly full, although the seat next to him was empty. He caught snippets of conversation, some in French, some in heavily accented English, which he recognized as a dialect from Great Britain, but he didn't know from where, and he didn't really understand the words. One French-speaking mother tried to settle her tired children, soothing them with assurances that soon enough they will be home in Montréal. A baby began crying but calmed once the train started moving. Conversation around him dropped in volume, became a background rumble. Evening fell gradually and with it the voices softened and stopped. He was left alone with his thoughts.

A hollow face stared back from the window as Paul tried to see through the darkness, looking for the shape of the landscape. They rounded a curve as the moon edged past the clouds and hit the Atlantic, lighting up a swath of ocean rolling toward shore. The man in the window disappeared for a time until the track turned back inland and the moon was gone. This time, he recognized him. It was Joseph. He could tell by the tightness of his jaw, the way those eyes accused him. Is there a room in his house for Joseph? If Paul could find a room for him, would he forgive Paul at last for being Maman's favorite son? Because that's it, isn't it? As he studied Joseph's face, he saw his own features, his own eyes burning, accusing, and realized he never understood Joseph's grief until now. He lifted his hand to the window. His brother's hand met his on the glass and Paul took hold. He could find a place for him, a room in his mind where he could visit Joseph the way he visited Stéphanie and the children — *oh God, my loves, my loves.* All the faces and voices crowded in on him. Rooms, so many rooms, but he couldn't have all these ghosts roaming at will, they would drive him mad. L'habitation Sablon loomed up, infused with unsullied childish memories. It was so large and accommodating, room for them all. Perhaps it was the old history with him, how they fought, the undercurrent of bewildered love, that was the reason the first room he made was for his brother Joseph. Paul tipped his head back and closed his eyes. He'd never been so tired.

HE WOKE BRIEFLY when a man sat in the seat next to him smelling of cigars and whiskey and began snoring almost as soon as the train moved again. It was morning when he next awoke and the man was gone. The train slowed as it came into Portland, Maine. The harbor was busy with steamships and short line tracks and longshoremen loading and unloading ships and containers.

He changed trains and by early afternoon he had arrived in Lewiston. Alcide greeted him at the train station, gripping his hand and kissing both cheeks. Emotion took both men, their tears mingled briefly.

A small boy—Paul guessed him to be about five years old—

stood by, watching the scene between the two men. He looked sad, but most likely because his father was sad. Paul smiled at the boy. "Who is this young man?"

"Paul, this is Raoul. He's named after his uncle Raoul, of course." Raoul smiled at Paul and took hold of his father's hand.

"Have you met your uncle Raoul?" Paul asked him.

"No," the child said, "Uncle Raoul lives in Guyane. That's in South America. It's very far away."

"Yes," Paul said, "further even than Martinique."

The mere mention of Martinique jolted him. And he could see his torment reflected in Alcide's face. *Maybe it was a mistake to have come here,* he thought for just a moment, before rejecting it. No, this was the right thing, for him, for Alcide.

The Dufail home, modest and middle class, was not a poor man's house. Alcide Dufail came to America for the same reasons Paul had: to learn the essential trades and business operations to build a future in the 20th Century. So his family connections, like Paul's, gave him entrance into the managerial world of the textile industry. Alcide's father had been a prominent négociant, an oil dealer, in Saint-Pierre, until his untimely death in 1875, when Alcide was still a toddler and Alcide's brother, Raoul, was not yet free of the womb. His Dufail ancestors were a mixed-race family, although by Alcide's generation the children easily passed for white. This was less important in the business world of Saint-Pierre, where the vast majority, rich and poor, were mixed, than in North America, where one drop of African blood marked you as less than human in some eyes.

Louise prepared dinner and after they had eaten the two Martiniquais retired to reminisce about their hometown and their youth, their own private wake, with no corpse in the living room, only in their hearts. Louise put Raoul to bed and spent the evening in the kitchen, making dessert for the church social tomorrow, cleaning up the dishes, and leaving the men to themselves.

"Do you remember when we were schoolboys, Paul?" said Alcide. "You were... what? Two or three years behind me? Were you Raoul's age?"

"Non," said Paul. "That was my brother, Mannie. I was a year younger."

"Oui," said Alcide, "and Joseph was the same year as my brother, Félix."

"Oui," Paul agreed, his mind going off on a journey through those years in the Parish school at l'Eglise du Fort. Happy years, mostly, until Eustase died. After that, Papa had taken them off to Bordeaux for most of a year, so that they could all forget. But in his mind, sometimes, he turned that around, telling himself that they had been in Bordeaux when his brother died, that they had rushed home to Saint-Pierre to be with him. It was as though he had deliberately chosen to forget those years before the hunting accident. Now, his memory played tricks on him. But he could never banish the image of his dying brother in Mannie's arms. And that always brought him back to reality, because he had been there, hadn't he? Not across the sea in the Métropole.

The evening continued like that, the two men recalling those boyhood years when life was carefree. Those days of wandering the hills with the other boys of the neighborhood, frightening each other with stories about snakes and zombis and evil spirits. Stories told by the older ones to frighten the younger, like the one about Père Labat, whose ghost ate bad children in the night, a tale which Paul and his brothers had learned from Daniel and Euphrasie at l'habitation Sablon.

But the conversation eventually led him down paths he didn't wish to go, and Paul abruptly excused himself, asked to be shown to his room.

"I am rather exhausted by this day," he said.

LATE AT NIGHT, having difficulty falling to sleep in this strange house, he found himself in a hallway of l'habitation Sablon. His ghosts mingled and watched him, expectant, patient as if it did not matter to them where he put them or how long it took him to assign them rooms like a paternal hôtelier.

Not at all what he wanted. But that's the way of ghosts, isn't it? How could he make room for them all? The Dupouys, Edith and Samuel and Raphaël and their many children—Léonie! He could never forget dear Cousine Léonie—the Dufail family and the Marlets, Étienne the bread seller, and Alexandrine with her cart of ripe fruits creaking along the cobblestones of the quartier, crying out, *mango, mango mi,* and all the children of his neighborhood who once greeted him on the street, *Bonjou, misye Poncy,* as he made his way to the rhumerie or to the market or to the tobacconist.

What would he do with all of these memories? All of these revenants walking through his dreams? He found himself traipsing through the dusty halls of l'habitation Sablon, peering into empty rooms, searching for forgotten artifacts to remind himself of happier days, only to be heckled by Maman and Joseph and Mannie at every turn. Little hands tugged at his shirt and said things like, Papa, what are we to do now? and he had no answer to their questions.

There were too many of them, and they all wanted his attention. Only Joseph in his own private room was quiet. Perhaps, he thought, if I give each one an empty room, I can visit when I please. So he went about assigning rooms, knowing the unruly creatures of his mind might resist. But what other option did he have? He introduced each of them to their designated room and tried as best he could to answer their objections. Last was Stéphanie and the children, to whom he provided an entire suite of bedrooms. The children grumbled. They did not know this house. He placated them by saying, *You may do whatever you like with your rooms, and when things become too boring, perhaps your maman will take you to the beach or shopping on Rue Sainte-Catherine. Alice, who had been gazing out the window, exclaimed, Bordeaux! Look, we are in Bordeaux!*

Stéphanie smiled a sad smile and he kissed her cheek. *I'm sorry I must leave, ma chère,* he said. *I must do this for my health, do you understand? I cannot be thinking of you always.*

Paul sought through the upturned faces for Maman. Once, he thought he saw Alice walking toward him and he turned around, not willing to face her just yet. Her voice called out, *Papa,* but he willed it away and kept walking, knowing that whichever way he went in these twisted corridors, they always took him to the same place.

At last he found Maman's room and he knocked softly. *Come in, Son.* He opened the door and stood still for a moment, looking out on Maman's little garden and the fields of wheat and looming above them in the background, Montagne Pelée. No more had he noted the volcano than it vanished, replaced by a painterly midwestern prairie sky.

How have you been, Maman?

I've been fine, Son.

You must be lonely here, Maman,

No, Son. That is you who is lonely. I am dead.

He nodded, acknowledging that sad truth. *Maman, you do not know how lonely I am. And how lost.*

Well, Paul, we must all go on, mustn't we?

He sighed, a long lingering sigh. When he looked through Maman's window, there was the mountain again, and the sound of distant rumbling, and a great chasm opening up in the earth. He looked away, refusing to see.

I must go Maman. It's time to go. He kissed her tenderly on the cheek, and turned toward the door, his heart racing, eager to flee this dreamscape.

MASS the next morning at Saint Peter and Saint Paul was followed by a French language liturgy, as the congregation prayed for the souls lost in Saint-Pierre. Paul was too far inside himself to listen to the words. And he was still too angry with God. Because what kind of God would do this to His people? He sat through the service like a stone, unmoving and unmoved.

It was only afterward as he prepared to board the train back to Manchester, when he felt the warmth of Alcide's hand and saw the kindness in Louise's face that he finally felt the comfort he'd come seeking.

It didn't escape his notice that comfort hadn't come in the form of God or Mother Church, but in the human touch.

O CANADA

Upon his return to Manchester, he found a letter from Clara waiting for him:

MY DEAR MONSIEUR PONCY,

I would have written to you much sooner, but I have been in so much shock that I could not find the words. Please accept my sincerest condolences. The tragedy in Saint-Pierre has been on all of our minds and I hope you are bearing up well under the weight of your loss. We have been praying for all the unfortunate souls, although that must not be much of a consolation in your time of need. Please know I am thinking of you.

Your friend, Clara.

HE GENTLY FOLDED the letter back into its envelope and set it on his desk. *Such a sweet girl. I have friends, don't I?* Clara and Albert and Annie, Alcide and Louise, Francine and her family, counting them was like counting his fortune.

Paul lay on his bed and allowed the sadness to wash over him. And then he slept, dreamlessly, his ghosts obediently silent behind their doors.

The next morning he returned to work, and for the next several months, through the fall and winter, and into the next spring, work became everything. Whenever he could, he toiled extra hours so he had little time alone to dwell upon the catastrophe. Clara and Annie both avoided further mention of the disaster in Saint-Pierre in their letters, for which he was immensely grateful. He returned their correspondence, asking about their families, telling them about the challenges of his new job for a manufactory, which now included occasional presentations to managers and fellow machinists in the railway repair shops. He traveled sometimes to Boston or Hartford or Chicago to talk about the ALCO locomotives. *I would rather be on the floor getting grease on my hands,* he wrote to the Bouleys. *But as an educated machinist with business knowledge, my superiors often push me far beyond my comfort level.*

In April, he received a letter from Albert, inviting him to the Jean-Baptiste Day celebration in Montréal in mid-June, which would coincide with the Boulé family reunion. Young Clara had already written to him, letting him know she would be attending the reunion with her grandmother. *Father, too, is going,* she'd said. Paul decided he must go. It would be good for his heart.

LITTLE ABOUT MONTRÉAL reminded Paul of Saint-Pierre, not least of all its size. He was uncertain why he thought it might. Perhaps because the two cities had been founded at the same approximate time by French colonists who left the Métropole for the New World. And perhaps there were moments walking the narrow rues of the old town, with their French architecture and cobbled streets, there came echoes of his hometown. But the wide modern boulevards of greater Montréal with their glass-fronted shops and luxurious sidewalks were thoroughly American. And missing too from these northern streets were all the black faces and the Caribbean sun and the soldiers and gendarmes lolling about the Customs House and Place Bertin, speaking a French he could understand.

But he was not unhappy with this. He had no real desire to bring back those memories here and now. Montreal was warm enough on this sunny June day. Albert and Annie, with four-year-old Olivia in tow, chatted amiably and pointed out landmarks to him as they strolled through the Ville-Marie, bringing a kind of unexpected happiness to his morning.

"There," Annie said, pointing out a towering cathedral, "is the Basilica de Notre Dame, and the hill beyond is Mont Royal. There are two cemeteries at the top of it, one French and one English. McGill University is there also, at the base, although you can't really see it from Ville-Marie."

Annie led them to Saint Henri Square to view the nine-meter-high statue of Jacques Cartier. Someone had defaced the concrete base of the statue with the words, *meurtrier des indigènes*. Annie apologized to Paul, as though she were an affronted Québécois, and not a Rhode Island housewife. Paul was touched and a little humored by this. "It's only true, isn't it?" he couldn't help saying. "Weren't all the Americas settled by murderers?"

Annie gave him a look and he hoped he hadn't offended her. These North Americans were so conservative in many ways, a fact that he kept forgetting. "I suppose that's so," said Albert, "but we wouldn't be here if not for people like Jacques Cartier."

"I can't deny it," said Paul, "but it's something to think about, yes?"

THAT EVENING they attended a concert at the Académie de Musique on Rue Sainte-Catherine, one of many events associated with the Jean-Baptiste Day celebration. The works were all French, by Fauré and Debussy, with one piano piece by a young composer named Maurice Ravel. Paul had never heard of him, but people in the audience seemed excited to see his name on the program. Albert and Annie, who had left Olivia with a Bouley relative, both demurred opinions on the music, giving Paul the impression they were uncomfortable with the subject, although they seemed to enjoy it. Paul, himself, was mesmerized. He had always only imagined such an experience: to hear a forty-five-piece orchestra playing the newest compositions from Paris.

He would have liked to stay out on the town and have a whiskey afterward, but Annie was eager to get back to Olivia. Tomorrow came the big parade and she wanted to be rested. The men agreed, reluctantly, and the three of them retrieved Olivia and returned to their hotel. While Annie put the little girl to bed, Albert nudged Paul and the two retired to the hotel bar where they ordered drinks.

"Just one," Albert insisted.

The two men reminisced about their time in Buffalo. "Our younger days," Albert said, as though it had been much further back in time than a mere two years ago. But it seemed long ago to Paul as well. It was, after all, a different life altogether. As much as he wished to erase the tragedy of Saint-Pierre, there would always be before the volcano and after the volcano.

Following a few more drinks, Albert said, "You remember Arthur's girl, Clara? She has turned into a fine young woman."

It was Paul's first clue — although he didn't realize it at the time — that Annie and Albert had a hidden motive for dragging him off to Montréal. Albert wasn't aware that he and Clara had been exchanging letters for some time now. "We have been corresponding since Buffalo. She is a sweet child."

"Well," Albert said, "she is no longer a child of fifteen. She is nearly eighteen now. That's what I was saying."

Yes, he supposed she was. He wondered why Albert insisted on getting this point across. "I look forward to meeting her again at the reunion tomorrow."

THE MORNING of the parade was bright and warm but for a light fog lingering over the river and the lower streets of Ville-Marie. The idea of a walk through the old town tugged at Paul, so he arranged to meet the Bouleys later near the Jacques Cartier monument. Something about the foggy narrow streets and the riverside. Maybe it was some memory of childhood, although he couldn't say; the sound of the water, the warm air of almost-summer.

As he drew nearer the water, a slight morning chill in the air reminded him that this was not like tropical Martinique at all. The fog near the river was more dense than it had seemed from above, and he could no longer see the other side of the river, just the vague outlines of piers and marinas and the big port farther downstream. As though from far away, he heard the familiar sounds of water lapping at boats, and voices, a man, a child, speaking in Créole and for a moment, despite the chill, he was home again in Saint-Pierre.

He continued along the narrow, cobbled streets, keeping a block or two from the riverside. He was afraid if he went all the way down to the water, the spell would be broken. In a doorway ahead, the face of a child peered at him in the fog. "Bonjou, Mesye," the little girl said in Kreyol before she ran off down the street, disappearing into an alley which led to the riverfront. Her footsteps rang on the cobblestones, echoed off the buildings around him.

He followed the girl for a moment, then stopped. He was seeing things in the fog, hearing voices that weren't there. And if they were real, then it might be best not to follow them. He was about to turn back when the child poked her head from a doorway, laughing. "Papa," she called in Kreyol, "can we go down to the beach?"

He tried to make out her features in the fog, but her face remained no more than an indistinct blur. "Yvonne?" he said, because it must be Yvonne. He had crossed, somehow, into that other world.

The little girl giggled and ran off to the end of the alley where it opened onto a quai. She crossed the quai toward a man, another shadow in the fog, scraping barnacles from the hull of an upturned fishing boat. "Papa," the girl repeated, "can we go down to the beach?" The man did not answer, but Paul could now hear voices of fishermen calling out the morning catch, and he smelled the salt air of the Caribbean sea. Suddenly, he felt light-headed. He could go no further. Hadn't he had left this all behind? These ghosts of Saint-Pierre. Back up the hill from which he had come lay the real world, and it was certainly beyond the time he had promised to meet up with Albert and Annie and little Olivia.

THE BOULEYS WERE WAITING for him at the Jacques Cartier monument when he arrived. Yesterday's errant message about murdered natives had been cleaned up, swept away with the trash so as not to mar the festivities. People were gathering in the park, streaming in from all corners of the city to see the parade. Excited children darted about, calling to one another in their local French, which still sounded to Paul like a foreign language, almost as exotic as the English with which he still struggled.

"Did you have a nice walk?" asked Annie.

"Yes, it is an exquisite day." And it was, though he shivered at the thought of the little girl in the fog and the memories she conjured. Had she actually been there at all?

From far away, he heard a brass band approaching. "It's coming," said Olivia, straining against her mother's hand, which held her back from running down the street, from getting lost in the crowd. "Can't we go see it?"

"Patience," Annie said. "It will be here soon."

As the parade arrived, the older children ran into the street, shouting, trying to find a better vantage point. The festive atmosphere drew Paul into its thrall. He realized he was feeling joy as the pageant engulfed him. A band played a quadrille as costumed participants carried aloft an enormous puppet and he was back in Saint-Pierre again. It was Mardi Gras and revelers called down from balconies and he and his girl wove themselves into the fabric of Martinique. He was part of that cloth. The moment passed with the beat of a drum — not a ka drum, but a big bass drum — and he returned to Montréal surrounded by French Canadiens fiercely celebrating their Frenchness on the rues and boulevards of the old city. *This is the real world,* he thought, and felt strangely at peace with it.

Paul gazed at Albert and Annie and smiled when Annie noticed him, then he took little Olivia in his arms, giving Annie a rest from the giddy girl, and held her high upon his shoulder.

"Can you see better now, ma petite chérie?" he asked.

"Yes," Olivia shouted, then she squealed as a float covered in orange and red flowers came into view, pulled by two prancing chestnut horses with plumes of white feathers waving on their bobbing heads, their bridles sparkling in the sun.

Paul laughed too. He had seen nothing like this before. It no longer reminded him of Carnival. But it felt a little more like home.

REUNION

The reunion began in the late afternoon at a Boulet residence in the fashionable village of Outremont. The large country home at the eastern edge of the ville beyond the slope of Mount Royal was already filling up with Boulet kin when Paul arrived with Albert, Annie, and Olivia. Several large tables constructed in the spacious yard were spread with various hors d'oeuvres, plates of bread, and pitchers of lemonade. A play area was sectioned off for the small children, overseen by two adolescent girls who seemed to take their duties quite seriously. Nannies-in-training, Paul thought. Or, on second thought, probably just mamas-in-training. Annie chatted with the girls for a time, giving Olivia a chance to become comfortable before leaving her to play with the other children. Albert wandered off to chat with his relatives.

Paul scanned the crowd, looking for the Mandevilles, but they were nowhere in sight. He was out of place among these strangers, yet it felt awkward to be following Albert around as he greeted extended family. Paul excused himself and found a chair in the shade where he could watch the guests arriving and mingling. He was reminded of the big family gatherings at the

Dupouy house in Saint-Pierre. He was feeling in the moment, comfortably surrounded by the buffer of his aloneness among these people, so determinedly French, though surrounded by the English, just as Montréal was surrounded by Rivière Saint Laurent. *I am,* he thought, *an island within an island within an island.*

"Monsieur Poncy!" A young woman, her dark hair swept up from her face, topped by a broad-brimmed straw hat was striding unevenly toward him as if over rough ground. She steadied herself with a beautifully carved walking stick.

He stood immediately. His friend was no longer a child. Clara was, in fact, a beautiful young woman, just as Albert had claimed. "Mademoiselle Mandeville. What a pleasure to see you again." He made a slight bow, a broad grin on his face. Paul recognized Arthur Mandeville, hands in pockets, standing next to Albert several yards away. They both smiled and nodded to him, or each other, he couldn't be sure. There was something almost conspiratorial about them. Paul turned his attention to Clara. "Sit with me?"

She sat on the grass without hesitation, tossing her walking stick aside. He sat next to her, leaving his chair empty. Clara regarded him thoughtfully. "I am so glad Albert and Annie brought you with them. How long are you staying?"

"A few days more. I will need to return to Manchester and my work, although at the moment I much prefer to be here."

"I expect Albert has planned things for you to see while you are here."

"Well, actually, no. Beyond today, nothing."

"It is not like Albert to be such a poor host."

"Albert is a fine man, but I much prefer to be sitting here on the grass with my dear friend," Paul said. Clara smiled.

They chatted peacefully for several minutes before two young girls appeared in front of them, plopping down like puppies. "Monsieur Paul Poncy, may I present my sisters the mesdemoiselles Berthe and Germaine. Berthe, of course you have met already."

"Did you see all the food? There is a whole pig!" The younger one broke in.

"No. I cannot believe it!" Paul exclaimed, raising his eyebrows dramatically.

Clara laughed. "We must show him. Come." Grabbing her cane, she rose with amazing dexterity, offering him a hand up, which he clasped as he sprang to his feet.

Once the roasted pig had been suitably admired, the sisters took off to join their cousins. Clara pointed out various aunts and uncles, their names and vocations. "Come. I must introduce you to Uncle Edgard."

Clara dragged him to meet her uncle, a young man with wild hair and handlebar mustache. "Uncle," she said, "this is my friend, Paul Poncy. He is a railroad machinist. Uncle is studying to be an artiste."

"Pleased to meet you, Paul," said Edgard. "Do you work for the Grand Trunk?"

"No, I'm employed by the American Locomotive Company in Manchester. Although I wouldn't mind hiring on with the Grand Trunk. They have one of the largest locomotive shops in North America. What kind of art do you study, Edgard?"

"Everything, I suppose. But I am, or intend to be, a portrait artist. Primarily oils. It is my strength, I believe."

"I think there will be fierce competition in the Mandeville family," said Clara with a little laugh. "Papa will want to photograph you, and Uncle to paint your picture. I suppose your choice will depend upon how much time you have to spare."

The men laughed.

"Now, if you will excuse us, Uncle," said Clara, "I must

introduce Paul to Uncle Antonio, if I can find him. Then we shall go to see Maman."

Taking their leave of Edgard, Clara introduced him to several other guests, including Uncle Antonio, a wiry young man with long limbs, chatting with Grandmother Boulet. He barely had time to say, "Nice to meet you, Antonio. A pleasure to see you again, Madame," when Clara dragged him off again in another direction. *The energy of youth,* he thought, feeling like an old man at twenty-five.

Eventually the two of them located Clara's mother sitting with a group of other women, baby Mathilde squirming on her knee. Paul thought Madame Mandeville seemed careworn, which he attributed to these energetic young daughters, one after another in age. Clara leaned her walking stick against the wall and offered to take the baby, but her mother demurred. "I am fine, dear," she said, smiling at Paul. "You two go enjoy your-selves. It is a pleasure to meet you, young man."

"Likewise, Madame," Paul said.

Just then, Therese Boulet entered the room, eyeing Paul. "Just the one I'm looking for. I need a strong young man to fetch some crushed ice. It's far too much for an old lady like myself to manage."

"Certainement, Madame," said Paul.

"Perhaps you and Clara might accompany me to the ice house, then."

"Avec grand plaisir, Grandmama," said Clara.

Clara grabbed her walking stick with one hand and Paul with the other and pulled him out the door.

PAUL OFFERED his arm and Clara took it. A good chaperone, Grandmother Boulet walked several yards behind the two young people, who were leaning into one another as they strolled along the graveled lane, unconscious at that moment that there existed anyone but themselves in the world. The late afternoon sun warmed them; the breeze was nearly stilled; all verbal conversation between them had stopped, letting in the sounds of the Montréal countryside, the soft rustling of leaves, the gravel crackling beneath their feet, the songs of sparrows as they skittered about in the silver maples which lined the drive. In the silence, Paul found himself at peace with this girl, with this family, with this place, which evoked again a feeling he could only describe as home.

Of course, he would have to return to Manchester in a few days. But there would be time to grow closer to Clara—if he decided that was what he wanted. The distance between Montréal and Manchester was nothing, really. And only a few hours further to Labelle. He looked at Clara to find her shyly looking back at him. When she smiled, he experienced a joy he hadn't felt in a long time.

They had nearly reached the street, when Clara said, "There is a play Friday night at the Monument-National. It is called *L'Aiglon.* Have you heard of it?"

"I don't think so," said Paul. "It is not the Sarah Bernhardt play, is it?"

"Oui," said Clara. "It may be the opportunity of a lifetime to see the great actress. There is an extra ticket, if you would like to go with me. Grandmama will chaperone."

"I would love to. But an extra ticket? For Sarah Bernhardt?"

Clara laughed. "Yes, Uncle Edgard has a season pass, but he can't attend. Grandmama had already purchased ours, so there's an extra, you see."

Paul smiled inside. He suddenly realized how much this week was being orchestrated to bring him and Clara together. It was charming, really. "I would love to go."

Clara leaned into him and whispered, "The Archbishop is having a tantrum about it, so some of the righteous might be throwing eggs at us as we enter." She laughed. "Grandmama says we can make an omelet with them."

"IT IS the tenth anniversary of the Monument-National," Clara informed Paul as they rode the trolley from Outremont. "It is the cultural center of Montréal, wouldn't you say, Grandmama?"

"For us it is," Madame Boulet said. "We built it ourselves. But," she sighed, "the Anglais... who cares what they think? We have the Societé and the Monument-National and will never forget Ludger Duvernay, bless his soul. Every 24 June, we remember his birthday because it is the day the Monument was inaugurated." As Theresa ended her rather stirring speech, Clara glanced up at Paul who seemed suddenly far away.

Ludger. He'd heard and read the name several times already. By now he knew Duvernay had founded the Sociêté Jean-Baptiste and he'd seen the image of the man printed on banners and posters, even a restaurant boasted his name and image. But this time, maybe because as Madame Boulet said Ludger, a black man wearing a straw hat was crossing the street and looked up at Paul as the trolley passed in front of him—for a heartbeat, it was Sylbaris crossing Rue Victor Hugo in Martinique.

"I have only been once to la Salle Ludger-Duvernay," Clara said. "It's most impressive." The excitement in her voice brought him back.

WHEN THEY WERE SEATED in their plush seats before the lights lowered, Paul opened the program. Several of Montréal's best theatre companies, he read, had called the Monument-National their home. The hall was indeed impressive, its walls lined in red velvet drapery and beautifully intricate woodwork. Paul had never been in such a large hall before. Most of the orchestral and parterre level seats were full when they arrived. The mezzanine where they were seated was still filling up. There were balconies, too, on either side of the stage, but they were hidden from the mezzanine.

"Tell me more about Ludger Duvernay?" Paul asked.

"He is the founder of the Jean-Baptiste Society," said Madame Boulet. "He was an early newspaperman who fought to protect French culture."

"I suppose that is important," said Paul.

"You don't sound so sure," Clara said with a little laugh.

"You and my granddaughter make a good pair," Madame Boulet said in an off-handed way.

"Oh, Grandmama, I know it's important. But we are all part of God's earth, French, English. Even Americans, I suppose."

Paul chuckled at that. "It seems to me all of this nationalism is promoted by the conservative clergy to keep the Québécois from straying from the Church. There was the same thing in Martinique. I am proud to be French, but I may not be a very good Catholic if I must listen to some of this nonsense from the pulpit."

"You certainly aren't afraid to share your opinion, young man," said Madame Boulet, lowering her voice. "I too am dismayed by the conservative zealots. There are too many of them about, even in my family."

"So tell me about this play," said Paul. "What is the Québécois obsession with Napoléon?"

"Napoléon," said Clara, "was the first French leader to

publicly acknowledge Québec. His son, Napoléon II, was called l'Aiglon, the play is about him. He once visited Québec, so this history is taught in our schools. He has become a symbol of our pride in being French, I suppose."

More *la Survivance,* thought Paul. It rankled his republican ideals just a little to think that those autocrats were so unquestionably venerated, but he decided to keep his opinion to himself. "I see," he said.

The lights went down and as he waited for the play to begin, Paul could not help but be keenly aware of the young woman sitting beside him. *Despite the terrible things that life can throw at you,* he thought, *it sends along beauty as well.*

He was delighted to see the famous actress, and when she first appeared on stage, costumed as the young Bonaparte, there was a sudden hush as the audience collectively held their breaths in anticipation. He quickly became absorbed in the drama, no longer thinking about the politics of republicanism, and when it was all finished, his thoughts lingered on the magic of the stage and how a woman of nearly sixty could make one absolutely believe that she was a young boy.

A magic like Saint-Pierre and Carnival, like Sophie dressed up as a man, and Paul, the doudou, weaving their way through the crowds along Rue Victor Hugo. He thought about how things are often not what they seem, and how one night can transform you. As he glanced at this brave girl beside him now, her excitement, her youth and beauty, he wondered if this might be one of those times when life would change him forever.

STRATFORD

Paul returned to Manchester happier than he'd been in a long time. Although they hadn't yet set a date—and no formal announcement would be made until he completed his apprenticeship exams and secured a solid job as a journeyman machinist—he was certain he had found the woman he wanted for a life partner. He and Clara had agreed to take their time, to get to know one another over the next year or two while Paul made a place for himself in the railroad industry, but he found himself eager to move on into that next part of his life.

It surprised him they had made the decision to marry so rationally. Despite his deep affection for this girl, there had been no grand romantic capture of his heart as there had been with Stéphanie or Amanda. Or the helpless, chaotic plunge of passion he felt for his first love, Sophie. It was more like he was building a partnership with Clara, something that would last for a lifetime. He thought about Papa and conceded that perhaps the old man was at least partially right. It wasn't about building your personal empire, as Anatole believed. But it was about survival and stability. And the kind of happiness that could endure.

Paul returned to his work with a renewed sense of purpose. By the next spring, he had passed his apprenticeship exams and paid the first installments of his journeyman dues to the International Association of Machinists and began seeking a position in Canada.

In the late fall, the Union presented him with an opportunity to advance his training in the Grand Trunk Railway Stratford, Ontario shops. He seized the job opening, which began in March, knowing that if he hesitated, someone else would quickly grab it. He would leave Manchester in mid-March and have a few weeks to settle into his new home. The Grand Trunk, about to embark on westward expansion, and desperately in need of journeymen machinists, offered a small stipend to help with relocation. Even though Stratford was actually further away from Clara in travel time, he would be in her country, to him a subtle, but important distinction.

THE TRAIN DEPARTED Manchester in mid-afternoon, heading south to Boston where he transferred to the same line that had taken him and Albert to Buffalo years ago. He could sleep through all that countryside between Boston and Buffalo and not feel like he was missing anything. He woke a few times, when the rhythm of the train changed abruptly and he got out once where the train was to stop for a good half hour. He smoked a cigarette and watched men shovel coal. The trains would all one day be running on diesel, but this one was still coal-fired steam. A few passengers came from the small wood frame station and disappeared into the train. He put out his cigarette and re-boarded. He thought about going back to sleep, but could not. Instead, he took the photograph from his bag, which Maman had sent him. It was the day he left Saint-Pierre and there he was with Stéphanie and all the children. Stéphanie held baby Yvonne on her lap, not even a month old. He tried again, but could not recall his little girl's face or imagine what she would look like if she were alive. The pain he still felt had lessened, it seemed. He replaced the photo in his travel bag and he watched his reflection in the window until Stéphanie appeared among the trees that raced by, anchored like a moon in the background. He closed his eyes.

There was a two-hour layover in Buffalo before he caught the train into Ontario and on to Stratford. Too little time to reacquaint himself with the city, but time enough to eat breakfast in the train station cafe and write a postcard to Clara. *"I expect I will learn new skills, and I'm determined to pass my Master's exam before I move on from Stratford. I'm lucky they agreed to take me into a training program, since it seems to be the only way for me to advance in my railroad career."* He knew it wasn't luck. He'd kept those letters of recommendation that secured him work in Woonsocket and Manchester. It seemed the Plissoneau name carried weight with the Grand Trunk Railroad, also. He supposed they'd contacted the Plissoneau firm to authenticate his letter, and he wondered what Georges thought of him still trading on his connections, still doggedly pursuing the railroad. Georges had never been the one to contact him in the United States. That had always been Samuel or Raphaël Dupouy. Would he be disappointed to learn that Paul had no intention of returning? He couldn't imagine living in Fort-de-France, so close to Saint-Pierre while fecund vegetation took over the empty streets and shattered buildings, grew over the bones and ashes of the dead. And perhaps he feared that most—to witness the total obliteration of his former life. There was no reason for him to go back, no reason at all. Martinique was a graveyard.

Paul shied away from these thoughts, stared out the train

window at the flat land that suddenly seemed to open up and go on forever on both sides of the train. On the map, this part of Ontario looked like an island between Lake Erie and Lake Huron. Paul knew glaciers pressed down on this land with their massive weight, but until now he had no comprehension of the scale. He had grown up in vertical topography, only the sea was flat and the plain de la consolation—those few acres bordering the Quartier du Fort. Here the world was horizontal. It stretched for miles and miles in every direction. Roads ran straight into the horizon. Horse-drawn dray carts with loads of lumber, hay, goods moving to and from train stations in small towns that popped up out of nowhere like those paper Christmas villages that unfold before your eyes.

The train overtook one-horse buggies driven by sober bearded men who, like the women with them, were dressed in grim black. A protestant religious sect, Paul thought, but couldn't remember which one. All headed to farms and far-flung towns, disappeared behind their individual clouds of dust that faded finally at the edge of the horizon.

At last, his new home came into view. Stratford, Ontario. Stratford-on-Avon in Canada. No Shakespeare, but perhaps the English bard's spirit lived here. Compared to Manchester, Stratford was clearly no more than an ambitious village, mostly catering to the farm trade and the employees of Grand Trunk's repair shop looming on the edge of town.

This is my new home now, Paul thought. *My new life. If I find no peace here, it will be my doing.* In that instant, he realized he must be truthful with Clara. *I must tell her about Stéphanie and the children.*

PAUL FOUND a room on Milton Street, between the railroad shops and what the locals referred to as the high street. A dollar and a half a week bought him a bed and two meals per day. Maisie Harrison, his landlady, bore a haggard, unsmiling face, but she seemed pleasant enough in conversation. He guessed the widow to be in her late forties. She changed the linens twice a week and expected promptness at mealtime, which suited him. His window afforded him a nice view of the large tree-covered park across the street. It was perfect for now.

He wrote to Clara often at first, then after a few weeks settled down to a letter on Saturday and a postcard on Tuesday and these he sent without fail. Before the winter set in, Arthur had moved the family back to Montreal and Paul half regretted his decision to move to Stratford. Had he stayed in Manchester he could have visited Clara more often. But his choice was made and his time with the Grand Trunk would be good for his career and their future. Paul faithfully put aside as much of his income as possible toward the day he and Clara would set up a household. There was little to tempt him in Stratford. In his spare time, he walked the streets of the village or went to the new public library searching for books in French and settling for reading newspapers and magazines in English. Occasionally, he would go to a tavern after work with a few of the men, but he wasn't often invited to join them.

Paul was one of several dozen journeymen who worked under Master Mechanic Patterson. They were machinists, boilermakers, blacksmiths and coppersmiths as well as indentured apprentices and general laborers. Altogether, there were over two hundred in the workforce. As a machinist, Paul belonged to an elite group in the shop. The International Association of Machinists represented all the journeymen, but there was a strict hierarchy among them. The title of Machinist conferred a special status. But it also brought resentment because of the higher pay rate and — to Paul's dismay — the treatment of less well-paid comrades by some of his fellow machinists who enjoyed lording it over their inferiors. It wasn't so different from the Manchester shop but here noticeably more grumbling came from the shop floor. Paul kept himself apart, feeling a certain detachment as one who is passing through. His reserve was clear and even the machinists who were not prancing about like petty lords didn't go out of their way to befriend him. When fall came and the cold bite of wind from the frozen north blew off Lake Huron, unimpeded by hills or trees, chilling him in his single bed, the idea of making Stratford home fled.

BY THE CHRISTMAS HOLIDAY, the rumblings and grumblings of the lower-paid shop workers became more intense, and had taken on edges that all but destroyed unity among the men, and even Paul could not ignore it. He was glad to escape for two weeks to Montreal to stay with the Mandevilles. He longed for Clara's companionship and was eager to set a date for their wedding. This time, his journey was through a landscape altered by snow that made the train into a giant snow plow. Blades affixed to the engine threw a constant spray of snow. He'd risen at 4:00 A.M., hours before dawn, to be sure to catch the 5 o'clock out of Stratford. He was asleep in his coach within an hour of boarding. The track followed the banks of Lake Ontario and then the Saint Lawrence. Perhaps it was halfway through his journey, Paul wasn't sure. He'd been reading, but paused to look out at the frozen river. A tiny house sat on the river amid drifts of snow. A girl was skating out from the bank to the house. A solitary house. A solitary child still far from the house, gone out of sight, obscured by evergreen trees and a bend in the track away from the river. How strange, he thought.

At the station in Montréal, Arthur and Clara met him with a horse-drawn sleigh and heavy robes to keep the cold at bay. Snow glittered in the light of streetlamps.

"It's beautiful," Paul said, "but it's brutal."

Clara squeezed his hand. Snow clung to her fur hat and the tips of her eyelashes. Paul leaned close to her ear and whispered, "You are beautiful." When he closed his eyes for a moment, he saw the skating child, the expanse of ice, the house in the frozen river.

On Christmas Eve, Paul walked with the Mandevilles to the parish church for midnight mass.

"Papa isn't particularly religious, but we always go. It is tradition," Clara explained.

The walkways were freshly shoveled. Paul himself had helped Arthur and neighbors clear the walk for a couple of blocks. The physical work momentarily pushed aside his apprehension about entering a church again. He had not been since the memorial mass at St. Peter and St. Paul in Lewiston.

"Oh," he said when Clara explained about Christmas Eve mass, "Maybe we could stay here and have a little time to ourselves?"

Clara shook her head. "Maybe you slipped some whiskey into the cider." She folded her arms across her chest. A steady look on her face. She didn't plead.

He could see the way it was. He drew a deep breath, "It was worth a try."

"Why don't you want to go?"

Paul would have told her. Not just about why he didn't want to go to midnight mass, but also about his children, their mother. He reached for his wallet where he kept their photograph. He had opened his mouth, but Berthe came running in all excited because Uncle Edgard had just arrived. Clara gave Paul a curious glance over her shoulder and followed her sister from the parlor to the kitchen where the younger children were all talking at once and everyone seemed to be laughing.

THE STRIKE

THOUGH CHRISTMAS HAD NOT BROUGHT peace to the shop, Paul was in better spirits and looking forward to being married in June and starting a family. He informed his supervisor that he and his wife would need a house and hoped they could live in one provided by the railroad. The company's simple two-story wood-frame houses were across the street from the shop. There weren't enough for all the families of the workers. Paul knew his odds weren't good, especially without children.

Patterson told him as much when Paul asked that his name be added to the list. "An apartment's the thing for you and your wife, Mr. Poncy. Though," he said, his ruddy face grown still, "some may find their names have slipped a bit and there's no telling what might happen between now and June. You keep your eye on what's important here and you might have a good shot at it."

Paul stepped out of Patterson's office high up where the Master Mechanic had a panoramic view of the workers below. At first glance, the shop floor seemed to be a chaotic jumble of half dismantled engines, parts strewn about, with men bent over their work or moving about the floor. But everything had an order when you knew what you were looking at, and from here you could not see, hear, or feel the dissatisfaction and resentment that was palpable when you were down among them. They would know, in the way secrets could not be kept, that he had put in for a house and everyone, even down to the shopboys, would figure that he'd get some special boost up the list because he was a machinist.

In the dark, between work and home, he felt himself being scrutinized. Conversations went silent as he approached. Paul couldn't blame any of them. Like him, they were working long nine-hour days with only a day and a half off each week. Sure, they were not breathing wool or cotton particles, but how different were these shops from the mills in Woonsocket? Or, for that matter, the sugar factories of Martinique? There were plenty of opportunities for overworked men to make mistakes that could cause them or their coworkers grave injury.

The bitter winter months passed, but the infighting and complaints from the workers increased even as the daylight lengthened. At local meetings, the men drew up a schedule of demands with the advice and aid of the Washington headquarters of the IAM. Higher wages and fewer hours topped the list.

The IAM and railway management prepared for negotiations. Shop stewards exhorted the men to turn their resentment away from their fellow workers and direct it toward their common enemy. This was made easier when the IAM announced apprentices would be admitted to the union, and the company's relentless efforts to weaken the union strengthened the men's resolve.

Seeing that the days were longer, the company increased the nine-hour weekdays to ten and from four hours on Saturday to five. He'd be working 55 hours a week now. April 1st was a Saturday and the first day of expanded work hours. Paul reported for work at seven to find what appeared to be the entire day shift, including apprentices, gathered outside the shop. "The night crew is still at work," one of the men reported.

"They say 7 o'clock. We're here, ready to work. What the hell are they up to?" one of the blacksmiths called out.

"Where are the shop stewards?" Paul asked.

The door opened and Master Mechanic Patterson appeared. "Apprentices, follow me." A few minutes later he came back and led the rest of the crew to the machinists' tool room. Inside were four shop police and a couple of men Paul had never seen before, probably sent from another GTR shop or headquarters. One of them held a sheaf of paper and the other a tray of fountain pens.

Paul folded his arms across his chest and spread his feet. From the corner of his eye, he could see he was not the only one to take a defiant stance.

As the last man filed into the tool room, one of the police closed the door and stood in front of it. Patterson cleared his throat. "These gentlemen have come all the way from our company's head office to meet with you men today. They're concerned, as we are, that you have some grievances. Because of our concern, we are giving you the opportunity to answer a short list of questions, which we'll ask you to sign."

The two company men were already passing out the documents and pens.

"As a sign of our good faith, you'll be able to keep the pen."

Paul raised an eyebrow. How much could the pen be worth? An hour's work? Less? He took the paper and pen held out to him.

"Please answer each question and sign."

The first question asked if he was content with current conditions at the Grand Trunk Railway shop. He answered no. The second asked why he was dissatisfied. That was easy enough as well. Wages were too low and hours too many. He'd barely read the third before a man in front of him and another from behind walked toward the door, still blocked by the guard. "We need to consult with our shop stewards."

"Where are you holding them?" from the back of the room.

The guard pulled his club out of the loop at his waist.

"Now there is no need for that. Just answer the questions and you'll be free to talk with anyone you want," Patterson said.

"I don't think so," Paul said. He read the third question out loud, conscious of his French accent. "In the future," he read, "should you find yourself dissatisfied with conditions at the workshop, will you be willing to take your concerns directly to the company?"

"I know you are eager to get to work," Patterson said, "and I'm afraid there is no time for you to talk this over. Answer the question, sign the paper and let's get back to work." All the guards had their clubs in their hands. Though with two hundred men packed into the room, the posturing was fooling no one.

Voices rose.

"That question there. It means we agree not to take our grievances to the IAM, don't it?"

"That's what it means."

"Well hell, I ain't signing this piece of shit."

The men became louder and angrier.

Patterson and the company men left the room, returning after a few minutes. "Very well. You may reconsider your answers."

As they left the room, each man carefully put the pen they'd used on a bench by the door. Paul found out later that most of the men answered as he had, citing dissatisfaction with wages and long hours and that they would not be willing to deal directly with the company. The apprentices had been given the same questions and as they were not yet members of the IAM, they had more to lose, yet also answered against dealing with the GTR. The union's position remained strong among the men.

When the IAM leadership sent word that the time had come for apprentices to be admitted to the union, a new energy filled the shop.

On 8 April, Grand Trunk called an "indefinite shutdown" of the shop for repairs. No one was fooled. It was a lockout and aimed to break the union's will. The men dug in for a prolonged battle, Paul among them. He thought about the salons in Stéphanie's garden and the youth that gathered there, earnestly discussing the rights of workers in the cane fields, sucreries, and distilleries and men like Sylbaris who handled the heavy barrels that went in and out of Saint-Pierre's harbor. Though he knew that with few exceptions, both those passionate youth and the workers they championed were victims of Mont Pelée, he felt a stronger connection to them at just this moment than he had ever before. Because of his family connections, he had never imagined that he would be on this side of a strike line. His privilege did not count for anything in Stratford. He might be a machinist with a certain valuable skill, but he was no one's cousin here.

The IAM called a special meeting and some men immediately pitched in for a strike fund, committees formed to persuade sympathetic business owners in Stratford to offer credit for the workers should the shutdown be prolonged or a strike called. With forty percent of Stratford depending on the shops, the proprietors knew when the strike was over, higher-paid union workers would continue to patronize the businesses that supported them. In addition, GTR had long-standing plans to enlarge the locomotive shops and had already petitioned Stratford's city council to have Nelson Street closed during construction. A larger shop meant more potential customers.

Better to be well-regarded and recommended than make enemies of the union men.

Paul was surprised at the festive air of the meeting. There was food and drink supplied by wives and daughters. Some time was taken up arranging a football match between the Scotsmen and the Englishmen to take place immediately after adjournment. Outside, the wind was blustery and Paul thought it was howling until he saw the bagpiper. It was more like a battle cry than music and he wondered if the man really knew how to play. But as the kilted piper walked away, about half the men who had been at the meeting followed as if captivated. He packed and lit his pipe and watched the parade march off to the playing field.

The "repairs" continued to keep the shop closed throughout April, though some of the gang bosses were "offered their pay"— an invitation to come back to work. They declined, choosing to stand with the men. The Stratford shops were not alone; over 2,000 members of the machinists' union working in GTR shops in Ontario and Québec raised demands for higher wages and reduced hours. Paul was proud to be among them. He could feel the power of this solidarity even if they didn't win, and there were no guarantees. GTR intended to delay a settlement for as long as possible. In Toronto, Division Superintendent Robb refused to consider the schedule of demands brought to him by representatives from the various shops, referring them instead to their local superintendents. When the company continued to refuse their demands, ninety percent of the union membership voted to strike and laid down their tools on May 5th.

I fear I must tell you that we will not be in a position to wed in June, Paul wrote to Clara. *I am not earning wages and am living on my savings. I am looking for other work, but we must be realistic.* He soon found that few jobs were available in Stratford, and Clara reluctantly agreed to put off the wedding until

November. He didn't have the skills of a tailor or shoemaker. He inquired with builders and found a little work wiring houses, but only enough to pay for his room and board. He wrote to his former employers in Manchester inquiring about work there, and by June, he was back at ALCO in New Hampshire.

Grand Trunk Railroad and the union finally came to an agreement in October. Paul learned some machinists had found work with Canadian Pacific during the strike and stayed on with that company after the walkout ended. Others had gone elsewhere, but he felt he would do better by returning to the Stratford shops, and when Master Machinist Patterson wrote to him that his position was still available and a company house besides — a concession to the union — he did not hesitate to return.

Everything would be back to normal in time for the wedding.

CLARA

In mid-October, a month before they were to marry, the icy mountain air had already begun to move down from the cold north of the Laurentides and settle into the crooks and crannies of the ville de Labelle. Once a beautiful little mountain hamlet, nestled in the lake region of Québec, it still held a certain charm in 1905, despite the ravages of logging, its principal economic activity. A few years earlier, a new covered bridge had been erected over the Rivière Rouge, just above the falls, and in 1902 the Sisters of the Holy Cross arrived and planned construction of a convent. Originally known as Iroquois Falls, the village was renamed in 1890 to honor its founder, Father Antoine Labelle, a colonial curé of dubious honor, who had led the drive to populate this frontier with Francophone settlers and push the last of the native people into reserves.

Clara Mandeville stepped cautiously from the front porch of her home and pulled her coat tightly around her shoulders, shuddering a little from the chill. She walked along the path to the gate, taking her time with each step, balancing her awkward progress with a wooden cane. She seldom needed her cane for a short walk, but the path was uneven and she'd fallen on it more than once.

The mail carrier, nearly as reliable as the mill's steam whistle, would be here at any moment. It was Thursday, and a postcard from her fiancé arrived nearly every week on this day. Clara would wait and catch the postman before eleven-year-old Germaine, with her prying eyes, intercepted the mail. Her little sisters were naturally curious about Paul, but it annoyed her no end when they snapped up the mail so they could tease her with it, as if she were a child herself, not nineteen and about to be wed.

As she waited patiently, Clara regarded the ugly, barren hillside of clear-cut stumps that loomed over the little logging town, with its muddy streets and shabby houses. She always longed for her Montréal whenever their household was in Labelle, but it felt a bit like a betrayal to her father's side of the family. After all, they were there in Labelle to be near his parents, because Grandpapa was the Notary for Mont Laurier.

For years, Clara's grandparents had maintained a large, comfortable home in the fashionable Mile-End quarter of Montréal, not so far from Clara's own childhood home in Outremont. Her grandparents also maintained a second residence in Labelle, near the village of Joly, from which they sometimes hosted family gatherings in the summer, when the weather was beautiful and the roads passable. Her grandparents' big house was on a lake, a few miles away, among other big, beautiful houses, not here across the street from a putrid lumber mill.

She was embarrassed by the raw ugliness of Labelle and said as much to Paul. He merely said, "Well, that's progress, ma chère."

"Well, the point is my family doesn't have to live *here*," she replied. "In this precise place, across the street from *this*."

But she knew, married to this man, she might well be living in places like this, raising her children on the edges of the industrial frontier, while he tried to shape the world in his image. *Why can't the trees be left to grow in the forest?* her heart asked. But of course she knew the answer to such a silly, idealistic question. Maybe she even knew such questions do not so much express concern for their subject, as for her wish to not see the ugliness left behind in the drive to build the cities and the towers and even second homes for people like the Mandevilles.

The Church said it was good. It is man's role to conquer the earth and bring it under God's dominion. So, it must be so.

The Mandeville family was relatively well off and comfortable. She should have been content. But even the squawking of the geese fleeing from winter storms was a nuisance to Clara at the moment. *What is this ennui?* she wondered. Was she getting cold feet? Sometimes she couldn't quite believe this mysterious Frenchman had actually chosen her, a girl whose life was twisted by polio, who had difficulty walking without assistance. *Surely there's a better catch out there than me,* she thought. *This is the twentieth century, after all, and a man can choose whomever he wishes to marry.*

She silently chastised herself for her self-deprecation. She knew she had much to offer a husband. It was just such a surprise to her, and she didn't entirely trust it.

Clara spied the postman coming up the boardwalk with a small bundle of mail in his hand. "Bonjour, Monsieur Thebault," she said. "Is there any mail for me?"

"Oui, Clara. There's a postcard from Stratford for you." He exhibited a warm smile as he handed her the mail. "Your wedding will be soon, yes?"

"In November," she said. "Just a month away."

"I'm thrilled for you, Miss Clara. Bonne journée."

Clara carried the mail back into the house and laid the

bundle on the entry table. Pulling out the card, she took it to her room, where she fell onto her bed. The card showed a row of buildings filled with shops and restaurants. Certainly, it wasn't Montréal, but it was clearly not a village like Labelle, either. On the back, Paul described the two-floor house that would be their first home.

PAUL WAS disinclined to talk about Martinique and no one, least of all Clara wanted to cause him pain, but she was very curious about his place of origin, and when she found Lafcadio Hearn's book about the West Indies in a Montréal bookstore, she bought it. Hearn's description of Saint-Pierre broke her heart. She was dazed by the thought that this marvelous place — and all those incredible women traversing mountain paths with a store of goods balanced on their heads — was gone. She forced herself to read the newspaper clippings of the disaster that she had saved. Some papers showed photos of bodies piled up to be burned because it was not possible to bury all the dead, though some effort was made to find and bury a few prominent white families. The pictures and articles broke her heart and she cried again as she did when she first read them.

Clara had worried over what to say in her first letter to Paul after the volcano destroyed Saint-Pierre and almost every living soul. Except for the prisoner, the black man whose solitary cell with only a tiny window and thick walls protected him from the terrible heat.

"What will I write to Monsieur Poncy?" she had asked her parents.

"You cannot console him," they replied. "Just say what is in your heart."

In the end, she had just said that she knew she had no words to comfort him, but she would continue to write if it pleased him. It was several weeks before a letter came from Paul. He made very little reference to the catastrophe. Just that he felt lost in the world and very much appreciated her letters.

She opened the drawer of her bedside table and lifted out a stack of postcards. She untied the ribbon that held them together and spread the cards out on her bed. His letters were often several pages, but the cards were usually brief and impersonal. Except for the one. She picked it up. The front of the postcard pictured a long industrial building, the shops of the Grand Trunk Railway in Stratford. Beneath the picture he had written: *"Portrait de la prison où loin de toi je passe mes heures à penser à ma C. Paul."* She sensed a deep sadness in the words. And she could see that sadness in him when she was with him. She wondered sometimes at his claim to be born in Bordeaux. He was so sensitive about Martinique; about his brothers who died in the volcanic eruption; about little things he had let slip regarding Saint-Pierre; about his school days. He refused to talk about it, about the horrible thing that had happened, and so she would have to honor that. Then there was the issue of his mother who lived in Oklahoma.

"Have you heard from your mother, Paul? Will she come to our wedding?" She had asked last Christmas, hesitating just a little, because his mother, Clémence, was such a mystifying subject.

"I don't think so," he said, a slight hesitancy in his voice. But he gave no further explanation.

Clémence lived in a convent or a Catholic convalescent home, or something, it wasn't at all clear to Clara. And Paul was never able or willing to explain to her satisfaction. Clara suspected that his mother was just a story, that she had died, like his brothers, in the volcanic explosion that destroyed Saint-Pierre.

She did not think the worse of him for these evasions. On the contrary, she thought she could imagine the pain that tragedy must have caused him. He only needed time to heal, that's all.

If ever one day he reveals this part of his heart to me, she thought, *then I will comfort him.*

A PROMISE

Master Mechanic Patterson allowed Paul a week to go to Labelle for his wedding. It was more than he'd expected so soon after the strike ended. The Mandevilles and Boulets greeted him with joy, kissing his cheeks, exclaiming over how well he looked. Clara's youngest sister, Mathilde, held her arms up to him. It was the most natural thing in the world for him to pick up this merry child and hold her on his hip as if she were his own. "Yvonne," he said, "how big you are." All the doors of the house flew open and there they all were, each one standing on the threshold of the particular room where he had put them, silent and staring. Then the doors slammed shut, the noise of Clara's family rushed back and he handed Mathilde to her grandmother, Therese. He wrapped his arms around Clara. "Oh, how I've missed you," he said.

They honeymooned for four days in Montreal, their hotel paid for by Clara's grandparents, before Paul brought his new bride home to Stratford. Clara had brought a large trunk full of her belongings. It pleased her that the house would be adequate for them, although not as spacious as she was accustomed. "It will do," she pronounced after inspecting it. Paul laughed, although her comment gave him pause. Eventually they would find something bigger and better, but it would have to do, for now.

By Christmas, Clara knew she was already pregnant.

FRANCIS PAUL PONCY *was born on 8 September 1906*. He was christened in St. Joseph's Catholic Church where they attended mass, Clara more faithfully than Paul. It was easy to register the baby's birth, there was no one to question his right to the Poncy name even if they had not been married. Those voices were silent when Paul bent over his new son who for a moment looked so much like André swaddled tight in blankets, his eyes dark with that flat unfocused infant gaze. Paul closed his eyes and kissed the little one's forehead. This one was safe. There was no volcano looming over his life, no fer-de-lance lurking in trees or in roiling masses at the bottom of a bouillon. Paul knew Clara worried about the baby. She had seen too many infants die in her mother's arms. But Paul assured her that this one, his son, was safe.

The echoes of Paul's old life were absorbed by the sounds of his life in Stratford, the warmth of his home and the delight both he and Clara took in the obvious heartiness of Francis Paul. Martinique fell back into the shadows. Old l'habitation Sablon took on a look of genteel disrepair when Paul chanced upon it in a dream or on waking before Clara stirred beside him and their day began. The door closed, the windows shuttered, trees and vines advancing across the estate, encroached from every side.

Clara had made friends with a couple of women from church. Sylvia Lewinski and Irene Donegal were also mothers. Sylvia's child, Jane, was a year old and Irene's Keiran, four months older than Francis. Sylvia fancied herself an old hand at parenting compared to Clara and Irene. They pushed their baby carriages through the park that spreads up from the Avon and fed the geese and ducks that waddled toward them. Clara hooked her cane over the handle of the carriage. It took some concentration to push and lean on the handle at the same time. Her friends were patient, but she could feel they pitied her and pity had always made her angry.

Sylvia's family and that of her husband were old Polish families, among the ones who established St. Joseph's in Stratford. "I knew I'd marry Benedek from the time we were little. Our grandparents came to Ontario together and settled in Stratford over forty years ago. St. Joseph's was all Polish families for many years."

Clara and Irene exchanged glances. They were both new to Stratford. Irene and her husband left Ireland because they had no future there. Irene missed her family and would likely never see them again. Clara felt a twinge because she was often sad to live so far from her own family, yet it was a simple train trip, half a day to Montréal, another to Labelle. It would be easier to be in Montréal again and go to the théâtre, galleries, restaurants. She sighed.

"I wonder if I will ever get used to living here," Clara said. "It is so different from Québec."

"It's hardly Ireland either. Though that's not so bad a thing," Irene said. "My belly is full and my baby is strong. He'll not be starving."

Clara didn't feel particularly close to the two women. Their husbands both were highly skilled furniture makers and worked in the same factory and were friends. Clara felt like an add-on friend, though she didn't mean to be ungrateful. She appreciated that they included her in walks through the park and sat with her in the parish hall as they repaired donated clothes to give to the poor or any of the other charitable tasks the women of St. Joseph's devoted themselves to.

She had a good husband, a strong baby, and so much to be thankful for. Yet, when she realized she was pregnant again only a few months after Francis was born, she felt overwhelmed. How was she going to manage two young children? Clara's mother had both her own mother and her mother-in-law to help, and as soon as she was old enough, she had the help of Clara, as well. She had never thought of herself as an invalid and no one in her family ever treated her like someone who couldn't take care of herself. But Clara had to be realistic. She had limitations and she could rely on her family.

"I need help," Clara told Paul. "I don't think I can manage two babies. Perhaps Berthe can come stay with us."

"But of course." They could make room in the little house. It would be good for Clara to have her sister there for companionship and to help with the children.

"Or I could go to Labelle."

"You want to leave? I know it hasn't been easy for you here without your friends and family. You must be lonely. But, surely, if Berthe came, it would be better." Paul could hear the pleading in his voice.

"I don't want to leave you, Paul. I miss my family." She felt tears coming.

Paul was suddenly terrified. Would he ever see her and Francis again? What would happen to them in Labelle? He could imagine a landslide of mud and stumps of trees engulfing that wretched little village, suffocating his children. He closed his eyes, clenched his fists. Maman stroked his hair and kissed his cheek. Framed by an open door, a buffalo wandered into view through waving grass and disappeared. He stared out of the door for a long time, but the buffalo did not return.

"Paul? Paul!" Someone calling his name. Who was there? He opened his eyes. Clara, of course, his wife.

"I'm okay. Just a little... I will miss you." Paul went to the baby buggy they used as a crib for Francis during the day so Clara didn't have to carry him up and down the stairs. He stared down at the sleeping boy. It was winter again. He could feel the cold through the curtains.

"I will write to Mama." Her eyes drifted to the newspaper she had placed on the table when Paul handed it to her so he could take off his boots and hang up his coat when he came home from work. She turned the pages, not really looking for anything, just trying to get the image of her husband sitting, so stiff and pale, out of her mind. Had she hurt him? She didn't mean to. An advertisement caught her eye. A contest to win a piano. *If I won it, I suppose I could give it away. Why not enter? I could win. I won that trip to the Exposition, didn't I?* As a child she had loved entering contests. It was a diversion full of possibility. A sort of gamble, but without really losing anything except the possibility.

While she waited for the winter months to pass and Francis to be old enough to stop nursing — for that time they agreed, Clara and Paul and her mother, it would be the best for her to stay with her family — she continued to scour the newspapers for contests. She often bought the *Toronto Star* or the *London Advertiser* — the local London, not the English one — just on the chance she might find a contest to enter. Maybe a new automobile or a trip to Paris or something equally exotic. It was something to do to keep her mind from her growing misery.

There was a distance now between her and Paul. He was as kind as ever and enjoyed his son. He came home on time every day from work. He even went to mass with her occasionally. Yet, every evening he settled in a chair by the wood stove and smoked his pipe in silence, staring out into space as if he were seeing something she could never see.

Finally, in April, after Francis was weaned from her breast, Clara packed bags for Labelle. Paul took a few days off work and rode with her as far as Montreal. It had been decided that Berthe would get on the train there and Paul would return to Stratford. With another child on the way, they really couldn't afford for him to take off more than a couple of days.

"I will write to you," she promised.

"Send me a telegram when the baby is born," Paul said. "I will come immediately."

They had not worked out her return to Stratford. Instead, they avoided the subject. In fact, Clara wasn't sure if she wanted to return to Stratford. But she didn't have a clue what she would do without Paul or how a twenty-two-year-old mother of two, a Catholic girl with children, could manage on her own without a husband. The thought startled her. Was she really thinking about separation? But it seemed too often in those quiet evenings when he went wherever it was he went as though she had no husband. And she had a family who loved her, and she needed her sisters and she wanted time to think about her life and her future.

WHEN CLARA LEFT FOR LABELLE, Paul knew it was about more than needing help with the babies. He knew it was about him, too. He thought he might be losing her. But he didn't know what to do. Before she left, he tried the best he could, yet he couldn't seem to get his past to leave him alone. He came in from the icy air with a chill through his bones. He kept the stove hot and felt the sun of Martinique on his skin when he closed his eyes, the rustle of birds taking flight, the shouts of children. And thinking about it only invited his ghosts back in the door.

"Papa, you're home," Alice Germaine would squeal. "We've been waiting for you all day."

Now that Clara and Francis were gone, he took to a new routine in the evening. After work, he would eat a light dinner at a café before purchasing a half-pint of whiskey and stopping at the tobacconist for pipe tobacco. Then he would go home, pour himself a whiskey and sit in his chair. He would load up his pipe and walk the halls of l'habitation Sablon. Imagining the faces of his brothers, cousins, his children, of Stéphanie, Maman. Hearing their voices, making them real again.

Real things have minds of their own and there were days when they followed him to work. Eustase first, maybe because he was the hardest to send away. Paul knew the danger in this and made it clear to all of them that these conversations were limited to the evening, when he was sitting in his rocking chair with his pipe, and although they were often unruly, this worked most of the time. Until something he saw or heard brought back Saint-Pierre, all in a rush. Out of the blue, as they say. Sometimes people on the street looked at him askance. Maybe they wondered if he was a returned soldier from the war in South Africa, or if he met some catastrophe as a boy. Would he have told them, if they asked? No matter, they never did.

At times like those, he felt as if he were one of those old men sitting on park benches lost in their past. Paul kept his concentration on the job. It was in those idle moments when he was alone on some street or café that he had to beware. Those were the times when the past would come creeping in.

And at night, alone in bed, he dreamed again, the liana and the snake pit and the ash. And that black hand reaching out for him. "Take my hand, Priest."

PAUL NOTED that the leaves were mostly gone from the oak trees, giving him an unobstructed view of the massive shop, it's windows glowing. Just there, across the street, work was going on through the night in the heat of forges, the ring of tools on steel, a kind of music. He thought about Clara and Francis and that soon there would be another baby.

Paul's mind drifted back to that dark night after he'd first heard news of the volcano, before his ghosts became unruly, popping in and out of his head, demanding his attention. Except for baby Yvonne, who refused to be seen. That night, in the awful emptiness, he had imagined them, their voices, the way they moved. He had left no memory untouched in his longing for them and his utter disbelief that everyone he loved was really gone.

At first his ghosts were tentative, uncertain of their place, maybe even reluctant. When had that changed? This evening it was Mannie who came unbidden, interrupting his thoughts. Paul attempted to wave him away. "Not now, Mannie. Can't you see I'm trying to think?"

"Think, little brother? You are trying to avoid me."

"Well, I have important things on my mind."

"More important than your brother and best friend whom you'll never see again? Whom you've abandoned for that fancy new world of yours? America has already seduced you away from your family, Brother."

"No, no, Mannie. Never. I could never forget you. But I can't bear it. I should have been there with you. With all of you."

"But you are alive, Paulie. That is a gift, not a curse."

Oh, but it *is* a curse, he wanted to say, but didn't, because he knew deep down that it was also a gift. Which only made the guilt that much more profound.

Mannie would not be the one to tell him that his survival was God's way of giving him another chance. That would be Léonie, who was suddenly standing in the room with her sister Alix, the two lovely blonde Biliotti girls side by side.

"You are being offered an opportunity, sweet cousin," said Léonie. It was not the Léonie of six or seven, but the pretty twenty-year-old he recalled, bidding him farewell at the docks in Saint-Pierre. "You must not lose your faith in God, Paul."

I have already lost it, he wanted to protest, but he could never be sharp with Léonie, second only to Mannie in his childhood affections. Instead, he rose to leave. "Bonne nuit, I must get my sleep."

"Bonne nuit, sweet cousin," the Biliotti sisters said, as he gently closed the door behind himself.

He would go to his quiet place and smoke for a while before turning in.

Perhaps one small whiskey.

ONE WHISKEY AND A PIPE LATER, he found himself right back in that house. He'd no intention of returning. But there he was, standing at the door to Maman's room. The old woman was the only one he wished to speak to—he wasn't ready for the others, for Stéphanie and the children. He knocked softly on the door and Maman said, "Come in, son."

He opened the door and there sat Clémence in her parlor, on one of her gaudy Rococo settees. It was the parlor of the house on Rue Castelnau, with that Gauguin reproduction hanging a little off-kilter in its ugly old baroque frame that Papa liked, and glass doors that looked out on the garden of bougainvilleas, magnolias, and banana trees. Beyond the garden wall, where one would expect the neighbor's garden or perhaps the Martinican forest there was nothing but wide open space, a meadow or a field, extending into the horizon in wave after wave of golden grain, reminding him of a painting he'd once seen in a museum—yes, that day in Providence with Lea, he recalled. *The Great American Prairie.* Oklahoma or some similar place. He couldn't recall the artist.

"Are you alright, Maman?" he asked. "Are you comfortable?"

"I'm fine, Paul. A little lonely, perhaps. I don't know whatever happened to Stéphanie and the children. I miss their little feet padding about the house, you know." She looked at him accusingly.

"I know, Maman. I will find them for you. I promise."

PAUL HAD ONLY JUST CLOSED the door to Maman's room when Stéphanie appeared suddenly in the corridor with Alice Germaine and her two young brothers.

"Mon cher," exclaimed Stéphanie, "there you are."

"Papa!" Alice Germaine squealed.

"We are so happy to see you," Stéphanie said, a big smile adorning her beautiful face—just as she had been, or had his imagination made her face more lovely?

"Where have you been, Papa?" Adrien said.

"Papa's been away in America," André Paul interjected with cocky authority.

"Yes, my loves," Paul said. "I have been far away in America, making money to send home to pay the rent and buy your food. How have you children been?"

A telling moment of silence ensued before Alice Germaine

cried out, "Oh, Papa, we've all missed you so much. Mémé Clémence said you would be home soon, but Uncle Mannie said it might be some time. There's been some sort of disaster."

No, no, he didn't want to talk about disasters. He quickly changed the subject. "Where is your sister, Yvonne?"

Alice Germaine shrugged.

"Yvonne?" Stéphanie shook her head in puzzlement, as though she didn't remember she had a second daughter.

"The baby, Yvonne," he said. But when he looked at them each, one after the other, there was no sign of recognition on their faces, just a look of alarm that they might have forgotten they had a little sister.

Deep sorrow overcame him, one that threatened to swamp the grief already encompassing this sad house. "You know," he said to the children, to divert them, "your Mémé Clémence misses you. You should ease her mind. Papa must return to America now. Work, you know."

He kissed Stéphanie tenderly, then the children, and he watched them enter Maman's room, trying to remember every little thing about each of them as they passed.

He had a living child now and another on the way. He owed them his attention. This time, when he took his leave of that house, he locked the door securely behind himself. He had no intention of returning.

THE TELEGRAM ARRIVED in late September. He had a new daughter. They would name her *Thérèse Marguerite*. They would call her Theresa until that day in the future when she insisted on the more traditional, although American, Therese.

Paul was filled with joy and determination. He had been given a chance to redeem himself. He attended St. Joseph's and confessed his many sins and made a vow to never abandon his children.

There was one thing he needed to do before he took the train to Labelle for the baptism. If he would never tell Clara about them, Paul reasoned, then he should not keep the pictures of them. There was also the bundle of letters he'd never been able to let go.

The night was cool. A fire was already lit in the stove.

It wasn't an attic, just a crawl space with a door you could only reach by standing on a ladder or a tall stool. The door was in the ceiling at the end of the second-floor hallway. The letters and the photos were as safely hidden away from his wife as they would be in a bank vault.

Paul opened the top of the stove and fed the letters into it. Then stood quietly, memorizing their faces, before he dropped the pictures of them into the fire, saving until last that photo of his family on the docks, Stéphanie with little Yvonne on her hip, bidding him farewell. Why, he asked himself, had he been so afraid to tell Clara? Because it hurts too much? No, if he were honest, it wasn't that. Because he and Stéphanie were not married? Though would it have really been necessary to tell her that? He thought of Lea Tambois and how she had reacted to seeing the photo he had kept in his wallet. "They are negroes."

mulâtre, he said to the flames. They just wouldn't understand.

AFTER MUCH HARD WORK, Yvonne screwed up her courage and pushed the raft she had made past the dangerous rocks and up alongside the *Liberté,* which rocked back and forth with the waves, threatening to capsize her little makeshift vessel. Up above, André and Maman hailed her as they hung onto the ship's railing. Thinking quickly, André ran off to find a rope to throw over the side. He came back with Étienne, and the old helmsman tossed the rope down to Yvonne.

"Hurry," said Yvonne. "Climb down to the raft and I will take you ashore."

"The tide is coming in," said Étienne. "Chief Navigator

Marcus thinks it may raise the *Liberté* enough for us to push away from the rocks if the wind is right."

Yvonne hadn't even thought about the Chief Navigator, she had been so focused on André and Maman. "Is the Chief Navigator alright?"

"Oui," said Maman gravely, "but he has broken his leg. I have bound it as best I can, but I'm afraid I am no doctor."

"Do you think this plan will work, Étienne?" said Yvonne.

"I think it might work with luck and good winds," said the helmsman.

Yvonne tied the rope to her raft so it wouldn't float away. She climbed up the rope and pulled herself on board the *Liberté*. Even though she was dripping wet, she hugged Maman and André with all of her might. "I'm so glad you are alright," she said. "I was terrified."

"Not all the crew made it, Mamzel," said a somber Étienne.

"What about Captain Marie?" Yvonne asked.

"Overboard," said André. "Probably eaten by the sharks." He didn't look very unhappy about this.

"What will we do with no captain?" said Yvonne.

"Who needs a captain?" said Étienne.

"But how can we sail without a captain?" asked Yvonne.

"We can all captain the *Liberté* together," said Étienne. "But if we *must* have a captain, I think it should be you, Yvonne."

"Me?" said Yvonne. "I'm just a little girl."

"We will all help you," said André, strangely in favor of this silly idea.

"I think we have all we need," said the helmsman. "We have a navigator, a helmsman, a cook, a swabbie, more than a half a dozen sailors, and Captain Yvonne."

"About the swabbie," said André, "we should all take turns swabbing the deck and cleaning the mess." Proud of his suggestion, he looked around at everyone for support, giving Yvonne his best big brother smile.

"I suppose that would only be fair," said Yvonne. "If we are all to share captain duties, then we should all share swabbie duties, as well."

So Yvonne had made her first decision as the new captain of the *Liberté*.

ÉTIENNE WENT to every corner of the ship and rounded up all the sailors. There were nearly a dozen of them. Maman helped Chief Navigator Marcus out on the deck with his broken leg. Helmsman Étienne explained the situation to the sailors, including the part about helping swab the decks, which brought several groans.

"And this is our new Captain," he said, putting his strong black hand on Yvonne's little shoulder. "Captain Yvonne."

"But she's just a little girl," said one of the sailors.

"She has to be better than Captain Marie," said another,

"Oui," said several more of the sailors. A great cry went up, "Vive Captain Yvonne!"

"Those who don't like it," said Étienne, "are free to leave the ship now."

Yvonne didn't think that sounded very fair since there was nothing to eat on this little island, and no fresh water to drink. "I think we should have a vote," said Yvonne.

Another cheer went up, and Étienne said, "Very well then. How many here accept Yvonne for your captain?"

Every sailor's hand went up.

"Then that's settled," said Chief Navigator Marcus. "I know Yvonne will be a very fair captain. Now the tide is coming in and we must be prepared to raise the sails."

~

THE SUN HAD GONE DOWN before the *Liberté* rose on the tide. She was soon clear of the rocks, but there was no wind to push her back out to sea.

"Oh no," said Yvonne, "our plan isn't working, Chief Navigator."

"Don't worry, Captain Yvonne," said Chief Navigator Marcus. "The ship will be up above the rocks for a few hours. Perhaps the wind will come up in that time."

"We should say a prayer to the winds," said Helmsman Étienne.

Yvonne didn't really think the wind could hear a prayer, but she said nothing. Who knows? She was just a little girl.

Chief Navigator Marcus smiled. "I'm sure the sailors will all be saying prayers this evening for the wind to come."

"And curses in the morning if it doesn't," said Maman.

Chief Navigator Marcus sighed. "Oui, Madame," he said.

Just then, Yvonne saw the corner of the Chief Navigator's map raise up like a ghost was about to turn a page.

"The wind!" she cried out.

Soon there was another gust. Then another.

"Tell the sailors to raise the sails," said Chief Navigator Marcus.

Maman ran out to spread the word. "Raise the sails," she shouted, "raise the sails."

The sails went up, and soon the *Liberté* was back again at sea to the cheers of everyone on board. The old helmsman broke out a bottle of rhum he had stashed away and Maman brought glasses and sugar for ti punch and two American root beers for Yvonne and André.

"Can't we have rum?" said André. "My sister is Captain Yvonne, after all."

"You are still only children," said Maman. "No ti punch for you."

André groaned.

And then they all raised their glasses in cheer.

"To the wind," said Étienne.

"To the *Liberté*," said Marcus.

"To Bordeaux," said Captain Yvonne.

"Hear, hear," said Maman, and they all laughed.

IT TOOK FOREVER to cross the Atlantic sea. But Yvonne felt confident that they were going to arrive safely. They would be in Bordeaux at Papa's house in time for his return. Nothing could stop them.

"Only about seven days to go," said the Chief Navigator, when Captain Yvonne met him on the bridge in the morning.

"Only about six days to go," he said the next morning.

"Only five days left," said Marcus the following day.

And then one morning, before she knew it, Yvonne woke up and washed the sleep from her eyes and climbed up to the bridge. There in front of her was a harbor and a great city larger than any city she had ever seen before.

"Bordeaux," she cried. "Are we here?"

Yvonne turned to see Maman standing behind her. "We are home, mon ange," said Maman, and Yvonne could see there were tears in Maman's eyes. Then she felt tears in her own.

They had arrived at last.

PART 7
LES ENFANTS PERDUS

THERESA MARGUERITE

Papa rocked in his oak chair, back and forth, back and forth, like the pendulum on the grandfather clock, all day and maybe all night for all Theresa knew. She wondered if he would ever stop again to eat or read his paper, or if he was stuck on some kind of track that wound endlessly through his inner world. Another Sunday had come and Mom wanted to attend Mass because the restrictions had been lifted, but Papa continued to sit there, distant, not looking up, unaware of the constant hubbub that arose around the activity and needs of his three youngest children.

Mom didn't try to persuade him to come with them. Instead, she went about rounding up the children for church, not wanting to be late for morning mass.

"Each of us has our own way of grieving," her mother said to Theresa by explanation, although the girl didn't entirely understand if she was talking about Papa or about herself or maybe even about all of them.

The truth of the matter, Theresa didn't want to go to church, either. She would rather stay home with Papa. The funeral had been on Friday, and she still remembered the horrible feeling that came over her when she'd walked into St. Bernadine's for Frank's service, and how that huge red-brick building felt like a tomb—as though the church itself was a giant mausoleum filled with all the departed of this sad world, all the victims from the Spanish flu, all the dead from that terrible war, all les enfants perdus like Frank, who would never be an adult. And even though Father Conneally had avoided saying any of that, her eleven-year-old mind had already absorbed enough of the cruelty of the world that she could hear the message in the silences between his words.

Her family didn't attend mass regularly, but today Mom worried about all of their mortal souls, not that she had ever spoken of such things in the past. At least not in Theresa's memory. "We must pray for your brother, Clair, as well," said Mom, when she laid out Theresa's dress on the bed.

"I will pray for him at home," she'd protested, refusing to move from the chair in which she had firmly planted herself. "And I'll pray for Frank's soul as well. But I can't go back there into that building."

Mom just shook her head, annoyed, but not willing to fight with her stubborn daughter. "All right then. I will leave Raymond at home with you and don't forget to wash the breakfast dishes."

Theresa sighed. But it seemed like a fair trade if she didn't have to sit in that pew thinking about her dear, dead brother.

RAYMOND HADN'T UTTERED a peep since her mother left the house. After finishing the dishes, Theresa curled up in her favorite spot on the couch, next to Papa's chair. She brought some books, including her English reader from Saint Catherine's, even though school had been shuttered for the past three months because of the flu. Some stories in the reader were silly, but some were good. She would finish them all, just in case. Uncertainty lingered in the air about when school might resume. Maybe next week. Maybe February. The adults were fighting about it and nobody could make up their minds.

Along with the reader, she brought *Pollyanna*. She liked it because it was about a girl who was crippled, like Mom, but who tried to see the good side of everything. She wished she could be like that, but it was hard to see the good side sometimes.

She had also grabbed Frank's tattered copy of *Peter and Wendy*. She felt guilty about having her departed brother's book, but he loaned it to her months ago when they were all first sick with the flu, and she knew he would want her to finish it. She felt a little like Wendy, herself, and sometimes she imagined her little brothers were the lost boys. And Captain Hook made her think of Papa's Marie Le Méchant and her pirate ship.

"Good morning, Papa," she said as she made herself comfortable. As usual, her father remained silent. She decided to not bother him, although it would be hard not to. He was right there next to her.

She started reading *Pollyanna* first, because she was almost done with it. But she would just start into a new sentence when Papa would mutter something under his breath.

"Yes, Papa?" she said, at last, thinking maybe he was talking to her.

Papa looked up at the sound of her voice, but she could tell he wasn't speaking to her.

"Alice," he said, speaking in French, "I'm sorry, mon ange. Papa's sorry he never came back for you."

Theresa was confused. What was this world Papa inhabited? A world where he had a daughter named Alice?

"Papa," she said, "are you alright?"

"Do you know the whereabouts of Yvonne, ma chère? I've looked for her everywhere."

Theresa didn't know what to do. Her father was clearly not talking to her, but to his phantoms.

"Papa, please come back home," she pleaded. "It's Theresa Marguerite, and I'm right here beside you."

"Alice," said Papa, "Would you help me find your little sister?" A silence ensued, then after a time Papa said, in a scolding voice, "Yvonne, your sister. How could you forget your baby sister?"

Papa continued like this for a time until Raymond started crying in his crib and Theresa left to go change her brother's diaper. A little later, she came back downstairs with Raymond in her arms and before returning to the couch went to the kitchen for some applesauce and a bib. Papa now sat calmly in his chair, his pipe unlit in his lap.

It was nearing Raymond's first birthday, and he had already taken a few steps, and you could almost hear words in his goos and gaws. He was quite a handful, but Theresa deftly fed him his applesauce, being careful not to spill any on the living room furniture, talking to him gently as she did. Papa was mostly quiet while this went on, until Raymond cooed, and suddenly Papa said, "Alice, is that Yvonne?"

"It is Raymond, Papa. And I am not Alice." She wanted to scream at him, but she restrained herself. "I am your daughter, Theresa."

Her father fell silent again. She didn't know if he heard her or not. She suspected he was still far away on his island, or wherever it was he went. Her anger turned again to sadness, as it always did. Sometimes she wished she hadn't been born.

~

WHEN MOM RETURNED HOME at midday, dragging the boys behind her, one arm around a bag of groceries, she looked frazzled and a little piqued. Seeing her, Theresa felt guilty for not going along to help with her brothers and the groceries, but she still would have had to take care of Raymond and how much could a girl be expected to do, anyway? Still, she decided it was maybe not a good time to talk about Papa.

Yet...

"Mama," she said when the groceries had been put away and the boys had gone off to play, "did Papa have other children before he had us?"

"Of course not. Where did you get that crazy notion?"

"He keeps calling me Alice. And he told me the other day he once knew a girl my age named Alice."

"Well, there is your explanation."

"But he said, *Papa est désolé de ne pas revenir.*"

"Who knows what your father means when he is talking to himself. Now help me with the déjeuner, s'il te plaît. After we eat, we will go see your brother in the hospital."

Soon her mother, too, looked far away, lost in some thoughts brought on by their conversation. Theresa scowled and went to work gathering the ingredients for sandwiches. Why did adults have to be so difficult, anyway?

MAMAN'S ROOM

TODAY, Maman's room was lit brightly with morning sunlight. Paul called out softly in greeting as he entered. When she didn't answer, he walked over to the glass doors to find her in the garden, sipping her café and browsing the newspaper. Clémence sat with her back to the door; a cut plum on one of her fancy plates, partially eaten. He watched her for a time, *display en vitrine.* Now and again she would gaze out at the prairie beyond the garden wall, and take another sip from her cup. The scene reminded him of home — home! — except the plum would have been a mango or a guava, and that vast plain would be the Plaine de la Consolation, with its cane and tobacco fields, stretching out to the slopes of the looming Pelée. For just a flicker of a moment, he saw the traitorous mountain flash before him until it blinked away again.

He did not want to think of the volcano today or any other day, for that matter. He was trying to find his Yvonne, lost somewhere in this house. How would he remember her if he couldn't find her? If he couldn't see her face? If he couldn't look into her little eyes.

He'd asked Alice, but she'd been no help at all. She couldn't even remember her own sister. Nor could anyone else, it seemed. Had he invented Yvonne in the same way he'd invented this house? Yet the Sablon house had been real, once, he was certain of that. Maybe not *this* house precisely. But the fact of it. And his little baby Yvonne in her mother's arms before that final goodbye two decades ago. She had been real, as well.

Had it been so long? Would his little girl be a pretty nineteen-year-old now, thinking about those things young women think about, their future lives and their friends and their beaus? Would she be flitting around the cobbled streets of Saint-Pierre, turning eyes and causing hearts to flutter?

Paul, you are such a romantic! He sighed and opened the glass doors and stepped out into the garden.

"Bonjour, Maman."

"Son, what brings you by this morning?"

"Have you seen Yvonne, Maman?"

"Are you still looking for this Yvonne, son? Remind me again who she is."

"She is my baby daughter, Maman."

"You have forgotten your child, son? *Mon Dieu.* How do you expect your mother to recall her if you cannot?"

Maman had a point. But hadn't she been with Yvonne all of those months after Paul left for America? Yvonne was only one more lost child among all the lost children of Saint-Pierre, but she was *his* baby girl. And if he lost her, then what did that mean for his still living children? Would he forget them, too, when they were gone? Would he forget Francis Paul in twenty years? Would he forget that handsome boy's face poised to bloom into a young man's? A bud plucked off before it could even flower.

"How are you doing in this place, Maman?" Paul asked. "Does it suit you?"

"You mean this prison you are keeping me in, son?" Maman

sounded a little bitter. "About as well as one could expect, considering the circumstances."

Paul was caught up short. Did Maman believe this to be a prison?

"This is not a prison, Maman. It is your childhood home."

"Phewf," said Maman. "Then what is this prairie outside of my window? Is this where you live in America?"

Paul thought about that for a moment. "No, not exactly. It's Oklahoma. But I thought it would be a nice place for my mother to retire."

"Have you ever been here, Son? It is unbearably hot and dry. And flat. And there are no mangoes anywhere."

"I saw it in a painting. And it was beautiful."

"So you haven't actually lived here. I thought not."

"Maman, you're not actually alive, so what good are mangoes? Aren't plums acceptable? And I enjoy looking out at the Oklahoma prairie when I come to visit you, because I can't bear the alternative. I want to think you are not so far away. And you can always visit with Tata when you are lonely, or with Papa, or Stéphanie and the children."

"Phewf," Clémence said again, raising her arms in a gesture of dismissal. "If this isn't a prison, then why do I hear rattling chains all night long? Why do I hear voices and cries of despair rising from the basement, Son?"

Ah, well. There were *some* prisoners here, but he did not want to alarm Maman with that.

"Those are only noises in the night, Maman. I shouldn't worry about them."

∼

PAUL KISSED his mother on each cheek and said, *au revoir. I will visit again soon.* But at the moment he remembered his goal

— find Yvonne — so he resumed his search, checking all the crannies and closets he could remember. He was amazed at how many such places there were and wondered if it was even possible to find them all.

He continued downstairs to the kitchen where he spoke with Emmaline, who complained as she pushed firewood into the cook stove, "If Master Anatole hadn't sent Sandrine off to Fort-de-France, she'd be here now to help me look after all these relations of yours," . The kitchen was unbearably hot, as kitchens in warm climates inevitably are, and Emmaline brushed away the heavy sweat which gleamed on her brow. "I have seen no small girl except for Alice, who isn't really that small anymore. Have you looked in the basement?"

He hadn't considered the basement. Its door, which lay just down the hall from the kitchen door, remained padlocked, he was certain. But who knows where little spirit children might get off to, slipping through cracks and crevices. And while he was at it, he could tell the basement's inhabitants to keep down the infernal racket so Maman could sleep.

Paul searched through his keys for the one he needed, and, finding it, unlocked the large padlock. He pushed back the hasp and turned the doorknob. The door squealed a little on its rusty hinges and opened onto a dusty cobwebbed staircase with old splintered wooden steps leading down into darkness. He lit the lantern which hung by the upper landing on a rusty nail. As he slowly descended, the steps groaned and creaked and sounded as though they might fall apart at any moment. They held, but not without a small fright or two along the way. As he reached the bottom step, the rattling of the chains had grown into an angry racket.

The basement halls, like those upstairs, were narrow and labyrinthine, as you might expect in a house of memory. He never knew where the next turn might lead him, if it led anywhere other than some completely forgotten dead end. His every footstep stirred up dust which hung in the lamplight and clung to his clothes. As a child, he hadn't particularly liked the basement. It seemed like a place for snakes, or zombis, or Père Labat. It was not suitable for much except hiding unwanted things in the dark.

Jean Joseph loudly clashed his chains against his cell wall and shouted out, "Let me out of here, you ungrateful little shit! Everything you have you owe to me and to your Papa. Everything."

Paul hesitated for just a moment before continuing down the hall, where he had imprisoned his grandfather years ago after that humiliating night at Stéphanie's salon. He stopped briefly at the old man's door. "Would you be quiet, for heaven's sake? You are waking the dead."

"You are waking the living, as well," came a voice from farther along the hall. Paul scratched his head, trying to remember who lived in the next cell. "Would you shut that old bastard up, Priest. I beg you. You know everything *he* had, he owed to *me*, don't you?"

The basement peeled with raucous laughter. Ah, yes. Sylbaris. Now he remembered.

THE BASEMENT

Jean Joseph became silent as a wharf rat, because he was not even a memory, after all, unless you give credence to such things as ancestral memory. He was simply a thought, albeit a very noisy one, perhaps filled in a little by family stories and that portrait on Papa's wall. Paul passed his grandfather's cell, ignoring the old man, to the dank room where he had lodged the troublesome Sylbaris. There was no lock on the door here. No door really at all. No chains because one no longer put black people in chains, did one?

"I hear what you are thinking, Priest," Ludger said. "You think I am a dangerous fool and you lock me in this basement with that bastard. You don't need chains because your thoughts are my chains. Yes?"

"I don't have time for this. I am looking for my daughter, Yvonne. Have you seen her?"

"The little girl, Priest? Why can't you just allow her to be free? Why must she also be chained to your memories like that old man?"

Because she is mine, he nearly said.

"She's no longer yours, Monsieur," Sylbaris said, hearing his unspoken thoughts. "The mountain has taken her."

"I don't wish to think about the mountain."

"Yes, another uncomfortable fact, like the black man in your basement."

"Alright, have it your way. An uncomfortable fact. The both of you are damnable facts but, fortunately for me, I only have to keep you down here. That volcano is far out at sea on the other side of the world."

"Are you certain about that, Priest? Are you sure it's not right beneath your feet?"

Paul thought for a moment about the small temblor he had felt in the night. *Ridiculous.* That was his house in California, a few hundred yards from the San Andreas Fault where it ran through the city of San Bernardino. He would not let this trickster make him think of volcanoes when there was a much simpler explanation.

Sylbaris laughed that belly laugh of his. "So, what do you think, Priest? Shall we go looking for your little girl? She is not the one I saw you with in that railroad town, is she?"

Winslow, Paul thought, recalling the circus, remembering the surprise of seeing Ludger Sylbaris there.

"No." Hadn't he just told this fool he was looking for Yvonne? "That was Theresa."

"Yes, your living child. The one you *should* be looking for." Sylbaris laughed.

"To hell with you," Paul cried out. Clearly, the man was playing with him.

"So, Priest, why have you not told your living children about these little ones from Saint-Pierre? Is it perhaps because you are ashamed of their black skin?"

"Connerie!"

"Is our little island an embarrassment to you, Monsieur?"

"Je le nie. I deny it."

Sylbaris shrugged. "If you say so, Monsieur."

After a long moment, Paul said, "I'll tell you what, Ludger. You try to keep your mouth shut, and I will allow you to join me in my search."

"Seems a bit of a contradiction, Priest, but very magnanimous of you to offer."

"Take it or leave it."

"I will try." Sylbaris shrugged, then added, "It's the best I can do, Priest. And better I suppose than sitting in the dark all day and all night. Biding our time, as it were."

PAUL AND SYLBARIS ambled through the dark corridors of the basement of l'habitation Sablon, stirring up dust and cobwebs, checking in abandoned closets and cubbyholes. Now and then there seemed to come a low rumbling from underground and the earth shook a little. Crumbling pieces of ancient brick and mortar filtered down, agitating the dust. Paul coughed and spit grit from his teeth.

Then the basement dissolved in a giant cloud, and the two of them were left standing on a familiar desert street. Horses, tied along the boardwalk, neighed and shuffled. A 1908 Hupmobile Roadster weaved down the broad roadway among the horse-drawn carriages, leaving a trail of smoke and fumes. Winslow, Arizona.

Beside Paul, the black man chuckled. It was not particularly an amused chuckle. "The very center of hell," Sylbaris hissed.

"The circus is coming," shouted a young boy running along the boardwalk. "The circus is coming."

"Ah, the parade." Paul recalled.

~

HE WAS HERE, again, a young man standing on the boardwalk with his arm around his pregnant Clara. Her sister Berthe firmly holding the hands of Theresa and young Paul as they squirmed in excitement, trying to break free, and here came the Barnum and Bailey Circus, led by a small brass band comprising a tuba, a big bass drum, two trumpets and a clarinet, followed by the Circus Master's wagon, the mustachioed maestro sitting above the driver, surrounded by beautiful young women crowned with ostrich plumes, and then came the sideshow wagons with billboards on their panels and more pretty feather-topped girls swinging from the rails. The wagons were pulled by big white horses and piloted by colorfully dressed young men in top hats. Next came the animals. Tigers and lions roared their anger from cages surrounded by cruel death-defying valiants whose whips kept the fearsome beasts in line. Following them, the elephants, adorned with brightly colored blankets, criss-crossed with gold and silver cords. The first elephant, ridden by a scantily clad girl gripping its neck with her bare legs and twirling a baton, and all the elephants which followed grasped with their trunk the tail of the one ahead, like a chain of young children fearful of being separated from their teacher. And at the very last came more sideshow trailers, shabbier than the first, acts whose run, Paul supposed, must be nearing their end, ready to be forgotten by the fickle public. Ready to disappear off the end of the train. It was the final one of these that brought the gasp from his throat.

The Miracle Man of Saint-Pierre, said the bright red letters on a yellow background, and there, bigger than life, was an image of a familiar, scarred black face from his past: Ludger Sylbaris.

~

THE CIRCUS MASTER would say that the Barnum & Bailey Circus train didn't so much roll as limp into Winslow, though the broken stay-bolts hadn't slowed it down. Nevertheless, the engineer insisted they stop the train because there was a Santa Fe machine shop in Winslow, and he didn't want to run the train all the way into San Bernardino with four stay bolts missing and steam and water leaking from the boiler. Sidelined in Winslow. This dusty backwater town of only 10,000 desert hardened, burned, weathered, and stubborn souls.

"How long?" the Circus Master asked. The three of them, engineer, Circus Master, and machinist, stood in the shadow of the engine as far from the firebox as they could manage and still see where the bolts had blown. The firebox was fiercely hot, but so was the sun a step or two away from the shadow.

"Four or five days," Paul answered.

"What is that accent?" the Circus Master asked. "Not Spanish is it?"

"It is French," Paul said, and he could see the Circus Master wondering what a French man was doing out here in the desert. Paul swept his thick dark hair back from his broad forehead, thinking for a moment he had a question or two of his own. The Circus Master saw the anticipation on Paul's face and waited, but the machinist neither asked his questions nor offered any more information. He didn't need to. The Circus Master had been touring long enough to know that stay bolts sheared or stripped often and the engine had to cool, which might take a day or two — at least in weather like this. Extract the sheared bolts, make new ones, install them, fire it up. You couldn't hurry it.

The Circus Master sighed and left the two trainmen. He

needed to get the crew started with unloading the animals, and they'd need a place to camp.

Several performers had disembarked, squinting at the sky, smoking their cigarettes. "Well?"

"A few days," he said. "Let's get the elephants and horses off the train. I'll procure a campsite."

"Boss," one of them had called, when he was only a few steps away, "are we going to have a parade or a walk?"

He considered for a moment. There wouldn't be much of a crowd here, but what the hell? They'd been traveling for several days already. If they went idle, no telling what mischief the performers, the crew, might get up to in this jerkwater, left to fill empty hours while Frenchie machined their train back onto the rails.

"Parade," he said.

At the noon meal, after the animals and wagons had been detrained, the Circus Master toyed with his food, let his gaze wander from table to table under the tent, waited until he saw that most had pushed their plates away, were leaning on their elbows or shifting about, restless. He stood, filled his lungs from his belly up and called out in the voice that stilled crowds from Maine to California, "Never before and never again may the fine people of Winslow, Arizona see the wonders of the world, the splendid spectacle that is the Barnum and Bailey Circus. You, my friends, will light up the world for them. For the rest of their lives, they will marvel at what they have seen, they will tell their grandchildren. Immortality. That's what it is. You will be carried into the future on the shoulders of memories. The memories you give them."

He was met with silence.

"The handbills will be delivered this afternoon. The parade is tomorrow morning. First performance 1400 hours."

~

CLARA WAS TOO exhausted from the parade and lugging around her not-yet-born baby all morning to attend the circus with them that day, but Paul couldn't keep himself away. He was determined, for some reason unclear to himself, to say a few words to Ludger Sylbaris. So he rounded up the children and their Auntie Berthe, and he paid the price for four tickets, ushering them all into the big tent.

At twenty, Berthe Mandeville seemed not much more than a child herself. Yet, he had been so much younger than that when he'd begun his relationship with Stéphanie. It jolted him to think about that. About those fierce passions of youth that take your life in unexpected directions. Perhaps he should have listened to his Maman and Papa. Perhaps he should have waited, but he would have missed the delight of knowing those children, of holding his babies in his arms.

They almost made this pain worth it. But if he had waited, if he'd gone off to America first, before trying to raise a family, then those children would never have been born to die so horribly. Except Alice was already born, and Adrien, and there would be no way to un-know them, would there? It was too late now for such foolish regrets. He couldn't undo any of it.

But he could forget what they looked like, forget their baby smiles. Like he had forgotten the face of his little Yvonne.

Paul purchased popcorn and peanuts for the children who were excited by the madcap clowns and the prancing elephants, but grew bored by the time the acrobats performed. They whined about going home, but Auntie Berthe shushed them. She wanted to see the aerialist gliding on their trapezes and high wires. But soon the children wore on her. So Paul sent them off, and then he left the big top in search of a bottle of whiskey, and when he'd loosened himself up a little, he'd locate his old acquaintance from home.

～

SYLBARIS PUSHED the straw hat up, revealing his broad forehead and the glint of sweat that beaded and rolled along his nose, filled the creases framing his mouth. Arizona. It might be a North American autumn, but it was warm in Winslow under the lamps that lighted the stage. The freaks waited behind the curtain. Listened to the rustle of customers, the bravado of boys, their shiny uneasiness.

Sylbaris shifted his weight from foot to foot, felt the scars stretch and scream. The stage master called out for the stilt man who slipped between the curtains, the Siamese twins, pig boy, the bearded lady. Soon would come "the miracle of Saint-Pierre," the signal for Sylbaris to step out holding the cotton fabric printed with palm trees and pineapple. Holding the edges together. *Keep them waiting. Maybe they know what they are going to see, maybe they don't. Anticipation,* the stage master says. *That's the main thing, like desire, good to have, better almost than the object itself, than the moment all is revealed.* Still, there was always a gasp when he dropped his cover and the crowd saw his scars rippling across his chest, his legs. A woman's sobbing when he turns and offers them his back. Someone always faints.

Someone always disappoints, as well. And often a bigot in the audience.

"It's a hoax. No damned nigger son of a slave could have survived that. A convict, no less. Sure he's got burns. I'd bet the coward slipped into that hell and pulled the jewelry right off of the corpses of the good people of Saint-Pierre. He was burned, looting and robbing the dead."

Sylbaris heard him as he waited, but he didn't move. He didn't flinch. He didn't even move his eyeballs. He stared steady straight ahead, as if the hate-filled man wasn't there. He didn't look at them, but he could feel the audience beginning to doubt. No one among the five or six people whose fascination with freaks had drawn them to his corner of the Greatest Show was arguing with the man. Ezekiel, the pitchman, was in the tent behind the platform Sylbaris was standing on. He was drinking whiskey and waiting until a few more people showed up before he came out and started reeling them in. It was still early in the evening. The sun hadn't even gone down yet.

Sylbaris had been sensitive to heat since the breath of Hell had rushed over him. And he could feel the heat of hatred rolling off the man in the audience. The man was drunker than Ezekiel at midnight. Still, he recognized that accented voice. The man might have spoken to him in Kreyol. He might have spoken to him in French. He didn't know what he would have said. How could you comfort a man who has lost his family and his world? How do you tell him, *Yes! Monsieur, I was there. Yes! I was in the cell under the morne. The window in that cell was so small when I put my hands around the bars, there was only room enough for a cockroach to crawl through the gap between my hands and the top of the window. Maybe if the window had been bigger my lungs would have been burned like those orphan girls at the convent across the street, whose screams I can still hear.*

Stumbling toward him through the back tent flap, the Priest spoke and so Sylbaris didn't have to. "Why didn't you die, you son of a bitch?"

"You don't know how many times, my friend, I've asked myself that same question," he said. "I have been just as angry as you. Not all the time. Just sometimes. Right now I'm just tired. I'm tired of standing here waiting for the sun to go down so that Ezekiel can open the flap of the tent and light the torches and bring me inside so I can stand on the stage and take off my shirt when I'm told to and turn around when I'm told to and walk forward and to one side and to the other, to show the people of this dusty little town the freak of nature that I have become because, I alone, a man from African people, survived when the nuée ardante came. No one else."

MAKO-BUROKWA OR A WALK IN THE DESERT

"So, Priest," Sylbaris said, "you have chosen a desert to make your home. I find this interesting. It is desolate, like your heart."

Paul squinted his eyes at his companion, wanting to say something unkind. Instead, he said, "This valley is quite pleasant. San Bernardino is on the edge of the desert, but not in the desert, precisely. It has qualities akin to Martinique, you know. Palms and citrus trees grow here. And avocats. Of course it is both much colder and much hotter, but one grows used to those extremes in America."

"I see," the black man said, a look of deep concentration pinching his face. "So you say we are looking for your daughter, the one you left behind in Saint-Pierre. Yvonne is her name?"

"Oui."

"And you think she is lost here in this desert?"

"She should be at l'habitation Sablon with her brothers and sisters." Paul looked in dismay at the sage and tumbleweeds and Joshua trees of the Mojave, wondering how it came to be that here he was on the high desert, walking with this devil from his past.

"Oui, your prison," Sylbaris said under his breath, because

there was no hiding his thoughts from these ghosts. "So, Priest, why are we here in this wasteland, then?"

"You've brought me to this place, Sylbaris. You tell me."

"Not I. I am just a figment of your delirium, am I not?"

"Then why am I here? Can you tell me that, Monsieur?"

"Perhaps," Sylbaris swatted away an aggressive fly, "you are trying to avoid something very painful."

"And that would be?"

"Perhaps it's that old man you have chained up in that basement. Or maybe something more tragic for you."

"Such as?"

"Such as the death of your son, Francis, perhaps?"

Paul winced. He didn't want to think about this.

"Go to hell, Sylbaris."

"It would appear that we have already arrived."

A silence descended on the two men as they contemplated that statement. After a moment, Sylbaris said, "Do you know of the mako-burokwa, Priest?"

"No, Ludger, but I suspect you are going to tell me."

"According to our Kalinga predecessors, when the Chemin, the spirit, leaves the body, it goes either to the Fortunate Isles, or it is destined to walk forever in the wasteland of the dead."

"Is there no possibility of redemption in this wasteland?"

"You mean like purgatory? Not after death. If you want to be redeemed, you must make amends in this life. But my point is that you and I are both like the mako-burokwa, the spirit doomed to walk lost among the dead, even though we are still among the living, Priest."

"Sylbaris," Paul warned, recalling Ludger's promise to not philosophize. "You promised."

"Mea culpa," said Sylbaris, in mock supplication, "I will shut up now."

~

"HAVE you ever thought about the end, my friend?" Sylbaris said a few moments later, as they continued their trek through the desert. "That someday there may be an end? And that God may not be there when you arrive? Perhaps it is the devil who greets you at the gate. Or perhaps there is no God or Satan but only the continuation of this wasteland, or perhaps there will be nothing at all." Sylbaris paused a beat. "Or who knows, maybe your little Yvonne will be waiting for you. Or Jean Joseph. Saint-Pierre redux." Sylbaris let out a laugh that would have shaken the rafters of l'habitation Sablon. "Wouldn't that be irony, mon ami? For both you and I? Old Saint-Pierre as the afterlife. *Imagine!*

"I've thought about my own end many times, Priest. It won't be in this cold, hellacious North America. I think it will be among the palms and the snakes, in some pit where I am condemned to toil, with consumption eating away at my tortured lungs. That is the fate of the black man, is it not, to die in the pit in which the white man has put him?"

"I did not come here for your philosophizing, Ludger. I came looking for my daughter, Yvonne, remember? She is perhaps about so high," Paul held his hand up to his waist before correcting it downward.

"So, you are uncertain of her height?" Sylbaris said. "Have you ever thought perhaps you have invented this little girl? As you've invented me?"

"No," Paul said. "My baby Yvonne lay sleeping in her mother's arms the day I left Saint-Pierre, Ludger. Maman and Stéphanie and Alice all wrote letters to me about her progress and her growth and her first little teeth."

"None of that, Priest, means she is real." Sylbaris glared at him, challenging him to dispute this proposition.

Paul refused the bait. He was too angry. *What does this insolent black man know about my reality, anyway?*

"Touché," he thought he heard Sylbaris say.

THE SUN WAS DESCENDING in the western sky, the mid-afternoon clouds gathering in their cliques, discussing whether to march on the citadel. A winter day on the desert. Paul continued along in deep thought. Or perhaps he was sitting in his chair in San Berdoo, his pipe in his hand growing cold. No matter. Was it going to rain, or not? Ça n'a pas d'importance.

"Pops," said the voice of his dead son, "who is Yvonne?"

Francis Paul was hiking beside him now, Sylbaris nowhere in sight. Paul didn't have the words to answer this boy. Why had he kept his living children from knowing Yvonne and André? Or from Adrien and Alice Germaine and their Maman? Had Sylbaris been right? Was he ashamed of them? Embarrassed by their skin? Or by his unconsecrated relationship with their mother? Because the pious North Americans would not understand, would they? They would use phrases like "living in sin" or words like "miscegenation" or worse vulgar epithets to describe these things he called love.

And so he had not done what he had needed to do. He had not revealed his former life and his private fears to Clara, who surely would have understood. Wouldn't she? He had not talked to his children about their brothers and sisters in Saint-Pierre. He had not told them that when you love someone, things like skin color or a priest's blessing shouldn't matter. That love was the important thing.

His lost children had become his private grief from another life that his current family knew nothing about—*could* know nothing about. In his sorrow and denial, he had said not a word to them. And now he had fallen too deep into the pit of denial to pull himself out.

And here was Francis Paul, Frank, the latest in his pantheon of ghosts, asking him uncomfortable questions, questions he had wished to leave buried.

What was he going to do with Francis Paul? There was no room for him at l'habitation Sablon. It was so full of the dead he couldn't even recall them all. How could he possibly fit another soul into that cramped space?

"Yvonne is your dead sister," he said, knowing this would not be the end of it.

"You never told me I had another sister, Pops."

"A brother, too. Long ago in Martinique."

"That was before Mom?"

"Oui." Paul was thinking again of Saint-Pierre all those years past. It was such a different world then, with such different dreams and forgotten expectations. He wasn't sorry he'd chosen America. He didn't regret he had this life, but he couldn't help imagining how everything would have been altered if he had returned to that other world of his youth, as he had promised to do. If there had been no volcano. Perhaps he would be building a railroad on Martinique. Perhaps he would be going home in the evening to Stéphanie and the children. To little Yvonne. But there would never have been a Francis Paul. No Theresa Marguerite or Clair, Art, baby Ray. No Clara. So which would be worse? If he had gone back, would he have this pain in his heart? Because he was certain it was worse to know and lose a family than to not know them at all.

"So why didn't you ever tell us you had a family before us, Pops? What happened to them?"

"They all died," he said.

"I don't understand. All of them?"

I don't suppose they teach children here about Mont Pelée, he thought. *A small mercy, possibly.*

"It was a great disaster, Son," he said.

"Like the San Francisco Earthquake?"

"Oui. Only ten times more people died when the volcano exploded in Saint-Pierre."

The boy became quiet for a very long time as he contemplated the loss.

"So when can I meet them, Pops?"

"I don't know. Their ghosts are in Martinique, and you are here in California." What else could he say?

"So, if I'm dead, where is God?"

"I don't know," he told the ghost of his son. "Perhaps there is no God."

"Then I don't understand. Why am I here?"

A CRACK IN THE WORLD

PAUL DISMISSED HIS DEAD SON. He had no answers for him. Did such answers exist? Would there never be a resolution to this pain he felt? He continued on for a time, thinking about his life, his dilemma, the words of Sylbaris bothering him. *Perhaps it's that old man you have chained up in that basement.*

Could it be true? Was he chained to the past in some way he couldn't explain to himself, let alone to his Clara and their children? Some sort of guilt clinging to him like a scab?

Sylbaris again walked beside him. He was holding a knife by its curved blade. A fisherman's knife like the kind a man might carry on the docks of Saint-Pierre. A familiar knife.

"Go ahead, Priest," Sylbaris said, offering it to him. "It has already drawn blood, once or twice." He laughed that demonic laugh. "A body should be easy enough to bury out here in this desert."

He pushed the knife toward Paul, who merely looked at it. "How do you kill a shadow with a knife? Even if you could, what justice can it bring?"

"I, for one, would enjoy seeing this particular ghost suffer. What do you have to lose?"

What did he have to lose, indeed? Paul took the knife. It felt strangely familiar in his grip, and as soon as it was firm in his hand, he discovered himself back in the basement of l'habitation Sablon, at the doorway of Jean Joseph's cell.

"There you are," the old man said, dragging his chains across the floor to stand just on the other side of the door. His grandfather's face peered at him through the barred window. "Have you finally come to your senses, boy? Are you going to set your old Pépé free?"

Paul held up the knife so the old man could see it. "I want to cut you out of the world, Grandfather, for all the pain you have brought me."

"It's because of me you are even alive, you little shit. Pain! You think life should be without pain? Even infants don't believe that."

"I thank you for giving me life, Pépé. It is a wonderful gift. But the gift you have given to the world, the suffering you have caused—"

"—Suffering? You have had a life of privilege and comfort, young man. You have been given every advantage."

He thought about Sophie, about Armand and Eugène and Désirée. About Stéphanie and that embarrassing evening at the salon. "At what cost, Grandfather? You've erected a hateful barrier between me and the people I've loved. I can't even talk to my living family about Martinique."

"It's only the grief, son. That volcano was a terrible tragedy."

"But it's more than the volcano. It's this shame I bear. I'm ashamed of you, and your legacy, which I carry around with me like a millstone. It is the shame of Martinique."

"You do not know how brutal the world is, Grandson. Your life has been sheltered in your limited world of republican liberalism. The blacks would have murdered us in '31, if we hadn't fled to the harbor. Your father, only seven years old, and your beloved Tata Elmire, eight. They barely escaped with your grandmother and uncles."

"And whose fault is it, Grandfather? Whose God loving fault is that? That's what happens when you enslave others. When you treat them like merde. Your chickens come home to roost."

"Those blacks were undisciplined children, Son. They needed to be taught about God and hard work. Even your liberated nègres are still enfants."

Paul laughed bitterly. How many times has this argument arisen in his life, spoken by his parents and his aunts and uncles and cousins, even by his friends? "And, in your need to civilize the blacks, you sent ships to Africa to buy them like cattle. How magnanimous of you. Doing God's work and all."

"It was not I who brought them to Martinique. They were already here."

"Ah, so we are going to blame your evil predecessors? I suppose you spoke out against their evil? Oui, old man?"

"Don't be stupid, boy. It doesn't suit you. Are you going to take me out of these chains, or are you going to cut me with that ridiculous—and I might add, useless—knife?"

Paul had forgotten that he still held the knife that Sylbaris had given him. He wanted, more than ever, to use it. He was about to answer the old man when the floor beneath him shook. The ancient walls of l'habitation Sablon creaked and groaned, showering him with tiny bits of broken plaster.

"What was that?" Jean Joseph asked.

"Just a small earthquake, Grandfather. Happens all the time."

"The volcano."

"Non. Just the earth slipping along its fault. What am I going to do with you Grandfather?"

"Use the knife if you must, Grandson. But you can't cut away your own memories, you know. You can't cut away Martinique. It will be with you until you die."

The earth shook again, this time a little harder, sending bits of crumbling brick down on him this time. From somewhere came the voice of a child calling out, "Papa. Papa."

"Alice," he said, "is that you?"

No one answered and he tried again, "Yvonne? Is that my little Yvonne?"

But there was still only silence, except for the old man, who had become restless and was again rattling his chains.

Paul searched through his keys and found the one that fit Jean Joseph's cell. He entered, realizing that he had never dared to come inside before, not since he had put the old man here so many years ago, imprisoned with his own ghosts to torment him. He took the key to his chains and released him.

"Thank you, Grandson," Jean Joseph said. "You won't regret this."

"Not so hasty, Grandfather," Paul said. "We are going to ask the others what they think I should do?"

"By all means, boy. Your grand-mère. Your Uncles. The King, if you wish. They will all testify for your old granddad."

"Those weren't the others I had in mind," said Paul. "I was thinking of the hanged men of Place Bertin. Perhaps we should ask *them?*"

The old man stared at him, unrepentant. "What do I care for their opinion? It means nothing to me. Nor should it to you."

From deep inside the cell arose the rustling and coughing and ahems of the other ghosts. Paul grabbed the old man by the arm and led him further into the cell, until they discovered themselves standing, suddenly, in Place Bertin itself. The blue sky and the Caribbean sea surrounding them, and the gallows looming like some dark hybrid thing, partly gallows and partly the guillotine the island had been too poor to afford, thrown together in a grotesque instrument of death. The circling vultures drawing shadowy spirals across the plaza.

He marched the old man forward toward the gallows as the ghosts of the hanged jeered and cried out "string up the old bastard," and, "tear him limb from limb."

The earth shook again, violently, nearly throwing Paul off his feet. He thought he heard calls of *Papa, Papa,* in the distance. It must be his Yvonne. "I'm coming, Yvonne," he answered. "Papa has something he must take care of first."

He remembered the knife in his hand. He had no use for it, so he threw it to the ground before shoving his grandfather toward the bloodthirsty ghosts.

The old man turned to face him. "You traitorous little shit."

His grandfather screamed more epithets, but enough was enough. "Pran li," he snapped in Créole. "He is all yours, now."

As the hanged men set upon his grandfather with blood-thirsty zeal, Paul turned away. The thought of the old man's suffering should have brought catharsis, but he found he had no stomach for it.

WHEN THE EARTH rumbled in earnest, Paul turned to see Pelée spitting fire into the sky on the northern horizon. He found himself on Rue des Bons Enfants, sprinting up the hill toward the family home. "Yvonne, André, Alice Germaine, Adrien," he called, "Papa's here to save you, my darlings."

Now the sky rained cinders and huge pieces of stone as he rushed toward the terraced houses ahead of him. "Stéphanie, Maman," he shouted as the world exploded around him. "Mannie, Joseph, Léonie, mon Dieu."

And there was a little girl running toward him crying out, "Papa, Papa."

"Yvonne," he sobbed, "my Yvonne. Papa's found you."

He ran toward her, and she ran toward him, but a great chasm in the earth had opened between them. Yvonne cried out, "Papa, Papa," but with each cry, with each step, the crevice widened so that the harder he ran, the farther away Yvonne seemed to be.

The earth shook again, and the banks of the great chasm crumbled, swallowing up the neighboring terraces, which burst into flames as they fell. The clock tower on the Church of the Fort came apart in pieces and tumbled into the abyss. The parishioners screamed and cried as they, too, were sucked into darkness. "Madame Pelée s'est réveillée," someone shouted, "Que Dieu nous sauve!" Panic overtook everyone as the chasm continued to grow, pulling in the streets and the dwellings and the shops of Saint-Pierre. Pelée, angry and unforgiving, rumbled and belched her fire in the north beyond the Plaine de la Consolation, which was now cleaved in two, like the hills of the Fort District, where, on the other side stood his heart. Yvonne. Crying out, "Papa, Papa."

The earth beneath him collapsed and he slipped over the edge. He grabbed for what he thought was a liana, but it was a power line, its end whipping and sparking. He let go. Above him, he heard a familiar laugh. Sylbaris. "It's too late now, Priest. You are falling. I hope, for your sake, there are no snakes down there."

FOR PERHAPS THE FIRST TIME, Paul realized there was nothing more he could do, no prayer he could incant, no wings he could sprout, no time machine that could transport him back to May 1902. Saint-Pierre and his family were all lost. Francis Paul, too, lost. You cannot undo what God has done. The tears rushed out like a small river, streaming across his face.

"Papa, Papa," came a child's voice again from somewhere far away. His small hope. But he wasn't ready yet to open his eyes and look at that other world. That world of the living.

"Papa, it's me, Therese Marguerite." He continued to cry as his daughter put her arms around him and gently stroked his forehead. "It's alright, Papa," she said. "It's just the fever come back again. It's alright."

TERMINUS, 1951

CLARA SIGNED her name to the entry coupon and slipped it into the envelope. She had a good feeling about this one. A Kitchenaid mixer with dough hooks, nesting bowls, the whole kit and kaboodle. It would be a good gift for Marguerite, or one of her daughters-in-law. Perhaps Mary, with her two little boys. She found Paul in his rocking chair, smoke wafting from his pipe. He smiled at her as she laid the envelope on the side table next to their wedding photo.

"Would you take this to the post office for me, dear? The walk will do you good."

"Of course."

"You should wear a jacket. It's cool out," she said and touched his shoulder.

He stood in front of the mirror in their bedroom and ran a brush over his salt-and-pepper hair. It had receded, making his high forehead even more pronounced. *My ears have grown,* he thought. He changed into a clean white shirt. To please Clara, he put on his lightweight suit jacket and dropped the envelope in his pocket.

~

THE TWO OLD men are sitting by the side of a river. It is a nameless river in a nameless place. An island, perhaps, in a sea, like the blue Caribbean Sea. Only this sea, if it exists, is as nameless as the river. The men sit on one of the large rocks which lay along the banks, smoking their pipes. Paul puffs on his favorite cherry-wood, purchased from the corner tobacconist in Los Angeles in 1948. Sylbaris holds a jewel of hand-hewn mahogany he carved years earlier at Morne Rouge, while recovering from the first eruption of Mont Pelée. He finished it the very day they took him from the parish church to the hospital in Fort-de-France, weeks before the mountain exploded again, more fiercely than the first time, sweeping away the villes of Morne Rouge and Ajoupa Bouillon.

Sylbaris, the black man, and Paul, the white man, breathe in the silence, listen to the water lapping against the rocks beneath their feet. It's been a long time, and words can wait for their proper moment.

Paul clears his throat, but doesn't speak.

"So," the black man says, finally, "have you figured it out yet, Priest? Is this heaven, or is it hell?"

"Ah yes," the white man says, leaving his thought unfinished.

Sylbaris laughs and says, "Or perhaps we find ourselves in the Fortunate Isles, and you are my slave, eh?"

"Now, there is a fantasy for you, Ludger." Paul is laughing fully now, and Sylbaris joins him with great guffaws.

"Yes, the béké priest is polishing my boots. I like this fantasy."

"I would happily polish your boots, my friend."

"Ah yes, and wash my feet, as well. But I want you to hear the crack of my whip, Priest."

Sylbaris smiles. It is the warm smile of old friends reminiscing. But there is a bitterness in it also. He picks up a small stone and skips it across the water. The two men resume their silence.

After a while, Sylbaris says, "The only thing better would be a pretty wasp to chase through the indigo, yes? Do you remember that sweet little câpresse in Saint-Pierre? The one who sat with us the day you cut me with my knife? She had eyes for you, and you were as blind as a rhum barrel. Before you arrived, I said to her, 'You know my béké friend studied to be a priest. He has God in him. Do you know why he quit the seminary?' Her eyes grew as big as mangoes and she said, 'Is he really a priest, Samson?' Some called me Samson in those days."

Sylbaris studies Joseph Paul's face, perhaps to see if he is properly offending his old friend.

"I said, 'No, but do you know why he quit the seminary, Cherise?' And she said, 'No, Samson, why did he quit the seminary?'"

Sylbaris pauses in his story. A long pause to draw out the drama.

Finally, Paul can wait no longer. "And so, what did you say?"

"I said, 'Because he is in love with you, dear, and wants to get you into his bed.'"

"You didn't!"

"Yes, that's why she flirted with you all evening."

"She wasn't flirting with me!" For several seconds Paul retreats in rêverie. He is trying to remember. Finally, he repeats, "She wasn't flirting with me. The two of you conspired to rile me up."

Sylbaris looks at his friend with a little sadness, but his eyes are laughing.

"When you took me up on my offer and arrived at that bar, my friend, I couldn't believe my eyes. I thought, what the hell is this crazy béké doing here in this working man's bar tonight? Maybe he wants to get himself killed. That would not be good, a white man killed in Lonbraj Ble. The gendarmes would shut it down for good, and where would poor Sylbaris get his rhum?"

"Yes," Paul said, "I was foolish to go there. Impulsive youth!"

"That's why I decided to be your protector. And that is when I discovered you were not just a crazy béké priest, but you did not even know whether you believed in God. Perfect, I thought. I also do not know if there is a god."

"I once thought I wanted to know why God allowed my brother to die a horrible death. I thought I might talk God with the common people. Such foolish idealism, yes?" Paul said, "And politics. Socialism. Republicanism."

"They are important questions, yes? If there was something in those days which drew me as much as rhum or a pretty woman, it was a good conversation about these wheels that grind the manioc. Even when I sit on the cold stone of the jailhouse floor, I am thinking these things. It is a curse which I blame on my granmé. She said to me when I was young, Sylbaris, you are the smart one. You will pass on the stories, the stories from the ancestors which have been told by many generations. By the ones from Mother Afrika. By the Indigènes. Those things which are lost to the people today. They are very important stories, oui? I say, yes granmé, and I believe it to be so. And I thought perhaps, here is a man of God, a man who has studied les questions anciennes. Perhaps he can help me remember."

"Merde, Ludger. That is not why you invited me into that bar. You wanted to scare the hell out of me."

Sylbaris laughs. "Yes, but that was not the only reason, my friend. Even before la catastrophe, I was already becoming mako-burokwa. The cards and the wasps, they are beautiful, but there is more to life than drunken foolishness. Years later, after

Saint-Pierre lay in ashes and I wandered the great wastelands, it was your doubt which gave me something to cling to."

"How so, my friend?"

"If a priest can doubt God, then perhaps a mako-burokwa can remember. And now, here I am with you in this place, a forgetful ghost, one destined, perhaps, to walk the afterlife alone. And yet, here you are as well. There must be a reason for this, yes?"

"But I can't imagine what it would be, Ludger. Aren't we just faded ink?"

"You are such a fatalist, Paul. That youthful idealism was not such a bad thing, you know? You are more than a bad poet's cliché. Why would your God put you in a prison from which there is no escape?"

"But we are in that prison, Ludger. We are born and we die. There is no escaping that." Paul looks at the river, and then the sky, and he laughs wryly. "I can't touch my grandchildren any longer. Not from this place."

"You are wrong, priest. You have already spoken to the future."

Paul sighs. "It is you, Ludger, who should have been the priest and philosopher."

"But who am I, Monsieur? Do I even exist, outside of your head? Perhaps, I am merely some nostalgia for your past, n'est-ce pas?"

"Perhaps."

"So, Priest, tell me about your life since last I saw you. It's been... how many years, now?"

"I honestly don't remember. But it was only minutes ago at that sidewalk café on Avalon I thought I had seen you. That our eyes met."

"Minutes. Years. What is the difference, now that we're gone?"

Paul shrugs, conceding this point.

"So, tell me, did you ever make things right with your young Theresa?"

Ah, well, Paul thinks with sadness. "Poor Theresa Marguerite. I am the reason her life has been so hard. I am the reason she left home to marry that brutal Englishman at the tender age of sixteen. *If only I had...*"

"*... not been wrapped up in hopeless pursuits,*" Sylbaris says, finishing his thought. "If only you hadn't been chasing after the dead ones, instead of loving the living ones, eh, Priest? And you never found her, your Yvonne, did you?"

Paul shrugs again.

"Perhaps you should finish her story now."

"Perhaps."

"I saw you there, you know, at that corner in Los Angeles." *82nd and Avalon.*

"Yes. As I remember, I was on my way to the post office to mail one of those contest coupons Clara loves. She enters every one she sees. I don't mind taking them, really, it gives me something to do besides sit in my rocking chair all day smoking my pipe. Then I saw you through the window. It was so unexpected to see you there. but I don't know what happened next."

PERHAPS IT HAPPENED LIKE THIS:

The old man might have avoided the car that has turned the corner a block away and is driving too fast, swerving a little. But he cannot believe that after all this time anything could prevent him from reaching the face he knows so well, impassive behind the glass, watching him cross the street in the golden light of early evening.

It is at the last moment he becomes aware of the automobile, sees dark faces through the windshield. Is that Ludger at the steering wheel? But didn't I just see him at the café across the street? Never mind, I must reach him.

The old man might jump back, save himself, but he looks again to the café window only a few feet away and he says in nearly forgotten Matinik, "Ludger, my old friend."

It may be his soul leaping toward the café window that speaks. It is possible that he is dead before the words he did not know he is going to say are there in his throat. Maybe he dies with them in his throat.

The other man, the man behind the window, considers the scene before him. The car careening to miss the old man doesn't miss him, comes to a stop on the sidewalk. People are cursing, screaming, trying to pull the black men from the car.

~

OR PERHAPS IT happened like this:

An old black man is sitting at that sidewalk café. He sees the man on the other side of the street. There is something familiar about this man, about that long, gaunt face. Could it possibly be the Priest, his old acquaintance from Saint-Pierre? He waves. His voice is old and weak, but he attempts to shout out, "Joseph Paul, it is I, Ludger Sylbaris." There is a flash of recognition on the other's face as he steps into the crosswalk.

That's when Sylbaris sees the car, weaving much too fast up the residential street. Go back, he wants to say. But he doesn't say it. He just watches as the car swerves around the corner, striking his friend. He hears the terrible thump as the body is struck, flying through the air to land on the pavement, not five yards away. He sees the blood seeping from the corner of Paul's mouth, the recognition slipping away. He hears the chemin leave the old man's body, crying, "Sylbaris, you are responsible for this!"

~

"YOU KNOW, my friend, the day you died," says Ludger, "I was sitting at that sidewalk café across the street. I saw you there, and I thought, My God, can that be the Priest? And the recognition was in your eyes, so I knew it was you, a ghost of my youth, come to me at the end of time to bring back old memories. And then, I saw that car, weaving down that street, much too fast. You were so intent on crossing the street to see your old comrade, eh, Paul?"

"Yes," Paul says, "I, too, saw the car, but my only thought was to get across the street, to shake your familiar black hand and reminisce about the glory days in Saint-Pierre. Ah, well, my friend, c'est la vie."

"Priest, you always trusted too much."

"Yes, perhaps you are right, Ludger. But if I didn't, I would not be who I am, and I would never have met you, yes?"

"Well, that might not have been such a bad thing." Ludger Sylbaris smiles.

"So, it was a sidewalk café, you say? I could have sworn I saw your face through the glass, on the other side of the window."

"Our memory plays tricks on us, Priest. Who knows this better than I?"

Paul wants to protest, but hesitates. "Ah, my friend, does it matter, one side of the glass or the other?"

"Which side of the glass, you say, Priest?" Sylbaris shakes his head in dismay. "Will you white people never understand?"

"Understand? What is to understand, Ludger?"

"Understand that yes, it matters. It is everything, which side of the glass you are on."

PAPA'S HOUSE

THE ADVENTURES OF YVONNE

Yvonne couldn't believe her eyes. They had arrived in Bordeaux! She was very excited to step off of the gangplank onto the quai. But she was also very sad. Now she must say goodbye to Chief Navigator Marcus, and to Étienne, the helmsman, who had come along to bid au revoir.

"I shall miss you, Chief Navigator, Marcus," she said, giving him a powerful hug. Tears streamed from her eyes.

"We will always remember you fondly, Captain Yvonne," Marcus said. There was a tear in his eye, too.

"And you, helmsman," she said in Matinik, as she hugged Etienne every bit as intensely as she had hugged the Chief Navigator. "I shall never forget you."

"Orevwa, kòmandan mwen. Se pou rèv ou yo feròs." Étienne said, which meant something like, *Goodbye, my captain. May your dreams be fierce.*

Everyone cried now. Maman and even—to Yvonne's surprise—André exchanged hugs with their departing shipmates and bid them all adieu.

And then they were off to explore Bordeaux and find their new home on Rue Sainte-Catherine.

RUE SAINTE-CATHERINE WAS a fancy street of boutiques and grocers and cafés. It reminded Yvonne of Rue Victor Hugo, only not as shabby. It seemed like every shiny store window mesmerized Maman. She would linger, looking at dresses and baubles, and say things like, "Oh, how lovely."

She asked Yvonne her opinion, but pirate captains were not so much interested in fancy dresses and such. "I want to see our new house," she said.

But there was no hurrying Maman. "Patience, mon ange," she said.

So Yvonne and André skipped ahead, no longer paying attention to Maman.

When Yvonne remembered to look around, Maman was nowhere in sight.

"Oh no, where's Maman?" she said.

Turning back, the two children cried out. "Maman. Maman."

They were about to give up in despair, when Maman emerged from a tiny boutique with a lovely blue dress draped over her arm.

Yvonne let out a sigh of relief. "We thought we had lost you!" she admonished.

"Je suis désolée, mes amours," Maman said. "You children must pay attention."

"Hmmph," snorted Yvonne. It was Maman who wasn't paying attention.

~

A SMALL PLAQUE with the number 13 adorned the door at Rue Sainte-Catherine, which was squooshed up between a clothing store and a boulangerie. The door was a faded aquamarine, which reminded Yvonne of the color of the Caribbean sea.

Maman knocked on the door and from inside came the sound of footsteps on the staircase. The door opened, and Yvonne was surprised to find Alice Germaine standing there.

They all squealed with excitement to see one another after such a long absence.

"Come upstairs. Hurry," Alice said. "Everyone's here now waiting for Papa. We will surprise him when he arrives."

When they all reached the top of the stairs, Yvonne was astonished again. What Alice said was true, *everyone* was here.

There was her older brother, Adrien. There was her Mémé Clémence and her Uncle Mannie and her grumpy Uncle Joseph and Uncle Auguste and Tata Rosa and all of their aunts and uncles and cousins whose names she couldn't remember.

There was even Emmaline, Mémé Clémence's old housekeeper, and the bread-seller who used to sell bread in front of their house on Rue Castelnau, and the mango lady.

And they were all waiting for Papa, who was arriving tomorrow morning. "He will have a special guest with him," said Alice with a wink.

That evening Uncle Mannie requested Yvonne tell her story of adventure on the high seas.

Yvonne didn't think of herself as a storyteller, so she was shy at first. But soon, everyone was clapping and oohing at the exciting parts and booing at Captain Marie.

When the story was over, Uncle Mannie hoisted Yvonne on his shoulder and the whole room sang *la Marseillaise*.

WHEN THE MORNING FINALLY ARRIVED, Yvonne could hardly contain her excitement. Papa would be here soon.

As they all sat in the parlor, waiting, her feet jiggled and she squirmed in her chair.

Maman said, "Calm down, mon ange. Papa will be here soon."

But Yvonne couldn't wait. To pass the time, Yvonne sang Kreyol songs she remembered from school. Sometimes Alice would sing along with her. Alice knew more songs than Yvonne, because she was older.

At long last, Yvonne heard the latch on the front door. Everyone in the room held their breath in anticipation as the door opened and closed again.

Then there came creaking footsteps on the stairs. Finally, the door at the top of the stairs opened and Papa walked in. Behind him stood a boy about Alice's age.

Yvonne ran to her papa and threw her arms around him.

"Papa, you're home."

Everyone clapped and laughed and started singing, *Ah! Mon beau château* loud enough to annoy the neighbors, who banged on the walls.

After things quieted down, Yvonne tugged on Papa's arm. "Who is that boy with you?"

Papa looked confused for a moment, as though he had forgotten. Then he turned and put his arm around the boy.

"Yvonne, Alice, children," said Papa. "I would like you to meet your new brother, Frank."

"A new brother?" Yvonne said. No one had told her about this.

"It's about time," Alice said.

"You have a new brother from America," Papa said.

"Oh," Yvonne said, a little worried that now there would be too many brothers bossing her around.

But then she remembered, she was *Captain Yvonne*. They wouldn't dare.

Yvonne reached out her hand to Frank, who took it in his own.

"You must be Yvonne," he said with a kind smile. "Pops has told me all about you."

"I'll bet he didn't tell you I was Captain on a pirate ship?"

"No," Frank said, "I would love to hear about that."

Yvonne pulled up a chair for her brother, and he listened carefully as she told her story for the second time in as many days. He was very attentive and cheered her on when she came to the rousing parts. When she finished her story, he hugged her and bid her good night.

"Sweet dreams, my Captain," he said, giving her a crisp salute. Yvonne grinned. She decided she was going to like this new brother.

THE NEXT DAY Papa rounded up Maman and all the children. "Family," he said, "today we will go to the seashore. We shall have Petit-déjeuner out this morning. And then we shall take a walk on the beach."

Papa and Maman and their five children walked through the cobbled streets of old Bordeaux toward the harbor. Yvonne skipped along happily, teasing the younger boys. Alice Germaine and Frank walked together like best friends, laughing and whispering secrets, the way older kids do.

Papa and Maman walked behind, arm in arm. When Yvonne looked back, Papa had a huge smile on his face. She had never seen such a big smile.

Here they were, Yvonne thought, all together at last, in the beautiful city of Bordeaux. The sun was shining, and the familiar smell of salt and fish greeted her from the ocean, which was just there on the horizon.

She imagined if she looked hard enough, she might even see Saint-Pierre and her blue Caribbean sea.

— fin —

CHARACTERS IN THE NOVEL:

Family in Martinique

Paul Poncy: Paul Poncy was the youngest son of the Poncy family, and the grandfather of co-author, Duane Poncy. He is the main character in *Ghosts of Saint-Pierre.*

Mannie: Emmanuel Poncy was one year older than Paul, and like most of the young men in the family, started out in the working world as an office assistant of one sort or another. He died in the eruption of Pelée in May 1902.

Joseph: Paul's oldest living brother died in the eruption of Pelée in May 1902.

Eustase: Paul's eldest brother died in a hunting accident at the age of twenty. Paul and Emmanuel were probably not actually present at his death as depicted in the book. He may have been accompanied by Samuel and Raphael Dupouy, who reported the death to the authorities.

Léonie & Alix: Léonie and Alix Biliotti were the daughters of Edith Dupouy and her late husband, Paul Biliotti de Gage. They died in the eruption, along with their other siblings.

Anatole & Clémence: Paul's father and mother. Clémence is said to have died in Oklahoma in 1910, but we have found not evidence of the veracity of this claim. It may have been part of Joseph Paul's dissembling and it is likely she also died in the eruption.

Granmé Jeanine: Rose Marie "Jeanine" Petit was the mother of Paul's mother Clemence. She was married to Étienne Clement Fauvé-Sablon, a small planter from Ajoupa Bouillon. *L'habitation Sablon* was on the Montauban River, which can no longer be found on the maps of Martinique. She may have died in the eruption.

Jean Joseph: Jean Joseph Poncy appears briefly as a ghost, along with his sordid story. His testimony before the Court of Orleans in 1832 played a role in the hanging of 24 insurrectionists after the 1831 uprising which burned down the Poncy house and many others. He was also involved in a very interesting case years before when his slave, Marcel, knocked him in the head and absconded with the old man's gold. Marcel and several accomplices managed to flee Martinique, but were tried and sentenced to hang in absentia. Jean Joseph's wife, Marie Jean Petit, died in Paris in 1833. Their three oldest boys, ages 8 – 11, were killed in 1817 while on their way to school in the Métropole, after the ship they were on broke apart in a storm while in port in Cherbourg, France.

Tata Elmire: Elmire Poncy, Madam Dupouy, was the nearest sibling to Anatole, and her children were all close family.

Edith Dupouy: The oldest of the Dupouy children, Edith was married to Paul Biliotti de Gage, who died in 1884. Ferdinand, Alix, Léonie and Valentine were her children. She died in the eruption along with all of her children.

Samuel Dupouy & Adèle Blondel de Rougery: The civil records list Samuel Dupouy as a stockbroker. He likely had many business interests, including the family Dupouy rhumerie. Samuel appears on just about all of the civic records having to do with his Poncy cousins. He died in the eruption along with all of their children.

Therese "Té" Dupouy & Gustav Caminade: Although much of Gustav's business was in Saint-Pierre, the family lived elsewhere on the island. They owned a retail food store and a small transatlantic shipping line. This family survived the eruption. Some of the children later married and lived in metropolitan France.

Raphael Dupouy: The family rum business was managed by Raphael Dupouy. The Dupouy Rhumerie was located at the south end of Saint-Pierre, not too far from the mouillage. He died in the eruption.

Stéphanie and the children: Stéphanie Grainau was the daughter of a policeman who fell in the line of duty in Fort-de-France when she was a child. Both her father, Antoine Charles Grainau, and her mother Marie Augusta Bouché are recorded in the records as being "Mulâtre." Her grandfather Eugene Faravoce Grainau was a successful businessman in Saint-Pierre. Her first two children, Alice Germaine and George Adrien have an unknown father or fathers. Paul Poncy is the recorded father of the other two, André Paul and Virginie Yvonne Poncy. All died in the eruption.

Madame Marlet: Stéphanie's aunt, Rosa Bouché was the widow of Henry Ange Marlet, an heir to a wealthy sugar estate. His father, a mulatto, was a well-known writer and politician in le Robert. Henry Ange Marlet was also a writer and worked for the Ministry of the Marine. Likely died in the eruption.

Family in America

Clara: Clara Mandeville was Paul's wife.

Theresa Marguerite: Paul and Clara's daughter, who is eleven years old when the story begins. She had two daughters, Bettie Lou and Dixie Lee, who make cameo appearances at the end of the novel.

Arthur Mandeville: Arthur Mandeville was a photographer in Montreal. His wife, Clarinda Charlebois was from Sainte-Anne-de-Bellevue, on the Isle d'Montréal.

Therese Boulet: Madam Mandeville. Arthur Mandeville's mother lived in the Joly district of Labelle along with his father, François Mandeville. François was the Notary for Mont Laurel.

Berthe Mandeville: Clara's younger sister was living with them in Winslow, Arizona in 1910 when Clara was pregnant with Clair.

Francis Paul: Frank, Paul's oldest son in America, died of the Spanish Flu in 1918.

The young Poncy children: Clair, Arthur, Henry, and Raymond were Theresa's younger siblings at the time of Francis Paul's death.

Other real (fictionalized) people

Ludger Sylbaris: the "Miracle of Saint-Pierre" was (arguably) the only survivor of the volcanic explosion which destroyed the city of Saint-Pierre. It is unlikely that Paul actually knew him, and he is used here in a symbolic way.

Vachel Lindsay: Paul did not know Vachel Lindsay, as far as we know. He was added for dramatic purposes.

The priests: Fathers Edouard, Napoleon, and Coneally were the actual priests at their respective churches. The fathers at the Colegio, however, are fictional.

The Tambois family: The Tambois family, along with their ages and occupations are real and were taken from the 1900 US Census. Paul was a boarder in their house at that time.

Albert and Annie Bouley: The Bouleys were neighbors in 1900. Whether Paul knew them is unknown, but Albert Bouley is a 3rd cousin to Clara's grandmother, Therese Boulet. The Boulets actually have large reunions like the one in the book, so it is not unlikely that Paul met her through this family connection. The Lanois family were boarders in the Bouley house.

Raoul Dufail: The Dufail family and the Poncy family were neighbors in Saint-Pierre. Raoul Dufail was one of the witnesses at the birth of André Paul Poncy. He actually married Marguerite Gemeau, the daughter of the cigar maker on Quai Peynier. The Gemeau's had also migrated to Cayenne. His uncle, Paul Dufail, was the head of surgery at the hospital in Saint-Pierre and died in the tragedy of Mt. Pélée.

Alcide Dufail family: Alcide Dufail, Raoul's brother, migrated to Maine in the 1890s, where he married Louise Lamarque. Their son, Raoul, went on to become an accomplished tenor and was one of the first musicians to be broadcast in a radio program in New York.

Invented characters

Paul's school friends: Sophie, Desirée, Armand, Eugene and other school friends were all invented for the story.

Philippe Guillaume: Stéphanie's revolutionary lover and father of Alice Germaine and Adrien.

Amanda Laviolette and friends: Amanda and most of the characters in the Buffalo scenes are fictional characters, except for Albert Bouley and the Mandevilles. And Vachel Lindsay, of course. We have no evidence that Paul was actually in Buffalo for the Pan American Expo.

BIBLIOGRAPHY

Further Reading

This novel took several years in the making. Although we began writing the current version in 2017, the original idea and research which went into it, began in the early 2000s. We would like to share some of those sources here, and if you want more, please go to our website at https://www.martinique.poncy-mclean.net.

Fiction

about Martinique and the French Antilles:
- *The Wide Sargasso Sea*, Jeanne Rhys, Norton & Co., 1999. This is an edition with a variety of critical essays, edited by Judith L. Raiskin.
- *Solibo Magnificent,* Patrick Chamoiseau, translated by Rose-Myriam Réjouis and Val Vinkurov, Pantheon 1997.
- *Slave Old Man,* Patrick Chamoiseau, translated by Linda Cloverdale, The New Press, 2018.
- *The Fourth Century,* Eduoard Glissant, translated by Betsy Wing, University of Nebraska Press, 2001.
- *Youma: The Story of a West Indian Slave,* Lafcadio Hearn, public domain.
- *Creole Folktales,* Patrick Chamoiseau, translated by Linda Cloverdale, The New Press, 1994.
- *Strange Words,* Patrick Chamoiseau, translated by Linda Cloverdale, Granta Books, London, 1998.
- *Texaco,* Patrick Chamoiseau
- *Climb to the Sky,* stories by Suzanne Dracius, translated by Jamie Davis, University of Virginia Press, 2012.
- *Martinique Snake Charmer,* André Breton, translated by David W. Seaman, University of Texas Press, 2008
- *Crossing the Mangrove,* Maryse Conde, translated by Richard Philcox, Anchor Books, 2011. Set in Guadeloupe.
- *Claire of the Sea Light,* Edwidge Danticat, Vintage, 2013. About Haiti.
About early 20th century in the America:
- *City of Light,* Lauren Belfer, Dial Press, 2010.

• *The Anarchist,* John Smolens, Michigan State University Press, 2018.

Non-fiction

• *Two Years in the French West Indies,* Lafcadio Hearn, Signal Press, 2001, from the original edition published in 1890.
• *Dangerous Creole Liaisons,* Jacqueline Couti, Liverpool University Press, 2016.
• *Sugar and Slavery, Family and Race: The letters and diary of Pierre Desalles, Planter in Martinique, 1808—1856,* edited and translated by Elborg Forster and Robert Forster, Johns Hopkins University Press, 1996.
• *Sweet Liberty, The final days of slavery in Martinique,* Rebecca Hartkopf Schloss, University of Pennsylvania Press, 2009.
• *Paradise Destroyed: Catastrophe and Citizenship in the French Caribbean,* Christopher M. Church, University of Nebraska, 2017.
• *Fire Mountain: How one man survived the world's worst volcanic disaster,* Peter Morgan, Bloomsbury, 2003.

Note: We have read numerous other articles and books not included here, but this is a list we thought would be most useful to potential readers who want to know more about Martinique and the times. A full list of bibliographical and genealogical sources as well as photographs may be found on our website at https://www.martinique.poncy-mclean.net

ACKNOWLEDGEMENTS

We would like to thank Duane's sister, Therese Poncy, for her valuable feedback and enthusiasm for our book. Also his dear cousin, Shelley Poncy, and her husband, Russell Hodgkinson, for lending us their house for two weeks while they vacationed in Mexico, so we could work on an early draft — and for listening to us read. We want also to thank our editor, Julie Tibbot for her valuable and insightful work, and to Clara-Julia Péru from the French-American School in Portland, Oregon, for helping us with our French and Créole. Thanks to Ellen Thomas of the Stratford-Perth Archives in Stratford, Ontario, and many more whose names we have forgotten: the museum guide at the Old Trails Museum in Winslow, Arizona; the librarians and assistants at the French-American Genealogical Society and the Museum of Work and Culture in Woonsocket, Rhode Island; and countless others on our research travels to Martinique, Canada, and the eastern United States. Also, we must not forget the many online genealogical researchers who have collaborated with us over the years on WikiTree and Geneanet. And not least, my late Aunt Margie for giving me the inspiration to research my family in Martinique.

We would also like to thank all of the friends and family who have encouraged our literary endeavors over the course of our writing career. Your comments, critique and thoughtful conversations give us the fuel to continue on our journey. Ger Killeen, Kate Saunder, Gabriele Hayden, Kathleen Ellyn, Paul Poncy, my late cousin, Patricia Ann Poncy, Alex Ryan, Roberta

Whitlock, in particular, and members of many critique groups over the years, you have kept us going.

We are indebted to you all. It takes a village to write a book.

Consider leaving a review of this book

Reviews are vitally important to authors, particularly those of us who are just starting out. We would much appreciate if you take a moment to rate and leave a few words about Ghosts of Saint-Pierre on Amazon, Goodreads, or your favorite book site. It doesn't have to be more than, "I liked this book," or "Recommended." This will go a long way toward helping others find our books. Thank you for reading!

ABOUT THE AUTHORS

Duane Poncy and Patricia J McLean live and write in Portland, Oregon., where they have long been figures in the local literary and arts community as activists, publishers, and hosts of fiction and poetry events. They are the editors of the acclaimed anthology, *Raising Our Voices*, and the literary journal, *Elohi Gadugi Journal, Narratives for a New World*.

www.ingramcontent.com/pod-product-compliance
Lightning Source LLC
Chambersburg PA
CBHW031237310726
48971CB00004B/1061